PUFFIN BOOKS

TIME RIDERS

2001 1912 1957 1941 2066

THE PIRATE KINGS

Praise for *TimeRiders*:

'A thriller full of spectacular effects' – *Guardian*

'Insanely exciting, nail-biting stuff' – *Independent on Sunday*

'This is a novel that is as addictive as any computer game'
– *Waterstone's Books Quarterly*

'Promises to be a big hit' – *Irish News*

'A thrilling adventure that hurtles across time and place at
breakneck speed' – *Lovereading4kids.co.uk*

'Plenty of fast-paced action . . . this is a real page-turner'
– *WriteAway.org.uk*

'A great read that will appeal to both boys and girls . . .
you'll find this book addictive!' – *redhouse.co.uk*

'Contender for best science-fiction book of the year . . .
an absolute winner' – *Flipside*

Winner of the Older Readers category,
Red House Children's Book Award 2011

ALEX SCARROW used to be a graphic artist, then he decided to be a computer games designer. Finally, he grew up and became an author. He has written a number of successful thrillers and several screenplays, but it's YA fiction that has allowed him to really have fun with the ideas and concepts he was playing around with when designing games.

He lives in Norwich with his son, Jacob, his wife, Frances, and his Jack Russell, Max.

Books by Alex Scarrow

TimeRiders
TimeRiders: Day of the Predator
TimeRiders: The Doomsday Code
TimeRiders: The Eternal War
TimeRiders: Gates of Rome
TimeRiders: City of Shadows
TimeRiders: The Pirate Kings

Sign up to become a TimeRider at:
www.time-riders.co.uk

TIME RIDERS

2001   1912   1957   1941   2066

THE PIRATE KINGS

ALEX SCARROW

PUFFIN

PUFFIN BOOKS

Published by the Penguin Group
Penguin Books Ltd, 80 Strand, London WC2R ORL, England
Penguin Group (USA) Inc., 375 Hudson Street, New York, New York 10014, USA
Penguin Group (Canada), 90 Eglinton Avenue East, Suite 700, Toronto, Ontario, Canada M4P 2Y3
(a division of Pearson Penguin Canada Inc.)
Penguin Ireland, 25 St Stephen's Green, Dublin 2, Ireland
(a division of Penguin Books Ltd)
Penguin Group (Australia), 707 Collins Street, Melbourne, Victoria 3008, Australia
(a division of Pearson Australia Group Pty Ltd)
Penguin Books India Pvt Ltd, 11 Community Centre, Panchsheel Park, New Delhi – 110 017, India
Penguin Group (NZ), 67 Apollo Drive, Rosedale, Auckland 0632, New Zealand
Penguin Books (South Africa) (Pty) Ltd, Block D, Rosebank Office Park, 181 Jan Smuts Avenue,
Parktown North, Gauteng 2193, South Africa

Penguin Books Ltd, Registered Offices: 80 Strand, London WC2R ORL, England

puffinbooks.com

First published 2013
001

Text copyright © Alex Scarrow, 2013
All rights reserved

The moral right of the author has been asserted

Set in Bembo Book MT Std 11/14.5 pt
Typeset by Palimpsest Book Production Limited, Falkirk, Stirlingshire
Made and printed in Great Britain by Clays Ltd, St Ives plc

British Library Cataloguing in Publication Data
A CIP catalogue record for this book is available from the British Library

ISBN: 978–0–141–33718–0

www.greenpenguin.co.uk

ALWAYS LEARNING   **PEARSON**

To Jacob — '. . . boys from the wharf . . .'

PROLOGUE

2050, Montreal

'How did we end up here? In this time, in this horrible mess?'

Waldstein studied his audience: rows of pale ovals receding into the dimly lit conference hall. A gathering of the brightest minds, innovators, businessmen, entrepreneurs at this, the world's very last TED Talk. There were going to be no more. Organizing them in this increasingly chaotic and dangerous world was becoming impossible.

The question he'd just asked, of course, was rhetorical. He was going to tell them.

'Greed. Greed and complacency. Back at the turn of the last century, when we were busy being very excited that we were all entering a new millennium, *then* . . . we assumed oil was going to last forever. We now know, of course, with hindsight, that as the clocks and calendars ticked over into the new century and everyone was celebrating at a party somewhere, we quietly hit the "peak oil" moment. The moment when mankind finally reached the halfway mark of this world's fossil-embedded fuel store.'

He paused for effect. The holographic autocue waited for him.

'The "tank" was half empty. There were a few geologists back then sounding the alarm, telling all who'd listen that we'd better get a move on and find a substitute for oil. But no one did

1

listen. Why? Because oil was still coming out of the ground easily enough and it was still cheap. Why upset the apple cart, right? Let's face it . . . at a fantastic party, who wants to listen to the guy in the corner muttering about the end of the world?

'We did nothing to wean ourselves off oil addiction. And so, fifteen . . . twenty years into the new century, when the big oil-producing nations started finding their oil wells drying up, one after the other, things started to turn nasty.

'That was the first Big Problem we should've fixed . . . and we didn't. The second . . . ? Again, back at the beginning of the century, there were economists calculating what the global population figure was likely to be for the middle of the twenty-first century – ten billion. *Ten billion*.'

His audience stirred.

'It turns out their estimate undershot by about a billion and a half. But who's perfect, eh?' Waldstein's laugh sounded dry and hollow. Certainly no laughs were coming back from his audience.

'Once again warnings were given. Ten billion? There's no way Earth's ecosystem could be leveraged to feed ten billion mouths indefinitely! But were people listening? Of course not. *You're telling me I can't have more than two children? How dare you! How dare you tell me what I can and cannot do!* So, that problem was never dealt with and not long after "peak oil" we had "peak food". . . "peak drinking water", all symptoms of a resource-exhausted world: a world desperately struggling to provide at least fifteen hundred calories every day to over twelve billion hungry mouths.'

Waldstein sighed. 'So, we had two big problems facing us: resource scarcity and a population explosion. Both could have been prevented; neither were. And these two problems were compounded by a third and final one.'

He thumbed his palm and a giant animated holograph appeared above his head, as large as the round stage he was standing on. An image of Earth playing through fifty years of gathered data: polar ice caps shrinking, the blue of the ocean swelling, expanding, like ink spreading across blotting paper.

'We let this world warm up too damned much. Some of that was down to burning all that oil – that certainly didn't help things much. But what really did it for Earth's fragile ecosystem was the sheer number of people on the planet. So . . . just when we needed as much land as possible to grow enough high-yield crops to feed us all, that lowland, that *farming* land, was being swallowed up by the advancing oceans. Farmland . . . and, of course, many of our great cities.'

He tapped his palm and flicked through shimmering slides: New York, now just the island of Manhattan protected by giant levee walls; New Jersey, Brooklyn, the Bronx, Queens . . . all now a mottled patchwork of submerged streets and rotting rooftops. London, a city of tenement blocks crowding each other like weeds straining for sunlight, emerging from a fog of pollution. The Thames, a menacing, swollen river again held at bay by enormous levee walls.

'The first fifty years of this century, we should have devoted to fixing these problems. Instead, what did we do? We fought like children. The First Asian War in the late twenties, over twenty years ago. Then the start of the various Pacific Oil Wars. The ten-year anniversary last week of the Thirty-Day War between the Arabian Coalition and Israel . . . and, God help us, that one wasn't even over oil . . . but something as archaic, as *irrelevant* as religious ideology! Over what name we should call a God that *doesn't even exist*!'

The hologram above Waldstein played a montage of images:

the rusting wrecks of tanks and mech-walkers, the irradiated ruins of Jerusalem and Damascus.

'Now we are where we are. Living in a world that we've exhausted. Poisoned. A world that some say is quite rightly turning against us. But this, in the much larger context of time, is merely another cycle. It's happened before. The dinosaurs had their time and now we've had ours. The world is simply rebalancing itself. Wiping the slate clean ready to start again.'

He was no longer reading from the autocue. The conference organizers had been given an advanced copy of his talk: some uninspiring, meaningless fluff about 'responsible entrepreneurialism in difficult times'.

What he wanted to say this morning – what he was going to say – was memorized.

'But, ladies and gentlemen, unlike the dinosaurs, we almost certainly won't be rendered extinct. We will, though, in the latter half of this century, *inevitably* experience a resource starvation that will whittle our numbers down to perhaps a few tens of millions. Perhaps even a few hundred thousand. And those that survive will adapt. Will hopefully be wiser and understand that this fragile world of ours must be treated with respect.'

Waldstein noticed his audience stirring uneasily.

He smiled. 'Yes, I'm sure you've figured out I'm no longer reading the text that was approved for today's lecture. But there is something that needs to be said . . .'

His gaze settled at the back of the audience, on the bank of cameras ranged there. This was going out on a dozen news-streams. Waldstein knew this was going to be seen live or re-streamed by virtually everyone on the planet – 2050, the last TED Talk. The very last of them.

A perfect platform for him.

'I'm afraid things don't look so good for us. Changes we can't avoid . . . are happening whether we like it or not. But here's the thing. I believe the Big Die Off will not be an end for us. It'll be a transition. A difficult one – a terribly hard one – but a transition, not an ending.'

Off to one side he could see movement, someone attempting to attract his attention.

They want me off the stage. They want me to finish.

'Mark my words, the next twenty years will be hard years for all of us. Painfully hard ones. As things worsen, there'll be those who will say that we could wind time back, use displacement technology to learn from all our stupid mistakes and have another go at these last fifty years, at making this a better world. To those people who will argue for that, I say this in response now . . .'

He wagged a cautionary finger at the cameras out there in the auditorium recording him. 'If we do that – if we actually are reckless enough to meddle with time – that foolishness will end up being the *biggest* of all our many mistakes.'

One of the event organizers – Dr Rajesh – was making his way across the stage towards him.

Waldstein nodded at the man. 'So, let me then finish . . .' It would look foolish if they attempted to force him off the stage. Foolish for him. Foolish for the organizers. The news story would be all about some undignified scuffle and not the message itself.

'*In conclusion*, I'll finish with this . . .' Dr Rajesh seemed to acknowledge that. He stopped where he was and allowed Waldstein to wrap things up.

'Ladies and gentlemen, we've made so many, many mistakes and in the coming years we are going to be relentlessly tempted to go back and try to undo them, for ourselves, for our children.

But time travel is an open doorway to Hell itself: a Pandora's box that cannot be closed once opened. If we dare to play God with this technology, then that really will be the end of absolutely everything. Quite literally *everything*: this small, remote, isolated blue ball of life we call *Earth* and everything on it.'

Waldstein hadn't expected much in the way of applause and he was quite right not to. He walked offstage, past an ashen-faced Dr Rajesh, amid a deafening silence.

CHAPTER 1

1889, London

7 February 1889

So, I sort of got into the habit of typing a log of 'agency' events
back in Brooklyn. I figured I might as well continue doing it here,
even though I'm not even sure we're 'in' the agency any more.

Anyhow, it's been a weird time. Compared to the time after we got
recruited up until coming here, it's been quiet. Peaceful even. All
of that time before relocating here seems like a blur. So much
happened to us. When I play the memories back – the Nazis, the
mutants, those dinosaur things, Colonels Devereau and Wainwright,
Adam Lewis – it's like some crazy B-movie. Those guys seem like
characters from a book. A book that'll stay with you for the rest of
your life.

Of all of them, though, I do find myself thinking about Adam the
most. I wonder if we could have let him stay with us, like we did
Rashim and that moronic robot of his. We could have, couldn't
we? I realize that now. But back then I was so certain that
everything had to be tidied up. Everything had to be put exactly
where it was.

So, I let him go back to work. I let him die.

Maddy looked at the screen in front of her.

And I miss him.

Such a stupid, stupid, girly thing. She'd known him for no more than two days. Two days and then he was gone. And here she was countless months — a lifetime and a half — later missing him. Pining away like some precious fairy-tale princess.

Pfft. As if they'd actually 'been' something.

Mind you, they might have. If she'd made a different decision.

'Sheesh, let it go, Maddy,' she chastened herself, then looked over her shoulder to see if SpongeBubba was listening. He had a habit of sidling up silently and just standing behind you, batting big-lashed eyes and grinning like a simpleton. But he was on the other side of the dungeon perfectly inert — eyes closed and one green light on his side panel showing he was in standby mode. The others were out. Rashim, Liam and Bob had gone out that morning to visit an illegal gambling house: their stock of money was running low. Sal and Becks were down at the dockside buying some food for supper.

Maddy was still feeling a bit twitchy about the female support unit. After all, the very same clone had been hell-bent on killing them all three months ago. They'd managed to decommission her, then *reboot* her: a rather messy affair that Maddy didn't really want to dwell on. The artificial intelligence that was installed in the unit right now was the default AI. Perhaps, at some point, she might try experimenting with installing parts of Becks's old consciousness, but for the moment . . . this felt safer. The downside was that the support unit was back to square one, learning from scratch how to appear less like an ice-cold, sociopathic killing machine.

So, Maddy was alone right now and had a chance to put her thoughts on-screen.

She deleted her last sentence: *And I miss him.*

Missing people? Falling in love? Having feelings? That was for real people with moms and dads, right? Not vat-grown meat products. Real people with real hearts and souls. She turned her attention back to the screen.

'Enough with all that dewy-eyed girl crud.'

We've been here in London for two months or so. Not bubble-days now, but actual, real one-after-another ones. I like that better. I like the fact that each morning I step out of our side door on to Farringdon Street and I watch the coaches and hansom cabs go past, and the traders setting up their stalls, that each day is a brand-new one with a possibility all of its own.

And that makes up for some of what I know now. So, I'm a 'product'. Liam and Sal too. And everything we thought of as our lives before we 'died' is a complete sham. But, like Liam says, 'We're here now. We've got each other.' He's right. The past may have been 'borrowed' from someone else. But screw all that: the future's ours.

She smiled. Wasn't it just? All theirs.

We have our new goal. We're not agents of preservation any more. Our role isn't to faithfully maintain a doomed timeline – to make sure the Titanic hits the iceberg, to make sure American Airlines flight 11 hits the north tower.

To make sure mankind destroys itself.

No.

We're going to watch. And wait. And perhaps, if the opportunity presents itself, steer this doomed world to a happier time in the twenty-first century. If that chance comes along, then we'll take it and to hell with 'history was only ever supposed to go one way'. Because, the way I see it, who knows what the 'right' timeline is? Maybe the virus that Rashim told us about – the Pandora Event, the complete annihilation of human civilization in the year 2070 – maybe that's a faulty timeline. Something that wasn't meant to happen. Maybe Waldstein is wrong to believe that's the destiny that must be preserved. And if that isn't enough to do my frikkin' head in . . . how about this?

Maybe Waldstein was never meant to have been born – never meant to invent a time-displacement device in the first place.

How's that for a complete head trip?

She closed the document. Enough head-scratching for one morning. She eased out of the rocking chair, not wanting to wake up SpongeBubba. She checked. His standby light was still on; his long-lashed plastic eyes gazed sightless out into the gloom.

Right now their dungeon still smelled of freshly pan-roasted coffee beans. Liam and Rashim's treat this morning before setting off: coffee and freshly baked bread with a thick slice of salted pork.

Maddy grabbed a shawl and stepped over to their low doorway. She lit the candle beside it, pulled aside a privacy curtain they'd rigged across the small archway then eased the door's bolt back, and the oak door creaked open. She checked that there was no sign of Delbert, their nosy landlord, or his string-bean assistant, Bertie, hovering in the space beyond. They used it occasionally to store some of their dubious wares and, of course, took every opportunity while they were fussing around in there to try to sneak a peek past their door and the curtain.

No sign of them this morning.

She stooped through the doorway, candle in hand, and stood up. The candle picked out the arching brick roof above her and the wooden packing crates of spices and luxury goods, shipped from all corners of the British Empire, that had all somehow managed to 'fall off the back' of various delivery carts. To her right a thin sliver of daylight smeared a dull glow across the scuffed and grime-covered paving-slab floor.

Maddy pulled a long iron key from the pocket of her dress and tugged the woollen shawl tightly round her shoulders. It was cold that morning. She approached the door – their own side door on to Farringdon Street – turned the key and, with a deep *clack*, the heavy door swung inwards, suddenly bathing the dim interior with daylight. She emerged, stood on the step up from the pavement and blinked at the bright morning.

Blue, a brilliant blue – postcard blue – sky above her. She narrowed her eyes against the glare of thick snow on the ground and on the rooftops and chimney pots where home hearths had yet to be lit. Farringdon Street was going about its business: ruddy-faced workers blowing clouds of condensation; a team of horses pulling a brewer's cart, steam rising from their flanks. A lovely, invigorating February morning, like something out of Dickens; like a scene from that Scrooge story. Maddy was almost tempted to summon some street urchin to her doorstep, toss him a farthing and ask him to go fetch her the large goose hanging in the butcher's window down the street.

She chuckled at that notion, blowing steam from her nostrils.

A man striding past in a dark morning coat and top hat touched the brim politely at her as he passed by. 'Lovely day, my dear, isn't it?'

'Yes,' she said, grinning at him. 'That it is.'

11

She watched the gentleman cross the busy street, weaving between delivery carts and hansom cabs, then filled her lungs with air that was crisp and cool and scented with the pleasing, ever-present – but never tiresome – tang of woodsmoke.

Oh God, I so love it here.

CHAPTER 2
1889, London

'Place your bets, gentlemen,' said the dealer. He glanced warily at the stack of chips that Rashim pushed forward across the faro table. The other players round the table stared wide-eyed at the size of his stack as Rashim studied the card deck intently.

'Good God, sir, that's a twenty-pound bet you're intending to place!' said the gentleman to his right.

Rashim shrugged distractedly, his mind on numbers.

The gentleman shook his head incredulously and looked up at Liam standing behind them. 'Is your friend normally so reckless with his money?'

'Oh aye. A real liability, so he is.' Liam patted Rashim's shoulder. 'But somehow the chap always seems to come good in the end.'

The five other players around the faro table, all of them smartly dressed gentlemen, held back from placing their bets, curious to see which number the stack of chips was going to be pushed on to. In the dimly lit room, smoke curled round the oil lamp above the table. Through tall, dark wood-panel doors came the muted hubbub of the clientele in the Long Bar: the well-to-do enjoying an expensive lunch before taking in an expensive matinee performance in the Criterion Theatre next door.

'And has he more money than common sense?'

Liam laughed. 'Well now . . . I suppose we'll see soon enough.'

'Gentlemen, will there be any other bets?' asked the dealer.

Ruddy faces around the oval table studied the stack, waiting to see which way Rashim was finally going to nudge it. Further back from the faro table, Bob's looming form blocked most of the pale light from the back room's solitary small and grimy window. Liam cast a furtive glance back at him and noted how many fingers he had extended on his thick thighs.

Liam patted Rashim's shoulder again gently, affectionately, as he spoke. 'Of course, I insist on coming along with him. He'd gamble away his family's entire fortune if I wasn't here watching out for him.'

Pat, pat, pat on Rashim's shoulder as he spoke. Three of them. Almost imperceptibly, Rashim nodded.

Three. He'd silently come to the same conclusion as Bob. A three: statistically the most likely card left in what remained of the dealer's deck.

'Mind you,' continued Liam, lifting his hand off Rashim's shoulder, 'I do wonder if someone up there is looking out for him. Luck of the devil himself, my friend here.'

Rashim gently pushed his stack on to the table's marked layout: the three.

The gentleman to his right looked up at Liam. 'Luck of the devil, you say?' He placed several of his chips beside Rashim's stack. 'Well, I'll have a little of that, then.' The other old men around the table chuckled among themselves and then followed suit.

The dealer cocked an eyebrow. 'All on the three, is it?'

Ruddy faces nodded.

He shrugged and then reached for the top card on the upturned deck. A ten of hearts. He slowly pulled it to one side to reveal a nine of diamonds.

'The banker's card is a nine, gentlemen,' he announced. Bets placed on a nine would have lost and been gathered by the dealer. He placed his thumb on the card, ready to slide it to one side to reveal the *Carte Anglaise* – the 'player's card'.

'And now we shall see, gentlemen,' he said, a hint of anxiety in his voice as he glanced at Rashim, 'whether the devil's luck is paying out today. Your card is . . .'

Outside the Criterion, Liam buttoned up his coat and exhaled a plume of breath into the cold air. He looked across Piccadilly Circus for a waiting hansom to flag down.

'Well now, I fancy that's another place we'll probably have to avoid visiting for a while. They'll not let us back in there for a bit.'

Rashim nodded as he folded the wad of notes away into a clasp and tucked it into the inside pocket of his waistcoat. All counted, the chips they'd won from the banker that morning amounted to just over seventy pounds, the annual wage of a clerk with change to spare.

Rashim buttoned his coat. 'I suspect we may have to start wearing disguises.'

Liam nodded as he waved his top hat to attract the attention of a cabbie dropping off a fare. 'Mind you –' he slapped Bob's back – 'how do we disguise this ol' meat mountain?'

Bob looked down at him. 'I could wear different clothes.'

'I think we'd need a bit more disguise than that, Bob. I can't think there're that many men in London of your height and build. Especially not with your charming good looks.'

Bob was, of course, essential. Not just as back-up for Rashim's card-counting, which on occasion had proved to be mistaken, but also as a guarantee that their winnings were paid promptly. One deep growl from him was usually enough to ensure they got what was their due.

'Perhaps we'll need to take Becks next time,' suggested Liam.

'I thought women weren't allowed in gambling dens,' said Rashim.

'Aye, well, we'll stick a fake moustache on her and put her in a suit. She's scary enough that no one'll want to look at her too closely.'

The hansom circled round, crossed the busy thoroughfare and presently the driver reined in the horses beside them. 'Where to, sirs?'

Liam pulled open the carriage door and let Bob and Rashim climb in. The hansom lurched over to one side under Bob's weight with the creak of suspension springs complaining. 'Take us to Holborn, my good man,' replied Liam. 'And don't spare the horses!'

He clambered in, closed the door behind him and the carriage pulled away into the bustle of traffic heading up Shaftesbury Avenue.

Rashim looked at him quizzically. 'Don't spare the horses?'

Liam shrugged. 'Is that not what posh gents of this time are supposed to say?'

Bob frowned as he ran a check on that. 'It is a cliché used in period films of the mid-twentieth —'

'Aw, come now, Bob . . . don't ruin the moment.'

CHAPTER 3

1889, London

'Information: this river used to freeze over every winter,' said Becks, pointing out across the Thames. 'The ice was thick enough for an entire marketplace to open up on it. It did this a number of times during the sixteenth century. Meteorologists called it "the Little Ice Age".'

Sal leaned against the wrought-iron rail of Blackfriars Bridge, thankful for her woollen mittens. Despite the warmth of the sun, there was a bitter chill in the breeze that gusted up from the choppy Thames.

'I see Maddy's downloaded some local history into you.'

'Correct. I have been updated with a detailed information package: London history 1500 to 1900.'

Becks sounded like Bob. In fact, more like Bob than Bob. Her AI was still young and unseasoned, unflavoured with all those small linguistic tics and nuances that the original Becks had managed to learn and mimic to make her sound almost human. But then . . . she wasn't *really* Becks, was she? She was another AI altogether, albeit one that looked identical to her. And one they'd decided to call the same name. Sal wondered if that was such a good idea. The support unit resting on the rail beside her was someone else. Perhaps her AI would eventually evolve the same way, and she'd end up very much like the support unit they'd once had.

'It's strange. I have to keep reminding myself that you don't remember anything that happened to us before we set up here in London.'

Becks nodded. 'Correct. Madelaine has discussed this with me. My predecessor's AI became unstable and unreliable.'

'She said she was all *lovey* over Liam.' Sal hooted softly. 'Go figure. Even a walking computer can fall in love.'

'Information: the expression of love was most likely a heuristically generated empathy feedback loop. A misfiring of a code function.' Becks looked at Sal with the same piercing grey eyes that had once been able to – almost – communicate something akin to warmth. 'My AI will be allowed to develop independently. This error should not be duplicated.'

Perhaps that was for the best. Another swooning support unit with the aching beauty of a fallen angel was probably the kind of distraction Liam could well do without. Sal watched a barge laden with sacks of coal approach the bridge.

'I sometimes wish I could "reboot",' said Sal. 'Empty my head and start over.'

'Why?'

The barge chugged beneath the bridge, its smokestack puffing a thick cloud of steam up at them. It wafted around them, a momentary fug of warmth tinged with the odour of burning coke. Sal flapped her hand as it cleared.

'Why, Sal?' repeated Becks. 'It is illogical to wish for data loss.'

'I wish I didn't know what I am. Not human.'

'Incorrect. You are human. Your brain is –'

'I'm a made-to-order human. A clone.'

Becks cocked her head. 'That *is* correct.'

'I guess I'm still finding it hard that I need to throw away half of everything I can remember. My parents. My childhood.

Everything up until the day I was recruited. And even that's fake.'

'I believe I understand,' said Becks. 'It is like having a folder full of questionable data.'

'Exactly. Except it's not so neatly organized. Even though my childhood is all false, it's part of what makes me who I am now. You know? It's why I talk the way I do . . . the accent.' Her Anglo-Indian intonation: it was still there despite her best attempts at trying to lose it all; to speak with an entirely neutral, unaccented voice.

'If all I knew was my life with Liam, Maddy and Bob . . . I think it would be much easier to cope. It's a bit like waking up from a dream. That bit when you've not quite woken up and what you were dreaming about still feels real?' Exactly that – a freshly woken mind sorting through a mixed-up bag of sensations and memories and then filtering out those that clearly couldn't possibly be true. Throwing away the nonsense of a dream – flying pigs, talking frogs, mushroom armies with machine guns – was far easier, though. Her fake life as an Indian girl in the year 2026 felt so completely real. The smells of downtown Mumbai: spices and sewage, the chemical tang of disinfectant and bleach from laundries. The acrid burn of exhaust fumes and plastics-recyc' plants breaking down plastic garbage for essential extractable oil. The sounds: the sputtering of go-ped engines, the shrill wail of police sirens, the clamour of hundreds of street pedlars, the hum of air-conditioners blasting warm air out on to already humid, muggy streets.

So hard to let go of that. It all seemed so real.

The barge tooted its steam whistle on the far side of the bridge, sounding a warning to another barge coming upriver.

It could be worse, Sal. Isn't this better? London 1889?

Both Maddy and Liam seemed to be revelling in it, savouring

every experience like tourists on holiday. And Rashim? He was just as bad; he seemed to be treating the experience like some extremely realistic Victorian London virtual-reality simulator. She envied all three of them. They were having fun.

Me on the other hand? I feel lost.

Lost. Like a ghost. Like some mournful spirit that hasn't quite realized it's dead and that it's time to move on.

A ghost.

'Sal?'

Becks had been saying something to her. 'Sorry, what?'

The support unit gestured to the hand baskets nestling in the snow at their feet. 'We should return. You are scheduled to make dinner.'

Sal nodded. It was her turn to cook tonight and she'd promised to make a rabbit stew. Several skinned rabbits – all muscle-purple bodies with fur booty feet – rested on top of a basket of potatoes, onions and turnips.

'Yes, all right.' Becks stooped down and picked up both baskets and Sal led the way back over Blackfriars Bridge, heading up towards Farringdon Street.

CHAPTER 4

1889, London

'I'm sorry.' Liam put his tankard down. It sloshed ale on to their table. 'Did you just say —?'

'The Fire of London, yes.' Maddy spooned some more stew into her mouth. 'Good this, Sal,' she said, her mouth crammed full. 'It's really good.'

'Back to the point, if you please,' said Liam. 'The Fire of London?'

'Yeah, why not?'

'Why not?' Liam looked round at the others. 'Um . . . let me see now. Oh yes . . . burning to death.'

'Oh, please. Liam, you can be such a dork.' She rolled her eyes. 'I'm not suggesting we stand in the middle of the fire. Clearly.'

'But this whole city burned down, didn't it?'

'No. Some of it did. And obviously we watch the fire from a part that didn't burn down. It's not complicated.'

'I think it would be interesting to see that,' said Sal.

Maddy nodded gratefully. 'Thank you, Sal. I think so too.'

'But why? Why go? Why take the risk?' Liam was flicking his spilled ale off the side of the table.

'We're not going to *burn*, Liam. Sheesh!'

'Well, all right, not the burning, I'm talking about the risk we take when we open a portal.'

Rashim nodded. 'He's right. It's not a necessary journey. Every time we open a window we broadcast a tachyon signature.'

'Yes and . . . sure, there's a small chance – a *small* chance – that someone might be looking our way at this time and spot it. But come on, guys, what is actually the chance of that?'

'There is no precise figure that can be calculated.' Stew dribbled from the side of Bob's mouth on to his chin as he spoke.

'Best not talk with your mouth full,' replied Maddy – with her mouth full. 'It's not a good look for you.' She turned back to Liam. 'We've been waiting here for what? Nine, ten weeks? If the agency had an actual fix on where we were, we'd have been visited again by now.'

'But one of their units *did* come through,' said Rashim, casting a glance at Becks. She was sitting beside Bob and spooning stew silently into her mouth, managing to make less mess than him.

'Well, OK, obviously back in 2001 it was a close thing.' Maddy winced. 'We must have left a trail behind us that they managed to follow. I mean, a stolen vehicle . . . I guess those support units must have tapped into police radio traffic or something and they somehow zeroed in on that school. But remember? Computer-Bob was instructed to wipe himself after the last window opened. So, there's nothing we left behind that anyone could use to find us.'

'Aye, but what if one of them got to him before he managed to wipe himself?'

Maddy shrugged. Her point was self-evident. 'Then we'd have had a visit already. Fact is we haven't. Which means, *obviously*, we lost them.'

'And we could be anywhere. Any-*when*,' added Sal. 'They don't know.'

'Right. The only thing that might help them close in on us

22

is if we go and do something really moronic that totally changes history and they track the origin of it back to this time.' She pushed her glasses up her nose. 'And I'm sure it doesn't need to be said, but that's something we, of course, are *not* going to do.'

'Still a risk, though,' said Liam.

'Ye-e-sss, but come on, a really tiny one. Crossing the street here is a risk. Using a public frikkin' toilet here is a risk.'

'More for us than you boys,' added Sal.

'Look, the way I see it,' Maddy continued, 'we're home and dry. We actually made it. We escaped whatever messed-up doomsday-loving Waldstein-cult-agency we were involved with and now we're free. And,' she said with a smile, 'as a bonus, we have a frikkin' time machine.'

'Which you want to now *play* around with?'

Maddy frowned. 'No, come on, Liam, that's not fair. You're making me sound childish. I just think we could take a peek, you know? Explore a little. Not too far back in time. And not too far away in distance. I mean, just think of all the things we could get a look at without pushing the displacement machine to its limits: the coronation of Queen Victoria, the execution of Charles I, the first stone of Westminster Abbey being laid. Shakespeare? How cool would that be? Meeting Will the Quill, giving him some story ideas?'

'Good God, yes,' muttered Rashim.

'Charles Dickens?'

Liam's face flickered with an idea. 'Charles Darwin?'

'There ya go, the monkey guy. We can see all these people and some of the great events and stuff that happened in London. Sure, I mean, we couldn't talk to them or, if we did, it would have to be in a very limited way and –'

'It would be inadvisable to talk directly with significant historical figures,' said Bob.

Maddy nodded. 'Fair point. But we could see them, couldn't we? Witness them and all their many great moments.' She pushed her bowl away. 'I never realized how much cool stuff has happened over the centuries here in London until I started trawling through our database. And it's all, like, on our doorstep!'

'Limiting the geo-displacement to just London will significantly reduce the energy burn,' conceded Rashim, 'and, of course, produce less of a trace tachyon signal.'

'That's my point. It's not like I'm suggesting we go swanning off to Ancient Egypt to watch the pyramids being built. Or go witness Neanderthal cavemen hunting woolly mammoths in Nepal. There's so much closer to home that we could see.' She shrugged. 'Why not? We owe nothing to anyone. We don't have the families we thought we had, leverage that might have been used against us. It's just us . . . and, provided we're not stupid, provided we're not hurting anyone, provided we're not changing anything, why can't we live a little?'

She directed her gaze at Liam. 'Hmmm, Liam? It's not like you to be the worrywart.'

He stroked his chin for a moment, weighing that up, then shrugged. 'Aye, living a little does sound good.' He grinned. 'Ah well, the Fire of London it is, then.'

CHAPTER 5
1889, London

'Everyone ready?'

The others nodded. Again forced to improvise, they wore clothes that could pass for the period – on this occasion the mid-seventeenth century – just as long as no one studied them too closely. Liam wore a loose linen shirt that spilled over dark trousers. Maddy and Sal wore long, coarse linen shifts and plain bodices that tightly hugged their waists. Only Rashim stood out, insisting that his silk-lined waistcoat would easily pass as a gentleman's doublet beneath his cape, especially if everyone around them was going to be distracted by the wholesale incineration of the City of London.

Since this wasn't a mission so much as self-indulgent sightseeing, Bob and Becks were remaining behind to watch the dungeon and operate the displacement machine.

'You all have your transponders safely secured?' said Rashim. The transponders were something Rashim had cobbled together from the various components they'd brought with them from the archway. Crude, simple and small devices the size of walnuts. Sal had hers inside a pendant that hung from a loop of chain tucked inside her dress. She absently felt for the bump beneath the cotton, resting lightly just below her collarbone.

'They're just a back-up,' said Maddy, 'in case we get separated.

And, of course, if that does happen, you all know the drill. Right?'

'We make our own way back to the rendezvous point and wait,' said Sal with a weary we've-been-over-this-already tone. 'Which is basically just outside on Farringdon Street . . . only two hundred and twenty-three years earlier than now.'

Maddy sighed. 'All right, then. Sal and Liam, you're up first.'

They took their places, side by side, within the squares marked on the floor. Both of them were standing on a small mound of dirt. To one side was a metal pail filled with a peaty composite of river silt and horse manure that Bob had scooped up earlier. Each opened window was going to result in a deeper and deeper trough being excavated out of the stone floor, so this worked as an alternative: standing on a mat of dirt, their feet were safely elevated from the floor so as not to bisect the bottom of the cubic volume being propelled through chaos space.

As always happened just before a displacement, Sal felt butterflies stirring in her belly.

It's only a second, she told herself. Less than that even. An instant. And yet it felt to her like several protracted minutes. She hated the total milky nothingness of it, nothing but a shifting, marbly, wispy snow-white.

Not exactly nothing, is it?

She shot a glance at Liam. He winked back at her. 'All right there, Sal?'

'I'm fine.'

He knew exactly what unsettled her. He'd told her he thought he'd seen them too: *something*, moving around faintly out there in that void. Nothing quite definable, nothing truly solid enough to offer the description of a shape of any kind. A thing – *things*, in fact, plural – that seemed to circle with malevolent curiosity, spiralling closely, but never quite getting near enough to be seen more clearly before they emerged on the other side.

But they were getting closer. Sal was sure of that. As if they – or it might be an IT, one thing stretched out into long tendrils that could be mistaken for multiple entities – seemed to be getting quicker at knowing she was sharing chaos space, spiralling towards her ever more quickly, ever more curious.

'Hands and feet inside, kiddies,' said Maddy. 'Hold perfectly still.' She looked at them both and grinned. 'And say *cheese*.'

Liam guffawed sarcastically. Sal cocked an eyebrow.

'Ten . . . nine . . .'

'You know what I think them things are, Sal?' said Liam quietly.

'What?'

'Lost souls. Ghosts maybe.'

Sal looked at him. 'Is that you *reassuring* me?'

'Well, my point is a ghost can't exactly hurt you now, can it?'

'That's not really helping.'

'. . . four . . . very still, both of you . . . three . . .'

Ghosts? In other words, things that were once people. Sal felt her stomach flop queasily. People. Perhaps the 'ghosts' of other people foolish enough to be doing this stupid thing. As Maddy counted down the last few seconds, her voice lost behind the hum of discharging energy, Sal wondered why the hell they were doing this.

Oh yeah, for fun.

And then she was experiencing that horrendous, vomit-inducing *drop*.

She kept her eyes clasped shut. Falling. Only it wasn't quite like falling; there was no sensation of wind rushing past her, no whistling roar in her ears. It was actually just weightlessness. And complete silence except for the thud of her own heart.

27

She counted in her head. Counted enough seconds to call it a minute.

Come on, come on. End! Please!

1666, London

Sal felt something tickling her nose and warily cracked open an eye. Hovering in front of her was a nugget of manure sprouting a twist of hay; equally weightless, it had risen up from beneath her feet and spun lazily in front of her. She welcomed having something else to look at. A universe with nothing in it but herself and a lump of rotating horse poo.

Then *thud*. Her feet made heavy contact and the turd splatted on to the hard-packed dirt between her feet. But still the milky, featureless dimension. Only it wasn't. Sal could smell burning. She could hear the clatter of a cartwheel, the snort of unsettled horses, voices raised in panic.

Liam emerged out of the swirling mist and grabbed her arm roughly. 'Watch out!'

He pulled her back up against a wooden-slat wall, and a second later a heavily laden cart, precariously top-heavy with furniture and worldly possessions, clattered noisily past them both. The driver was slapping the hindquarters of his horse with a cane.

'Move out of the way up there!' he called to another pair of figures staggering towards them through the fog of smoke. Sal quickly recognized them as Maddy and Rashim.

The four of them were reunited amid curls of acrid smoke.

'Jesus, I can't frikkin' breathe here,' rasped Maddy, holding her arm over her nose and mouth.

A strong gust of wind flushed the smoke aside and they found themselves in a narrow street. On both sides, towering wooden-slat buildings tilted towards each other across the street; their increasingly overhanging layers, topped with roofs of thatch and wooden tiles that almost met, cast the narrow cobblestone and packed-dirt street in perpetual gloom.

'That way . . . I think,' said Maddy, pointing. 'It should take us down to the river.'

They hurried after the cart as it rumbled and bounced down the narrow street. Above them, lead-lined windows hung open and anxious faces peered out at the thick pall of smoke above the rooftops. Banks of it, like cloud banks, filled the afternoon sky.

Others began to fill the narrow street, spilling in from side alleys and even narrower rat runs between tall, leaning shanty-buildings made of wood with thatched reed roofs. Everyone was hastily heading in the same direction, south, instinctively drawn towards the river's edge. They were all laden with possessions, bundles of family heirlooms, and carrying their children, taking their babies away from the ominous, advancing smoke.

Jostled, bumped, compressed into an increasingly dense, surging river of people, they were finally ejected on to a broad wharf that stepped down towards the river, platform by platform, rickety stairwell by rickety stairwell, to a confusion of jetties on high-tide stilts that emerged from the river's edge into the Thames like the teeth of a comb. Each jetty was flanked by all manner of lighters, dinghies and fishing boats that bobbed heavily on choppy waters beneath the unsafe overloading of people and their possessions.

Maddy studied their surroundings. Ahead of them, the river; beyond it the distant, chaotic shanty town of wooden buildings on the south bank. To their right, a crumbling, low stone wall followed the line that would one day be Farringdon Street – the remains of a Roman wall that once marked the pre-medieval boundary of Londinium. It ran down to the river.

To her left, looking eastward along the riverbank, she could see a bewildering encrustation of timber warehouses and yet more jetties, the forty-five-degree angles of many dozens of loading cranes, the vertical, swaying lines of hundreds of masts. London along the riverbank resembled a confusing, randomly intersecting, precariously leaning lumber pile. A mess of shacks, warehouses, tall six- and seven-storey timbered tenement houses, half built on land, half built on slime-covered stilts that descended into the river.

Beyond, a mile upriver, Maddy could see London Bridge stretching across the Thames, an ordered procession of sturdy stone and brick archways, topped with the same chaotic timber jungle of towering stacked houses. Once upon a time it was just a bridge; now the bridge itself had grown almost a whole town's worth of homes on top, like the bottom of a ship's hull growing a colony of barnacles.

'Let's head along the river,' said Maddy, pointing towards London Bridge. 'We can get a closer look.'

CHAPTER 6
1666, London

'Jay-zus, there goes another one!'

Three hours had passed. Liam and the others watched in silent fascination as a team of the watch, the city's volunteer firemen, secured half a dozen long-poled fire hooks. The hooks were gaffed over the frames of several top-storey windows. Then the men firmly grasped the bottom of the poles, five or six to each one, and at the blast of a horn they tugged in unison with a chorused grunt of exertion.

The five-storey tenement building – its upper floors projecting out precariously, making it look recklessly top-heavy and ready to tumble over of its own accord – creaked as the structure flexed. Another synchronized grunt rose from the men as they tugged again in unison, and they heard the first snapping of timbers at the very top. Wooden roof tiles began to cascade down on to the street.

'Hoy! All below!' shouted the watchman with the horn. 'She's coming down!'

The whole building swayed and flexed disconcertingly for a moment, then the entire rear timber wall began to peel away from the top. The roof, suddenly without support, collapsed in on itself with a deafening crash, dust billowed out of the open windows and a shower of shards and splinters rained down. Then the wall being tugged by the fire hooks groaned and began to fall outwards. The watchmen beat a hasty retreat as it slowly arced out, like peel from an apple, teetered and then fell to the ground, shattering into brittle fragments and shards across the wharf. In several places the wharf was smashed through, structural beams crashing through the planking itself, down through the criss-crossed lattice of wood pylons and struts and splashing into the Thames below.

Liam whooped excitedly at the spectacle of it. All that remained of the tall building was one stubborn far corner, two storeys high, which wavered for a moment then it too creaked, groaned and finally folded in on itself and, with a crash, became part of an untidy, jagged mound of splintered lumber.

Through the cloud of swirling dust where the building had once stood they could see a horizon of huge rolling tongues of orange flame, whipped up by a fresh westerly breeze that was pushing the fire eastward. The flames were leaping greedily from rooftop to rooftop. Showers of sparks and tufts of blazing roof thatch danced in an updraught of hot air, effortlessly leapfrogging the firebreak gaps of the buildings that had already been pulled to the ground.

Maddy glanced to their right. London Bridge, just beside them, a towering wide structure that reached confidently across the river on its stone and brick base, was already on fire. The tall, top-heavy spires of tenement housing on the northern end of the bridge were now burning ferociously. Earlier they'd watched as teams had frantically attempted to pull down enough buildings to create a firebreak that would save the bridge. But the effort had turned out to be too little, too late.

Below the bridge, near the base of the brick archway stanchions, all manner of boats had begun to gather. None of them were *directly* beneath the bridge for fear that the flaming debris now raining down might land on them and set their tar-painted decks alight. Dinghies criss-crossed between the larger boats across choppy waters as enterprising oarsmen raced each other towards floating valuables that had been tossed from the windows above.

And now Maddy could make out individuals trapped in the tenement buildings already on fire. People were desperately hanging out of wide-open windows that spewed thick columns of white smoke, waving their arms, waving rags, screaming, pleading for help.

My God.

She'd witnessed scenes like these before in news footage from Manhattan: workers in smudged office-white shirts and loosened business ties precariously dangling out of the waffle framework of the World Trade Center. Waving for attention as they became framed, engulfed, overpowered by billowing clouds of grey-black smoke.

All of a sudden this didn't feel so much like historical sightseeing but the worst kind of awful voyeurism.

She saw a woman finally letting go of a window frame. Dropping four, five storeys plus the height of the bridge itself down into the Thames. In one arm she held a bundle of rags. The other arm flailed to keep herself upright. She disappeared into the water and Maddy didn't see her emerge.

Another person dropping. A man, his clothes, or perhaps it was his hair, on fire, left behind a drifting vapour trail of smoke. In the air she could smell it – burning fat. Above the cacophony of human voices, the roar and crackle of flames, she could hear the squeal of pigs, the shrieking of other trapped animals. And that's what she hoped was the source of the odour of cooking flesh. But that was denying the obvious. It was just as likely the smell of *humans* cooking too. She felt like throwing up.

Her eyes met Liam's. He'd just seen the same things as her:

33

people desperately leaping for their lives, quite possibly knowing the jump was futile, probably fatal, but unable to withstand the searing heat of the flames a moment longer. He could also smell the same thing; he was wrinkling his nose.

'I've seen enough,' said Maddy. Her voice was lost in all the noise, but all the same he seemed to understand what she'd just said. He'd seen enough too. This little field trip was a bad idea. Come to think of it — a pretty *sick* idea actually. That's what the grimace on Liam's face was telling her. That he'd come to the same conclusion. Maddy tapped Rashim's and Sal's shoulders. They both turned.

'We're going back!'

'OK,' said Sal. Her face told the others that. *That's it, enough.*

'Rashim? We're going!'

She turned and led the way westward along the wharves at the river's edge. Other people were streaming the same way. The fire seemed to have consumed the entire city to the east of London Bridge and, like the herd instinct of wild animals beating a retreat before a raging forest fire, the people all around them sensed this was no longer a place to stand and passively watch events unfold. The flames were coming this way, fanned by a lively, gusting breeze rolling in from the Thames, pulled in by the inferno as it sucked hungrily on fresh oxygen.

Maddy clattered down a flight of rickety stairs to a lower wharf, to their right the open cellar and workshop of a cooper. A craftsman inside was busy packing the most valuable tools of his trade, his wife loading their life's possessions into barrels that Maddy guessed were going to be dropped into the water and floated across the river. The others right behind her, Maddy fought her way past people trying to clamber down further flights of steps towards the water, where dinghies and lighters bobbed and oarsmen offered their taxi services at grotesquely inflated prices.

She ducked under some beams supporting the shack above and found the small wooden platform came to an end. Ahead was a stepladder that took them back up again to 'street level'. At the top she was gasping, jostled by people carrying sacks of goods and possessions on their backs. Moving along the river's edge was effectively an assault course of platforms, steps, ladders, stairways, beams, struts, barrels, loops of hemp rope hanging from beams above, low enough to garrotte the unobservant.

Another five minutes of climbing, clambering, ducking and weaving and they were back up on a cobblestoned quay so congested that people near the edge were in danger of being shunted over the side, down on to the shingle roofs of the riverside shanty town below. Maddy was utterly spent. She doubled over, hands on her knees, and retched.

Liam was beside her, gasping for air himself. 'Don't bleedin' stop!'

'I . . . I need . . . I need to catch my breath!'

Rashim and Sal joined them, the three of them forming a tight knot round Maddy, amid a surging river of people.

'The fire is moving faster,' said Rashim. 'Faster than we are!'

Maddy stood up to look. She nodded. It was. The temperature of the air had risen noticeably. The cautious retreat of the people around them was now beginning to turn into a panicked rout.

The sky was no longer a looming telltale bank of low-hanging smoke, above smouldering thatch roofs; instead, it was now a clearly visible churning wall of flames. Houses that, earlier in the day, had taken half an hour for the fire to catch, get a grip of and consume until they collapsed were now spontaneously igniting ahead of the flames, so hot was the ambient air temperature.

'Why did we get so close to the fire?' cried Sal. 'We're *too* close!'

Maddy shook her head. It didn't make sense. 'It wasn't meant to have reached this far yet! I thought we were safe west of the bridge!'

'Well, we're not!' cut in Liam. 'Come on! We *have* to keep moving!' He grabbed her arm, tugging her after him as they moved once more with the flow of people.

All of a sudden, above the screams of panic, the roar of pursuing flames, they heard the unmistakable crack of a single musket shot. The sea of fleeing Londoners stalled.

Ahead of them Maddy could see people had stopped and were backing up. Beyond them was an open space: twenty feet of vacant quayside littered with abandoned carts, bundles of rags and a line of soldiers, the King's Guard, in dark green tunics and iron breastplates, muskets presented forward.

Another crack of a musket. A warning shot over everyone's head. A captain of the guard on horseback emerged from behind the line of his men and gestured at the stalled crowd to back up the way they'd come.

'No further!' he bellowed as the horse beneath him jittered nervously. 'You must all withdraw the way you came!'

Angry, anxious voices from the crowd chorused their indignation.

'Back I say!' He coaxed his horse towards the people. 'Back, or make your way down to the river! There are boats, lighters waiting for you! But you cannot take another step this way!'

Liam craned his neck to see better. 'Why aren't they letting us through?'

'I don't know,' replied Maddy. She turned to look for another direction in which they could head. Behind? No. Back that way they'd face a wall of increasingly unbearable heat; she could already feel it on her cheeks. To their left was the edge of the quay, and beyond it winding stairways and creaking ladders, timber rooftops leading down through the stepped shanty town to the already overcrowded jetties. And right? It was blocked by the stone front wall of a large storehouse. Narrow rat runs either side of it would take them northwards up into the city where the fire was already burning and spreading down towards the river. It seemed they were in a rapidly shrinking pocket, and the only way out was being blocked by these soldiers.

Half a dozen more guardsmen emerged from the large double doors of the storehouse, running swiftly to rejoin the others. One of them said something to the captain. He suddenly reined his horse in.

'Get back! All of you fools! Get back! On the King's orders . . . and for the love of God . . . you people must GET BACK!' The captain swung his horse round and spurred it savagely, clattering back towards his men.

Maddy glanced at the storehouse doors, left open. What were they running from? Because they'd just come out fast, running like a raging bull was hot on their heels. It was dark inside the storehouse. She heard the captain bark an order and, with a clattering of plate armour, the rattle of harnesses and buckles, the soldiers lined up across the quayside began to withdraw hastily. Once again, she looked back at the dark interior of the storehouse and saw something fizzing, sparking, flaring across the floor.

Oh my God . . . is that —?

CHAPTER 7

1666, London

Liam was lying on his back, his fuzzy, concussed mind recalling a moment of déjà vu; a moment like now with him lying flat on his back, stunned and winded, and looking up at the dark sky. Last time he'd experienced this, he'd been looking up at a blue sky over the medieval city of Nottingham, arrows silently flitting overhead like summer bees. Now he was seeing a swarm of fireflies lazily dancing down towards him like snowflakes.

Pretty. He grinned groggily.

He lay there for what seemed like ten lazy minutes but, for all he could determine, might have been ten seconds. Smoke billowed across his field of vision and he sensed sluggish movement all around: people like himself knocked flat by something, and now, with their ears ringing, beginning to stir. He eased himself up on to one elbow to look around and take stock.

The crowd he'd been wedged right in the middle of moments ago was gone. In its place was a dust-covered carpet of bodies, some stirring like him; some writhing in agony. Some perfectly still. And, nearer to where the large storehouse had stood moments ago, some in pieces. The storehouse was gone. In its place was a dishevelled mound of stone and wooden beams from which rose wisps of smoke and dust that spiralled up to join a mushroom cloud that was slowly drifting westward.

He felt a hand on his shoulder shaking him roughly. He turned to see a ghostly, powder-white face. For a moment he didn't recognize the man. Then he noted the clipped beard, the long dark hair pulled back into a tidy ponytail, now grey with dust.

Rashim was saying something, his mouth flapping, but his voice sounded like it was arriving from afar, down a long pipe. Faint, muffled and lost amid the whining burr of white noise in his ears. Liam guessed what he was shouting. 'I think I'm OK.'

Rashim was pointing to something. He felt Rashim touch his ear and then presented the tips of his fingers coated with startling, livid red blood. He was shouting something else.

Liam shook his head. 'I said I'm all right!' he shouted back. 'I just can't hear too well!'

Rashim grabbed his arms and hefted him to his feet. He had a better view of things now. Thirty, forty – maybe more – bodies littered the cobblestones around them. Those that hadn't been killed or wounded or simply knocked flat on their backs by the blast had retreated. Many of them had leaped over the quayside down on to the shanty buildings and several of those flimsy structures had collapsed under the impact.

'Where's Maddy? Sal?'

Rashim shook his head and said something in reply. Gone? Did he just say '*gone*'?

Liam felt the blood drain from his face. *Gone*, as in *dead*? He looked around him at the bodies. 'Where the hell are they?'

Rashim punched his arm to get his attention. 'I . . . think . . . they . . . ran!' he mouthed carefully. Liam looked again at those around him. Some of them were now getting to their feet, others unable to. He saw a young man his age sitting up and staring down, wide-eyed and uncomprehending, at a foot-long shard of wood embedded into his chest just below the collarbone. Blood jetted out in lazy arcs on to his lap.

Jay-zus.

A woman nearby or, more precisely, the top half of a woman.

But, and he felt a guilty stab for feeling almost elated with relief, no sign of Sal or Maddy. The shrill ringing in his ears was beginning to subside. He could hear Rashim now.

'They ran. I think.'

'Which way?'

'I don't know. The blast knocked me over too. I didn't see which way.' He looked towards the edge of the quay. 'Perhaps they went over the side?' Rashim turned back to him. 'What now?'

Liam didn't have the first clue.

'We can't stay here! The fire's approaching.'

The roaring he still had in his ears was, he realized, not the tail end of concussion, but the proximity of the fire front. The riverside building they'd passed, just before the now absent storehouse, a grand three-storey, stone-built merchant's house, was burning. He could hear glass shattering from the heat, the timbers of the gable roof inside snapping and giving.

Ahead of them he saw the soldiers lining up again. They'd retreated fifty yards further back along the quay and he saw several of them hastily rolling barrels into the open doors of the next building along.

He understood now what they were up to. A firebreak: they were attempting to create a much wider firebreak to contain the fire. The half-measure fire gaps they'd seen being deployed near London Bridge were clearly not enough. More than one building's worth was needed to save what was left of the city west of this point. But now they were resorting to desperate, more drastic measures to do it: gunpowder instead of fire hooks.

And, with the flames advancing so quickly, he suspected the captain and his men were under strict orders not to delay lighting their fuses under *any circumstances* . . . even if that meant the deaths of innocent civilians.

'Liam!' Rashim grasped his arm. 'We have to move!'

A portion of an overhanging wall at the front of the merchant's house collapsed on to the cobblestones below, sending a shower of sparks into the air and unleashing a roiling inferno within the building. Exposed to these closer flames, Liam could feel his face burning from the heat.

'Over the quay!' he gasped. 'That's the only way!'

CHAPTER 8

1666, London

They raced towards the edge of the quay, but others nearby had the same idea and a logjam built up round the top of a narrow wooden stairwell that creaked alarmingly under the weight of so many people using it at the same time.

'Liam!' barked Rashim. 'The roof!'

Beside the creaking stairwell was the flat timber terrace of a building a twelve-foot drop down from the lip of the quay. Rashim swung his legs over the side and leaped down. Liam joined him a few seconds later, the flimsy planks wobbling unsteadily beneath them.

'Jay-zus, it feels like it's ready to give!'

The heat in the air all around them was making the already summer-dry wood even more brittle. In many places scorch marks and small patches of smouldering timber indicated where tufts of burning thatch had landed and started work on the beams and planks. Liam found a ladder leading down inside the wooden shack and led the way.

They emerged on to a plank walkway already swaying under the weight of dozens of other people burdened with leather buckets and cloth sacks of valuables. The walkway – supported on wooden pylons and cross-beams tethered together with hemp rope – sloped downwards, turned left and dipped more steeply, before it evened out and joined a narrow jetty.

As they pushed their way past a man trying to drag a heavy oak casket behind him, they heard an almighty crash from above, and a shower of sparks billowed over the side of the quay, raining down on to the wooden shacks.

They forced their way on to the jetty, a standing space no more than forty feet by fifteen, and already almost completely filled with people, crates, barrels, goats and chickens in wicker baskets. Around the jetty, a dozen vessels of varying sizes were bobbing and swaying as agitated negotiations were conducted across the water, with extortionate 'rescue fees' being called out by the boatmen.

Liam could see the boats were all keeping a wary distance from the desperate people on the jetty; the crews were holding oars, clubs and coshes, one of them even had a sabre, ready to fend off a last-minute rush. Looking up behind him, he could see the roof of the shack they had jumped down on to a minute ago was already sprouting yellow flames. The rest of this ramshackle shoreline was going to be on fire within the next ten minutes. There *was* going to be a last-minute scramble, a point at which those on the jetty weren't going to care whether they might be coshed, clubbed or hacked at . . . the heat was going to be too much for them.

They needed to negotiate their way on to one of these boats. Now.

'Rashim!' He glanced at his friend's expensive tailored waistcoat. 'You look rich, come on!' He grabbed his arm and shouldered his way through the baying crowd towards the nearest boat, bobbing three yards to the right of the jetty.

He cupped his hands. 'Hoy! Hoy! Over here!'

One of the boatmen looked Liam's way.

'I have a *gentleman* here! A gentleman who needs a boat!'

Heads on the jetty turned towards them. Anxious faces, angry faces.

The man on the prow of the boat craned his neck, got a good look at Rashim and grinned. 'Aye, there's space here for a gentleman!'

'And his *servant*?' pleaded Liam.

'That's up to the gentleman!'

Rashim followed Liam's nod. 'Yes! Of course! Passage for two!'

'Forty pounds for the both!'

Rashim looked at Liam. 'We don't have any —'

'Jay-zus!' hissed Liam. 'Just agree, will you? We'll worry about that later!'

Rashim turned back to the boatman. 'It is a deal, sir!'

The man on the prow nodded at Rashim. 'Throw me ya purse!'

'No!' bellowed Rashim indignantly. 'Absolutely not, sir! I will only pay once we're aboard!'

The boatman relayed that over his shoulder to another man at the back of the boat who appeared to be the sailor in charge of the small vessel. He craned his neck curiously to get a better look at Rashim then eventually he nodded.

'You'll 'ave to swim to us!' the boatman called out. 'Ah'll pull you in!'

Just then they heard an almighty crash. Liam turned and saw the rickety stairwell they'd nearly taken down from the quay collapse in on itself. Forty or fifty people busily picking their way down the uneven plank steps disappeared along with it. The roof of the shack they'd descended was now a crackling inferno. He could feel the heat singeing his hair.

Liam was about to leap into the water when he felt a hand grab his arm roughly. He turned to see a red-haired woman, her crimson face blotched with soot and damp with rivulets of sweat. 'Take ma baby with you! Please!'

She pushed a terrified young boy forward. By the scrawny size of him, he was ten, maybe eleven, years old, with a tuft of blond hair atop a skinny frame of raggedy, patched clothes. He clung to his mother with the same savage desperation as she was clinging to Liam's arm.

'No, sorry . . . no, I can't!'

'Please! For God's sake have mercy for 'im!'

'I'm sorry!' He tried peeling her vice-tight fingers from his arm.

'Liam!' snapped Rashim. 'Come on!'

'Go!' he replied. 'Jay-zus! JUST GO!'

Rashim jumped into the swelling water and began to swim for the boat.

'God help ya, he's just a child!' the woman screamed into Liam's face. 'He can work for you! For your master!'

'No, I can't! I'm sorry, miss . . . now please, let me –'

He turned to see Rashim reaching out for the paddle of an oar being extended down into the water.

The woman released his arm, but then placed both hands on the sides of his head, turning him to face her, to really look at her. To *see* her. To know her . . . if only for that instant.

'*God help me*, he is all I have! All I am . . . please! If you do one act of kindness in yer life, let this be it!'

Liam looked down at the boy, but saw only hair; the boy's face was buried in the folds of the woman's dress, his arms wrapped round her.

Ah Jay-zus, Liam, you flippin' idiot . . .

He found himself nodding uncertainly. 'Aye, all right.' He reached down and grabbed one of the boy's stick-thin arms. The woman let out a choked gasp of relief.

'No! No, Mama! No!' The boy struggled to shake off Liam's rough grasp.

The woman, sobbing, fought with her child, wrenching his arms from around her waist. 'You let go now! Let go!'

The boy squirmed and screamed as Liam and the woman wrestled him off her. Liam twisted his small arms until he feared one of them might break, then he had him, trussed in his arms, a thrashing, crying, kicking bundle of twigs and rags.

The woman dropped down to her knees and grasped her son's face in her hands. 'William, my darlin' . . . my love! My baby! You're going with this kind young man! Be very good for 'im!' She quickly kissed his forehead then stood up and once more held Liam in an intense gaze.

'God will bless you, sir!' Her heat-blotched face, damp with streams of sweat and tears, betrayed the oddest contradiction: heart-rending grief . . . and elation. Unbridled relief.

'God will always bless you for this!'

A loud crash to their right. Liam saw a billowing cloud of sparks descend on to the jetty. The people, the animals, screamed in fear and agony as a roaring plume of flame coiled up into the evening sky, the temperature suddenly shooting up.

'LIAM!' Rashim was calling him. He could see Rashim slumped half in, half out of the boat. 'COME ON!'

There was not another second to waste. Liam leaped into the water, pulling the struggling boy with him. The cold water of the Thames was an instant relief from the now unbearable heat. With one arm, he pulled deep strokes through the water, dragging the boy behind him. Two, three, four . . . then his arm smacked against an oar extended towards him. He grabbed hold of it and pulled the boy up until he could reach for it too.

The boat was now beginning to draw away from the jetty. With a sense of urgency, oarsmen on both sides were pulling in unison to distance themselves quickly. Liam turned to look back and could see why. The jetty was being abandoned. The water around it frothed with people leaping for the river.

As a pair of hands roughly grappled for him, Liam pushed the boy forward. 'Take him first!'

The boy – nothing to him but wet rags and emaciated skin and bone – was pulled easily out of the water. A moment later a big butcher's hand grasped his and, with the last reserve of will and energy he had left, Liam worked a leg over the edge of the boat and rolled wet and coughing into the swilling bilge.

'That was close!' panted Rashim. 'Look.'

Liam wearily pulled himself up to look back over the retreating prow. The jetty was receding quickly, but even so, he could feel the heat on his face as if he was staring into the open belly of a baker's oven. In the gathering gloom of the evening, unnaturally dark from the low ceiling of thick smoke blocking out the late summer's evening dusk, he saw that flames were sweeping down from the riverside inferno and beginning to engulf the jetty. He saw the silhouette of a goat pulling frantically against its tether, chickens in a basket, their feathers alight, wings flapping in confusion and agony. And a solitary human figure sitting on the side, perfectly still, watching the boat recede.

The boy pulled himself up from the bilges, coughing, spluttering, but desperate to catch sight of his mother. Liam turned the boy's shoulders towards him. 'Hey.' He cupped his small oval jaw in a firm grasp that kept him from looking back. 'You don't need to see this, lad.'

A strong gust of wind stoked the flames and they swung round together, changing direction, and the woman was suddenly lost from view, embraced by flickering tongues of orange.

The boat rocked and swayed as it retreated towards the middle of the river. Silent . . . it was almost completely silent except for the soothing swoosh of oars being dipped into the water. Liam heard the clump of boots on wood, sloshing through bilge water, and then felt a hand on his shoulder. He looked up to see the man he'd glimpsed from afar, nodding acceptance of their transaction: a tanned face beneath a tricorn hat, a dark goatee, not unlike Rashim's, but long enough that it was braided with a ribbon. 'Now then, your master said he'd entrusted you with 'is purse of money, when we was pulling him aboard.' He grinned. 'Somewhat trusting of the gentleman, I'd say.'

Liam looked up at Rashim, who shrugged less than helpfully.

'I . . . well . . . now see, there *is* some money, sir. But it's not exactly on us.'

The captain pursed his lips with disappointment. 'Hmmm . . . you know, I expected something slippery like that. Not to worry.' He grinned again and looked at Rashim and the boy sitting beside Liam. 'I do believe there's some coin to be made here all the same.'

CHAPTER 9

1666, London

'Oh crud, where the hell are they?'

Maddy squinted to try to make sense out of the shadows. It was fully night-time now, but the sky wasn't dark or peppered with stars; instead, it was a dull cauldron amber, the glow of London alight bouncing back off the bottom of a thick unnatural cloudscape.

They were bathed in a sickly sulphur-coloured twilight, an end-of-world vision. Like an Impressionist painting of Hell or Constable depicting Armageddon with a palette of only crimson and sepia. And beneath a bloody sky the north bank of the Thames churned with people fleeing west, towards them. A seething, roiling mass of figures with not a single torch or oil lamp among them – there was light enough.

In the distance, a mile away, London Bridge was an arc of fire that reflected in the restless, choppy water. And the river itself seemed to be a logjam of boats from dinghies all the way up to a few square-rigged ships.

'Can you see them?' Sal shook her head.

Maddy couldn't understand what had happened to them. They'd been all together in that press of people. Then the explosion and she had figured out what that was now: demolition charges, far more efficient than men with hooks. She'd guessed what was coming a few seconds before they went off, time enough to pull Sal down to a crouch. Then the stampede had happened, people flooding towards the quay and the multitude of creaking stairs, ladders, wobbling walkways down to the river's edge. But somehow they'd found themselves pushed to one side with a rat run beside them. Instinctively, she'd led Sal that way, away from the herd.

Stupidly.

They were heading towards the fire front and very quickly found themselves running a gauntlet of flames between two tall buildings completely on fire. She'd felt her hair singeing, her skin beginning to blister and, for a moment, halfway down the narrow run, was considering this was where both she and Sal would die. Oddly, she'd assured herself that at least their deaths would leave nothing behind that could contaminate history. Just bones and charcoaled flesh. That would be it.

Her blouse was riddled with scorch-rimmed holes where embers and sparks had settled and burned through the material. The hem of her dress was burned up one side, all the way up to her thigh. It had caught and, as they'd sprinted for their lives, she'd been frantically patting the flames out before they engulfed her.

And now, somehow, they were here, alive. The flaming gauntlet had ended with a courtyard filled with ponies snorting, thrashing against their tethers and scraping the cobblestones in distress and panic. They'd pushed their way through, jostled and bumped by the horses' flanks, and eventually emerged on to a small area of inner-city pasture. It was filled with soot-covered people doubled over, coughing smoke out of their lungs, tendrils of smoke rising from everyone; winged collars, bonnets, cuffs, skirts, tricorn hats and flourishes of lace gently smouldering, waiting patiently to be patted down and extinguished.

As for Liam and Rashim, Maddy could only guess that the

surge of people had led them towards one of the myriad ways down to the riverside, in which case they were somewhere among the press of fleeing people picking their way through the assault course of the waterside shanty town. Or perhaps a boat had rescued them and somewhere out there, on that armada of vessels criss-crossing each other's paths, they were both waiting to be put ashore. Quite probably equally anxious about the fate of her and Sal.

'Jahulla!' Sal spat soot out of her mouth. 'Why did you take us so close to the fire?'

Maddy shook her head. 'I . . . I didn't think it had spread that far.'

She had a map. A map from the database that had shown cross-hatched areas depicting the fire's progress over the three days. Either the Wikipedia article was inaccurate or she'd been looking at the wrong map. Either way she'd messed up. Messed up and nearly killed them.

Jesus. And this was supposed to have been 'fun'.

You complete failure, Maddy. You frikkin' idiot.

'I'm sorry, Sal. I guess . . . I guess I screwed something up.'

Maddy led Sal out of the open area and down into a narrow cobblestone backstreet. Top-heavy houses, dark and vacated, leant over them like curious silent giants.

The scheduled return window was due any minute. They weren't entirely alone standing here on this quiet avenue. There were people a little way further along, fearfully looking eastward, watching London burn and praying the drastic firebreaks ordered by King Charles II earlier that evening were going to prevent the fire front advancing their way.

In any case, in the half-light they were probably not going to notice a momentary shimmering sphere and suddenly two fewer people in the world. No.

'What are we going to do? Are we going back without them?' asked Sal.

Maddy was considering the very same question. 'I think so. They're not lost, Sal. Remember? Rashim's transponders?'

Yes. That's what they would do. Go back and get the signal array pointing this way, sniffing tonight for the faintest telltale whiff of a solitary tachyon particle. This was, after all, the precise reason they'd all been issued with one, because something like this was bound to happen.

Because you're not a complete failure, Maddy. Because you were cautious enough to realize this could happen. Right. It was *her* idea for Rashim to knock up something cheap and cheerful.

If they were alive, they'd be broadcasting a signal they could zero in on to get them back. And, even if they weren't alive, they'd probably still be broadcasting . . .

Don't go there, Maddy. They're alive, OK? Just separated. That's all.

'Any second now,' she said. 'We'll zap back home and we'll locate them, Sal. No sweat.'

'I hope so.'

Maddy patted her. 'Sure we will. Liam always finds a way, doesn't he?' She forced a reassuring smile, but it was probably too dark to see, and felt just about as reassuring as a wink from a used car salesman.

'Until one day he doesn't,' Sal replied.

Just then they felt a puff of air in front of them and in the middle of the cobblestoned alleyway a dark six-foot-diameter sphere danced like a film of oil on water. Maddy could see the faint glimmer of an electric light bulb, the outline of Bob and Becks waiting to welcome them home. Maddy stepped through first and Sal followed her. And then it was gone in the blink of an eye, the beat of a heart.

Only one person noticed it: a woman hanging out of the narrow window of her home, directly above them. A woman anxious about her watchman husband, called to his duty and somewhere out there fighting the flames. She puzzled over what she thought she'd just witnessed in the alley below, puzzled for all of a couple of minutes and then a neighbour called up to inform her that her husband and the rest of his watch crew had been seen coming this way.

News was – or at least the hopeful rumour was – that the King's orders for drastic last-minute measures, for the gunpowder demolition, *might* just have done the trick, at least in terms of preventing the fire spreading any further westward. The woman barely heard that part. The word was her husband was alive, and that's really all she wanted to hear.

CHAPTER 10

1666, somewhere in the English Channel

Liam was aware of three things, one after the other in quick succession. Firstly that his head was throbbing. It seemed to be contracting and expanding with metronome regularity, like a blacksmith's bellows. With each throb, another dull wave of pain and nausea coursed through him.

Secondly that his nose and throat were clogged, almost completely blocked, with a syrupy-thick mixture of soot and snot. He hawked back some phlegm into his throat and almost immediately regretted it for the jarring pain in his head that it caused and a burning sensation in his nasal passages.

Thirdly that the world seemed to be swaying. His limp body, stretched out on the wooden floor, was slowly rocking from one side to the other as the world beneath seemed to want to gracefully lean to the left then to the right. That really wasn't helping at all with the nausea. He felt ready to casually heave his guts on to the rough floor beside his face, except for the fact that he suspected the gently rolling floor would tilt the vomit back towards his open mouth. He groaned miserably.

'Liam? Is that you?'

'Ishh meee,' Liam groaned in answer. His cheek pressed against rough planking that was rubbing his skin raw as his body rocked to and fro.

'Thank God! I was concerned you might be brain-damaged.'

Liam recognized the male voice: slightly effete, particular and precise in the way he spoke. Rashim. He cracked open one eye and instantly winced at the bleary stars and streaks of daylight that lanced across his blurry vision. He snapped his eye shut. That was daylight, a painful sliver of it.

'Where ishh thish plashe?' Liam slurred, still unable and unwilling to lift his head. His lips were pressed against the floor, dry and cracked. His own voice was a spike to his temple.

'At sea,' replied Rashim. 'I think.'

Liam's ears were still ringing ever so slightly. A faint, high-pitched whine like a dog whistle. But for the first time he noticed other sounds: the regular rhythmic creak of wood, the hiss and thump of sluggish waves against a hull.

He finally decided he had enough resolve in him to lift his head off the floor, feeling a wave of dizziness and nausea overtake him as he clambered on to unsteady hands and knees. He retched, producing a drool-thread of saliva and bile that swung from his mouth then dropped to the wooden floor beneath his spread palms. With eyes narrowed against the daylight, he looked up. He saw Rashim huddled against a wooden bulwark, arms wrapped round his knees. And beside him a sandy-haired boy, in more or less the same posture.

'Who's *he*?'

Rashim shrugged. 'He hasn't spoken to me yet. Maybe he'll tell you who he is.'

Liam let that go for the moment as he looked around. Planks of rough wood made a low roof, crossed with thick oak support beams. The wooden floor was a mess of coils of rope, barrels stacked on their sides and tethered together to stop them rolling. Large cloth sacks were piled up like bodies in a mortuary.

A ship. It looked like one of those old sailing ships. Yes, of course it was an old one. He remembered now, they'd gone back to 1666 to witness the Fire of London. Clearly they weren't back in the dungeon, so they were obviously still in 1666.

'What happened?'

'What do you remember?'

'The fire. Maddy's genius idea to make us a part of it.'

'What's the *last* thing you remember?'

Liam sat back on his haunches, wiping drool from his mouth. His head dipped low between his shoulders as he fought another urge to retch. He remembered an explosion. A big one. Being knocked off his feet and on to his back by the force of it. Then chaos. People panicking. He remembered that. A stampede towards the edge of a road or a quay of some sort and a steep drop beyond.

'An explosion. We all headed down to the river's edge, didn't we?'

Rashim nodded. 'That's quite correct.'

Liam could picture the panic, the wobbling world of rickety wood. Down on to a pontoon now, packed with baying, pleading people and surrounded by bobbing boats that rocked on water sparkling with the glints of reflected flame.

'We managed to get on board one of them boats, didn't we?'

'You agreed a price and we were pulled aboard. Yes.' Rashim rolled his deep hooded eyes. 'And you assured them I was a rich gentleman carrying lots of money.' He sighed. 'I'm not really sure what you thought the next step of your plan was going to be.'

Liam winced, cradling his thumping head. 'I got us away from the fire, didn't I?'

'This is true.'

'So, I saved us –'

'And this little mute urchin, for some reason.'

'But we're *alive*! We're safe, aren't we?'

'Hmmmm . . .' Liam sensed an ironic tone in Rashim's voice. 'Alive, yes. I'm not entirely convinced we're saved, though.'

The worst of the nausea was beginning to subside and Liam bum-shuffled across the coarse wood until his back rested against the bulwark, next to the boy, sandwiching his small frame between them. 'So, where the hell are we, Rashim?'

'You don't remember any more?'

'I think I remember swimming for my life.' He closed his eyes. The boy, *this* boy, he'd been dragging him along behind. Liam tried to remember more, but that was it.

'The boat that rescued us and about a dozen other people went downriver,' said Rashim, 'to some place called Tilsbury and their ship. They let the others off. Not us, though.'

'Jay-zus! Why the bleedin' hell not?'

'That's pretty much, word for word, what you screamed right in the face of the boat's captain.' Rashim turned to look at him. His wan smile seemed vaguely sympathetic. 'Before one of his men clubbed you over the back of the head with an oar.'

Liam winced. He'd thought his pounding head had something to do with the percussive impact of the explosion.

'No money,' continued Rashim. 'No getting off for us. I now have the distinct impression we're hostages of some sort.'

'What?'

Rashim shrugged. 'We're now a part of their *cargo*.'

'Jay-zus! What happened to honest-to-God charity? Doing a good deed for people in need!'

'Quite.'

Liam twisted to look out of the small hatch on his left. The hatch was ajar, the shutter gently banging against the frame with each slow roll. For the first time he noticed a six-foot-long thick cylinder of iron on a sturdy oak chassis, over small iron-rimmed wheels.

'Hang on.' He touched it warily, almost hoping it would vanish under his fingers and all of this would turn out to be a bizarre hallucination, a dream. 'This thing's a cannon,' he muttered.

'One of many,' said Rashim, nodding across the floor. Liam turned to look round at the space he'd woken up in. The low roof, the ropes and barrels. And yes, other trapdoors, other cannons, twelve down their side, another twelve along the other.

'This is . . . this is a gun deck?' Liam shuffled round to sneak a look out of the shutter beside him. He could see a deep, rolling blue sea and foam splashing up the side of the wooden hull towards him. 'And we're on a ship . . . out at sea?'

Rashim nodded. 'I do believe you've managed to catch up with current events.' He offered him a sardonic smile. 'Welcome, Mr O'Connor, to our *current* miserable predicament.'

'Jay-zus. Out of the bleedin' frying pan into —'

'The pirate ship. Or worse . . . slave ship.'

'Whuh?' Liam looked at him. 'We're *slaves*?'

Rashim shrugged. 'I'm sure we shall find that out soon enough.'

CHAPTER 11

1889, London

They emerged from their separate square-column fields back into the dungeon. Maddy waved at Bob to stop what he was doing.

'Don't bother resetting for the other two . . . we've lost them!'

Both support units and SpongeBubba froze. Even the flickering statistics displays on the monitors behind them seemed static.

'What happened to the others?' asked Becks.

Maddy offered a potted explanation between gasps. 'Bottom line is,' she finished, 'we got separated in the panic. And we need to find out if they're OK.'

'The transponders,' said Bob.

'Exactly, we need to zero in on them.' She looked across at Sal. 'We may even need to open up a portal right in the middle of flames, you know . . . if they're trapped or something!'

Bob nodded. 'I understand.'

Maddy made her way across to the computer table and sat down in the rocking-chair. 'Computer-Bob, you know all about Rashim's transponders?'

> **Affirmative, Maddy. A drip-rate signal of 1ppm per millisecond.**

Jesus. One tachyon particle per million. That was as slight as natural background radiation. 'How easy is it to pick up a signal as weak as that?'

> Not easy unless you know precisely where and when to look.

'I believe that was the point,' said Becks, wirelessly picking up on the exchange. 'Dr Rashim Anwar did not want you to be broadcasting your location too loudly.'

Maddy opened her pendant, pulled out her transponder and looked down at it absently. 'How long did he say these things' batteries will last?'

> Approximately five years.

More than enough. More to the point, though, was locating them right now. The transponders might be chirping away quite happily, but there was no knowing if Liam and Rashim were OK. Hurt or worse.

'OK, aim the array for about one mile due east of here and for about nine in the evening of the second of September 1666. That's when things went pear-shaped.'

> Affirmative.

Sal perched on the edge of the table. 'You know if we find their signal, and it's not moving, what that might mean?'

Maddy did know. They'd have to go and look all the same. They'd have to be sure. And, if their worst suspicions were confirmed, they'd need to reclaim the bodies. The thought unsettled, no, *shook* her.

'Oh God, Sal . . . what if they *are* dead?' Her voice wobbled uncertainly. 'Then it's my fault. I've got them killed and for why?' She balled her fist and banged it on her thigh. 'Because I was getting *bored*! Because I wanted to do some frikkin' sightseeing!'

Hadn't Liam said it was an unnecessary risk? Hadn't he said that? And she'd just bulldozed that quite legitimate objection of his aside.

Jeez.

'Maddy.' Sal leaned forward, her voice softened. 'If that's what it is. If . . . you know —' she didn't say it, didn't say *if we find them dead* — 'if that's what we end up finding, then you shouldn't do this. You can't do this.'

'Blame myself? Why not? It's my stupid fault!' Tears now. That just made her angrier. 'I'm a support unit. Right? Someone, somewhere, *designed* me.' She laughed humourlessly. 'Then why the hell did they design me to be so frikkin' stupid!'

Here it was. After so much together, after surviving mutants and monsters, Nazis and Neanderthals, tyrants and dinosaurs . . . it was a small dose of plain ol' home-grown stupid that was going to put an end to them. Because just the two of them, two meatbots and a walking filing cabinet wasn't a team any more. That was just two lost girls and a brick prison cell full of misplaced tech.

Computer-Bob's cursor skittered along the screen. Sal noticed it. She tapped Maddy's arm to alert her.

> **I have located two transponder signals.**

'Are they together?' asked Sal.

> **Affirmative, Sal. Approximately within a yard of each other.**

Maddy wiped her face dry, leaving smeared tracks of soot on her cheeks. 'Are they moving?' A far more important question.

> **I will need to make a second scan, but advance the time.**

'Advance it by a . . .' She found her glasses on the table and fumbled them on. 'Advance it by a minute.'

> **Affirmative.**

Both girls stared in silence at the screen, waiting anxiously. Becks and Bob joined them, standing either side of the rocking-chair. So easy to interpret that as a gesture of emotional support, of shared anxiety. So easy to think that, but then you had to remember they were meat machines: the lab-grown equivalent of a pair of sociopaths. Killers without conscience. All that made them not dangerous was a single friend–foe flag buried somewhere deep in the code of their artificial intelligence.

> **I have the same signals. Their geo-coordinates are identical. There is no movement.**

A minute's not enough. A minute could be the pair of them floundering, wondering which direction to run. 'Advance it by five minutes.'

> **Affirmative, Maddy.**

Another agonizing wait.

'Come on . . . come on,' Maddy muttered at the dialogue screen. Finally the cursor blinked and shuffled along its command line.

> **Signals reacquired. Five minutes' advanced time.**

'And?'

> **The geo-coordinates are different. Approximately two hundred and fifty-seven feet south-east of the previous reading.**

Maddy gasped air out of her lungs. 'They're alive!'

Sal smiled with obvious relief. 'Headed southwards. After that explosion they must have been carried towards the river.'

'Yeah. But that's not a great place for them to be stuck.' The map she'd had of the progress of the fire indicated that the flames had destroyed everything right up to the water's edge. 'We need to open a window down there.'

'It was well crowded though,' said Sal. 'Hundreds of people trying to get boats to rescue them.'

'I know, but we can't just leave it to chance that they find their way on to one. We've got to do something to help.'

'That would be inadvisable, Maddy,' said Bob. 'Opening a window in the middle of a crowd of people.'

Inadvisable and quite probably very messy. And, God knows, they might end up turning Liam and Rashim into human lasagne if they opened right on top of them. They could look into the future, though – Liam and Rashim's near future – to see if they manage to get rescued.

'Advance the clock by another five minutes . . . no, actually, make it ten.'

> **Affirmative.**

'If they're still stuck there,' Maddy said, 'then I say, screw it . . . we open a window a dozen yards out into the river. And I'm sorry if we end up chopping someone in half or putting a hole in someone's boat and depositing several dozen gallons of river water here in the dungeon . . . whatever. That's just tough.'

Sal nodded at that. Maddy twisted in the chair to look at Bob and Becks. 'You two aren't going to give me any grief over that call, are you?'

Both support units shook their heads. 'Their safe return is desirable,' said Becks evenly.

'Good to know you care.' She turned back to look at the screen eagerly. 'Come on, computer-Bob, what have you got?'

Another minute passed, then finally the cursor shifted once more.

> **Information: the signals have gone.**

'Gone? What do you mean, gone?'

> **I will have to widen the search field. One moment.**

'Maybe they got a boat?' said Sal hopefully.

'Or made their way along the river's edge? Maybe they're trying their luck further along.'

Possibilities. The clutching-at-straws type. But then there were other possibilities, *probabilities*. The flames had been moving frighteningly fast. Ten minutes could have seen the fire sweeping down into that quagmire of wooden buildings, incinerating everything in its path. Rashim's transponders weren't magical amulets – they weren't Frodo Baggins's ring – they were an even mixture of RadioShack electronic components and cannibalized bits from the future. Heat, enough of it, and they and Liam and Rashim could quite easily be cinders.

> **I am unable to pick up any signals.**

'Oh God!' whispered Sal. She buried her face in her hands and began to sob.

Liam's a survivor. Of that Maddy was certain. A born survivor. Or at least engineered that way. He wouldn't just stay there, frozen to the spot, waiting to die. At the very least he'd try – he'd jump in the river. He'd do something.

'No.' Maddy shook her head resolutely. 'No, goddammit, no, that doesn't mean game over. It means we have to look harder! Widen the search pattern. Maybe those transponders are malfunctioning, shorting out in the water or something.'

> **The signals are very weak, Maddy. We need to know quite precisely when and where to aim the array in order to pick them up.**

'So, we do a pattern search! Starting right now. Several miles up and down the river, either way. We use the last verified signal as the point of origin and we pattern-out from there. OK?'

> **This will take some time.**

'So get going, then!'

> **Affirmative.**

She turned to Sal, and rested a hand gently on one of her shaking shoulders. Her turn to be supportive, to be the strong one. 'Come on, Sal. Liam's a fighter. He's no idiot. I tell you what he's done . . . he's talked his way on to a boat and it's just sailed out of range, that's all. We'll pick him up again.'

Sal nodded. 'Yeah . . . yeah, I suppose.' She looked up at Maddy hopefully, her face now streaked with watery soot.

'Snap.' Maddy smiled. 'Now we've *both* got girly wet-with-tears faces now.'

CHAPTER 12

1889, London

Hissing rain. A constant swish of drizzle, punctuated with the heavy *tap, tap, tap* of fat, lazy drips from the top of the door frame to the puddle at her feet. Sal watched from the doorstep as Farringdon Street got on with its busy day. The beautiful snow was being turned to a dispiriting grey slush.

She wasn't alone this morning. The tall, stick-thin young man who worked for their landlord shared the doorway with her.

'I do hate the rain,' said Bertie. 'This freezing rain. It seems to get itself into all and everything.'

Sal nodded. The beautiful snow-white and blue-sky day yesterday had made London look like a picture postcard.

Bertie smiled clumsily at her. Something to fill the awkward silence. 'So, how go the doctor's experiments back in your lock-up?' he asked, tipping a nod at the gloom behind them.

'Oh, you know . . . OK, I guess.'

'I find modern science such a fascinating subject. I feel we live in such a wonderfully fortunate time.' Bertie shook his head in wonder. 'It seems not a single month passes without some incredible new invention or discovery being announced in the science journals.'

She noticed the smile on his pale skin. Not the cynical and lecherous grin of a young man trying to work his charm on a young lady, but rather an expression of innocent wonder. Boyish marvelling at exciting possibilities.

'I look at the light bulbs and other devices that use the electric power, those noisy horseless carriages, those cylinder-playing phonographs . . . and I feel like I am looking directly into the future. Quite exhilarating, I find.' He looked down at her. 'Tell me, do you ever wonder what the far future would look like? For example –' he gestured out at the street – 'what London would look like a hundred years from now? Or a hundred and fifty years?'

A hundred and fifty years? She did the maths. *2039.*

'I fancy all this old grime-covered brick and cobblestone would be long ago done away with. Replaced with tall, smooth towers of marble and steel. Perhaps every last man would have his own horseless carriage.' He looked up at the rain-heavy clouds. 'I could imagine the sky would be full of flying devices carrying people from tower to tower. Carrying people to work. Who knows? It could be that no man would even need to work! It might all be done for us by machines, by mechanical servants!' He laughed. 'Wouldn't that be such a sight!'

Sal nodded along with him.

'What about you, Miss Vikram? What do you think the future might be like?'

She wondered what to say, what to tell him. That the future would be utterly bleak. That, in many ways, the seeds of humankind's destruction were being sown, even now at the latter end of the nineteenth century. This Victorian world – Bertie's world – was on the cusp of discovering and utilizing the energy free-ride that was *oil*. And this world would *accelerate* throughout the twentieth century. Population levels would explode. Like some hardy, shrivelled weed in a plant pot gorging itself on freshly added mushroom compost, the world was going to flourish and bloom and grow far too large for its little pot. Then, eventually, having leached the last nutrients from its soil, it was going to turn on itself, cannibalize itself and eventually die.

She wondered how to tell him that. That, even now, mankind's clock was ticking down the time it had left to live.

'I think the future will be . . . *interesting*, Bertie.'

'Herbert.' He shrugged self-consciously. 'I hate that Del always introduces me as Bertie. It sounds like the sort of name you'd give to a terrier.'

'I'm so sorry, *Herbert*.'

He waved her apology away as a nothing-to-concern-yourself-about. 'I think it would be such an exciting prospect to imagine somehow being able to travel forward in time. To see what future we make with one's own eyes.' His eyes widened. 'Think of this! Perhaps a hundred and fifty years from now men will have invented transport that will take us to other planets entirely. The moon . . . Mars! Imagine that! Planets where perhaps other intelligent beings might be living right now, looking back at us and wondering what we must be like. What a thought!'

Space travel. Sal nodded and smiled again, not wanting to steal that naive optimism for the future from him and reveal that the best we were ever going to do was to reach our nearest neighbour, the moon. Walk around on it for a bit, pick up a few stones, plant a flag and then go home again. That was going to be the crowning glory of humankind, our one big foray off this world, leaving one dusty old American flag behind, and a few footprints that would never blow away in a fresh breeze on that sterile, lifeless rock. Footprints that were almost certainly going to last longer than humankind.

'Hey, Sal! Sal!' Maddy's voice echoed out from the gloom inside. 'Sal! We've found them!'

Maddy stumbled out of their dungeon, the low oak door clunking heavily against the brickwork. 'We've picked up a sig–' She spotted Sal had company in the doorway on to the street.

'Oh! Sorry . . . I . . .' Her jaw hung slack. Awkward.

Herbert looked at her then Sal. 'Ah, I presume this is to do with another one of your *confidential* scientific experiments?'

Sal smiled up at him. 'I'm sorry, Herbert, I probably ought to go and . . .'

'Yes. Yes, of course.' He nodded and bowed slightly. 'You have matters to attend to. It was a pleasure chatting with you, Miss Vikram.'

'Sal,' she replied and smiled. 'You can call me Sal.' She grasped his proffered hand. 'And it's been a pleasure for me too.'

Maddy acknowledged Herbert with a quick wave, ushered Sal back inside, then closed and bolted the door behind them. 'Computer-Bob picked up a signal,' she said, leading Sal over to the table and monitors.

'So, where are they?'

Maddy sat down in the rocking-chair. 'Computer-Bob?'

> **Yes, Maddy?**

'Put the location data up on the screen again.'

A monitor to their right flickered as a display appeared showing a string of numbers that both girls recognized as a time and location stamp. Sal squinted at the numbers. 'Isn't that a week *after* the fire? Am I reading those numbers right?'

Maddy nodded, frowning. 'Yeah, it's about that.'

'And the location? I'm not too good at making any sense of those numbers. That's not London, is it?'

'It's not here, that's for sure. Computer-Bob, can you put those geo-coordinates on to a map, please?'

> **Affirmative.**

69

On another screen a map of the world appeared, and then a moment later a red dot glowed on it. Maddy's response was to snort. Not a laugh so much as a nasal retort. 'What the . . . ?'

Sal muttered a curse under her breath. Not a Hindi one but one she'd already picked up from the milling crowds of dockmen and traders of London. '*Beggar me.*'

She looked at Maddy. 'What are they doing in the middle of the English Channel?'

Maddy cocked an eyebrow. 'Beats me.'

CHAPTER 13

1666, somewhere off the English coast

'Come on, you pasty-faced lot, the captain wants to get a look a' ya.'

Liam looked up at the sailor leering down at them. He had a face that seemed to be all beard with a ruddy-coloured, bulbous nose poking out of it, like an egg sitting at the bottom of a nest. A man anywhere between thirty and fifty, if Liam was trying to pin an age on him, but then it seemed to be that everyone in this time looked a decade or more older than they were.

'Get a leg up, then!' he growled, nudging Liam with his boot.

The boy got to his feet first and offered Liam a small hand to help him up. Liam smiled at him. That gesture – the extended hand – was the first time the boy had even acknowledged him since their escape from the fire. He grabbed the hand and groaned as he got to his feet. His head still throbbed every time he dared to move. Rashim followed them and they clambered up a ladder after the sailor, emerging into broad daylight.

'Good God,' uttered Rashim at the spectacle.

Liam's eyes wandered up the spider's web lines of the shrouds as they converged fifty feet above beneath the crow's-nest. The mainsails ballooned and rippled slightly, more than amply filled with a stiff westerly wind. All around them, the main deck was busy with men at work. For a moment, though, the bustling activity ceased as every last one of them, perhaps a hundred men in total, stopped what they were doing in synchronicity to get a look at them.

'Come on, ladies!' barked their escort. 'Yer not being paid to gawp like old women!'

'Ain't been paid nothin' yet anyways!' shouted someone from above.

'You'll be paid with my boot up your arse, Thomas, if you don't get them loose lines squared away!' Their escort muttered a stream of profanities under his breath and then beckoned Liam and the others to follow him. 'Come on! This way!'

They picked their way through a circle of men sitting cross-legged on the deck, splicing rope ends, all beards and sunburned foreheads. Liam offered a polite smile and 'excuse-me's as they stepped through. They were headed towards the aft of the ship, up some steps and on to a smaller raised deck. A crewman with a weather-tanned face and a dark blue cloth cap stood at the helm and grinned at them.

'New blood, is it?'

'Aye,' grunted their escort as they passed him. He led them up to a small oak door and rapped his knuckles on it. 'Captain Teale! I have yer stowers 'ere!'

Liam heard a muffled voice from within. Their escort quickly opened the door, ducking his head as he led them through. Liam's eyes adjusted to an interior gloom again. They were in a cabin twenty feet long and about fifteen wide, tapering at the far end. A row of small lead-lined windows wrapped their way round the end of the cabin, letting in a modest amount of light. Sitting in a chair, and slumped over a navigation chart spread out across a table, was the ship's captain, his face hidden beneath the dipped brim of a tricorn hat.

He looked up at them and now Liam could see his face. Unlike the rest of the sailors he'd seen so far, the captain's face looked a little softer, a little plumper, a little less weather-worn. He sported a beard and moustache trimmed neatly round his pursed lips, the beard long enough beneath his chin for the bristles to be twisted into a tidy braid, tied off with a yellow ribbon.

'My name is Captain Jack Teale. Captain of this vessel, the *Clara Jane*.' He studied them silently for a moment. 'Well,' he said finally, 'you're clearly not the usual kind we pick up: wayward dregs and scoundrels.' He took in Rashim. 'First mate here said something about you, sir, supposedly a gentleman of means.'

'I . . . well, I . . . think there was a misunderstanding the other night.' He looked to Liam for help. 'When we were rescued.'

'Aye, that's the thing,' cut in Liam. 'We were in a tight spot, so we were. That fire in London was completely out of –'

'Oh, indeed. I saw it. Quite something to behold. Tragic actually,' Teale conceded. He shrugged. 'But also something of an opportunity. We made some decent coin ferrying and "rescuing" that night.' His eyes narrowed. 'But it seems not with the three of you. Your negotiation, so I've been told, was somewhat less than honest.'

'I'm sorry.' Liam shrugged. 'I had to do something. It was that or burn to death.'

Captain Teale smiled. 'Can't say I blame you that much. I'd have done very much the same in such a desperate quarter.' He sat back in his chair, removed his tricorn hat and scratched at his scalp beneath long dark hair which, like the beard, was twisted into thick braids. 'The fact of the matter is I'm not a philanthropist, I'm a businessman, and this ship is a private enterprise. So, you'll be obliged to earn the fare you promised, before I think about letting the three of you go on your way.'

'Earn our fare?' Liam looked at Rashim, then back at Teale. 'What, as part of your crew?'

'Aye.'

'Uh, can I ask . . . for how long?'

Captain Teale ignored that. Instead, he was now studying Rashim. 'Now, sir. A gentleman, is it?'

Rashim offered a tentative nod.

'A gentleman without a single coin on him, so it seems.' Teale drummed his fingers on the table. 'Unfortunately for you. But I shall assume you to be educated? Well versed in current affairs? In words and numbers? Languages? Sciences?'

'Yes. Yes . . . of course.'

'Good,' replied Teale. 'Perhaps you might offer me a little decent conversation. The animals out there on deck are little more than shaved monkeys. Good men to be sure, but not gentlemen.' His eyes settled on Rashim's waistcoat. 'If I may, sir, that is a very nice doublet. I've not seen one cut quite like that before.'

'It's . . . uh . . . it's the latest fashion in Italy, I believe.'

Teale raised his eyebrows in appreciation. 'That so?' He got up, came round the chart table, bumping his hip clumsily on the corner. 'Ah, beggar me! Damned ships are all hard edges and rough corners.'

He stood in front of Rashim, rubbing his thigh. He reached out and ran his fingers over the fine silk. 'Very nice. Take it off, there's a good chap.'

Rashim glanced anxiously at Liam. The waistcoat contained his transponder, tucked away at the bottom of an inside pocket.

'I'd like to hang on to it, if that's OK with you?'

Teale raised an eyebrow. '*Oh-kay.*' The word was new to him. 'Ohh-kayyy? What is that? Italian?'

'No, not really.'

Teale cocked his head. 'I'll have the garment, if you please.'

'I'd really rather hold on to it.'

'You'll remove it or I'll have Mr Reynolds here remove it for you.' Teale shrugged. 'And, to be honest, he's not exactly light of hand. 'Twould be a shame to rip such a nice thing, don't you think?'

Rashim looked at the sailor who'd escorted them. The man scowled at him and growled.

Actually growled.

'All right, all right.' He unbuttoned the waistcoat and then hesitated a moment before handing it over. For a moment, Liam wondered whether Rashim was going to ask to retrieve the transponder first. But that would be foolish. This captain would probably mistake it for a piece of jewellery and insist on keeping it too.

Teale took the waistcoat, put it on over his own burgundy shirt and buttoned it up. 'Very nice. Very nice indeed.' He smiled, not unkindly, at Rashim. 'Thank you. Let's consider this a first instalment of money owed, shall we?'

'Can I ask how long you intend to keep us aboard?' asked Liam again.

Teale turned to look at him. 'Well now, sir, that all depends on how quickly this enterprise turns a profit.'

'So, what, uh . . . what exactly is this enterprise?'

'Is your servant here always so damnably precocious with his questions?' he asked Rashim.

'I . . . yes, I suppose he is.'

'Do you not thrash the impertinent fellow?'

'No. I don't *thrash* him. It's not that sort of a relation–'

'If he is indeed in your employ, sir –' Teale looked bemused – 'taking your wage, you're damned well entitled to thrash him.'

'No.' Rashim looked at Liam. 'We're not so much master and servant. We're more friends. Travelling companions actually.'

'And this small boy? Whose property is he?'

'Just another companion,' answered Rashim.

'*Companions*, eh?' Teale shook his head at the oddness of it all, then turned to Liam. 'As you're now a part of this ship's crew, you'll be addressing me as *Captain* in future, or – if I'm in a more genial mood – *Skipper*.'

Liam nodded. 'All right, Captain. May I ask again, what is this enterprise?'

'Since you ask,' Teale said with a shrug, 'our enterprise is relieving overladen Spanish merchant vessels of their burden.'

'So, this is a pirate ship?' asked Rashim.

'Good God, sir, no!' snapped Teale. 'Nothing so . . . so *criminal*! No, this is a *privateering* vessel. We have the King's blessing, of course!'

'Not yet we ain't,' grunted Reynolds.

Teale waved the man's comment away. 'Pfft! Mere paperwork. We shall have that trifling matter sorted soon enough.' He turned to Liam. 'Meanwhile my first mate, Reynolds here, will find some duties for the three of you to do. I'm not sure precisely what . . . messing around with grubby yards of rope of some kind, I fancy.'

He stepped back, looked down admiringly at his new waistcoat and straightened it. 'Now off the three of you go. Go and be useful.'

Reynolds led them out of the captain's cabin. They stooped through the low door and stood back out on the raised stern deck. Liam looked down the length of the ship, a hive of activity, every sail out now and filled as she ran before the wind, sloughing through choppy water at a fair clip, sheets of salty spray fanning up either side of the ship's prow.

Reynolds grinned at them with a gap-toothed mouth. 'Right then, you little beauties, you're all mine.'

CHAPTER 14

1889, London

'This is completely crazy! Where are they going?'

Maddy and Sal studied the monitor in front of them. Computer-Bob had lost the signal as it blipped its way past the end of the crinkly coast of Cornwall. Lost it because there were any number of directions the blip — clearly a ship of some sort — could have gone. North up into the Irish Sea. South down towards the coast of France. West out into the Atlantic or innumerable headings in between those compass points. For the last seventeen hours computer-Bob had systematically been sweeping the sea to the south-west of Britain in a spiral search pattern radiating out from the last point they'd had them on-screen. Searching in ten-square grids, moving forward in day-chunks of time for each grid location. The further Liam and Rashim moved away in time and space from their last contact, the greater the chance they were going to be lost completely.

Seventeen hours of agonized waiting and watching as computer-Bob painstakingly generated a grid pattern that overlaid an image of the Atlantic Ocean. There were squares colour-coded to indicate the grid locations searched, and the dates they'd been searched for. There was some best-guessing involved too: the speed at which a ship at that time might travel, assumptions that it would travel in a straight line and not be randomly zigzagging.

Guesses. And that's what was disconcerting. Guesses. That's all they could work with. But now, after so many hours taking turns sleeping and watching and hoping, now they finally had a fix on them again.

Sal looked at the square that was flashing on the screen. It was two-thirds of the way across the Atlantic. The time-stamp indicated that four months had passed for Liam and Rashim.

'Four months?' Sal shook her head. 'It wouldn't take a sailing ship that long to cross the Atlantic, would it?'

'I don't think so. Old sailing ships weren't *that* slow getting about, were they? Maybe they've been somewhere else. Or perhaps they've been there and back and set off again? I don't know.'

'Well, whatever, so now we have them, why don't we just open up a window and go get them?' asked Sal.

Maddy shook her head. 'We can't: the signal's a moving target. Think about it, Sal. We open up a portal and step through and we're just as likely to find ourselves dropping into the ocean in the ship's wake than we are stepping on to it.'

'Maddy is correct,' added Bob. 'Even if the portal correctly opens on the ship, if it is still in motion, there is the possibility of a density merge with part of the ship or even one of the ship's personnel.'

'Right. And I don't fancy ending up spliced with a sweaty sailor.' Maddy was chewing on a matchstick. She so very much missed the plastic biro caps she was used to gnawing to a jagged nub. 'What we need is for them to get wherever they're going. They've got to stop at a port or bay somewhere, right? I mean, this is some old seventeenth-century sailing boat, so they'll need to stop for food or water, or shore leave.'

Bob nodded. 'Waiting for the target to become stationary would be the most advisable course of action.'

'We've got to just sit tight, Sal. Sit tight and make sure we don't lose track of them again. At least for the moment they're out at sea, so presumably they're going to follow a straight line since there's nothing to dodge round.'

One of the monitors displayed computer-Bob's dialogue box.

> Correct. I have reversed the search from this current location, regressing by time and location, and now have identified three other locations the signal has travelled through.

On the map, three of the grid squares across the Atlantic turned red. Each of them indicated they were several days apart in time. The three squares were more or less in a straight line. The tangent of the line was a downward slant pointing roughly towards the south-east coast of America to the tip of Florida.

Sal frowned. 'They're going to Florida? What's there?'

'Disneyland!' said SpongeBubba. The unit had waddled across the floor, drawn by idle curiosity to the others gathered round the table. 'Skippa's going to Disneyland!'

Sal looked at Maddy. 'Do you know how to turn this stupid thing off?'

'SpongeBubba? Over-ride command menu. Guest administrator.'

SpongeBubba's eyes swivelled to look at Maddy intently. 'Password?'

'Obi-Wan Kenobi.' She looked at Sal. 'Rashim told me.'

'What's that mean?'

Maddy tutted. 'That Rashim's a nerd.' She turned back to SpongeBubba. 'You good to go?'

'Menu options available. I am listening.'

'Standby mode, please.'

The lab unit slumped slightly with a wheeze of servo-motors then was perfectly still.

'Rashim told me the command list.' Maddy turned back to the matter at hand, grabbed the mouse and began to scroll down the map on the screen. 'Florida. Or they could just as easily be heading towards the Bahamas.' She zoomed out slightly. 'Or anywhere in the Caribbean in fact.' She frowned. 'Jeez, look. That's a whole bunch of islands right there. They could change course somewhere in there and we could easily lose track of them again.' She winced. 'If we knew more about what their situation is, what kind of boat they're on, maybe we'd get a clue as to where they're headed.'

'Information,' said Becks. 'They may not even be alive.'

The girls turned round to glare at her. 'For Christ's sake, Becks!'

She looked at them impassively. 'Maddy, it *is* a distinct possibility to consider. It has been four months in their time.'

Maddy spat a small splinter of wood from her teeth. 'Well, let's assume for now that they're alive, shall we? Liam's lasted that long before, and in far more hazardous times.'

Becks nodded.

'Right.' She turned back to look at the map. 'I just wish I knew more about this period of history. You know . . . as opposed to relying on whatever we've got on the database. Which probably isn't going to be much.'

'We could open a pinhole view,' said Sal. 'Maybe we can get a close enough image of what's there,' she added, nodding at the blip on the screen. 'Who knows? We might even catch a glimpse of Liam.'

'True.' Maddy nodded thoughtfully. 'It's got to be worth a try, I guess.' She leaned forward. 'Computer-Bob, how accurate is the signal?'

> I can attempt to triangulate this last signal. It may be possible to be quite precise.

'How precise? I mean, are we talking an image taken within

a yard of the transponder signal? Or a hundred yards? Or a mile? What?'

> **I cannot say before calculation.**

Maddy ground her teeth with frustration. 'All right, you do that. Let's see if we can get a look.'

> **Affirmative.**

An hour later they had a candidate location: a string of coordinates that computer-Bob estimated was within fifty yards of the signal's origin.

'A single signal. That's all we seem to have here,' said Maddy. 'Liam's or Rashim's?'

'The transponders aren't that sophisticated, Sal. Rashim had them leaking a breadcrumb trail of tachyons, that's all. They don't say *whose* breadcrumb trail, I'm afraid.'

Neither of them decided to say out loud whose signal they hoped they'd locked on.

'It's possible one of them has failed or got broken,' she added. 'That they're both together still.'

Sal nodded. 'Yes, of course.'

'OK, Bob, let's grab an image and see what's what.'

> **Affirmative.**

The distant rhythmic thud of Holborn Viaduct's generator was momentarily blocked out by the hum of energy discharging into the displacement machine. A hum that lasted a second, no more. On one of the monitors in front of them a pixelated image began to appear. They waited a few moments as image compression adjusted itself and the blocky image resolved into something clearer.

A square of deep ocean blue.

'Sea,' said Sal. 'Jahulla!' she cursed, forgetting for the moment her vow to abandon the Hindi she'd been programmed to use. 'We missed the ship!'

'Not necessarily. Maybe we just need to adjust the viewing angle. Bob, can you do that again and give us the reverse angle?'

> **Yes, Maddy.**

They waited, then again the second-long hum, and a few moments later a new image began to arrange itself on the screen beside the first. Blue again, but this time with a blur of something dark running diagonally across it.

She looked at Sal. 'What is that, do you think?'

'A rope?'

She nodded. Yes, it could be. A bit of rigging perhaps. A spar of wood. Something boaty, she guessed.

'Maybe we're far too close. Can we do another? Offset the pinhole by, let's see, twenty, thirty yards?'

> **We can obtain another image, Maddy. But each time we open a pinhole we're discharging our own minute trace signal of particles. This will compromise the accuracy.**

'Do one more. Back up by twenty yards so we can get some more detail.'

Computer-Bob once more released a short burst of energy into the displacement machine and, a moment later, a third blurry image assembled itself on-screen. This time they had something quite clear: a boat. A very small one, little more than a dinghy, with a solitary mast and a triangle of cloth. And there, sitting at the back of the boat, the head and shoulders of someone wearing a hat.

Maddy squinted at the pixelated image, trying to squeeze more detail from it than was actually there.

Liam? Is that Liam?

'Just one of them,' said Sal.

'There could be someone else in that boat out of view. Lying down, sleeping or something.'

'Bob, can we go in a bit closer?'

> **Information. The precision is already being compromised. If we get too close, we might endanger the person in that image.**

He was quite right, of course. Too close and, with decreasing precision each time they took a snapshot, they might just open a mini-portal right inside whoever that was, almost certainly killing them.

'Someone on a dinghy in the middle of the Caribbean. That's really not a great deal to go on.'

'It doesn't look good,' said Sal. She studied the image again. 'Is that even Liam or Rashim?'

Maddy couldn't tell. It was a blurred bunch of pixels of a person's head and shoulders; even if the image had a greater granularity and there were more details to pick out, the face was shaded beneath the brim of a three-cornered hat. A dark smudge that, quite frankly, could be anybody.

'All right, this probably isn't helping much. I guess we'll just have to keep tracking this signal until it comes to a full stop somewhere. Meanwhile, maybe we should read up a bit on the history.' She looked up at Sal and the two support units. 'You should go to the British Museum reading room. Take these two munchkins with you to look at whatever history books they have on pirates and stuff. They can scan 'n' brain-dump the information for you.'

She looked at Bob and Becks again, standing like useless bookends behind them.

'Besides, looks like the pair of them need to be taken out for their daily walkies.'

CHAPTER 15

1889, London

Sal's head was swimming. They'd spent the afternoon in the British Museum's reading room ploughing their way through all the books on piracy that the librarian had been able to muster. Unlike trawling through modern-day encyclopedias or databases, the information was haphazardly organized at best: a *mélange* of personal accounts, biographies, works of dubious fact – more likely fiction – ships' logs, clerks' accounts of court cases, diaries, despatches from governors and ambassadors, and most of this material in a flamboyant and inventively spelled language that seemed to require several readings of any given sentence to actually extract the meaning.

The clarence carriage rattled noisily over tram rails as they turned right off Southampton Row on to High Holborn.

'So, I hope you two at least managed to make sense of all those books.'

'Affirmative,' rumbled Bob.

'We are collating the data,' said Becks, her eyelids fluttering like some Jane Austen heroine about to fall into a theatrical swoon.

'We are currently assembling a database of the social, political and economic conditions of 1667.'

'Cross-referenced with acts of piracy in the areas of the West Indies, the Caribbean and the Indian Ocean,' added Becks.

'Great,' said Sal with a nod. Not for the first time, she wondered why whoever had 'designed' her had not thought to give her a computerized mind. But then perhaps that made sense. Bob and Becks were essentially walking, breathing, eating, farting computers. Designed to process data, not so great at intuitive thinking. And that was something reassuring. That perhaps she was more *human* than she'd been feeling lately. More human than 'product'.

'So, what situation is Liam facing, then?'

The clarence creaked as Bob twisted in the leather seat to face her. 'Can you be more specific, Sal?'

'No. Not really. Since I haven't got a clue about this time. I mean . . .' She tapped her gloved fingers on the sill beside her with frustration. 'Is there a war going on or anything?'

'There has been a recent war,' replied Becks. 'A proxy war between England and Spain fought mainly along the various trade routes across the Atlantic. Both sides attempted to sabotage the other's ability to maintain effective trading conditions with their colonies.'

'The war with Spain ends in 1660 after the death of Oliver Cromwell in 1658,' added Bob. He looked at Sal. 'You know about the English Civil War?'

'Not really.' Sal made a face. 'Is it relevant?'

Bob cocked his head. 'What is relevant is that after the Civil War the leader, Oliver Cromwell, being Protestant by religion and secular in his authority, was ideologically opposed to the Catholic Spanish-Habsburg Empire. After Cromwell's death, we have a destabilizing power vacuum within England that could have led to the country falling back into a state of civil war again.'

'This power vacuum ends,' said Becks, 'with the restoration of the monarch. Namely King Charles the Second. Charles the

Second is Catholic and inclined towards peace with Spain. So, the war between these two countries ends in 1660.'

'So, there's not any war going on when Liam is?'

'Not officially,' said Bob. 'But it does continue in a covert manner in places like the West Indies, the Caribbean, along the coast of Central America. Independent ships are given licences by regional colonial governors to prey on the merchant ships of other nations. These licences are called *letters of marque*.'

Becks nodded and continued. 'Ships with this licence are known as privateers. And in the year 1667 the governor of English-held Jamaica – Sir Thomas Modyford – is granting these licences to as many ships as apply for them, in order to attack Spanish merchant vessels.'

'King Charles the Second instructs his governor to stop doing this,' said Bob, 'as it is endangering the peace with Spain. But the governor of Jamaica ignores this.'

'Why?'

Bob looked at her. His eyes flickered as he retrieved data. 'Jamaica was only recently captured from the Spanish in 1655. The Spanish, despite the peace, want it back. Governor Modyford fears they will attempt to retake it. His only way to defend the island and its principal settlement, Port Royal, is to attract a fleet of privateers with a vested interest in it remaining under English control: to remain a safe haven for privateers.'

Sal nodded. 'Right.' She looked out of the grubby window as they clattered up High Holborn. 'So, Liam and Rashim are heading towards a part of the world where there is something like a war still going on?'

'Affirmative. A proxy war,' corrected Becks. 'A privatized war.'

Sal sighed. 'Why is it that this kind of screw-up, when one

of us ends up stuck somewhere, never happens in somewhere peaceful and safe and, you know . . . generally nice?'

Both support units shrugged. 'We don't have the data to answer that,' said Bob.

The clarence dropped them outside their side door in the shadow and beneath the broad iron arches of Holborn Viaduct. Sal paid the driver, unlocked the small arched door and let them in. The dark hall beyond was thankfully empty. She rapped her knuckles on the smaller arched door to their dungeon.

'Maddy? Hello? We're home!'

She heard the faint tap of a footfall inside, the *snack* of a bolt sliding quickly and the door creaked open. She could see Maddy's face lit by a gas lamp. She was grinning excitedly.

'You're looking happy. What is it? What's happened?'

'We've got a steady, motionless signal. Computer-Bob's locked on to it and says it's viable and safe.' She ushered Sal and the other two inside. 'We're good to go back and get them!'

Maddy centred herself in the square marked on the floor. She'd already had Sal on her case arguing that it made sense to send just the support units. It wasn't exactly a complicated mission as such. Just home in on the signal and, hopefully, come across Liam and Rashim and bring them back. No complicated, tactical decision-making required, just a straightforward go-and-get. But she rationalized, not entirely convincing Sal, that it made sense to have a pair of human boots on the ground. What if something had gone wrong: if Liam or Rashim were hurt or in a bad way? She even considered the possibility that Liam might have 'gone native', and might need convincing to come back with her. After all, how many times had he told her in the last few months that he wished he'd stayed on in Nottingham as the sheriff?

'I'm ready,' she said, sucking in a breath to steady her nerves.

Bob readied himself in the square next to hers. 'I am also ready,' he grunted.

Bob and Becks had given Maddy a half-hour briefing on where they were going. Port Royal. She wasn't sure whether she felt terrified or thrilled at what they'd told her. She was trembling, that much was true.

'A minute countdown,' said Sal. 'Maddy, seriously . . . Bob and Becks can do this.'

'It'll be fine, Sal.' She offered a flickering smile. 'So, it may be a bit rough and ready, but I've got Bob with me.'

Rough and ready? From what the support units had told her, Port Royal sounded like some sort of Wild West frontier town. Lawless, chaotic. But then she'd quickly had a look at a map that Becks had Bluetoothed on to one of the monitors. There were streets, with names like Queen Street, Lime Street, York Street. There was a courthouse, a church, a merchants' exchange, even a school, for God's sake.

Jesus . . . if kids can survive living there, I'm sure I'll be fine taking a five-minute stroll.

'It'll be fun,' she added, more for her own benefit than Sal's.

'Forty-five seconds.'

Yep. Fun.

Just like going to watch the Fire of London. That kind of fun?

She silenced that hectoring voice in her head. That was a screw-up, maybe not even hers, though. The map depicting the fire's progress over time must've been wrong. After all, come on, fire's unpredictable. No fire this time. Just a rather lively and lawless town, and surely no worse than Rome under Caligula had been, right? Surely no worse than that?

'We're at thirty seconds,' said Sal. 'Hands and feet . . . ?'

Maddy nodded. She placed her hands by her side. She looked

down at her clothes. Again, they were going into a past that they were not specifically dressed for, but wearing clothes generic and nondescript enough to pass, hopefully, without attracting any attention. A plain brown dress with a cinched-tight corset, laced boots and a white linen bonnet. Her glasses, of course, were sitting on the desk. She wasn't planning on reading anything and Bob's eyes were going to be better at scanning the world for Liam than hers anyway.

Three feet away, Bob was dressed equally neutrally. A pale grey linen nightshirt with a belt cinched round his waist, into which was slotted a butcher's knife, and dark pantaloons tucked into a pair of dockers' boots. His thick, dark, coconut hair could do with trimming, she noted, as Sal marked a ten-second warning.

'And . . . remember, return windows in one hour, two and twenty-four hours as agreed,' she called out above the increasing hum of energy getting ready to discharge.

Maddy nodded. She could feel the hair beneath her bonnet lifting from the nape of her neck as static electricity danced around her.

'Five . . . four . . . three . . .'

Once more into the milk . . . here we go.

CHAPTER 16

1666, aboard the Clara Jane

Liam sat cross-legged on the deck working in a small circle with three other crewmen, carefully re-nipping the buntlines. His lap was filled with coarse, scratchy, thin strands of hemp rope that he deftly wound in a coil round the end of the much thicker rope – the buntline – and secured firmly in place.

The men worked methodically with him, sharing dirty stories that he imagined would turn both Maddy and Sal crimson with disgust and outrage. Across the deck, William – the young boy he'd saved from the fire – was working alongside the ship's cook, scouring and cleaning pots and pans with sand and seawater.

William was speaking now. Not many words at any one time, and always in reply rather than initiated, but at least it meant the trauma he'd experienced hadn't rendered him some kind of mute.

A brisk downdraught from the mainsail above cooled them all and sheltered them from the baking sun, tossing Liam's mop of hair from one side to the other. On the foredeck one of the sailors was playing a fiddle, something light and whimsical that reminded him of Cork, or rather, his coded memories of Cork. The ditty came and went as the wind carried it.

He finished securing the end of the buntline and stretched his aching back, casting a glance at the quiet industry going on all around him. Maintenance mostly. Another team of men were busy tarring the shrouds and anchor line, another group securing the stitching around the hemline of a sail. And all of them were gently leaning into the soothing sway of the ship as she crested and broke through shifting hillocks of deep blue sea.

Under slightly different circumstances, Liam decided, *I think I could get used to this.*

'Liam, lad, those ladies' fingers of yers holdin' up to the task?' asked one of the men sitting beside him. Henry Bartlett — formerly pressed into His Majesty's Royal Navy for a number of years, but now enjoying the much easier regime of a privateer.

'Aye, it's hard on your hands, so it is.' He looked at the blisters on his fingers. 'I'm pretty sure I'll never be able to play Mario Kart again.'

Henry and the others laughed at that. Not that it made any sense to them.

'There ya go again with another one of yer pecul-ee-ar sayin's.'

That seemed to be the trick, of course. That seemed to be what worked. His peculiarity. The men around him, the crew by and large, seemed to have warmed to him, even to Rashim. Born out of curiosity mainly, in the way a pack of laboratory monkeys might view a new plastic squeaky toy thrown into their cage. Liam had quickly figured out that the best way for them to be accepted – adopted more like – by this intimidating crew of grizzly veterans and lowlifes was not to try and blend in, but instead to stand out. *Be eccentric.* They seemed to love that. Although Rashim (equally odd in their eyes) they viewed with some caution. He seemed to have acquired the role of 'Captain's Regular Dinner Guest'. While Liam was one of the lads, albeit an extremely odd addition to their fraternity, Rashim was still held somewhat at arm's length.

'Here,' said Henry. He reached for the large flagon of

watered-down ale that sat on the deck between them and passed it to Liam.

'Thanks.' He took a swig. Something of an acquired taste. But marginally better to suffer the sun-warmed sour and yeasty flavour of ale than the bottom-of-the-pond tang of the ship's store of drinking water.

Nearly a month now, Liam figured. A month since they'd set sail from London and yet how quickly the shipboard routine had begun to seem quite normal. The first few days had been the hardest to cope with. He'd been unwilling to accept they were stuck there, every minute looking across the ship's decks, impatiently waiting for a portal to open; to see the shimmering image of Maddy frantically waving at them to hop through and come on home. But Rashim had pointed out – and had to do it several times – that there was no way they could safely do that. A portal was a fixed object in space. Not something that was going to travel along with the ship. If they even managed to precisely target a portal on the ship, it would be like a giant cannonball travelling down the length of the moving vessel, sucking whatever it bisected along the way (hull, deck, mast, rigging, sailor – or parts of sailor) back to 1889. Worst-case scenario: the portal might gouge enough of the ship to actually sink the thing.

'*We're stuck with this situation until we get a chance to go ashore*,' he'd told Liam. '*We'd better get used to it.*'

Just then Liam looked aft and saw Rashim emerge from the captain's cabin, shaking his head and muttering something to himself. Liam excused himself, got up and made his way to join him.

Rashim nodded as Liam leaned against the gunwale. 'How was this morning's meeting?'

'I have a horrible feeling we're being captained by a complete amateur.' He looked out at the rolling sea. 'He hasn't the first idea about navigation. It's guesswork with him.'

'But he knows where we are, right?'

'His best guess was worryingly approximate.' He looked at Liam. 'Somewhere along the west coast of Africa. I've tried the best I can to narrow that down a bit. I think we're somewhere along the coast of Sierra Leone . . . or whatever that place is called right now.'

Captain Teale should've taken the ship out to sea by now; they had passed the correct latitude to bear west towards the Caribbean on the far side. Teale had said he was waiting for a favourable wind. The real reason, Rashim suspected, was that Teale had got a last-minute case of the jitters at the thought of crossing the Atlantic and successfully navigating them into the Caribbean.

'You know, he has no idea how to determine longitude or latitude. Which, I think, is why we're hugging the coastline of Africa like a bunch of beginners,' he said, nodding out at the faint grey outline of land on the horizon. 'This way he doesn't need to even look at a chart. He's fine as long as land is in sight.' Rashim laughed. 'Very scientific, eh?'

'That's a bit worrying.' Liam looked at him. 'But you're helping him figure out how to get to the Caribbean, right?'

Rashim shrugged. 'I'm doing what I can. I'm trying my best to work out how to use the *backstaff*. They don't exactly come with a user manual.' He shook his head. 'It's bad enough we got press-ganged on to a pirate ship, but to be press-ganged by a bunch of amateurs?'

Liam nodded. If it wasn't so worrying, it would be kind of embarrassing.

'Oh well, look on the positive side, Rashim. The first time we put ashore, hopefully Maddy will be able to pick us up.'

'Only if she knows where to look. And that's a long shot.'

Liam tapped his waistcoat. 'We've got our transponder thingies.'

'Still a needle in a haystack if she doesn't know precisely where to look.'

Liam clapped him on the back. 'Relax. You'll learn. She always figures it out.' That came out sounding a little too cavalier. There were almost as many screw-ups as home runs thus far in their short history together. Perhaps marginally fewer of the screw-ups.

'Eventually,' Liam added under his breath.

CHAPTER 17

October 1666, aboard the Clara Jane

The gruel tasted better than it sounded or even looked. Or perhaps it was just that Liam felt insanely hungry. The fresh air, of course. That and the fact that every moment of each day the constant shifting of balance to accommodate the gentle roll of the *Clara Jane* worked on the entire body and demanded every muscle do its part. It was no surprise, then, that each evening, by the time the ship's cook was boiling up something in his pots and the smell of whatever stew, gruel or pottage he was cooking floated up from below decks, Liam was ready to clean his bowl whatever he was served.

He looked out of the cannon porthole. The sun was low, an orange beach ball rolling along the horizon. Warm, diagonal, almost horizontal slants of light spilled in through the gun portholes and swept light searchlight beams across the wooden deck, glinting off chains and belt buckles, making pairs of eyes squint momentarily.

All but the duty watch were below decks sharing the day's main meal. The gun deck was a clattering scrape-tap chorus of wooden spoons on tin bowls, and the murmur of conversation.

William, having finished helping the cook serve the crew, sat down beside Liam with his own bowl of gruel. He looked up at Liam. 'Is it good? Do you like it, sir?'

Liam nodded. 'Very tasty.'

'I helped Cookie make it,' he said, spooning in a mouthful.

'Good job you made of it too.'

'Thank you, sir.'

Liam shook his head. 'Just call me Liam . . . like the others, that's OK.'

'Oh-kay?' The boy looked up at him. 'What does that mean?'

Liam shook his head. 'Nothing . . . just how they talk where I come from. It means all is well.' He watched the small boy eat for a while. 'How are you doing, lad?'

The boy paused thoughtfully, his jaw working for the moment on a nugget of pork gristle. 'I miss my mother so much.'

'That's perfectly understandable.'

William looked up at him. 'Do you think she . . . ?'

He's asking me if she's alive.

'If she escaped the fire?'

The boy nodded.

'It was hard to see what was going on . . .'

Tell him a lie, for God's sake.

'I saw most of those people jump in the water as the flames came down to the jetty. Your mother amongst them.' He nudged the boy's arm gently. 'I'm sure, no, I'm *certain* she got scooped up by one of them boats. Aye, and there was a lot of them around.'

'I hope so.' His voice was a whisper.

'You know what I think, William? I think in a couple of years' time you'll make it back home to London. You'll be nearly a young man by then and you'll find your mum and she'll be so proud of you. So proud of her son, the big, strong, swashbuckling sailor.'

William frowned. 'What does *swashbuttle* . . . ?'

Liam grinned at that. 'Nothing. Another stupid word we use where I come from.'

William gave that some thought. 'Where do you come from? You talk so differently to the others.'

What to tell him? Well, not the truth obviously. But, even then, what Liam used to consider the truth, a childhood lived out in Cork, was all someone else's fantasy. Someone's best guess at what Cork was like at the turn of the century, a mixture of clichés and stereotypes.

'Ah, it's a place called Williamsburg. No one I meet has ever heard of it. Funny little place, it is . . . with all sorts of odd sayings and goings-on. What about you, William?'

'Me and mother live with me uncle. He's a cooper.' He corrected himself. '*Lived*.'

'You got a father?'

'Father died after the Big War.'

Liam had to think about that for a moment. The Civil War, that's what he was talking about.

'Mother says he died for Mr Cromwell. She says he got hit by a musket ball that broke up inside him. It just took a few years to happen. He finally got sick and died when I was a baby.'

'I'm sorry, William.'

William shrugged. 'I never knew him.'

Across from Liam, Rashim sat next to Henry Bartlett who seemed keen to find out about Rashim's regular conversations with their captain.

'So, Mr Rach-eee . . .'

Rashim closed his eyes. *Oh please . . .*

'My name's pronounced *Rashim*,' he said. 'A "*sh*" sound. Not a "ch". And, by the way, that's my given name, not my surname.'

Henry dipped his head in apology. 'My 'pologies, Ra-*sheeem*. So it seems the captain 'as taken somethin' of a shinin' to yer. What is it you gents spend all the mornin' talkin' about?'

Rashim wondered how honest he should be. The crew, it seemed, had faith in Teale to lead them to good fortune and great riches. He had to wonder why though. Behind the closed door of his aft cabin, Captain Teale was a nervous wreck. The façade, there at first for their first few morning meetings, had been one of bravado and cockiness. Teale came across to Rashim as a member of the lower gentry born with that inbred self-belief that he had only to bark loudly and common men would follow.

Rashim had learned a little of Teale's background. He'd served as a cavalry officer in the King's army during the Civil War. A young man, then, reckless and brave. And once, after the Battle of Naseby, kissed on the cheek by King Charles I in gratitude for his hopelessly romantic bravery, leading a charge that routed a dangerously close line of musketeers and all but decimated his own company of horsemen in the process.

After the war, Teale's fortune hadn't been so great. The modest family wealth had been confiscated by Cromwell and Teale had been forced to earn a living for the first time in his life. At first the captain had been guarded with Rashim, telling him how he'd been a successful businessman, learning the 'art of making money' from the grubby merchant classes. Refining the process, adding some glamour and elegance to the marketplaces he frequented, buying and selling commodities at great profit.

But then the posturing and boasting began to give way to a more honest account of events. None of his commercial ventures had been particularly successful. His last endeavour had been a catastrophic failure. He'd used family connections to be granted a licence and thousands of acres to set up a sugar-cane plantation in Jamaica. And then, using his considerable salesman's skills, he had talked a number of Bristol merchants into pooling their money and investing in a merchant ship loaded with slaves, seeds, equipment and money destined for the Caribbean to set up the plantation. Teale assured them all they were going to double, nay, quadruple their money within two years of the plantation being established. And, of course, Teale, for his business genius, his handy royal connections and setting up the entire enterprise, would receive a tidy commission on that.

But the ship had been raided by buccaneers. They lost everything. Even the ship itself. Teale left Bristol the night he got the news. Left before his consortium of investors got wind of the same information and came after him for his blood.

Down in London, he learned about a new opportunity: the business of privateering. Men no better than him, certainly less educated and in some cases with little or no maritime experience, were making their fortunes raiding Spanish ships. Under Cromwell's rule, licences to raid and plunder overladen and underprotected Spanish ships were being granted letters of marque as quickly as the ink could dry.

It was Teale's bad luck, though, that before he could get himself into that line of business, Cromwell died and shortly after a monarch was reinstalled. Charles II, being Catholic and rather sympathetic to King Philip IV of Spain, stopped granting these licences after the Spanish king complained.

'However, my second cousin, Lord Modyford, at present the governor of our recently acquired British outpost at Port Royal, Jamaica, is still granting letters of marque to men he can trust.'

That was Teale's *unique* angle. A guarantee to any crew of cut-throat buccaneers, scurvy sea dogs who would follow him that he could use his family connection to obtain a privateer's licence and they could plunder away, raid fat Spanish ships to their heart's content with a mere piece of paper protecting them from being considered 'pirates'.

It hadn't taken Teale very long to convince another group of merchants to part with their money, to provide a schooner – the *Clara Jane* – and to talk a crew of experienced sailors into coming aboard and setting sail for Jamaica.

Rashim had asked why, if he'd had no problem getting a crew, he and Liam had been press-ganged aboard. Teale explained that the ship had been ready to set sail from Tilbury when news of the fire in London reached them. His crew had decided there might be some easy pickings to be made heading back upriver: some looting, some ferrying at exorbitant cost. Teale had shrugged. 'Misfortune to one is profit to another. It actually seemed rather too good an opportunity to miss out on.'

Apparently the *Clara Jane*'s shore boat had earned them nearly a hundred pounds of rescue fees that Sunday night. Not a bad start for their adventure on the high seas.

'Well?' Henry Bartlett nudged Rashim for an answer.

'You want to know what do we talk about?' Rashim hoped his casual shrug looked convincing. 'High culture. Poetry. Shakespeare. You know, that sort of thing.'

'Poetry, eh?' Henry laughed. 'Our Captain Teale's a right bleedin' gentyman dandy, ain't 'e?' He slurped a spoonful of his gruel. 'No matter. Captain's a right smart fella. An' well connected. I 'eard say 'e's family to the King himself or somethin'.'

No, it wasn't poetry. Or Shakespeare. Captain Jacob Teale was beginning to discover that maybe there were some things a noble-born gentleman wasn't going to be instantly adept at. And it seemed maritime navigation was one of those.

'*I still can't make head nor tail of these confounded contraptions!*' Teale had confessed to Rashim only this morning, glaring at the backstaff sitting on his table. '*And these charts? God help me – they are but meaningless scribbles to me.*'

'You really have no idea how to navigate this ship?'

'No, sir, I do not!'

'Well, er . . . does anybody on this ship know how to navigate it?'

'Well, I was rather hoping you might, Mr Anwar.'

CHAPTER 18

1666, aboard the Clara Jane, somewhere in the Atlantic Ocean

'It looks like we're not going to the Caribbean any more.'

Liam looked at Rashim. 'What? You're kidding! That's where all the crew think we're headed!'

'Best keep your voice down,' whispered Rashim.

It was dark and Rashim had just come out of another meeting with the captain. The sun had left a stain on the horizon that was fast fading, and above them, in a cloudless, dark blue sky, the stars and the moon shone clear and bright. Below decks, they could hear the crew noisily going about their supper ritual: the clang of pots and pans, raised voices, laughter, the clatter of dice across a barrel top. On the foredeck now it was just the two of them, the night watch up above on the mizzenmast and the helmsman aft. A gentle breeze was luffing the sails lightly and the sea itself was flat, subdued like a chastened child.

'Teale had a complete meltdown this evening,' confided Rashim. 'You know I said he hasn't got the first clue how to locate latitude or longitude and he wants me to learn it for him.'

'Yes, but you said you could get us to the Caribbean . . .'

'Well, I thought it was just that he couldn't navigate but I think he can't bring himself to steer this ship out to sea. I mean, beyond the sight of land. Though he won't admit it.' Rashim sipped his tankard of watered-down rum. 'I presumed when we hit the equator, or some point shortly after, I could navigate us across the Atlantic.'

'Well, that's what some of the lads have been asking about,' said Liam. 'When exactly do we strike out west?'

'The answer is we're not. Teale's decided we're continuing south instead.'

'South?' Liam consulted a mental map. 'You mean south . . . as in down to the bottom of Africa?'

'All the way down, round the bottom and up into the Indian Ocean.'

'Why?'

'I think the real reason is he's scared witless at the idea of crossing the Atlantic, though he won't come out and say that, of course. But the reason he's planning to give tomorrow, when he assembles the men, is that there are even better opportunities for fabulous wealth raiding Arab ships in the Indian Ocean.'

Liam digested that for a moment. 'The crew will be, well . . . I mean, they all signed up for Jamaica.' But then actually, no, thinking about it . . . they'd all signed up to make a pot-load of money. After a moment's sharp intake of breath they'd probably decide it didn't matter where they were going, just so long as they were doing it somewhere easy, and still under licence as privateers, not pirates. That was the important thing. None of them wanted to live the rest of their lives with an arrest warrant hanging over their heads and, inevitably one day, a short sharp drop at the end of a rope.

'There'll be grumblings,' said Liam. 'But that silver-tongued fella? You know, I've got a feeling he'll sell them on the idea somehow. They all seem to think he's God's gift.'

'He's a smooth talker.'

'Aye and a moron by the sound of it.'

'Indeed. In my time he'd have made a perfect digi-tech salesman.'

Liam shrugged. 'In my time he'd have made a perfect balm and potion salesman.'

The lazy sea lapped softly against the hull beneath them, and Liam gazed out at the dark water, a vanilla glint caught every now and then of the moon above.

'That might mean we hit land sooner rather than later.' He looked at Rashim. 'That's a chance, right?'

'Chance for a portal? Possibly. But only if they're still managing to track us.'

Liam nodded. And, if they did open a portal, chances are one might open right beside Teale, since he was wearing Rashim's waistcoat. 'If we do stop ashore at some point, you and I'll have to stay close to the captain.'

'All the men assembled, are they?' Captain Teale turned towards the ship's quartermaster, Francis Woodcock. The men referred to him as 'Old Tom', on account of his being neither called Tom nor that old. Liam was still trying to get a handle on what passed for humour among his shipmates.

'Aye, Skipper, all present and accounted for,' barked Old Tom.

Teale stood by the railing of the afterdeck, looking down on the entirety of the ship's company, eighty-six men assembled on the main deck before him. The helm was looped off to stop it spinning and the ship's sails were dropped. The *Clara Jane* was at rest, gently lolling on a calm sea.

'Gentlemen,' he started, 'as some of you I am sure have marked, we have been maintaining a southerly course and not, as expected, heading west out to sea.'

'Aye!' someone called from the back. 'And when do we turn?'

104

There came a ripple of voices across the deck, all of them wondering aloud the very same thing. The crew, none of them navigators, were all savvy enough to notice the sun had been rising on the port bow and setting on the starboard and, of course, there on the port horizon there was still the faint, grey pencil-line of land.

'I know you men all signed on to voyage across the Atlantic and to make your fortunes from whatever hapless Spanish merchant ships we encounter in the Caribbean. And this, as God is my witness, we shall eventually do. However . . . it is my decision, as captain of this ship, that our commercial enterprise will start with a small detour.'

'Detour?'

'You men, I am sure, will have heard tales of the immensely rich trade routes between India and Arabia. Ships laden so heavily with silks, wines and coin that they wallow like calf-bearing heifers. The Indian Ocean is a rich and fertile hunting ground for us and an opportunity for this crew, this ship, to make good fortune.'

'We want *Spanish gold*! Not spices and materials for ladies' dresses!' called out Henry Bartlett. Several of the crew cheered that, and not in a light-hearted way, Liam noted. There was palpable discontent stirring among the men.

'That way takes us to Cape Horn!' shouted one of the men.

'Aye and we'll have to put ashore for supplies somewhere. There'll be savages an' man-eaters an' the like!'

The mood was turning ugly.

'This ain't what we signed on for, Teale!' cried Henry. 'This ain't what none of us came aboard for!'

Jacob Teale stroked his Cavalier whiskers thoughtfully, a thumb hooked into the hip pocket of Rashim's waistcoat. Maintaining a very deliberate air of nonchalance, he waited until the chorus of barracking voices eventually died down, rather than shout over the top of it. He waited until he had absolute silence.

Oh, he's good, thought Liam. There was an air of the frustrated thespian about the man.

'Gentlemen, gentlemen,' he began calmly. 'We *will* get our hands on gold, more gold than you men could possibly conceive. More gold, I imagine, than this schooner could safely carry. For every Arabian barque heading one way with trade goods, there's another returning with a hold full of coin. We shall all return to England as rich squires. Each man here will have enough booty that he shall never need to work another day of his life. Each man here will live out his life enjoying fine things, wearing fine clothes. Enjoying fine women!'

Liam noted a few of the men considering that – picturing that scenario in their minds.

'And mark this, gentlemen, and mark this well, for I know this weighs heavily on the mind of each man here. Every last ship in the Indian Ocean is considered fair game with or without licence from the King. These are Moors, Muslims . . . ships of Arabia and India. We shall not be branded pirates for the plundering we do, but instead we will be welcomed home as heroes!'

A roar of approval erupted from some of the men. None of them wanted to be branded a pirate. It meant only one thing: a life lived entirely on the run. Henry Bartlett had told Liam the main reason he'd been so keen to sign up to Teale's ship was the assurance the captain had made that, with his connections, the ship was *guaranteed* a privateer's licence.

Teale picked out the man who had talked of savages. 'And you, sir, you fear a few dark-skinned barbarians?' He threw his head back and laughed. Liam winced at how cheesy a stage laugh it was, but then suspected none of these men would have seen Errol Flynn or Douglas Fairbanks playing the swashbuckling daredevil in some flickering black-and-white movie.

'I'll wager a single shot from one of our cannons will cow them. They'll scatter like rabbits; that or they'll bow to us as if we are gods!'

Some more of the men cheered at that.

'Gentlemen, we will make ourselves rich in the Indian Ocean this year. Then next year, I promise you, we shall cross to the Caribbean Sea with our fortunes and buy plantations and build spectacular mansions and be *kings* of all we survey!'

A roar of voices erupted across the deck, even Henry Bartlett nodding appreciatively at that.

'We shall be kings among pirates!' Teale added. And, with that, he had the entire crew like putty in the palm of his hand.

Liam looked sideways at Rashim. 'Blimey, he's almost got *me* convinced.'

CHAPTER 19

1667, aboard the Clara Jane, somewhere off the west coast of Africa

It was only two days after Captain Teale had reasserted his authority with promises of inconceivable wealth for all that one of the men aloft, repairing a sheet bracket on the foremast, spotted sails on the horizon south of their position.

Teale was keen to make an early start to their adventure, so with the wind in their favour he decided to give chase. Every last sail and outrigger was fully unfurled and let out, and the *Clara Jane* bore down on it with the sheets taut and thrumming with tension, the bow carving through the deep blue sea, leaving a long trail of foaming water in their wake.

Old Tom barked orders for the ship's kegs of gunpowder to be rolled out of the armoury and cracked open, and for the *Clara*'s two dozen long-barrelled muskets to be primed and distributed to those members of the crew who made the most convincing case that they could hit a target.

Henry Bartlett shoved a cutlass into Liam's hands and passed a hatchet to Rashim. He was grinning like a loon. 'About bleedin' time we had us some action!' He moved on, handing out weapons from the small cache he held in his arms. Young William was following behind him, laden with flintlock pistols dangling from long silk ribbons slung round his neck.

Liam looked down at the curved blade in his hands. 'I'm not sure if I'm excited or absolutely terrified,' he muttered.

Rashim nodded. 'I'd rather not get my hands bloody if it is possible. I'm not good with blood.'

An hour after first sighting the ship, they were close enough to make out some detail on it. Teale had invited Rashim and Liam up on to the foredeck to enjoy the chase with him. 'Damned good sport this is, eh, gentlemen?' He pulled a spyglass from his belt, extended it and braced himself against the foredeck's handrail as he squinted into the lens.

'Triangular-shaped sails. And quite low in the water. Looks like a Moorish ship to me.' He passed the spyglass to Old Tom. Tom studied the ship for a moment. 'It's a dhow, Skipper,' he said. 'Two masts, lateen sails. Perhaps a couple of hundred tons.'

'Now is that big?'

Tom shrugged. 'She's a fair size.'

'Will she have cannons?'

Tom looked at his captain incredulously. 'She's a merchant ship, Skipper . . . of course she don't have no bleedin' cannons.'

Teale nodded assuredly. 'Well, yes, indeed. As I very much suspected.'

The pursuit lasted into the afternoon: the dhow ahead of them had clearly spotted them in its wake and every one of her sails was out.

'She's tending towards port!' called out Tom.

'That's *left*, isn't it?' muttered Rashim. Liam nodded.

'Those *Moors* are trying to make a run for the mainland!' bellowed Teale, nodding at the coastline of the continent. It was much closer now, perhaps no more than half a dozen miles to port. Rashim had told him his best guess as to where they were was somewhere off the north-west coast of Africa: about as useful as saying New York was somewhere on the right-hand side of America.

Teale turned to Rashim and Liam. 'Damnable cowards will try to make for some cove or inlet to lose us. Ha! 'Tis just like hunting fox!'

If this really was Teale's first time commanding a ship, Liam wondered how the man could be so certain of that fact, or of *anything* actually.

The arrogance of the aristocracy. Give a man a lifetime of being told he's a better man than most and he'll believe he can do anything, Liam decided.

The dhow was close enough now that Liam could make out some detail without the aid of a spyglass. Three burgundy-coloured triangular sails, a long, low, galleon-like hull that rose up and overhung at the rear — it reminded him of the too-close-together buildings of London, upper floors almost meeting each other above the narrow streets. He could make out the movement of individual crew on the rigging frantically trimming the sails to make their best speed.

Old Tom shook his head and looked up at the *Clara*'s wind-tell pennant, snapping and fluttering towards port. A south-easterly wind, pushing them towards land. He looked confused.

'What is it?' asked Liam.

'She should be making better speed than that. She's rigged fore and aft. The wind's begging her favour more than it is ours.'

Teale slapped his shoulder. 'She's stuffed to the rafters with our booty, Tom! Didn't I tell you! These ships are like cattle fattened for slaughter!'

Another hour passed with the *Clara Jane* crashing energetically through the ocean in hot pursuit as the sun above them passed to its zenith. Teale ordered the helmsman to steer port-side of the dhow, in an attempt to get between it and land to herd it out to sea. Now they were as close to land as they'd been in three weeks. Liam could pick out individual trees and the humps of craggy rocks, the pale line of beaches and breaking surf. The coastline here was arid, rocky and, more to the point, treacherous: headlands tipped with craggy, weather-worn spurs of rock like long, bony fingers reaching out to sea. And at the end of them the ocean foamed and boiled round rocks just beneath the surface.

'Captain Teale,' said Rashim, 'are we not getting a little *too* close to the shore?'

Teale leaned over the rail to get a better look at the water to port. 'Perhaps you're right.' He turned to the helmsman. 'Southward now and no closer to the shore!'

'Aye, Cap'n.'

Ahead of them the dhow was now only four or five hundred yards away.

'What's that?' said Liam. He pointed to a faint line trailing behind the dhow. A faint line that angled down into the water, and there he could make out something churning the water white and leaving a wake of foam. Rashim followed his finger. 'Yes, now what the hell *is* that?'

Teale trained his spyglass on it. 'It appears that they are dragging something behind them.' He chuckled. 'The fools have most probably hoisted their valuables over the side hoping we shan't find them when we board her.'

'Stupid idiots. But that'll be draggin' her . . . slowin' 'er right down,' muttered Tom.

Liam looked at Rashim. '*Deliberately?*'

Rashim understood his meaning instantly. 'Oh God . . . do you think . . . ?'

'She's bait?' Liam was about to answer, when a voice cried out. 'She's coming about!'

111

The dhow had severed its dragline and was now cutting sleekly through the water as it turned a hundred and eighty degrees, its burgundy lateen sails fluttering manically for a moment as they lost the onshore breeze, then snapping taut as they filled; the dhow heeled over hard and was now bearing down on them.

Teale stared at the approaching ship, goggle-eyed. 'I'll be damned! The fox has turned!'

'It's a trap!' said Liam.

'Don't be silly, lad!' he called over his shoulder. 'There's not a single cannon on that ship!' He turned and grinned at Liam. 'We outgun those fools.'

Liam looked at the dhow; it was hurtling straight towards them. At the rate it was approaching, Teale's twelve cannons would be lucky to get one volley off on target before the thing was upon them.

'Tom! Our guns are all ready, aren't they?'

'Aye. Gunner and crew're standing by for your orders, Cap'n.'

Teale smiled. 'Then let's swing her around and give those Moors the cannon!' He turned to the helmsman. 'Steer her to the right.' He gestured towards the open sea. '*Starboard*, that's it . . . hard to starboard!'

The helmsman at the wheel hesitated. 'But . . .'

Teale strode across the foredeck and wrenched the wheel from his hands. 'This is no time to dally, man!' He spun the wheel and the *Clara Jane* began to sway slowly round.

'WHAT?' Tom spun round to look at his captain. 'What are ya doin'!' he screamed at him.

Teale glared at his insubordinate tone. 'Good God, man, I am turning the ship so we can give them a damned volley!'

'Look!' barked Old Tom, jabbing a finger up at the sails. 'Ya turned *into* the wind!' All of their sails were flapping and rustling listlessly and the ship itself wallowed on the swelling sea, robbed entirely of its forward momentum. The turn to starboard was painfully slow – if at all.

'We're sittin' heavy as a rock now, ya fool!'

Meanwhile the dhow scythed towards them, no more than a hundred yards away. Quite clearly she wasn't a mere merchant's trade ship with no more than a dozen or two crew on-board. Liam could see that now. Her deck was lined with men, among them the glint of swords, hatchets drawn and the barrels of one or two flintlocks readied.

'They're corsairs!' bellowed Henry.

Liam looked at Tom and Captain Teale.

'Corsairs?' Teale had gone as white as a sheet.

'Bloody pirates!' muttered Tom. 'First ship we try an' plunder and it's another load of pirates.'

'Oh, marvellous,' hissed Liam, wishing not for the first time that they'd taken Bob and Becks along with them to enjoy the Great Fire of London.

CHAPTER 20

*1667, aboard the Clara Jane,
somewhere off the west coast of Africa*

The dhow gracefully, *artfully*, cut in towards the landward side
of the *Clara Jane* and mere seconds before their hulls made
contact the lateen sails were slacked off and left to flutter as
momentum brought the dhow alongside with quick and well-
practised precision and the hulls bumped heavily, causing every
man to stagger to keep his footing.

A dozen grappling hooks arced across from the dhow and
tangled with their rigging and the first muskets began to fire
with a *fizz-boom* of powder igniting.

Liam watched the dhow's crew stream aboard the *Clara* —
fifty . . . sixty of them, maybe more. Not quite as many
in number as them, but they all looked so much more
ferocious, so much more ready for this fight than the crew of
the *Clara*.

Liam looked at Rashim, his face almost as pale as Teale's. 'You
OK?'

Rashim nodded quickly, licking his lips anxiously.

It was right then that Liam felt it — recognized that something
in him was so very different. The last time he'd faced the threat
of imminent violent death — the possibility that at any second
he might be disembowelled by the chance sweep of the cutting

edge of someone's blade – he'd felt the urge to vomit, to evacuate his bowels. This time . . . ?

I'm all right. I'm not actually scared.

Perhaps knowing what he was. Knowing that he was a meat product . . . ?

I'm just like Bob. I'm like Bob. I'm like Bob. I'm indestructible.

Maybe he was. Maybe not. But hadn't he taken what would have been a mortal wound back in Ancient Rome and recovered from it?

Liam found himself grinning. *My God* – he panted, hefting the cutlass in his hands, feeling the weight and the balance of the blade – *I can do this*. He turned to Rashim. 'Stay up here on the foredeck!'

'Uh? Wh-where are you g-going?'

Liam pointed his blade down at the squirming mass of men on the main deck. 'To fight!'

Rashim grasped his arm. 'It's . . . Liam, it's *dangerous* down th-there! You could get –'

'Rashim.' He eased his friend's hand off. 'I'm not even human. Not really.' He laughed, perhaps with just the slightest note of bitterness, regret. 'It's not like I've ever really lived anyway.' He patted Rashim's shoulder firmly. 'You stay up here! You stay safe. And make sure Will stays below deck.' He turned and jogged across the afterdeck and slid down the ladder on to the main deck.

He came almost immediately face to face with a man taller and wider with a dark-skinned face and dazzling blue eyes framed by a mop of black coiled hair. The man raised his weapon, a long-handled machete, and swung it down at the junction of Liam's neck and shoulder. He blocked it with his cutlass, feeling the blade vibrate jarringly in his hands. The man had a dagger in his other hand and went to thrust it at Liam's hip.

'No you don't!' Liam wrenched his cutlass down, still locked with the man's machete, pulling him off balance. The dagger thrust went low and wide. And Liam found his elbow made hard contact with the man's jaw. The blow knocked him backwards and he was bracing himself against the edge of the *Clara*'s gunwale. Liam stepped smartly forward and shoulder-barged into him. The man lost his balance, flailed a moment before toppling backwards over the edge and disappearing into the dark gap between the two ships' bumping hulls.

Liam turned to his left and saw Henry Bartlett ferociously swinging a fire axe at two other corsairs, useless roundhouse sweeps that were merely keeping them at bay. The two were grinning, toying with Henry, knowing he wasn't going to be able to keep that up forever.

Liam's feet stubbed against a body on the floor. A face he recognized if not a name he could remember. The dead man had a flintlock pistol on a ribbon round his shoulder. Liam stooped down and grabbed it, yanking it free of – *Jason*. That's it . . . *his name was Jason*.

He aimed down the pistol's long barrel at one of the men taunting Henry and, hoping the hapless Jason hadn't had a chance to fire it before going down, he pulled the trigger. The flintlock clacked down, powder fizzed for a heartbeat and then the whole pistol bucked in his hand as a dense cloud of smoke erupted from the end.

'Jay-zus,' he hissed. His hand and arm tingled from the recoil impact of the weapon. The smoke was a languid, blue-white mushroom cloud that refused to clear. Impatiently he stepped through it to see the man he'd been aiming at drop down heavily on to one knee, clutching at a gaping, ragged wound in his chest.

Liam dropped the pistol, a useless encumbrance now. Henry Bartlett caught Liam's eye briefly and nodded a thanks at him before advancing on the other corsair with his wildly swinging axe.

Liam looked around, quickly trying to gauge the way the skirmish was going. The knot of men had spread out across the entire deck: now no longer a tight scrum but several dozen individual duels. Men fighting each other with snarling ferocity – dirty, ugly fighting. Not the athletic cut and thrust of swordplay peppered with the exchanged quips of dashing men he'd seen in so many cable-channel movies; no, nothing like that.

This was one man on top of another, pumping a knife again and again and again into the other's neck. This was one man beating another's head to a messy pulp with the heavy wooden butt of a musket. One man gouging at another man's eyes. A man firing a flintlock pistol point-blank into the back of the head of another, spattering skull and brain tissue across the deck.

God help me. Liam was horrified. Disgusted. But also, he realized with a sting of guilt, he was utterly exhilarated.

The fight seemed to be evening out. There were fewer corsairs than crew, albeit the Moorish pirates were clearly battle-hardened and experienced and ready for this fight. But the *Clara*'s crew were fighting for their very lives, not just for a prize but for a payday. And right there was the shift of balance – what would determine who was going to win this short fight.

It was down to survival.

Liam found himself looking for another to fight, bizarrely, for a moment, like being at a dance and looking for a partner. His gaze locked on another man. Younger this time. Perhaps his exact same age. His young face, all smooth coffee skin on which the first bristles of manhood were attempting to grow. Liam and the young man advanced on each other. The struggling, squirming, screaming, braying world all around them faded to

117

a muted periphery . . . as if somehow, someone had slowed time down to a crawl, dampened the noises of the world and just left the rasping breath of Liam and this young man.

The young man nodded at Liam. An odd gesture of formal greeting – a courtesy extended to someone he intended to kill in cold blood.

Liam nodded back. 'Aye, well . . . let's be having you, then.'

The young man held a scimitar, a curved sword, already smeared with someone else's blood. Somehow that made this easier. There was a moment, a fleeting second just then, where Liam wondered whether he could kill this young lad. His age, his build, dark scruffy hair: he seemed almost a mirror image. Liam wondered if in another place, another timeline, they could be friends, brothers even. A stupid thought to have. Especially right now when this could only be a fight to the death. He looked again at the bright smear of blood. The blood made it possible. Seemed to grant him permission.

Let's get this over with.

Liam lunged forward, swinging his cutlass around, aiming at his midriff. The young man blocked it and their blades rang deafeningly in this lonely world of theirs. The corsair swept his blade around in the opposite direction, looking for a chance to get to Liam's right side. He swept low in response, their blades clattering and ringing again, both sword hilts locked.

Both young men leaned in towards each other, looking to push the other off balance. Liam could feel the young man's hot breath on his cheek. It was almost an intimate embrace. And that's when he noticed the young man was trembling. Quite terrified. Liam cursed under his breath. He glanced again at the rivulets of blood on the scimitar.

He's killed already. He's got blood on his hands. He's a valid target.

Liam brought a knee up and caught the young man in the

groin, winding him. The embrace unlocked and the young man backed up a step to buy a second or two to recover. But Liam advanced quickly, taking the advantage. He swung his cutlass down. The young man hastily parried, deflecting Liam but not stopping him. The edge of his cutlass ricocheted off the scimitar's guard and carried on down in a sweep that curved inward, biting deep into the calf of the young man's right leg. He cried in pain and flopped down on to one knee, a flap of skin and muscle exposing a sliver of bone. Liam must have cut a tendon, a hamstring, a muscle.

Now Liam had a height advantage. And mobility. The young man tried a quick, low thrust to Liam's groin, a roll-of-the-dice chance to turn his fate around. But Liam deftly stepped to one side and, with the young man's reach fully extended, there it was for the half a second it was going to be offered, the young man's wholly unguarded neck and shoulder.

Liam thrust his blade down. Brutally. Hard. Hacking deep into flesh, cartilage and bone. The young man looked up at Liam, the cutlass buried deep in him, with brown eyes that watered. Brown eyes that seemed to want to communicate something: anger? Regret? Forgiveness? Blood streamed from his mouth and his eyes began to roll, and then he flopped sideways on to the deck.

Liam stared down at his body, transfixed, as a pool grew beneath his torso. Maybe he wasn't so very young, Liam decided. Maybe he just looked young. Maybe there was something of a life lived there – before such a bloody end. Liam aged him up from sixteen, to twenty, to twenty-five in three blinks of an eye.

Does it matter how old he was?

Liam looked again at the bloodied scimitar lying on the deck. *He was a valid target.*

CHAPTER 21

1667, aboard the Clara Jane, somewhere off the west coast of Africa

The hatchet felt clumsy and heavy in Rashim's sweat-damp hands. He didn't think he was going to be able or even willing to kill anyone with it. He doubted he'd be able to do little more than flail it around in front of him and try to look intimidating at the same time. Down on the main deck, he caught a glimpse of Liam amid the churning mass of bodies, parrying and thrusting, his blade already speckled with blood.

Oh God, help me. I'm scared.

His legs felt like they were going to give way beneath him. On the rough wood of the deck beside him, Old Tom was rolling around with a pirate, locked in an embrace, both men grunting and gurgling as they tried to strangle each other. Captain Teale seemed to have recovered some of his composure and was now fending one of them off with a skilful display of swordsmanship. It seemed the only person on either ship not now locked in a personal struggle for survival was Rashim.

He looked around the ship. It appeared this struggle could go either way. Bodies were beginning to pile up on deck: the wounded, the dying, the dead; bare feet and boots were slipping in growing smears and pools of blood.

It was right then that his peripheral vision registered

something on the horizon: the signature shape of triangular sails emerging round a spit of land. Two more dhows were heading straight towards them.

It was *a trap. This whole pursuit was a trap.*

That had been the corsairs' game plan: to raise every sail and make it appear as if they were desperately trying to escape, while at the same time covertly slowing themselves down, luring Teale's ship ever closer to shore, to where more of them were waiting.

'Captain!' Rashim shouted. 'CAPTAIN TEALE!'

'Goddamn it, man!' shouted Teale over his shoulder as he parried a blow. 'Can you not see I'm busy?'

'There're more of them coming! We have to break this off!'

But Teale was otherwise engaged, his blade rattling against the edge of another. Rashim looked again at the two dhows; they were bearing down fast. If the same numbers of corsairs were on each of those ships . . .

We're going to be overwhelmed.

He looked around frantically for something he could do. Run? Save himself? Swim for it? He stepped across to the gunwale at the edge of the afterdeck, looked down at the choppy water below. He could jump over the side. Perhaps he might be able to make for the shore. Then what? Be alone there? Stranded? And then how long before he was chanced on by more men like these to be killed or more likely sold on as a slave.

The corner of one of the dhow's released sails fluttered across the narrow space between the ships, whipping loosely, taunted by the lively breeze. And a thought came to Rashim. Something Old Tom had said a few days ago, when a bare candle flame had been left carelessly close to a barrel of caulking tar.

Fire is the thing all sailors fear the most. Loose fire on a vessel is what has sent all too many men to the bottom of the ocean . . . Never mind a storm or unseen rocks, it's fire a seaman fears.

The dhow's loose sail. Rashim had an idea. He turned and ran to the low door to Teale's cabin, kicked it open and ducked inside. He found what he was looking for – a large oil lamp in a brass and glass cage, swinging from a hook on a rafter. He grabbed it, opened the lamp's door and pulled out the ceramic flask of oil inside.

Back outside, he raced for the edge of the deck, sidestepping Tom on the way, and leaned over the gunwale. He reached out for the corner of the fluttering burgundy sail.

'Come on!' he hissed as it danced and flapped a yard beyond his reach.

No good. Not quite close enough. He wasn't going to grasp hold of it. Even if he did, it was as likely the heavy material tugged by the wind would pull him over the side. Rashim cursed. Change of plan. He pulled the wick from the top of the flask. Oil sloshed around heavily inside; the flask was over half full.

I could throw it at the sail? Yes. He could try and douse their sail with oil. But an ill-judged swing of the flask and the oil inside could easily end up missing the flapping sail and splashing down into the sea below.

Rashim held the flask carefully in both hands, one grasping the handle and one cradling the base of the flask. Another gust of wind caught the material; it fluttered and bulged and flopped across the dhow's foredeck. Wrong way.

'Come on! *Come on!* This way!'

The wind freshened again and the dhow's foresail rippled and fluttered and then mercifully bulged out over the gap between the ships' hulls towards Rashim.

Now!

He swung the flask and a yellow arc of lamp oil splashed out, bridged the gap and soaked into the dark material. 'YES!' he whimpered. He dropped the flask on to the deck. Now all he needed was a flame.

'A flame! A flame!' he muttered to himself. 'I need a goddamned flame!' He looked around. For so much acrid gun smoke still wafting across the decks there wasn't a single source of flame or ignition to be seen. Then he noticed Old Tom, bulge-eyed and purple-faced, still wrestling on the deck with his assailant, a flintlock pistol peeking from his belt. Rashim scooped up the empty flask at his feet, hurried over and, with an almighty swing, brought it down on the back of the head of Tom's would-be strangler. The pirate flopped forward on to him and, gasping for air, Tom pushed the unconscious body off to one side.

'Curse ya! Yer might've . . . bloody well . . . done that . . . sooner!'

'Your pistol!' said Rashim. 'Did you fire it yet?'

Tom was on his hands and knees, retching. Coughing. Spluttering. Rashim didn't have time to wait for the man to recover. He wrenched the flintlock out of Tom's belt.

'Hoy! Hey! The piece is . . . mine!'

'I need it!' Rashim checked the weapon as he hurried back towards the edge of the deck. It was mercifully still primed and ready to fire. Again he leaned against the gunwale, as far out over the side as he dared. He wasn't hoping to ignite the sail with the ball of hot lead fired from the pistol. At best all that was going to do was nip a tidy hole through the fluttering sail. No. If he could fire it close enough to the oil-sodden material, the foot-long tongue of sparks and flame might just catch it.

Might just.

Once again he was at the mercy of the teasing wind. It pulled the dhow's foresail back across its own deck, coyly taunting Rashim as it hung there lifeless and rustling. Rashim shot a glance towards the shore. The other two dhows were closing fast.

'Goddammit!' he hissed. 'Will you please come *here!*'

He felt a breeze cool his damp cheeks and, once more, the sail snapped to life, fluttered, ballooned, then finally swung back towards him. Rashim stretched even further, his arm fully extended, one leg on tiptoe, the other raised, attempting to counterbalance his weight; an ill-timed bumping of hulls and he'd be over the side. He pulled the trigger and the pistol kicked in his hand. A mushroom cloud of blue-grey billowed out, completely obscuring Rashim's vision. He pulled himself back, righting his balance, and frantically wafted at the smoke spinning and twisting in front of him.

And through it now he could make out that the sail had swung back over the dhow's foredeck. If it had been night-time, dark, he'd have known if the sail was alight. However, in this glaring midday sunlight, any flame was almost invisible. But there it was, he saw it – the burgundy sail darkening as if a pot of ink had been spilled from the other side and was blotting through the material. A ragged hole appeared in the middle of the blot and then smoke, all of a sudden lots of it, and finally the first hint of a tongue of orange flame began to curl up the material.

'*Yes!*'

The sail was well and truly alight. Old Tom staggered over to join him, and understood in an instant what Rashim had been up to. 'Clever man!' he huffed, still struggling to get air down his bruised and battered throat. 'Very clever.'

'But look!' Rashim pointed. 'There're two more of those ships! See?'

Tom squinted. The other two dhows were little more than a quarter of a mile away, a distance they were going to cross in mere minutes. He cursed. 'Then we're done for unless we can get under way right now.'

The foresail was now billowing smoke across both decks and, through the fog of it, Rashim could hear the corsairs beginning to call out to each other. Shrill voices were raised in panic. The effect was almost instantaneous: a ripple of voices crying out in alarm. Their ship was their livelihood and a mad scramble began as they disengaged from combat and swarmed back over the gap between hulls to their own ship in an attempt to cut the flaming sail free and jettison it before the fire spread any further.

Old Tom was quick to react. 'Cut those grappling lines!' He grabbed the ship's helm and spun the wheel full lock to get the *Clara Jane*'s turning momentum going once again. Far too sluggishly, an angled gap began to open up between both hulls as the schooner lolled lifelessly to its right and the sails rustled and shifted unhappily, uncertain which way to fill.

'Go on, find the wind!' hissed Old Tom. 'It's right there, old girl! Find it!'

Teale joined them beside the helm, anxiously shooting a glance at the approaching dhows. 'You are turning us *towards* those rocks!'

Tom cursed. 'God help us, we need motion, Teale, you imbecile. *Motion!* Doesn't matter which damnable way we head!'

CHAPTER 22

1667, aboard the Clara Jane, somewhere off the west coast of Africa

The *Clara Jane*'s sails began to fill and catch the westerly wind, pulling her sluggishly around to face the craggy shoreline. The sea directly ahead of them was a frothing white foam of waves breaking across treacherous shallows and smashing against sharp knuckles and fingers of protruding rock.

'Turn away!' cried Rashim.

'Not yet!'

'You'll run us aground!'

'Aye, mebbe.' Old Tom shot a glance at the approaching dhows, now no more than a couple of hundred yards from them. 'But we'll be done for, for sure, if we stay bobbin' dead in the water.'

He kept the wheel locked fully to port until it looked as if the ship was going to ride right up on to the rocks, then, at the very last moment, with the schooner now crashing forward through the water well and truly under sail, he spun the wheel hard to starboard, once again full lock. The *Clara Jane* arced slowly round to the right, every last man on the ship wincing with expectation and bracing themselves firmly, waiting for the inevitable crash and splinter of the ship's keel on the rocks below.

Rashim felt something, a bump, a scrape, an agonizingly long vibration, beneath his feet.

God, we just hit something.

But the *Clara Jane* continued its painfully slow U-turn crawl around until the last spit of rocky shoreline ahead of them eased off to their left and the prow now began to bear south-south-west towards the pair of dhows bearing down on them.

'We're . . . uh . . . now we're heading right towards them!' said Rashim.

The *Clara*'s prow settled on the narrow space between the two boats and then Tom straightened her heading.

Rashim frowned. 'No, hang on . . . you're taking us *between* them?'

The schooner heeled over on to its port side as the sails now filled and the yards swung round on their braces, the ship closely hauled and sailing as tight to the wind as a square-rigger could go.

'They got no cannons on-board, we'll be fine,' said Tom. 'Just keep your head down from musket fire as we sail twixt 'em.'

Liam pulled himself up the ladder on to the afterdeck to join them. He looked back at the dhow they were leaving in their wake. The flames from the foresail had spread to the mainsail and he could see the pirates clambering up their masts, hacking ferociously at the rigging to cut the burning material free before the flames could spread across to the aft sail.

'Nice job, Rashim.' He grinned at the smoke wafting from the dhow. 'Aye, that was quick thinking.'

Rashim looked at Liam, noticed his shirt spattered with blood. 'Good God, Liam! Are you wounded?'

He looked down at his shirt and shook his head sombrely. He shook away the image of that young man: those brown eyes imploring Liam to remember him, be *haunted* by him, forever more. 'It's not my blood.'

Teale adjusted his waistcoat, placed his tricorn hat back on his head and joined them. 'Marvellous work, you men!'

'We ain't home and dry just yet, Teale,' growled Tom, nodding at the scene in front of them as he handed control of the wheel back to the helmsman. The other two dhows were now looming up on either side of them. For a moment it looked as if the *Clara Jane* was going to collide head on with the one on the port side, but it turned slightly off wind to avoid them, and a moment later they were racing into the space between both vessels, three hulls hissing through choppy water mere feet apart from each other.

Musket fire crackled from both of the low-decked ships as the corsairs chanced opportunistic shots up at them from either side.

'Heads down, men!' barked Teale, keen, it seemed, to be heard and seen reasserting his authority on the afterdeck.

Another crackle of gunfire and Liam felt a pulse of hot air on his left cheek as a musket shot whistled past him. 'Jay-zus!' He and the others ducked instinctively.

They're targeting the helm! No sooner did Liam have time to think that than another shot buzzed through the air and embedded itself firmly in the chest of the man holding the wheel with a heavy *thwack*. The man flopped back from the wheel and on to the deck, quite dead as he hit the wood. The *Clara Jane* immediately swung to port, the wheel spinning with a clattering of spokes.

Liam leaped forward and grabbed it with both hands, straining to haul it back and correct the ship's course. Another couple more shots whistled through the air comfortably high above his head as they finally pulled clear of the two ships. Liam was about to turn round and whoop defiantly at them when a final parting shot was fired from the transom of one of the dhows. A moment later Liam felt his temple had been smacked with a mallet. He vaguely sensed himself spinning, then a moment later he was staring at the blur of the deck right beside his face, watching a pool of his own blood spread out and soak into the rough wood and thinking, *Please . . . not my head again . . .*

CHAPTER 23

1667, Port Royal, Jamaica

Chaos space was mercifully quick this time. Travelling through it, Maddy had clenched her eyes shut and concentrated on the errand at hand. That horrible transition through non-space had seemed to last no more than a couple of heartbeats. Perhaps that was the trick. The more you focused on that awful milky whiteness, tried to make sense out of it, the longer your perception of the time you spent in there. Or maybe it wasn't just *perception*: maybe you really were in there for longer, as if chaos space itself was in turn curiously studying this person who dared to trespass through it – holding on to them for longer than was necessary before finally becoming bored, and tossing them out into the real world.

Maddy's laced boots impacted with a jolting thud on to hard dirt. She kept her eyes shut, savouring the immediate sensation of sun-warmth on her face, the pink glow of daylight percolating through the veil of her eyelids. Directly above her, she could hear the twittering of exotic-sounding birds. To her left, the gentle roll, draw and hiss of lazy waves nearby. And, not so far away, the sounds of settlement life: somebody chopping wood; the metallic *tink-tink-tink* of a blacksmith's hammer; somebody playing a fiddle; the bark of a mongrel dog. The call of a foreman and the chorused *harrumph* of men hefting something heavy and their groan of relief a moment later. And, faintly, the snap and flutter of flags, pennants, sails caught by a fresh breeze; the tap and clank of ropes and blocks against wooden masts.

She inhaled deeply and realized how used to London's overpowering odour of burning coal and coke she'd become. Here was an entirely new bouquet of smells. A hint of salt – yes, the sea, of course. Woodsmoke – always present, *when*ever they seemed to visit. But over the top of those two odours was the acrid tang of pine tar being cooked in pots somewhere.

'Maddy?'

Bob's deep voice broke the spell. She opened her eyes. They were standing in the small stone-walled graveyard of Port Royal's 'old' church. Above them the fibrous fronds of a palm tree swayed and rustled impatiently.

'Yes, yes . . . I'm good.' She adjusted the tie-strings of her bonnet beneath her jaw; already they were irritating her. 'Which way do we go?'

Bob pointed across the small graveyard – humps of sunbaked orange dirt marked with paupers' wooden crosses and dotted with several other palm trees in which colourful birds hopped and chattered to each other. 'Three hundred and sixty-three yards in that direction,' he said.

'So precise?'

He shrugged. 'The signal is clear.'

'After you, then, big boy.'

Bob strode across the graveyard towards a sun-bleached wooden gate that creaked as he pushed it open to reveal Port Royal's main street.

'Wow,' Maddy uttered.

To their left was the squat stone structure of the church. Its front looked across a narrow strip of dirt and dried grass on to Port Royal's high street. On either side of the wide and arrow-straight dirt thoroughfare, wooden buildings jostled with each other on tiptoes to lean over it. Almost as ramshackle as the Thames-side shanty town, the two-storey timber buildings slanted like a mouth full of uneven teeth. Not so much as a single right angle could be seen between them and all of them were top-heavy with upper floors that extended over the street like the bowsprits of Spanish galleons moored side by side. Small leaded windows were flanked by green-painted wooden storm shutters flung wide open. All of the windows were open too, to make the most of the fresh breeze. From them, drapes and linen curtains fluttered in and out like wagging tongues.

The street – though it hardly deserved to be called one – was unpaved. Several deep ruts ran down it like tram tracks, carved by wagon wheels on a day when rain must have rendered this street a quagmire, but was now baked as hard as concrete. Here and there tufts of dry grass sprouted from cracks in the dirt, and every few feet were wheel-flattened pancakes of horse manure. It was busy mostly with foot traffic and a few traders' carts, most of them pulled by hand, some by oxen. One or two of the more wealthy-looking denizens were trotting up and down the street on horseback.

Bob nodded to their left. 'The signal is coming from that direction.'

They headed north-west, up the high street. Maddy noted, with some relief, that there were a fair number of women to be seen, not perhaps as many as on any given London street, but at least some. Many of them wore threadbare dresses of colourful silks and velvets, their faces powdered white, cheeks rouged an unnatural doll-like pink.

There was no mistaking their profession.

To their right they passed the governor's mansion. Like the old church, made of stone, it was coated with lime-coloured paint, almost eye-wateringly bright in the glare of the noon sun.

The grand building was fronted by a tidy, well-kept garden tended by a handful of Negro slaves. A low stone wall topped by wrought iron with a gate midway ran along the front. Directly outside it, two soldiers wearing crimson tunics and dark, broad-brimmed felt hats wilted in the hot sun.

To their left they passed a meat market. Low wooden shacks with grass awnings on stilts out front, beneath which hung rows of wild boar carcasses, buzzed by a cloud of flies. Smoke billowed from the doorway of a shack where all manner of meat was being dried and smoked. The pervasive odour of boiling tar almost, but unfortunately not quite, covered the smell of offal festering in a bucket left in the sun.

Nice. Maddy resorted to mouth-breathing.

A little further up the high street, the bustling market-town ambience of Port Royal began to give way to something else. The calls of merchants and traders were replaced by the raucous hubbub of voices shouting over each other. They passed a tavern whose clientele had spilled out on to the dirt track of the high street. Roughly hewn log benches and tables, improvised from barrels and casks pulled out from inside and spread out along the side of the street, were occupied by men sprawled, bleary-eyed, in the sun. Every last one of them seemed to have a long-stemmed clay pipe sticking out of their bearded faces, puffing blue-grey threads of tobacco smoke before them.

And fewer women, Maddy noted unhappily.

Further along, the street narrowed and they found themselves with taverns on both sides of them. The spillage of clientele all but met in the middle of the dirt track, creating, in effect, an outdoor tavern that choked the flow of pedestrians both ways, causing people passing through to have to weave between the knots of drinkers and duck through lazy clouds of pipe smoke.

With an unsettling jolt, the truth settled on Maddy like a brick dropped from above.

I'm surrounded by frikkin' pirates. That's what they almost certainly all were. Only not the fun-loving, ahoy-me-hearties, salt-of-the-earth types that have a habit of cropping up in movies. No. These men looked like hardened criminals, like seventeenth-century versions of modern-day trouble-spot mercenaries. The kind of glassy-eyed psychopaths drawn to hotspots like Bosnia, Iraq, Afghanistan as much for the adrenalin rush of killing as for the money.

Real-live, nothing-like-the-movies pirates.

And right then Maddy made the big mistake of making momentary eye contact with one of them.

CHAPTER 24

1667, Port Royal, Jamaica

'Hoy! You there!'

Maddy wanted to quicken their pace through this knotted chokepoint. Bob was just in front of her, a big wall of muscle going nowhere. Their way through the sprawl of drinkers was blocked by a man coming the other way, pulling a handcart laden with bales of cotton.

'Hoy! You! Missy!' The pirate had now got up off his perch and was weaving his way towards her. 'Jus' wanna talk to yer, me luvvy!'

Come on. Come on! Maddy ground her teeth and thumped the small of Bob's back. 'Bob! Let's go!' she hissed at him.

'The way ahead is blocked,' rumbled Bob in reply over his shoulder. 'I am just letting this trader come through to clear the –'

'Jesus! Screw being polite! Just go!'

'Miss!' She felt a heavy hand land on her shoulder. Not just land, the hand grabbed her shoulder roughly and twisted her round.

She felt a fetid blast of stale, rum-soaked breath in her face. 'Lovely pretty rose, y'are!' he grinned, all gums and one yellow tooth leaning like the last drunk at closing time. 'Wha' a luv-er-ly beauty!' His tanned face creased with an even wider grin. 'Buy yer a tankard of kill-devil, my dear?'

Maddy shook her head. 'No, I'm quite all right, thank you.'

The man's eyes rounded at her diction. 'Proper-sounding lady, aintcha?' His firm grasp moved from her shoulder to her arm and he tugged her towards him. 'Come on, love. Come meet the lads!'

Maddy grabbed his hand and twisted one of his fingers sharply. 'No thank you!'

He laughed at that and for a moment she thought her forceful and spirited rebuff would be met with a respectful nod and a pardon me. Instead, still laughing, he reached out and grasped the neckline of her dress and yanked at it roughly. Buttons popped off, exposing the top of her modest cleavage. Instinctively she covered her half-exposed chest with one hand and slapped his face with the other. And that just seemed to encourage him. He reached under her bonnet and snagged a fistful of her hair. 'Come on, luv! Let's meet the boys!'

'BOB!' cried Maddy as she staggered after the man.

The support unit spun round at the sound of her shrill cry. 'STOP!' he boomed.

The man turned to look over his shoulder at Bob. Eyes widening again this time as he took in the size of him. 'Go an' bugger off!'

Bob cocked his head – quickly filing the interesting term. 'Release her immediately!'

The pirate, quick from practice or a lifetime's habit, whipped out a long knife from his belt and pointed it towards Bob.

'There will be extreme violence unless you release her,' replied Bob, almost apologetically.

The man chuckled at that. 'Extreme violence, is it?'

'Correct.'

The hubbub of voices all around them began to quieten, curious eyes – passers-by and drinking pirates – settled on the momentary stand-off.

Maddy, doubled over, whimpered in pain. His fist clenched even tighter in her hair, tugging sharply at her scalp.

'Oh, I'm goin' to tap yer with a nasty scar, mate, 'less you turn around and leave us right now!'

'Negative.' Bob narrowed his eyes. 'You have three seconds before the extreme violence begins.'

The pirate laughed, a little nervously this time, his hand flexing, adjusting the grip of his knife. Of course, now there was no place for him to go but onward. The matter of losing face was more to the point than the squirming girl at his side. But he decided he needed both hands so he pushed Maddy roughly at one of the tables. She fell across it, knocking jugs and tankards of rum on to the dirt road.

'Come on, then. Let's 'ave yer!'

Bob calmly took a step towards him. Within range for a thrust, the pirate lunged forward with the blade aimed at Bob's midriff. Bob swiftly side-stepped, moving with an agility and speed that the pirate clearly hadn't expected for someone so large and top-heavy. Bob grabbed the man's extended arm in one ham-shank fist and gave it a sharp twist. The sound of a bone snapping filled the momentary silence in the street.

With his other hand, Bob grasped the man's extended upper arm and, twisting, as if he was about to give him a Chinese burn, he pulled apart. The pirate dropped to his knees, screaming, clasping his bloody stump.

'You were warned,' rumbled Bob. He looked for Maddy. She was being held down on the table by several other men. Bob looked sternly at them. 'I can continue with this.'

Heads around the table shook; they instantly released their hold of her and she struggled off the table and staggered back to rejoin Bob. She passed the whimpering pirate, rocking backwards and forwards in agony. On impulse she swung a booted foot at him, catching him firmly in the ribs. Not that he seemed to notice. The bloody stump of an arm was a more pressing matter to him.

'C-come on, Bob,' she said in a strangled voice, doing her best not to let the shock of the moment lead to tears. At least not here. Not now. Not in front of these animals.

Bob put a protective arm round her shoulders and they resumed their progress up the high street, this time not having to weave their way through: a respectful gap was now opening up before them. Fifty yards more and then Bob indicated a side alley on their left. 'The signal is coming from this street.' They turned into it, Maddy relieved to no longer have a street full of eyes burning into their backs. She took a few deep breaths to steady herself, relieved, pleased with herself that she wasn't about to start crying. She clasped her hands across her exposed chest – no worse than the ample cleavage on show by the women who plied their trade in this town, but far more skin than she was comfortable revealing.

'God!' she gasped. 'I . . . I thought I was about to be . . .'

'The threat has been neutralized.' Bob looked down at her in an almost fatherly way. 'You are quite safe now.'

She grasped one of his fists, her hand almost entirely lost in his. 'Thank you, Bob.' She squeezed one banana-sized finger. 'We'd be nothing without you. Just a bunch of bumbling teenagers.'

Bob considered that for a moment. 'You are praising me?' From Liam, from Sal, he was used to that manner of heart-felt gratitude. But from Maddy it sounded odd. He was used to her acerbic comments, asides that he'd learned to categorize and file under [SARCASM].

'Yes, you dummy. Thank you.'

He nodded. Pulled up an appropriate response. 'You are welcome, Maddy.'

'Now,' she said, sucking in one more breath and composing herself, 'it's down this way, is it?'

'Affirmative.' He consulted something internally then appraised the narrow alleyway. Mostly single-storey wooden shacks that leaned towards each other, this narrow dirt rat run was almost completely in shadow.

'I believe the signal is coming from that building,' he said, pointing to one halfway along on the right.

Maddy held her breath as they picked their way forward, past steaming pools of human and animal effluence and puddles of stale urine, the decomposing body of some cat or dog buzzed by a cloud of flies. Ahead of them, somehow, she was convinced the news wasn't going to be good. She was almost certain they weren't going to find Liam and Rashim happily toasting each other for being so jolly clever and surviving near on six months in this godforsaken place.

But wouldn't that be cool? To open a creaking doorway and find the pair of them waiting impatiently for their rescue. Both of them tanned and weathered by months on the high seas, perhaps Liam's pathetic tuft of chin-hairs grown into something more impressive. And stories to tell of their adventures.

'And about bleedin' time!' Liam would probably say with that dumb-ass, half-cocked smile of his the moment he clapped eyes on her.

It would be cool, but she was pretty certain none of that was going to happen. One transponder signal, that's all they were picking up, which, of course, could quite easily mean one of them had got lost, broken or malfunctioned. But Maddy had a growing sense of dread that it meant one of them had come to grief.

Bob finally stopped outside the shack he'd pointed out. 'The signal is here,' he said.

'OK.' She licked her lips anxiously. 'I suppose we'd better see.'

CHAPTER 25

1667, Port Royal, Jamaica

Maddy rapped her knuckles on the wooden door. 'Hello? Anyone in there?'

The door creaked inwards. Inside it was dark and a foul smell wafted out, accompanied by a cloud of buzzing flies. She pinched her nose against the smell, stooped and stepped cautiously into the low-ceilinged shack. 'Hello-o-o?'

Inside, as her eyes adjusted to the pale light coming in through the open doorway, she could see a dirt floor that sprouted ankle-high tufts of grass and weeds. It was insufferably hot within: no breeze, no flow-through of air to take the edge off the oven-like heat. And the smell . . . She caught another overpowering waft of a heady brew, like a rotting meat pie. And stale sweat. Human faeces.

'Ughhh,' she gagged. 'Smells like something's dead in here.' She winced at saying that. As if voicing that aloud was making it that much more likely.

Please don't let me find Liam or Rashim in here. All of a sudden finding them was the last thing Maddy wanted. Because with this smell . . . ? It meant only one thing surely.

Bob ducked down low and squeezed into the small shack beside her, squinting to make sense out of the gloom. A tatty curtain of stained, threadbare linen hung across the room, suspended from a sagging rope. She looked at him, knowing that behind that material they were going to get an answer. As she reached for the curtain, her mind flashed up a possible scenario: Liam's rotting carcass.

No, not that, please.

She swept the material aside. The rear of the shack contained little more than a hammock strung from one creaking wall to the other. It bulged with the deadweight of a body. Maddy took a tremulous step forward, not wanting – but needing – to see what was in there. She leaned over the hammock and in the dim light could make out a barefoot man in dark leggings and a pale linen shirt which perhaps, once upon a time, had been white, but now looked a sweat-stained shade of lemon, punctuated with a dozen other stains of varying colours. She forced herself to look up at the body's face.

And heaved a sigh of relief. It was neither Liam nor Rashim.

'Thank God!' she blurted.

At the sound of her voice the body lurched suddenly, the hammock swinging, the shack's entire timber frame creaking; dust cascaded from the dirt and straw roof. The man's eyes snapped open wide as he sat bolt upright. 'Who . . . the devil –?'

Maddy stepped back. 'Sorry! Sorry! I thought you were dead.'

The man swung a bare foot over the side to steady himself and got up, but he misjudged his step and tumbled to the ground. She caught a waft of stale spirits, mixed with the cloying stench of a body and clothes that hadn't seen water or soap in a while. He pulled himself up on his elbows and looked up at her through yellow dry stalks of light-starved grass and weeds. Then vomited. And then passed out.

'He's blind drunk,' said Maddy. She squatted down over him,

mouth-breathing once again. Bob hunkered down beside her, studying him. 'The transponder is on him somewhere.' He began to rifle through the man's clothes and pockets.

'My God! Look! It's there!' She reached out for the man's left ear. The transponder was dangling from a hoop of metal. 'He's wearing the thing as a frikkin' earring!'

It took them the better part of an hour to rouse the man from his drunken stupor. Bob went back to the high street and returned with a leather bucket of drinking water, which they used to douse him. After he'd come to, he drank feverishly, slurping from the bucket's ladle, washing away a bad case of dry-mouth. He was badly dehydrated, not just from the booze; the heat inside this shack had been slowly cooking him. He drank several pints' worth of water before he was halfway ready to speak to either of them.

Sitting outside on the stoop of his shack was better than enduring the stench inside, but not much better. Maddy decided it was about time for some answers. She held out the transponder in the palm of her hand. 'Where did you get this?'

He blinked bleary, unfocused eyes at it. 'Tha's mine,' he slurred and wiped his mouth with the back of a hand that was shaking.

'No, it's not. It actually belongs to a friend of mine. Where did you get it?'

He scowled at her. ''S all I got left, Goddamn you. It's mine . . . give it back.'

She grabbed the collar of his shirt in her fist. 'You can have it back when you tell me where you got it!'

He looked up at her. A pitiful sight. He was emaciated and clearly hadn't eaten for days, if not weeks. An unkempt beard was hiding cheeks hollowed out from malnutrition, and glassy, red-rimmed eyes sunk deep into dark sockets glinted wetly up at her.

'You got any of the decent stuff, m'dear?' He smiled pathetically. 'Just a li'l drop to tide me over?' His hands were trembling with the shakes.

'What? You mean something like rum?'

'Yes! R-rum . . . just a drop . . .'

'Bob?' She looked up at the support unit. 'Go and intimidate someone, will you?'

'You want me to acquire some alcohol?'

'Yep.'

'Affirmative.'

She watched Bob until he turned out of the rat run and on to the high street. 'So, while we're waiting, you can tell me where this *earring* came from.'

'Aye, I'll tell ya.' The man snorted drily, humourlessly. 'From a man I'll kill with me bare hands if the good Lord ever sees fit to place him before me.'

'What man?'

'A treacherous, devil-eyed snake. Evil incarnate. The Devil himself, so help me.' He hawked up some phlegm and spat it out on to the dirt beside him.

Maddy was getting exasperated. 'Describe him to me.'

'Dark as night, with the smell of sulphurous Hell about him.'

'Dark? You mean dark-skinned?'

'Aye.' He narrowed his eyes at her. 'You know they say the good Lord burns dark the skin of sinners, so he does. Burns the skin black as night to mark 'em as evil.'

She had no time for that kind of stupid. 'Tall? Thin?'

He nodded. 'Aye . . . I'd s-say tall.'

Rashim? Had to be. 'Was he with someone else? Another man? Young, white?'

'Aye, there was the two of them. The pair were a p-partnership of evil.'

Maddy sat back, relieved. That had to be Liam. Then at least the pair of them were together. That was something. 'Where are they? Do you know? Are they alive?'

'T-took everything I h-had, so they did. *Everything.*' The man's face began to crumple and tears leaked out of puffy eyes down his sallow face into the bristles of his beard. 'T-turned them all a-against me. And after I *trusted* them . . . after I *rescued* them.'

Maddy heard raised voices coming from the high street followed by the crash and splinter of something landing on something else. A moment later she saw Bob's lumbering outline returning down the rat run with a clay jug swinging from one hand.

She wondered whether it was a good idea to let this poor wretch descend back into a drunken stupor. But then she could see he was trembling badly with the shakes: withdrawal symptoms. Here was a man intent on drinking himself to death; someone with nothing left but a desire to waste away to a pickled stick; to vanish from the face of this earth amid a spirit-infused fog. So be it.

Bob joined them and squatted down beside Maddy. 'I am reliably informed the beverage in this container is rum.'

The man's eyes widened with childlike glee at the word. He beckoned the jug towards him with gimme-gimme hands that flexed open, closed, open. Maddy took the jug, picked up a battered tin mug and poured a small measure out and handed it to him. Just a bit to deal with the shakes, no more than that. For now.

'Now, please . . . start at the beginning.'

The man gulped it down and almost immediately seemed a little better for it.

'I'll start with me name, which is Jacob Cuthbert Teale. Although, for a while, before those two demons took my ship off me, I used to be known as *Captain* Jack Teale of the *Clara Jane*. My ship, my crew . . . *my venture*.'

He sighed. 'Then things began to go wrong . . .'

CHAPTER 26
1667, aboard the Clara Jane, somewhere off the west coast of Africa

For the second time, Liam found himself coming to with a head that felt like some small malicious troll with hobnail boots was marching bloody-minded loops round the inside of his skull. He opened his eyes to see Will leaning over him, damping his forehead with a wet sponge. The young boy's face creased into a grin.

'Master Liam, sir . . . how do you feel?'

His mouth was dry, tacky, thick with mucus. 'Like hell. Is there any water?'

William nodded, dipped a ladle into a water bucket beside the hammock and lifted it to Liam's lips. He slurped from it thirstily.

'We thought you was goin' to die,' said Will quietly. 'There was so much blood.'

Liam hesitantly raised a hand to feel his head. His shaggy hair was matted with dried blood. He could feel a ridge of puckered flesh atop a large swelling and winced as he probed it.

'Ouch.' A few more head wounds like this one and he figured his skull was going to end up looking as misshapen as an old potato.

'Master Rashim said you was very lucky, sir. The musket ball was a glancing blow, he says.'

Liam wondered. Perhaps it was that. But then again, perhaps, like the support units, he'd been designed with a thicker skull. That left him with a queasy follow-on thought that perhaps the inside of his skull was just like Bob's: a largely empty space in which sat a small nub of brain tissue linked to a dense silicon-wafer computer. Something Maddy had wondered about before.

He sat up in the hammock. It creaked under his weight. He looked out past one of the *Clara*'s cannons through the open gunport at darkness outside. Night.

'What . . . what happened?'

'We escaped them Moors,' replied Will. 'The men are all saying it was a brave and clever thing Master Rashim did, setting that ship afire.'

Brave? Clever maybe. But brave? Liam vaguely recalled Rashim had been quaking in his boots just before the fight. If either of them could actually be described as brave, surely it was him, hurling himself into the thick of that fight alongside all the other men of the *Clara*. Inwardly he sighed.

'Yes, Rashim's a very brave man.'

'Master Henry says we was awful lucky. Says they was probably slavers. If them other two ships had caught up with us, we'd all be dead or slaves in chains by now, bound for Arabia.'

'How long have I been out?'

Will cocked his head. 'Out?'

'Unconscious.'

'Just been this afternoon and this evening, sir. We only lost sight of 'em sails an hour ago.' Will shook his head. 'Was a frightful frantic chase out to sea, sir. Frightful.'

Liam nodded. 'I can imagine. Where's Rashim?'

Will looked uneasy.

'What's up?'

'Everyone's all havin' a meet up on the deck.' Will was speaking in a whisper. 'They're not very happy with our captain.'

Captain Teale glared through the open door to his cabin at Rashim and Old Tom standing outside and at the men assembled sheepishly down on the main deck. 'And what is this about?'

Rashim could smell alcohol on his breath.

'The lads ain't happy,' said Tom. There was a hint of apology in his voice. Even though he too had been quietly grumbling about Teale's incompetence, the thought of a ship's natural order of hierarchy being called into question made him unhappy. Mutinies were never a good thing. Mutiny led to chaos. Chaos aboard a ship at sea was a recipe for disaster.

'*Unhappy*, are they?' Teale looked questioningly at them both. 'And they have sent you two as their spokesmen to bring me this news, have they?'

Rashim nodded. 'They . . . well, they're concerned with some of the tactical judgement calls you've been making . . . sir.'

Both Tom and Teale frowned, confused, and Rashim mentally kicked himself for using such an anachronistically modern phrase. 'Concerned with some of your decisions.'

Teale scowled. 'It's not their damned business to question my decisions. I am the captain of this vessel, their superior, and they will jolly well do as they are commanded!'

Old Tom pressed his lips together grimly. 'The men won't . . .' he started.

'The men won't *what*?'

Tom shuffled uncomfortably. 'The men won't have that, sir.'

Teale's cheeks pinked with rage. 'They will do as they are blasted well ordered to do or, so help me God, I will have any man who refuses arrested for mutiny and insubordination! And on our return to England he shall be tried and hanged as a mutineer!'

'I suspect these men won't really care about that,' said Rashim. Teale's bluster was looking thin.

'They don't see this ship as being covered by naval, maritime . . . or any law for that matter.' Rashim glanced back over his shoulder at the men gathered silently on the main deck. Several oil lamps flickered among them, catching the impatient glint of eyes.

Teale seemed to sense that bellowing and bluster weren't going to get him anywhere right now. 'A word in private, Mr Anwar?' He smiled courteously at Tom. 'If that's all right with you?'

Old Tom was taken aback by Teale's sudden polite deference. He cleared his throat and shuffled. 'All right, sir. If that's what you want.'

Teale stepped back into his cabin and gestured for Rashim to come in. Once inside, Rashim gently closed the door. 'I should caution you,' he began, 'the men are very angry that you led us into an ambush.'

Captain Teale's stern scowl evaporated in an instant. 'Oh God have mercy on me!' He took four steps across his cabin and slumped down in the chair beside his navigation table. 'I . . . I thought I had the measure of this captaining-a-ship foolery! I . . . I thought – damnation!' He glanced up at Rashim. 'I have confessed to you already . . . I *daren't* steer this ship all the way across the Atlantic!'

'But,' Rashim persisted, 'that was your original goal, was it not? To sail to the Caribbean and obtain a privateer's licence?'

'Yes!' Teale snarled angrily. 'Yes! Dammit, man . . . that was the *intention*, so help me. But I . . . I simply can't!'

'Why not?'

Teale reached for a tankard and slurped at the dregs of wine in the bottom. 'Curse you, Rashim! Do I need to spell it out to you, man? I am afraid! I have a mortal fear!'

'Of what?'

The captain turned in his chair to look out of the aft windows. Outside it was all but dark now and there was nothing to see. 'Land! Or more to the point, losing sight of it!' He slammed his fist against the table. 'I can make no sense of these navigation devices! The charts and maps confuse me! But above all . . . I cannot cope with the notion of nothing but sea within my sight!' His skin glistened with nervous sweat. 'Look at me! I am undone! I am in pieces!' He glanced back again at the windows, but they merely reflected the gloomy cabin, the oil lamp on the table and Teale's glistening face. 'We must turn back soon. Back towards the land! Before we are too far out to sea!'

'But the men won't accept that. They won't turn back. They're afraid of the corsairs.'

Teale was beginning to rock backwards and forwards. 'They must be told! We have to go back!'

'The men will almost certainly mutiny if you go out there and issue that order! More than that, I suspect they'd kill you. Or at least throw you over the side.'

'My God, man! Can they not see? Can you not see? We may lose our way and never see land again!'

Rashim took a step forward. He looked down at the charts and navigation devices. 'Is this your problem? You're afraid of being lost? Forever?'

'Yes! Worse than damnation in Hell! To be forever at sea! My God, just look at all the blue ink on that chart, sir!'

'No, look, see . . . the ocean isn't infinite,' Rashim said with a smile. 'Actually it's not as big as you think. Really.' He traced his finger across the map. 'At the very least, if you just keep heading west, you'll hit land eventually. You can't miss the Americas.'

Teale sat forward. 'Rashim, you said before . . . you said you could navigate us there. Can you truly?'

He shrugged. He'd already figured out the principles of navigation. It was just elementary arithmetic after all. But the practice of taking accurate readings on a swaying boat . . . that was another matter entirely.

'I suspect I could get us roughly, I suppose, *roughly* in the region of the Caribbean.'

Teale reached out and grasped his wrist. 'Then you, sir . . . you should be my first mate. Take charge of this navigation!' He nodded, encouraged by his idea. 'And the men would approve of that! You are well liked by them! Aren't you?'

'I wouldn't necessarily say that I'm *liked* –'

'After today's heroics –' Teale grinned a little maniacally – 'they *will*, I'm sure, and they will welcome you as my second-in-command!'

CHAPTER 27

1667, aboard the Clara Jane, somewhere off the west coast of Africa

'I really don't understand,' said Liam. 'I don't understand why you're helping him. The fella's a complete idiot, so he is.'

Rashim braced his elbows against the rail of the foredeck as the *Clara* rolled energetically over the back of a languid ocean swell. He squinted into the backstaff's horizon-vane viewing slit as he tried to take another reading. 'He is not a fool, Liam. But –' he shrugged – 'he is definitely no sailor either.'

'But *you* could be the captain of this ship right now. You, not that pompous twit.'

Liam knew the mood of the men aboard the *Clara*. They easily shared their thoughts with him now. He was well and truly one of them; he had earned their respect and confidence fighting those Moors, battling shoulder to shoulder alongside them.

'They were all ready to vote you in to replace Teale as captain. That's what they wanted.' Liam nudged his arm affectionately. 'They obviously think you're naval officer material.'

Rashim sighed. The nudge had put him off. He hunkered down once more, bracing himself against the rail to try and get his reading.

'But we need Teale,' he said. 'He is the one that has valuable family connections with the governing authorities in Jamaica.'

Liam took Rashim's point. No Teale, no letter of marque . . . no privateer's licence and the moment the *Clara Jane* attacked a merchant ship, Spanish or otherwise, they'd be branded as pirates and would forever more be fugitives from the law. None of the crew had signed up for that. And that one thing was the only reason they were prepared to continue tolerating Teale as captain. This uneasy situation was eased somewhat by the fact that Teale was keeping a very low profile, staying in his cabin, letting Rashim take charge of navigation and Old Tom, as quartermaster, manage the crew. Most of the time, Rashim said, he was either drunk or asleep. That's how he was dealing with his morbid fear of being out of sight of land – his nautical agoraphobia – blotting it out of his mind with rum.

'But the point is, Rashim . . . if you had taken charge, you could have ordered the ship to head to the nearest chunk of firm land and weigh anchor. You could have taken back your waistcoat off Teale, and Maddy would have had a fair chance of getting a steady fix on us and bringing us home.'

Rashim looked at him. 'There is a lot of supposition right there, Liam. We do not know for certain that the transponder in my waistcoat is still working, or that the signal is clear or strong enough for her to have zeroed in on it.' He kept his voice low. The nearest men were breaking salt encrustations from the rigging blocks on the deck below, out of earshot, but the fluttering wind could carry an ill-chosen phrase across the decks in a moment of pause and stillness.

'If she lost track of our signals, even for a moment – and, thinking about it, Teale was zigzagging us all over the place in the first few days out from England – for her it would be like trying to find a needle in a haystack. Liam, I made those transponders as something we could use to find each other if we got separated in a crowd, not for tracking someone across world-spanning oceans.' He stood up straight, adjusted the viewing slit on the horizon vane. 'I think we have to accept the possibility that we might be on our own.'

'Great.' Liam sighed. 'Ah well . . . not like I haven't been lost in this kind of mess before.'

'Lost? You mean with no pick-up data? No rendezvous point? No time-stamp?'

'Aye, lost . . . *completely* lost in time.'

'One of your missions?'

'Aye. It all started as a simple mistake, overlapping of fields, and Maddy accidentally blasted me and a bunch of other people back to the time of the dinosaurs. Sixty-five million years ago, if memory serves me.' He tugged at the hank of grey hair at his temple. 'That's how I got this. The stress she put me through.' He laughed drily at that.

'Good God! But . . . how did you —?'

'How did she find us?'

Rashim nodded.

'Well now, I had Becks with me. The "Becks" before the one we have now. She was able to calculate *when* we were.'

Rashim shook his head. 'That is not possible. Surely. Not from merely looking around at where you are. Geological time is on a completely different scale. I can't see how you could identify a precise date, let alone a year.'

'She based her calculation on the rate of tachyon particle decay. And it wasn't exactly precise. She narrowed it down to the nearest thousand years or so.'

'No, Liam . . . no, that *is* precise. In the grand scheme of things . . . over millions of years . . . to narrow it down to a particular thousand years. Quite incredible.' He made a face. 'If only we had one of those support units with us . . .' He turned to Liam. 'You sure you cannot do something like that in your mind?'

Liam cocked an eyebrow. 'I know I'm not exactly a normal human, but, Jay-zus, I'm not a walkin' calculator either!'

'Sorry.' Rashim realized he'd been thoughtless. 'My apologies, Liam. That was insensitive of me.'

Liam shrugged it off. 'Nah . . . don't worry about it. I know what I am and I think I've dealt with that now.' He grinned. 'Mind you, it might've been handy if they'd built me with a computer lodged in me head. But I suspect I'm all mushy stuff up top. I suppose I was designed to think like a human, not a machine. That's Bob's job, so it is. Mission priorities, databases, picking up signals an' all that.'

'Anyway,' said Rashim, 'if somehow Maddy is still tracking the signal, then that waistcoat of mine is on the same boat as us, whether it's on my shoulders or Teale's. It is not going anywhere without us.'

Liam pursed his lips. 'I just can't see why, if she is tracking us, she doesn't have a go at opening a portal.'

'We're a moving target. Far too dangerous. We'd end up merged with something or turned inside out.' Rashim smiled. 'I can happily wait a while.'

Liam looked down at the rolling deep blue sea, being carved by the sharp prow of the ship. He listened to the slap of waves against her hull, felt the faint spray of water on his cheeks. From above them, they could hear the thrum of taut halyards, the snap and rustle of the sails. 'I suppose we could be stuck in a far worse place than this, Rashim.' He breathed deeply. 'I could get quite used to this.'

Rashim nodded thoughtfully. 'I would not return to my time. Not even if I had the choice.'

'It was really that bad?'

Rashim gave the question some quiet consideration. He gazed out at the foam-flecked sea, the warm turquoise sky. Beautiful unpolluted colours that seemed to belong to another planet entirely.

'I grew up in a world that knew it was counting down time. We all realized we'd passed a point of terminal systemic decline. That all that was left was managing our own end.' He gave a wry smile. 'The world was like one big departure lounge for humanity. All of us waiting for the inevitable final collapse.' He pointed at the water below them. 'The oceans were blighted with toxins, algal blooms killing all the life below. I recall holo-pics of the Atlantic and the Indian Oceans; they were a rusty-red, not this lovely blue colour. Red with toxic algae.'

He shook his head sadly. 'Do you know, Liam, in my time there was a floating mass of plastic in the Pacific Ocean. I mean, an *island*, five hundred kilometres across and at least several dozen metres deep of rubbish that had accumulated and been caught in the spiral tidal geysers of the Pacific. At its centre, the rubbish was so deep that people could walk across it. Set up camps on it even. It was a monument to our stupidity. An artificial island, as big as a country, of floating trash – that's how badly we messed things up.'

Liam tried to imagine such a thing on the horizon ahead of them: a floating island of fetid rubbish. Most probably buzzing with clouds of seagulls and flies. 'Nice.'

'I know the past can be a barbaric place. I knew that when we were setting up Project Exodus. We picked Ancient Rome and we knew we were heading for a time that was brutal and violent and primitive. But at least it was a time where there was hope still. Not just then, any century in fact, right up until the twentieth century, before the discovery of oil, the development

157

of mass industry, before the explosion of the world's population . . . up until then we still had an unspoiled world with as yet largely untapped resources and endless potential. The twentieth and twenty-first centuries, in the hands of a smarter species than humans, could have been remarkable. They could have been the two centuries that turned Earth into the home world of a civilization that could have stepped off-world on to others. Perhaps even taken some faltering footsteps beyond this solar system. Instead, we just trashed our planet. Rendered it inhospitable.'

He sighed. Finally he smiled at Liam. 'I could get quite used to living in this time too.'

CHAPTER 28

1667, aboard the Clara Jane, the Caribbean Sea

'By my calculations, Captain Teale,' said Rashim, checking again, walking the dividers carefully across the chart, 'we are no more than five or six days away from Jamaica.'

Teale nodded. 'Fine. Jolly fine work there, Mr Anwar.'

His words this afternoon weren't slurred nor did they carry across the chart table along with the pickling stench of rum. In fact he was stone-cold sober. Rashim looked up at him and saw that he also looked extremely agitated.

'Perhaps I can fetch you another bottle from below? There are still a number left.'

Teale shook his head. 'I . . . perhaps later.' He sat forward in his chair. 'Rashim?'

'Yes?'

'I . . . how can I say this?' Something was clearly on his mind. 'Is it fair to say we have become good friends?'

Friends? Rashim wasn't exactly sure that was the word he'd use. The man was pleasant enough, charming when it counted, and certainly had the charisma of a showman.

'Friends . . . uh . . .' Rashim offered him a flickering smile. 'Of course.'

'I believe I can trust you, Rashim . . . trust you more than I can those feckless rascals outside. May I share a delicate matter with you?'

He decided, for the moment, to play along. 'Of course.'

'A secret. I can trust you with a secret, can't I?' Rashim nodded.

Teale pressed his lips together. 'I have not been entirely truthful.'

'About?'

Teale flashed a cavalier smile. 'About one or two matters.' He shuffled uncomfortably in his seat. 'I . . . I am not quite as well *connected* as I may have suggested.'

'What do you mean?'

'I sense you are as much a free-spirited man as I am. A fellow adventurer. A chancer? Hmm?' Teale's comradely chuckle sounded forced. 'To be sure, is this not a golden time for those minded to seek adventurous opportunities? Is this not a time when a man from humble beginnings can make something of himself?'

'You were saying something about not being quite so well connected?'

Teale grinned, tapped the edge of the table with his fingers, like a poker player about to reveal a cunning hand full of aces. 'I have played a rather devilishly clever charade, truth be told. A bold game, Rashim. You see, I am not born of nobility. I admit I have no family link with anyone notable. Not even with the governor of Jamaica.'

Rashim stared at him.

'The art of ingenious deception, my friend. The bigger, the bolder, the more extravagant the tale, the more an audience is ready to believe in it. Indeed, it was such tale-telling to an audience of gullible merchants in London that provided us with the funding for this ship and her victuals! This whole enterprise!'

Teale's smile spread across his face as if he'd revealed the devastatingly funny punchline to a marvellously hilarious tale.

'Hold on. You said . . . all those things you told me. Fighting for the Royalists as a cavalry commander? Your family background? Your family fortune –'

'Embellishments. Truth be told, my good friend, my craft is the stage.' He raised the tricorn hat off his head and held it to his chest, as if humbly acknowledging the roaring applause and adulation of an adoring, penny-a-seat audience of theatre-goers.

'I am an *actor*.'

Liam cursed under his breath. 'You've got to be kidding me. Seriously?'

Rashim nodded. 'I am quite serious. None of anything he said was true. None of it. The man has been hustling everyone from the very beginning.'

'But . . . but surely that idiot must have realized as soon as we arrived in Jamaica and he tried to get a licence off the governor . . . ?'

'His *plan* – for want of a better term – was to hope we got lucky before arriving. He was hoping we'd have some plunder aboard that he could use as a generous bribe to grease all the appropriate palms.'

'Jay-zus . . . what a completely sleazy, slimy –'

'Basically a conman. A trickster.'

'Aye.' Liam looked at Rashim, then his face suddenly creased into a smile. He found himself laughing.

'What? What is so damned funny?'

'Well, I suppose it's just . . . I suppose *ironic* is the word. Of all the people to be press-ganged by, we end up getting press-ganged by a *pretend* pirate.' His laugh dwindled to a wry smirk. 'It just seems to be the story of my life, so it does. One big fat lie after another.' He wrinkled his nose dismissively and chuckled again. 'It's laugh or go quite mad.'

'Hmmm, good to see you are taking this so seriously.'

'Oh, I am, or I will . . . just give me a moment.' Liam wiped his bristly chin with the back of his hand as he gazed out across the main deck, as busy in the evening as it was in the day with the crew at work patching and repairing.

At what point do I wake up and find all this is some bizarre bleedin' dream? That I really am just a normal lad from Cork . . . and all this is just the result of eating a bad bit of pork too late at night?

'You know, those fellas are so very much going to want to kill him when they find out,' said Liam finally. 'They're not going to be happy chappies.'

'You are thinking we should tell them?'

Liam shrugged. 'If Teale's no longer of any use to anyone, here's our chance for you to be voted in as the captain and, of course, for us to get that waistcoat and transponder back.'

Rashim narrowed his eyes. 'Yes, that is true. But . . . if we tell them, I do not want to be responsible for the man's death.'

'Neither do I. We'll have to play this very carefully, though. Those fellas're going to be hopping mad, so they are.'

Liam was quite right. The men were baying for Teale's blood.

'Hangin's too good for that lying scum!' roared Bartlett.

The others nodded. Liam had called the meeting down on the cannon deck, in an attempt to be discreet and out of earshot of Teale who, he imagined, was drunk again right now, or more likely fast asleep for the night. But the roar of anger and indignation was surely carrying topside. Perhaps it was covered up by the sound of Cookie banging pots and pans up on deck as he rinsed them in a casket of seawater.

'Lads, lads . . .' Liam raised his hands to hush them. He was a little taken aback at how ready they were to quieten down and listen to him. Like a class of unruly schoolboys, the noise was all bravado and front. Yes, they were angry. But even more so they were unsettled, unhappy . . . without a leader, a little frightened even. 'Lads, I think our first business should be to elect a new captain of the ship. Then let whoever that is decide Teale's fate.'

'Aye,' said Old Tom. 'Ship needs a captain or we're just a rabble at sea.'

'Quite,' agreed Liam.

'In that case, I put meself forward,' said Henry Bartlett. He looked around at the others. 'C'mon, boys, who's with me?'

A few hands were raised tentatively, a dozen perhaps. Henry scowled at the others. 'That's all, is it?' He spat on the deck. 'I've served in the King's navy. Been at sea more'n fifteen years. More than most of you lot!'

'How about you, Tom?' called out one of the men. 'Will ye put yer name up?'

Tom laughed and shook his head. 'I know me way round the deck, but I'm no navigator. Nor am I a businessman. And that's what we need, boys, someone who knows 'ow to make us money.' He offered Henry a polite nod. 'An' Henry here . . . good, solid man tho' he is . . . I don't see as the kind that's gonna make us rich as gentry.'

He turned to look at Rashim. 'But this 'ere gent – Mr Anwar – is the one that picked our course across the sea. He may look as soft as unbaked dough, have the hands of a woman, but 'e's got the knowings of navigation for sure.'

The men looked uncertainly at Rashim. Old Tom's endorsement certainly carried some weight, but then they were wary of handing over their command to yet another silky-tongued gentleman who might just as easily turn out to be another inept poseur, like Teale.

163

'I'll second Tom's nomination,' said Liam quickly. 'He may not have Henry's years of experience at sea, but he's smart, so he is.' Liam realized he was slipping into using modern language again. *Smart*. The crew would be looking at Rashim's — now somewhat grubby — tailored Victorian dress shirt and wondering what the hell that had to do with anything.

'He's clever. *Canny*.'

'Aye,' agreed Old Tom. 'Bright as a button.'

All eyes fell on Rashim and he stirred self-consciously. 'Well, I wouldn't exactly —'

Liam cut him off. 'Tom's right.' This really wasn't the time for Rashim to get all modest and self-deprecating. The men needed a leader. 'Rashim got us here. Picked up the skills of navigation in *just a few days* and got us safely to the Caribbean.'

Liam knew the skill wasn't quite the dark art that these mostly illiterate men thought it was. Arithmetic, common sense, a rudimentary knowledge of world geography . . . and the ability to read and write. That's all. But they didn't need to know that.

'I vote for Rashim,' said Liam.

'You're his indentured servant, ain't yer?' said Henry. 'Much as I likes you, lad . . . how do we know he 'asn't put you up to vote for 'im?'

'Liam's not my servant,' said Rashim. 'Never has been. We're just friends.'

'That's right. And I'd trust this man with my life.' Liam looked at him. *I would too*. Odd that. How long had they known each other in *real time*? A few months?

There was silence below decks. The crew gathered round a solitary oil lamp that swung gently from a rafter, the only sound the creaking of the *Clara* as she swayed on a docile tropical sea, and the clatter of Cookie up on deck.

'So, let's call the vote,' said Old Tom finally. 'For Mr Henry Bartlett . . . let me see your hands.'

This time there was even less of a show of hands for him: nine.

'For Mr Rashim Anwar?'

Liam and Tom both raised their hands, followed tentatively by one or two others. Liam craned his neck to look past those gathered in a knot round the lamp to the rest of the crew crammed in the narrow space all the way down the gun deck. He saw a few more hands raised further back and counted twenty in total. Not all of them. Not a landslide, not by a long way, but more votes for Rashim than Henry. The majority of the men hadn't voted.

Still unsure of Rashim.

'Any other names?' called out Tom. 'Come on . . . now's the time!'

Silence.

Tom looked at Liam. 'Then, as I see it . . . we have our new captain.'

Liam grinned and started to clap his hands. But then quickly stopped when the entire crew looked at him as if he'd grown a second head. 'Ah . . . I see.' He lowered his hands and tucked them into his pockets. 'We . . . hmmm, I guess we don't do the hand-clappy thing right now, then? Fine.'

'First business, Skipper,' said Bartlett. 'What we gonna do about Teale?'

Rashim cleared his throat. 'OK. Well, uh . . . let me see . . . I am not too sure. What do you chaps think?'

Jay-zus. Liam shot Rashim an incredulous frown. *Hardly an inspiring heroic-leader-of-men start.*

CHAPTER 29

1667, the Caribbean Sea

Jacob Teale was beginning to feel that the worst of this wretched nightmare was behind him. According to Rashim, they'd successfully crossed the ocean and entered the Caribbean Sea. There were islands everywhere here according to the various weather-beaten and suntanned sea dogs Teale had encountered in the inns and taverns in London. A man could navigate by eye, hopping from one cove to the next, and never need to stray out into the dark blue water beyond sight of land to make a living here.

He allowed himself a small smile. A man like him, with a quick tongue, a natural charm, the charisma and presence of a heroic leader, could make himself a fortune in these opportune waters. Just so long as he didn't squander money and chance on drink. He vowed that tomorrow not a single drop of rum or any other grog left aboard would pass his lips. They'd be arriving at Port Royal, Jamaica, tomorrow and he needed to be on his best form when he stepped ashore. Teale had little doubt in his ability to talk his way into the governor's mansion and, once there, to convince him that a written licence to plunder Spanish ships was his divine right and would yield him a steady flow of bribe money.

Perhaps, slightly trickier, was his crew. Teale suspected his magnetic spell had worn a little thin with them. There'd been a few mistakes . . . and he certainly hadn't shown the best side of himself these last few weeks, lying up in this cabin, drinking himself into a stupor day after day. Meanwhile, Rashim and Old Tom had been effectively 'captaining' the *Clara* between them. He'd had a fleeting concern that maybe Rashim might be a potential threat to his leadership. The man was undoubtedly clever and had a gentlemanly 'air' about him that this crew of gutter dogs instinctively deferred to. But he was no leader of men, that much was sure. His voice was almost feminine, his manner faltering and vaguely apologetic. The scum of this crew, petty criminals and scoundrels the lot of them, responded only to confidence, the loud bark of a man who was sure of himself. Anyway, not that any of this mattered. The moment he wafted the signed letter of marque in front of these men, they'd be his.

Teale settled back into his cot for the night, satisfied that, despite a rather unsatisfying start to his adventure, things were going to turn out just fine. And that's when he heard the muffled sound of many boots climbing the steps up on to the afterdeck. A moment later his door swung open. Not even a polite knock first.

'What the devil is this!' he snapped angrily.

Two men stepped in, one of them holding an oil lamp. From its guttering light he could make out one of them was the young Irishman – O'Connor or something similar, wasn't it? And the other was . . .

'Rashim?' He sat up on his bunk. 'Damn you, man! How dare you barge in on me like some –'

'Get up!' said Liam. 'Now.'

Teale's eyes widened. His lips quivered with outrage. 'God's bones! How dare you! I'll have you lashed for insub–'

'I'd get up right now and do what we say, if I were you,' replied Liam.

Teale did get up. 'You, sir . . . I shall have Tom clap you in irons.' He cupped his hands. 'Tom!'

'Aye?' Old Tom emerged from behind the other two.

Teale eyed all three of them, standing in the doorway of his cabin. He could see beyond them: the afterdeck was crowded with men peering in. 'Tom? What is the meaning of this?'

Tom smiled, all gums and black teeth. 'Lads has voted you out as captain.'

'Voted! *Voted?*' He spluttered the word. 'What is this? Some handmaiden's embroidery club? This is my damned ship! I organized this venture! I –'

'The men voted you out,' said Liam, 'and voted Rashim in.'

Teale's incredulous eyes met Rashim's. 'Is this true?'

He shrugged in response. 'Uh . . . yes, actually.'

Liam took a couple of steps forward. Close enough that he could lower his voice. 'The men really, *really*, want to slit your throat and throw you over the side. But Rashim –' he looked back at him – '*Captain* Rashim has issued his first order . . . that we give you one of our pinnaces with sails and oars and some water.'

Rashim nodded. 'That's quite right.' He tried to rustle up a more commanding voice. 'Those are, in fact, *my orders*.'

'And, if I were you,' added Liam, 'I wouldn't waste time arguing. The men are in an ugly mood. The sooner we have you off this ship and on your way, the better it's going to be for you.'

Teale snarled under his breath. 'You men! You men outside!' he barked suddenly. 'Any of you who will arrest these traitors right now will NOT be considered a part of this foolish mutiny! The rest of you I shall have flogged as –'

Liam shook his head and tutted. 'Teale, look, this really isn't helping matters.'

Five minutes later they had a pinnace bobbing beside the

Clara, a rope ladder flung over the side and the crew had begrudgingly lowered a cask of drinking water into the bottom of it.

Teale hesitated by the ship's rail. 'You know . . . the moment I step ashore, I shall report you all as pirates! Brigands! Mutineers!' He turned to stare at the assembled men. 'I will have an audience with Governor Modyford! I will have his ear and I will have him assemble a fleet of ships to hunt you all down! You will be pursued relentlessly. There'll be no cove, no island, no port that you can hide safely in!'

Liam noted the effect Teale was having on the men. That roaring voice of his, the tone of absolute certainty in it, that what he promised was going to come to pass. The jeering of a few moments ago had dwindled to an uncomfortable silence.

'You'll hang because of these two!' he said, glaring at Liam and Rashim. 'All of you simple-minded fools will hang because of *them*! And your carcasses will rot in gibbet cages as a warning to others!'

'Jay-zus,' Liam muttered to himself. *We need to get him off now.*

He grabbed Teale's shoulder. 'Right . . . that's enough rubbish from you.'

'My waistcoat!' said Rashim quickly. 'We need it.'

'Oh yeah.' Liam began to pull the garment off him.

Teale slapped his hands away. 'Unhand me, you common ruffian!'

'The captain wants his nice jacket back,' said Liam.

Teale shook his head casually. 'It matters not to me.' He unbuttoned it, shrugged it off his shoulders, handed it over and then laughed. 'I shall merely reclaim it from your dangling corpse, Rashim. Of course, I shall be sure to have it laundered before I wear it again!'

Liam grasped his shoulders and pushed him back towards the

rail. 'I think you should leave now,' he hissed quietly at him. 'Before someone takes a shot at you.' He made sure that Teale saw the handle of the flintlock pistol tucked into his belt.

Teale managed a smirk. 'I talked several dozen bankers and merchants into giving me this ship . . . I can certainly talk a foolish old bewigged scrap-island governor into signing your death warrants.'

'Well, good luck with that.' Liam shoved Teale back so that the man had to swing a leg over the rail.

Teale hesitated, clinging on to the top of the rail. 'These two fools will be your doom! Mark my words . . . the last face you will see, besides the magistrate and the hangman, will be mine!'

Liam pulled the pistol from his belt and aimed it at Teale's face. 'Go.'

'And you, Mr O'Connor sir . . . I shall be sure to ask to pull the lever on *your* execution!'

'You just don't know when to be quiet, do you?' He cocked the pistol and Teale finally began to climb slowly down the rope ladder. At the bottom he sat down heavily on the plank thwart.

'Mark me carefully, gentlemen, within the year . . . you'll all be bones held together by rotting flesh!' he called up to them. 'Every last one of you are dead men from this moment!'

Liam aimed his pistol down and pulled the trigger. The still night was split with the crack and boom of the shot and a puff of wood splinters erupted from the plank that Teale was sitting on. He got the message. Hastily grabbing the oars from the bottom of the boat, he began to row.

Liam and Rashim watched him paddling out into the darkness, listening to the dip and pull of the oars until the flat stern of the pinnace was lost in the night.

'That could have gone better,' said Rashim quietly as he pulled the waistcoat over his shoulders. The rest of the crew were staring sullenly out at the darkness. No whooping of joy. No cheers for the new captain. The mood was oppressive. Foreboding.

'Aye. Well, it's all done with now.'

Rashim fidgeted and fussed beside him. 'You know, he's ruined the cut of this thing. And there's buttons missing.'

Old Tom called the men to order. 'To your berths now, boys! Busy day tomorrow.' He nominated the night watch and the men quietly, gloomily dispersed, leaving Liam and Rashim alone, standing in the waist of the ship, staring out into the darkness.

'Ugh . . . and it reeks of alcohol and sweat now,' clucked Rashim.

'The transponder?'

'Oh yes.' He smiled skittishly. 'I almost completely forgot about that.' He unbuttoned the waistcoat and reached one hand inside and fumbled for the small secret slit of a pouch.

'You got it?'

Rashim fumbled some more, his fingers probing the silk lining. 'Er . . . the pocket's open. It is unstitched.' Liam remembered he'd sewn a few stitches of thick cotton to close the pouch for safekeeping just before they'd set out to watch the Fire of London.

'What?'

Rashim cursed and pulled his hand out. Empty. 'The thing has gone.'

Liam slowly lowered his head until his forehead thumped softly against the wooden gunwale.

'Great. Just great.'

CHAPTER 30

1667, Port Royal, Jamaica

Maddy stared down at him. He'd passed out again. The rum had revived his wits long enough to tell them what they needed to know, and now ex-captain and would-be adventurer Jack Teale was just another spent wreck, just one of so many other pirates lying drunk in doorways and on porches, like the weather-worn hulls of one of any number of sun-bleached dinghies washed up, beached and abandoned on a high tide.

Maddy looked at the snoring man. *He won't last much longer.* Either he'd die of malnutrition or more likely in some brawl attempting to steal someone's swag for the price of one last bottle of rum.

She stood up and looked at Bob, relief etched on her face. 'So . . . now we at least know they're both alive.'

'And they are in the vicinity.'

'Vicinity. You mean, like, somewhere in the Caribbean?'

'Correct. Nearby.'

'That's a helluva lot of *nearby* in which to try and find them, though.'

Somewhere in the Caribbean. Or at least they had been when they'd cast Teale over the side. And how many weeks ago, she wondered, was that? They could have sailed on elsewhere since then. They could even be sailing back across the Atlantic by now, perhaps trying to make their way back to Holborn,

London. But then hadn't Jack Teale told her his crew had firmly set their resolve on making their fortunes here in these waters? If Liam and Rashim were in charge of this ship now, that's what they'd *have* to promise their crew: that they were here to stay. Surely, their men, in newly rebellious mood, would mutiny against them if they issued orders to sail straight back the way they'd come?

'I wonder . . . why didn't they just come ashore here in Port Royal? And, you know, wait for us to zero in on them and pick 'em up?'

'I do not have adequate information to answer that, Maddy.'

'I was thinking aloud,' she replied absently. She stroked her chin. More to the point, why did they *give* Jack Teale this transponder? That's what he'd said. It was a *gift*. And yet this small walnut-sized chunk of circuitry was their only link. Their only hope of being tracked down and found.

What are you two idiots playing at?

Something occurred to Maddy just then. Something more than a little disconcerting. Perhaps at some point over the last few months – months to Liam, mere hours for her and Sal – Liam had finally decided he'd had enough and gone 'rogue'. She recalled how often he'd dwelled all misty-eyed and nostalgic on the six months he'd spent in twelfth-century Nottingham playing at being the big sheriff: the stand-in lord and commander-in-chief of all he surveyed.

God, he'd loved all that, hadn't he? The swords, the armour . . . the being in charge. And how many times had he said he'd go back there in a heartbeat if it wasn't for the fact they had a job to do saving the future?

But there isn't a job to do now, is there? Not really. We're kicking our heels. We're little more than time tourists with a machine to take us wherever we want.

She smiled sadly. She didn't think she could blame him if that's what this really was. If this was an opportunistic bid by Liam to escape from their eternal trap. After all, now they knew the truth of what they were: that none of them had actually *chosen* to be TimeRiders. The choice, after all — their recruitment moment — had merely been a programmed memory. Someone else's 'choice', certainly not theirs. No different to an author voicing the words, thoughts and feelings of a character. And that made them little more than sock puppets.

So . . . maybe that's it, then. Isn't it? He's made his choice. He doesn't want to be found.

That was Teale's account of events, admittedly a somewhat biased and bitter recollection of the last few months . . . He'd told her how he'd saved Liam and Rashim from the fire, how they had become the best of friends and then all of a sudden they'd turned on him, staged a mutiny and kicked him off his own ship. It certainly did sound as if both Liam and Rashim were very much embracing the idea of being swashbuckling pirates in charge of their very own ship and their own destinies. She could imagine how appealing that might be for them, particularly Liam: a wide-open horizon full of adventure and the freedom to sail off in any direction he chose.

God, what's not to like about that?

Maddy envied them that and found herself wishing she could be out there on the open sea alongside them, a sword and flintlock in each hand, *yee-haaing* and *ahoy-ing* alongside the pair of them. She envied them then wondered if, after all they'd been through together, Liam would really bail out on her and Sal, just like that.

I nearly did. Twice.

She recalled both times clearly: in the battlefield ruins of New York, when she'd thought that their team was finally incapable of functioning any more. And then in Boston, so close to reclaiming her old life again – or so she'd hoped.

Maddy looked at the transponder and realized, with a painful tug, that this was finally it. After all this time a parting of the ways.

Obviously this wretched drunk lying at her feet had no idea at all what the small device was. As far as he was concerned, it was shiny and looked pretty and made a very fetching earring. She thought she understood then why Liam had given it to Teale. His decision was made. Perhaps he suspected she'd try and persuade him to come back to London with her if she caught up with him; suspected she'd manage to convince him out of duty, loyalty, obligation, and this was his way of avoiding that. His way of ducking out of that situation. His way of finally cutting free from the agency – for what it was. No tearful goodbyes this way, no arguments. Just this. He knew that Maddy would find and follow the transponder's signal and eventually recover it. This was what he was telling her.

Please, Maddy, don't come looking for me. Don't take me back. I'm happy here.

This was his final goodbye.

'Bob?' Her voice sounded thick. She cleared her throat, determined she wasn't going to get all emotional. At least not right now, not in this God-awful place. And certainly not in front of this dumb-ass rack of muscle and bone.

'Yes, Maddy.'

'I think we're all done here.'

'We are returning?'

'Yes.'

He frowned then rolled a thick eyebrow up. 'Without Liam and Rashim?'

'Correct, without Liam and Rashim.'

That seemed to confuse him. 'We will return to London and begin a search for the signal on the other transponder?'

'Yeah . . . yes, I guess so,' she replied absently. But in the back of her mind she wondered whether, instead, she might have to start thinking that the time had finally come to accept this was all over now. Whatever purpose they'd once had had run its course and now they were on their own. Maybe, just maybe, she was simply going to go back to 1889, pick out somewhere, some time, for herself where she'd like to live out the rest of her days, open a portal and do as Liam and Rashim had done: bail out. Sal could do the same if she wanted.

And Bob and Becks?

They could do whatever the hell their mission-oriented bot-heads told them to do actually. They could sit in that dark dungeon for the rest of their unnaturally long lives, staring at computer screens and collecting dust for all she cared.

'Come on, Bob . . . we're done here. Let's go back.'

CHAPTER 31

1667, the Caribbean Sea

Be careful what you wish for . . . you might just get it.

That's what Liam was thinking as he watched some of the crew of the *Clara* row ashore on their water run. The last fortnight, stormy weather and a strong, prevailing northwesterly wind rolling in across the Atlantic had pushed them down to the south-eastern extent of the Caribbean, not so far from the shoreline of the Spanish Main. A hundred or more miles off track. Rashim's navigational skills were looking decidedly amateurish.

The casks of drinking water were now all but empty or what was left was spoiled and needed replenishing. Liam and Rashim had decided this small unnamed island with its tall, jungle-covered peaks and sheltered lagoon would make a suitable place to stop and restock. Not only did they need to fill up on drinking water but their supplies of food – victuals, as Old Tom called them – were down to virtually nothing. The last couple of days, Cookie had resorted to making a broth of the last few rotten potatoes, thickened with the powdered remains of their oats.

They were going to have to hope this island would offer some wild boar, perhaps even a turtle or two.

Liam had quietly advised Rashim that the foraging party was best led by Henry Bartlett. The man was proving to be something of a liability. Disgruntled at not being voted captain, he was beginning to make trouble, to sow seeds of discontent among the crew, and Liam thought the best medicine was to keep the man busy with something rather than have him idle and muttering and grumbling to those willing to listen.

They watched Henry and a dozen other men as their two boats laden with empty water casks finally rode up on to the beach and they splashed out into the shallow water. The men going with Bartlett had been handpicked by Liam: men who *weren't* particularly close to Henry, weren't part of Henry's small (but growing) band of disgruntled fellow *mutterers*. The last thing they needed was for them all to be together ashore for a couple of days to voice their shared discontent, to egg each other on and hatch plans.

'This isn't going very well so far, is it?' said Rashim.

'They're a hard lot to please,' replied Liam. It didn't help that every man aboard this ship had been given the hard sell by Teale back in London: promised that the waters of the Caribbean were awash with gold and easy plunder. That getting rich would be as easy as plucking low-hanging fruit from a tree.

The last few days, barely a fortnight since Teale had been ousted, they'd experienced one misfortune after another. Firstly a storm that had seemingly blown up out of nowhere, cracking a yard in half and damaging all the rigging attached to it. Then a mishap with one of the ship's casks of gunpowder going off. Luckily, the majority of the store of powder, still waterlogged from the storm, had failed to ignite alongside it. But the explosion – caused, Liam suspected, by some careless fool tapping the ashes from a pipe where he shouldn't have – had been enough to kill one of the men (presumably the idiot with the pipe) and wound a couple of others.

Finally . . . they'd run aground on a sandbank. Been stuck on it for several days while the crew had been forced to offload everything that could be removed to lighten the vessel, then every man mustered to work chest-deep in the water to rock the schooner inch by inch backwards into deeper water.

As Rashim had pointed out, not the best start. Truth was they were in a pretty sorry state. Some of the men wanted the ship to head to the nearest port – presumably with the intention of abandoning the *Clara* and trying their luck on some other ship, preferably one captained by someone who knew what he was doing and, better still, with a licence to raid and plunder Spanish ships.

Even if they went to a port, they had no money. None at all. Liam imagined there would undoubtedly be some sort of mooring fee, or a local tax or bribe that would have to be paid and, failing that, he presumed their ship would be confiscated in lieu of payment.

'What we need is a win,' said Rashim. 'Just a small win.' He turned to Liam. 'To show the men our luck has changed for the better.'

'Maybe . . .' Liam started voicing a thought that hadn't quite crystallized in his mind yet.

'Maybe . . . what?'

He shrugged. 'Maybe we just need to cut ourselves free from all of this.'

'What do you mean?'

'I mean . . . what if we just sailed into a port, rowed ashore and just . . . I dunno, abandoned this ship. Let someone else take charge of it. Let Henry take charge of it, since he wants that so badly.'

'Then what?'

Liam pursed his lips. 'I don't know. I'm just making this up as I go along.'

'We are stuck, Liam. We are stuck in this time and, if we did as you suggest, we would be stuck here with nothing but the clothes we stand up in. We would be beggars in a place that I am sure has little charity going around.'

Liam nodded. 'True.' Rashim was right. The *Clara*, sorry state that she was in right now, was their only asset. The only thing they could use as leverage in their situation. And their 'ownership' of her was only by the current consent of the crew. One more stroke of bad luck and they could just as easily turf Rashim and him over the side and vote someone else in to run the ship.

'All we need is one easy victim,' said Rashim. 'Then, with a little money, we could turn this all around. I am sure of it.'

Liam smiled. 'You're actually loving this really, aren't you? *Captain* Rashim?'

Rashim ignored that. 'I have had some ideas.'

'Ideas?'

'Yes. Ways we could have a definite tactical advantage over all other ships. Ways we could modify this ship to make it unbeatable. Make it . . .' Rashim narrowed his eyes and gazed out across the lagoon at the beached dinghies. 'Make this ship *legendary*. But we would need money first.'

'*Legendary?*' Liam cocked an eyebrow. 'Come on, what's going on in that head of yours?'

'Yes, legendary, Liam. We are stuck here. Both our transponders are gone. I cannot even confidently assure you that they were powerful enough for Maddy to track anyway. For all we know, she could still be scanning up and down the Thames for us right now. Or she may by now think we were caught up in the fire. Dead.' He swiped away a damp curl of dark oily hair from his face. 'Liam, we are stuck here, are we not?'

'Aye, for the moment, I suppose.'

'But . . . could we not make our mark?'

Changing history. Sure. Liam nodded. It's not like he hadn't resorted to that before. He'd created a fossil with a get-me-the-hell-out-of-here message. He'd signed a museum visitors' book with a coded version of a similar message. But what was out here in this tropical wilderness that could effect the same result? They could carve messages into palm trees, leave notes buried in treasure chests and hope some future treasure hunter might find one and take it to an anonymous little oak doorway beneath Holborn Viaduct. But really . . . ? The chances of that?

Then Liam laughed. Laughed at his stupidity. He had it . . . what Rashim was getting at. *Make our mark*. Make themselves a legend. Become a story recorded in history books. Books that Maddy and Sal might read. Perhaps even create a time wave that Sal would pick up on — a clue that they were both alive and making their presence felt.

'Liam, using a few modern . . . *refinements*, we could make our ship infamous. The scourge of the high seas.' Rashim grinned rather self-consciously at the cheesy phrase. 'You and I, Liam . . . we could be kings of the pirate world.'

'Pirate kings, huh? You sure this is all about getting Maddy to find us . . . and not about you living some personal *Captain "Blackbeard" Rashim* ego trip?'

'It is to that end. To give something for Maddy to spot.' He gave Liam an indulgent wink. 'But . . . but also . . . I mean, *pirate kings*? You and I. Would that not be quite something?'

'Aye . . . it would.'

They gazed out at the men on the beach, already splitting up into several parties to scout the island for a source of fresh water.

'All we need is that one easy victim to start us off,' said Rashim. 'A little money.'

'You going to tell me what your ideas are? You know, for making us so super-invincible?'

Rashim tapped the side of his nose. 'I am still refining my ideas. Soon.'

'Well, I'm going to suggest an idea.'

'What?'

'If we're going to make this ship famous . . . *infamous* even . . . then I suggest we change her name.'

'To what?'

Liam rolled his eyes. 'Well, obviously to something that will jump out at Maddy and slap her in the face.'

Rashim looked none the wiser.

'The *Pandora*, of course.'

CHAPTER 32

1667, the Caribbean Sea

'She's badly crippled, Skipper,' said Tom, passing the spyglass to Rashim and pointing across the flat sea towards the pale dot of a sail on the horizon.

Rashim squinted into the lens for a minute before passing it on to Liam. 'His eyes are better than mine.'

Liam took it and settled on the distant smudge of billowing canvas. The ship loomed in and out of view as their own vessel rocked gently. He braced himself against the rail and adjusted the spyglass's focus. He could make out a high-sided merchant ship. And there, fluttering from the mizzenmast, he could make out yellow and red colours on the listless flag. 'Spanish?'

'That she is, old-style carrack,' said Tom. 'And see? Her foremast is snapped above the yard.'

Liam nodded. 'Aye, she does look a pretty sorry sight.' He lowered the spyglass. 'Storm damage, do you think?'

'Most likely,' grunted Tom.

The storm that had whipped up last week had come without warning and passed quickly. It had been a terrifying few hours during which they'd bucked and rolled and large swells had crashed over the low waist of their ship. Perhaps the storm had been more severe further west and south towards the Spanish Main.

'Do those Spanish ships not travel in flotillas?' asked Rashim.

'Most times. This one must'a been left behind. Too slow for the others. They don't like to waste no time 'anging about in these waters. Straight an' as quick as they can out into the Atlantic.'

Liam turned to Rashim. 'Looks like our first bit of good luck. Some easy pickings.'

'Indeed.' Rashim took a deep, steadying breath. 'I suppose we'd better get our hands dirty, then.'

Tom grinned.

Three hours of pursuit later, a single warning shot from one of their port-side cannons and the carrack had eagerly lowered her sails. Now she bobbed listlessly a hundred yards across the water from them. Liam convinced Rashim that now was as good a time as any for him to try and look the part of the fearless, swashbuckling leader of a band of bloodthirsty buccaneers. So, he stood at the prow of the leading pinnace, doing his best to play the part, one booted foot resting haughtily on the gunwale, a hand resting on the hilt of the cutlass tucked into his belt.

As they pulled alongside the hull of the carrack, a rope ladder was tossed down over the side to them. After a moment's hesitation, and goaded by a look from Liam, Rashim led the way up, finally at the top swinging his legs over the rail with as much commanding presence as he could muster. Before him, on the main deck, the carrack's entire crew were assembled, their weapons in a tidy pile on the planking at their feet. Fifty pairs of anxious eyes silently rested on him.

Rashim fought the urge to offer them a polite little wave while he waited for Liam and the rest of the boarding party to clamber up and join him.

'And what do I do now?' he muttered under his breath to Liam as he took his place beside him.

'I don't know. Ask who their captain is, I suppose.'

'Right.' He cleared his throat. 'Who is in command here?'

One of the crew on the main deck took a step forward. A short stocky man with long dark hair silvered with strands of grey and a tidily clipped moustache. He dipped his head politely. 'I am Captain Juan Lopez Marcos.' He pulled a sword from his scabbard, an unpolished, dull-edged blade, and offered it hilt-first to Rashim. 'I surrender this ship to you.'

'Right . . . very good.'

Behind him, Rashim heard the rest of the boarding party clamber over the rail. He heard one or two of them whoop excitedly as they spread out across the deck and began to eagerly rifle through the crew's possessions.

The Spanish captain took a faltering step closer to Rashim. He spoke with a lowered voice. 'We offer no resistance, *señor*. I ask . . . only that your men exercise *restraint*.'

'Yes . . . yes, quite. Of course.'

'I . . . we carry a cargo of wines, foods, a little coin. I must inform you there is no gold aboard our ship.'

'Well, we'll take a look for ourselves all the same,' replied Rashim.

'*Señor*?' The Spanish captain looked anxiously at the Englishmen as they raced each other eagerly up the ladders to the aftcastle and forecastle in search of booty. 'I must tell you, there are women and children aboard our –'

His words were interrupted by a shrill scream and, a moment later, Henry Bartlett emerged from a cabin door on the raised aftcastle deck dragging a young woman out into the daylight by the arm. 'Look what I found in 'ere, lads!' he roared triumphantly. He rough-handed the girl by the shoulders and thrust her towards one of the other men, then reached back into the gloom of the cabin and pulled another girl, whimpering with fear, out into the glare of the midday sun.

They heard further whoops of delight from the other end of the ship as one of the men emerged with a long-necked, bulb-bottomed bottle of wine held aloft in each hand. 'There's crates an' crates of the stuff!' He stuck the neck of the bottle into his mouth, pulled the corked stopper free with his teeth and upended it into his mouth, a deep plum trickle of wine spilling from his lips and soaking the front of his blouse. The men of the boarding party chanted and roared encouragement as he chugged his way through it.

'*Señor*?' Captain Marcos implored Rashim with spread hands. 'Your men? I beg of you . . . please?'

Tom and Liam drew up either side of Rashim. 'You should let the lads 'ave a bit of fun, Skipper,' cautioned Tom. 'This is what they been waitin' a long time for. This is what they been expectin'.'

Several more men raced up the ladder to the raised deck of the forecastle, disappeared inside the cabin door and emerged a few moments later cradling more bottles in their arms. The men started passing the bottles around, several casually tossed across the main deck and dropped, shattering glass on the deck.

Liam leaned towards Rashim. 'This could get out of control if we don't nip it in the bud.'

'I know . . . I know.'

Up on the aftcastle Henry Bartlett had been passed up a bottle and now uncorked it with his teeth, spitting the cork out on to the deck, upending the bottle and drenching his lips, his face, with the ruby-red liquid. 'Bee-oootiful drop!' he spluttered loudly. He then reached out for one of the young women standing beside him and grasped her by the upper arm. 'Come on, me fair Spanish lovely!' he roared. 'Show me a little of yer Spanish mane.'

His friends on the main deck cheered that.

'You're right, Liam, we have to stop this.'

'No.' Tom shook his head slowly. 'Best leave 'em be, Skipper. I tell ya, yer'll have a mutiny on yer hands if you order them to —'

The girl began to scream and struggle as Henry dragged her towards the open cabin door. 'Rashim!' hissed Liam. 'Jay-zus, do something!'

Rashim winced. 'I . . . they won't . . .'

'Oh for . . .' Liam cursed under his breath. He strode across the deck and grabbed the rail of the ladder leading up to the aftcastle. 'Henry!'

Henry wasn't listening — he was wrestling with the girl. Her hands had grasped the door frame and he was trying to prise her fingers loose. Liam hauled himself up the ladder. 'Henry! HENRY!'

The man looked over his shoulder at Liam. 'What?' Bartlett grinned at him. 'Come on, lad, she's part of our booty!'

'Bartlett.' Liam's voice hardened. 'Let her go!'

The good-natured smile disappeared from Henry's face. 'Now that's no way to talk to a good friend.'

'Captain's orders,' said Liam. 'There'll be no mistreatment of these people. They surrendered. The ship is ours and the cargo is ours. The crew and passengers are —'

Henry spat on the deck and swore. 'These two lovelies are ours, Liam. Fair 'n' square.'

'You let her go now, Henry . . .' Liam's hand rested on the handle of the flintlock tucked into his belt. The gesture wasn't wasted on Henry.

'Or what?'

Liam realized the entire ship was silent. The noise of the other men, the excited whooping, the chatter, the clunk and patter of boots and bare feet on deck, the noise of wooden crates being prised open . . . even the swill and swoosh of upended bottles: all of that had stopped. All eyes and ears were on the pair of them.

'Don't make this more than it needs to be, Henry. Just let her go.'

'Yer not the captain . . . lad.'

'He . . . he's a-acting on my orders, Mr Bartlett,' called out Rashim. Liam inwardly winced at the uncertain wobble in Rashim's voice. Hardly the most commanding presence.

Henry let the girl go and she hurried across to her friend who consoled her in her arms as her shoulders shook and she sobbed. He turned to Liam, took a challenging step towards him.

'See, Liam lad . . . things is all a bit different now,' he said. 'What we just done this morning, that makes us criminals, don't it? No longer laws an' rules now. Yer friend down there's only the captain cos we *let* him be the captain.'

Henry raised his voice. 'Ain't that right, lads? It's the crew what makes the decisions now! By our vote!'

Several of the men, those who'd already got a good way through the bottles they were holding, cheered that.

'An' we all earned this booty, *proper earned it!*'

Another cheer from below.

'So . . . why don't yer step back down an' leave us be?' Henry had mirrored Liam's gesture and rested his hand on the wooden handle of his pistol.

Liam realized this was the line, the thread-thin line, the boundary that defined who was in charge of their ship. And Henry Bartlett had planted two bold feet across that line.

This is it . . . this is where he's going to openly challenge Rashim. You can't back down now.

'Henry . . .'

'Liam . . .' Bartlett grinned.

Liam pulled his pistol out and held it ready, half-aimed, its short barrel wavering in the space between them. 'Give me your weapon and return to the boat!'

He suspected Henry had come to the very same conclusion; this was his perfect moment. Back down now and he was going to lose face among the supporters he'd managed to gather over the last few weeks.

'Ain't gonna do that, lad!' he announced loudly. Softly now: 'Liam . . . don't make me do this. You know I like you.'

'And I don't want to do this either, Henry, but . . . you know I can't just stand by and let you . . .' He glanced at the sobbing girl, perhaps a year older than Sal. Her small frame, black hair and dark skin . . . it could almost be her.

'We're here to steal Spanish booty, to make ourselves rich men. That's what we're going to do. And no one who isn't standing in the way needs to get hurt in the process. Jay-zus, Henry . . .' He sighed. 'I've seen there's enough needless cruelty in this world without us adding to it.'

Henry Bartlett pursed his lips thoughtfully and looked down at the deck, giving that notion some consideration.

Silence, except for the gentle creak of the carrack as it swayed on the subdued sea, her slackened sails fluttering and rustling. The sobbing had subsided and now both girls stared with frightened, wide brown eyes at the stand-off that would decide their fate.

'Aye,' said Henry presently, with a sad and weary nod of acknowledgement, ''tis a cruel enough world.' With a sharp tug, he pulled the flintlock out of his belt.

The *crack-hiss-boom* filled the silence and long, still seconds passed as the blue-grey cloud of gunpowder smoke swirled, twisted and finally cleared.

Liam watched Henry Bartlett staring back at him as a thick

dark rivulet of blood trickled down his chest. His mouth hung open and snapped shut like a turtle's beak several times. Then finally he rocked back on his heels and collapsed on to the deck.

Liam realized his mind was empty. A void. No horror, no shock, no self-loathing. Nothing. He hoped that would come later. Because if it didn't . . . what did it mean? That he'd finally become some sort of killing machine? Finally become a support unit?

I want to regret this later. God help me . . . I want to regret this.

CHAPTER 33

1889, London

'He wouldn't do that!' said Sal. 'He wouldn't just leave us without even saying goodbye.'

'Don't you see? That's exactly what he's done.'

Sal shook her head. 'No. I don't believe that. I don't know how someone else has ended up with the transponder thing, but it's not that . . . not Liam trying to shake us off.'

'Think about it, Sal. He's been gone several months, not just twelve hours. That's enough time to think about things, to wonder what you really want out of your life.' Maddy realized that since they'd escaped from 2001 and settled here in London their time had been pretty much fully occupied with fixing themselves up to be functional, or at least semi-functional, again. Several months stranded on the deck of some boat? Perhaps that had given Liam some perspective: time to *really* think what he wanted to do with the rest of his life.

'He's been gone into the past for six months before. He came back to us, so why would he suddenly not now?'

'Because this time, Sal, he knows exactly what he is.' Maddy laughed bitterly. 'This time he knows there's no O'Connor family back home to protect from the timeline going bad. There's no Mom and Dad to worry about. No loved ones. No hometown to pine for . . . and want to preserve and protect. He has nothing and no one to worry about.' She shrugged. 'He's realized he's free.'

She sat down in the rocking-chair. 'And you know what? I can't say I blame him.'

Sal slumped down in the armchair opposite her. 'You . . . you're sure?'

'No, I'm not sure. I'm never *sure* of anything! That's what's so frikkin' tiring: second-guessing *everything*. Never knowing anything for certain and having to give things my best goddamn guess.' She sighed. 'But we know he gave that man his transponder, Sal. Handed it to him as a gift, for Christ's sake! *Here y'are, fella, all yours, so it is*,' she said with a half-decent attempt at Liam's accent. 'What the hell do *you* think that means? Huh?'

Sal bit her lip silently. She shook her head.

'Now I don't know if that's Rashim's influence,' Maddy continued. 'I don't know if Liam has always secretly wanted to be a pirate. For all we know maybe he's taken a blow to the head, lost his memory and doesn't even know who he is or what his little gift was. But it seems to me the one thing we *can* infer from this is that he's deliberately given away the one way . . . *the only way* . . . there is for us to find him and bring him home.'

'I just . . .' Sal shook her head again. 'I just don't believe he'd do that without finding some way to let us know.'

Maddy spread her hands. 'Maybe he tried. Maybe he wrote a note. Maybe he's deposited some carefully coded message somewhere and something went wrong and it's sitting on the bottom of the ocean in a little green bottle, yet to be found.'

Or perhaps it had been found and was a curious little cryptic exhibit in some maritime museum somewhere. Without the Internet, they were blind here to such minute changes in the timeline.

'So, you say we should just give up on them?'

'I don't know, Sal. I don't have any ideas right now. I suppose there's no harm in letting computer-Bob scan away to his heart's content. Who knows, he might pick something up.'

'Meanwhile?'

'Meanwhile . . . ?' Maddy looked across at her, exasperated. Angry. Wanting to snap at Sal and tell her that she didn't have anything left to offer. That maybe it was Sal's turn for once to come up with a bright idea. But that burned away quickly.

They sat in silence for a while. A clock ticked noisily in the corner of the dungeon. Bob and Becks sat still like shop mannequins, silently conversing or file-sorting between themselves. SpongeBubba shuffled from one pad-foot to another in the far corner, his bulging eyes blinking anxiously above his frozen plastic toothy grin.

Finally Maddy spoke again. 'Meanwhile . . .' she began, 'maybe you and I should think what we want to do now.'

Sal looked up at her. 'You mean . . . leave? Like Liam?'

'I suppose that's what I'm suggesting. Yes.' She smiled hopefully. 'Unless, you know, unless you like it here? I mean . . . *I* quite like it. The clothes . . . the sights, the things going on in the world now. It's a pretty exciting time, if you think about it.'

'What about watching out for more contaminations?' Sal cocked her head. 'Or at least watching out for the bad ones and putting them right?'

Maddy wondered if Sal was hanging on to that, a need for a purpose. A reason to exist. The mission to save mankind from itself – whether it deserved saving, or even still needed saving – that's what had held them together so far, wasn't it? Without 'the mission', they were nothing. Perhaps there was a way they could go on. 'Recruit' or, more accurately, *grow* a new Liam. Maybe, if she dug deep through computer-Bob's database, there was information on how they could go about doing that. Not for the first time she wondered if there might be spare versions of them lying in storage somewhere: little foetuses frozen in tubes. Perhaps in that safe deposit box in San Francisco, right at the back, there might be another casket containing Liams, Sals and Maddys. Hadn't Foster mentioned to them that there had been a team before theirs? A team that had come to a rather unfortunate end. She shuddered as she recalled Foster's words . . . they'd been 'torn to pieces', he'd said. Ripped apart by that ghostly, ephemeral mist that Foster had called a 'seeker'.

A version of me, a version of Sal . . . torn to pieces. She recalled the faint outline of that apparition, drifting towards them in the darkness of the archway. She'd sensed, somehow, that it seemed to be drawn to them, seemed to know them. And that, for some reason, made it even more terrifying. Quietly, unspoken, Maddy had begun to have her own suspicions as to what that thing was. That it was once a human. A person who'd travelled time once too often and become lost in chaos space. Perhaps even . . . one of them. A previous incarnation of one of them. Maybe that was what ghosts were. A real phenomenon, people from all times, from other timelines, other possible dimensions who had become trapped in that ghastly place and were trying to escape it, drawn like moths to the light by portals opened every now and then.

'Maddy? What are we going to do? What about . . . our mission?'

'The mission,' she repeated, fiddling with her glasses unnecessarily. The lenses didn't need cleaning but her hands needed something to fuss with.

'With just us two and Mr and Mrs Meatbot?'

Maddy wondered now if they'd already pushed their luck

further than was wise. Here they were safe from Waldstein. Here they were where no one from the future was ever likely to come looking for them. Both of them alive and with enough resources to live well. With future knowledge, they could make themselves fabulously rich if they wanted to. And, sheesh . . . couldn't a couple of young ladies with suitcases full of money have a pretty fabulous time in 1889?

She breathed a cloud on to each lens, then rubbed it off and put the spectacles back on the bridge of her nose and tucked a loose strand of hair behind her ear.

'Oh, Sal, I think that idea's pretty much finished with now.'

CHAPTER 34

1667, Port Royal, Jamaica

Rashim felt all eyes on them as they dropped anchor a little way out from the north docks overlooked by the low wooden palisade of Fort James. Fifty yards away, the carrack did likewise, both ships gently swaying in unison as the mild current pulled them taut against their anchor lines. From the afterdeck Rashim could see the business of Port Royal: teams of dockmen working along the shorefront loading and unloading the merchant ships tied up along the wooden docks; water pens containing what appeared to be enormous turtles, and men wading shin-deep in the warm water among them.

He could see men shading their eyes to look up at these two new vessels cautiously anchoring out in the bay.

'We're taking a risk,' muttered Liam.

They'd had that discussion the night before, both coming to the conclusion that this was their best option, and yet now, with so many curious pairs of eyes in the distance settling on them, it was beginning to feel a somewhat foolhardy choice of action. At this moment, with this captured Spanish merchant ship anchored beside them as conspicuous evidence, they were pirates. Criminals. And, as soon as they set foot ashore, there was the possibility they'd be arrested and clapped in irons.

Rashim stared across the water at their weather-battered prize. 'We have an offering.'

Liam nodded. 'Aye, it's amazing what a big fat bribe can do for you.' He grinned at Rashim. 'Just make sure you don't call it a bribe.'

Half an hour later their two pinnaces were tied up on the north docks and they made their way down Queen Street towards the governor's mansion: Liam, Rashim and Tom, the Spanish captain and the two young women passengers. And behind them a handcart draped with a tarpaulin and pulled by two of their crew, young William entrusted with walking behind the cart and watching that no curious hands reached out from the onlookers either side and probed beneath it.

Outside the grand stone building of the governor's mansion, the captain of the guard scowled disapprovingly at them for a long while as he weighed up Rashim's request for an audience with the governor. 'He doesn't normally choose to breakfast with common criminals,' the young officer muttered coolly.

'Then tell him he'll be richly rewarded for his valuable time,' said Liam, gesturing at the covered cart. The officer turned his ice-cold gaze on Liam for his impertinent interjection.

'Yes,' said Rashim. 'Quite right . . . *richly* rewarded . . . for his time.'

The officer sighed, rolled his eyes. 'Very well.' He turned on his heels and disappeared into the cool shadows of a cloister, a receding clack of echoing boot heels on stone paving.

As they waited in the baking sun, Rashim fussed with the garments he was wearing. The carrack had been carrying some of the personal effects of Captain Juan Marcos. A rather fine wardrobe of clothes among them. He was now wearing a long frock coat with an elaborate ruff of lace around his neck and his cuffs. Hardly practical for the tropics. Beneath his tricorn hat, crowned with a plume of ostrich feathers, his scalp itched from prickly heat, and beads of sweat were already dotting his forehead.

Liam had chosen to dress less flamboyantly. After all, he was merely the first officer. The lesser man. Still, he'd dispensed with his Victorian dress shirt and waistcoat, and like Rashim wore a double-breasted frock coat, but unbuttoned to make something of the light breeze stirring the palm trees overhead. No stifling, scratchy layers of fancy lace and no fancy floppy hat on his head.

'You look hot,' he goaded. 'And uncomfortable.'

Rashim tugged irritably at the stiff collar round his neck. 'Very.'

The captain returned a few minutes later, looking annoyed. He adjusted his powdered wig. 'Apparently he *will* see you . . . that is, if the conversation is genuinely to be a rewarding one.' The officer was obviously quoting the governor's response word for word. But the disapproving tone was all his own. He nodded to Rashim, to Captain Marcos and to the two women. 'You will come with me, please.'

'Hey, hang on. I'm coming along too,' said Liam.

The officer's eyebrows rose sceptically, irritably.

'Yes. He is my partner,' said Rashim quickly. 'My . . . uh, my co-captain, if you will.'

'*Co-captain*? And what the devil is one of those?'

Rashim shook his head; the term was ill-chosen. 'He is my second-in-command. I need him to . . . I would *like* him . . . to come with me.'

'As you wish.' The officer looked past Captain Marcos and the young ladies at the cart and the two men who'd been pulling it and William. 'But not those scruffy herberts over there. They'll surely put Sir Thomas off his mangoes.'

Rashim nodded. 'Fine.'

The officer led them through the cool shaded gloom of the cloisters, into an entrance hall, up broad marble stairs into a hallway and a high-ceilinged stately receiving room, then out on to an awning-covered balcony overlooking the cloisters and a courtyard garden full of fruit trees, and lively with the chittering of parrots and parakeets.

At a large round oak table bedecked with silverware and a platter of brightly coloured tropical fruit sat Sir Thomas Modyford, recently appointed governor of the recently acquired colonial territory of Jamaica. Fat to the point of being almost round, he sported a tidily clipped beard and the combed-out flare of a King Charles II styled moustache. A luscious mane of curly nut-brown hair tumbled down on to his ample shoulders. Hair that Liam mistook for real until he scratched at his scalp beneath and the whole extravagant wig shifted.

He dabbed at his mouth with a napkin and sat back in his chair. 'So, to whom do I owe the pleasure of this far-too-early-in-the-day intrusion on my time?' He addressed his question to Rashim.

'Well, Your . . . uh . . . Your Honour, I would like to introdu—'

'The appropriate honorific, sir, is . . . Your Excellency.'

'Sorry, Your Excellency. I am Rashim Anwar, I'm the . . . well, I am the captain of the ship that has just anchored out there in your harbour.' Rashim nodded across the enclosed garden, across the ramshackle rooftops of Port Royal towards the low walls of Fort James and the turquoise waters beyond.

Sir Thomas Modyford twisted in his seat and squinted out at the blinding daylight. 'Ah, indeed, I spotted you fumbling your way in a little earlier. Is that carrack with you as well?'

'Yes, sir. Sorry . . . Your Excellency.'

Modyford narrowed his eyes as he studied both the ships in the distance then turned to examine his visitors. He looked at Rashim and Liam, then past them at the Spanish captain and the two women with him. 'Let me hazard a guess . . .' He sighed. 'You are yet another boatful of common criminal scoundrels looking to make your fortunes from stealing and looting, and you wish me to legitimize your enterprise, hmmmm?'

'We . . . uh . . . we are rather hoping to seek a letter of marque, Your Excellency.'

Modyford chuckled sarcastically and his ample form wobbled beneath a silk robe. 'You and every other ne'er-do-well. It seems I have acquired something of a reputation as a genial host for common, gutter-dwelling criminals.' He removed his wig with a casual swipe and tossed it to the servant standing behind his shoulder. His head was tufted with a thin fuzz of grey hair, lank and damp with sweat. His scalp was blotched with scabs and sores. 'Damned thing makes me itch like a pox-infested harlot,' he grumbled.

Liam stifled an urge to snigger.

'Well, here's the thing, gentlemen –' *gentlemen* being said with a hint of distaste – 'I do not hand out a licence to every Tom, Dick and Henry who comes asking. I have to exercise a certain degree of restraint. With our new King's recent restoration, I must be cautious. He seeks a peace with the King of Spain. They are, after all, both jolly good Catholics.' He ran a hand over his damp scalp.

'I may not have seen eye to eye with that godless oaf Cromwell, but at least he had a better understanding of our predicament out here. This island of Jamaica, we hold for the moment . . . but I suspect King Philip of Spain would very much like to have it back. Since our King Charles is attempting to extend the hand of friendship to Spain, he has had to rather publicly denounce the practice of licensed piracy against Spanish merchant ships. So . . . I am forced, to some degree, to follow his lead.'

'But if you granted us –'

Modyford raised his hand to hush Rashim. 'However, this

colony needs defending and King Charles sends me nothing, no ships, no soldiers. We are very much on our own out here. All I have, to retain this outpost of His Majesty's, is a handful of soldiers and several undermanned forts in rather poor condition. However, what I do have at my disposal is a motley collection of buccaneers and privateers who think of Port Royal as their home. For want of a better term, they are my "militia". I would not trust any one of those vagabonds with my purse, but I can count on them not wanting the Spanish to take back this island.'

He sat forward and reached for a grapefruit.

'What I need is to be cautious to whom I grant a licence. Port Royal must not appear to King Charles to be a haven for criminals, a den of lawlessness. It cannot seem that the situation here is . . . out of control. It is a matter of some *delicacy*.'

Liam understood what he was getting at. 'You need gentlemen . . . not roving bands of bloodthirsty crooks.'

Modyford scowled at Liam's unsolicited contribution. But after a moment he nodded. 'Indeed. *Privateering*, gentlemen, is what keeps this colony going. It is a thorn in Spain's side and an awkward embarrassment to our King. But provided it is not excessive, provided there are no glaring atrocities that force King Charles to have to step in and put an end to it . . . then I have some degree of latitude.'

'Which is why we have brought this gentleman with us,' said Rashim. He turned and gestured to the man to step forward. 'This is Señor Juan Lopez Marcos, captain of the vessel we . . . uh . . . we *salvaged*.'

The Spaniard stepped forward and bowed formally. 'Greetings, Your Excellency.'

Modyford nodded politely back. He turned to Rashim. 'And why have you brought him here?'

Rashim was about to explain, but the Spanish captain spoke

first. 'My ship, *San Isidro*, was raided by these men, Your Excellency. But . . . I must report, they demonstrated clemency and chivalry.'

Modyford pursed his lips. 'Really?'

'Yes, Your Excellency. This man –' he nodded towards Liam – 'risked his life to protect my lady passengers' safety. He killed a crewman . . . one who threatened to . . .' He struggled to find the appropriate, palatable word.

Modyford silenced him with a wave of his hand. 'I understand.' He regarded Liam approvingly. 'Good man.' Then he turned to Rashim. 'And you have firm control of your crew?'

'Yes. They all signed on to crew the ship, provided their activities remained on the right side of English maritime law. They do not wish to be branded as pirates, Your Excellency.'

'Hmm . . . that definition is a somewhat flexible one.'

'They are good men. Reliable men.'

'You understand you and your crew have taken a rather foolhardy risk presenting yourselves to me like this? Your raiding of this captain's ship, without licence, was clearly an act of piracy. I am obliged to enforce our King's policy, when presented with such an undeniably clear case of wrong-doing . . . which you have both admitted to in the presence of witnesses. You understand this?'

Rashim and Liam both nodded.

Modyford steepled his fingers beneath his ample chin as he gave the matter several moments of silent consideration. Finally he spoke. 'Señor Marcos, you and your ladies will be my guests until we can arrange passage for you on the next ship back to Spain.' He pushed his chair back, stood up and turned to the servant behind him. 'Show them out. They must be hungry . . . arrange some food for them.'

The servant nodded and came round the table to escort them out.

'Your Excellency,' said Marcos, 'I humbly ask you to show these men mercy as they did to us.'

'It is under due consideration,' said the governor drily and he nodded at his servant to lead the Spaniards out.

Alone at last, Modyford looked at Liam and Rashim. 'Well now . . . what am I going to do with you?'

'We . . . did mention to the officer who brought us up that your time would be . . .' Liam bit his lip, cautiously feeling his way. 'How exactly did we phrase it, Rashim?'

'I think the phrase was . . . richly rewarded?'

Sir Thomas Modyford's stern expression seemed to darken and Liam wondered whether they'd just made a gross miscalculation. Perhaps their none-too-subtle suggestion of a bribe had condemned them.

But the slightest curl of Modyford's lip suggested otherwise. 'Hmm . . . well now, that certainly might help.'

CHAPTER 35
1667, Port Royal, Jamaica

Liam sucked in a lungful of air and savoured the distinctive odours of the port all around him. The rich tang of tar as men worked up and down the wharf to caulk the hulls of their ships, an ongoing and never-ending process that ensured a watertight bond between hull planks. The all-pervasive undertone of salt in the air that seemed to cling to everything ship-borne. The odour of woodsmoke curling out of chimneys across Port Royal. The slightly less appealing stench of ripening meat from the market down the way as the mid-morning sun worked on the last unsold carcasses left hanging on butchers' hooks.

He remembered this sensation from a moment that felt like a whole lifetime ago: a sense of belonging in the right place, belonging to the right time. And, with a smile now, he had the very same thought as he'd had when gazing out across the rooftops of the city of Nottingham.

This'll do me.

'Hoy! Mr O'Connor, sir!' It was 'Gunny' – James Gunn and, coincidentally, the ship's head gunner and only properly trained gun-master – hanging from a sling alongside the prow of their ship. 'How's she looking?'

Liam looked up from the dockside at the man holding a caulking brush in one hand and a small bucket of white paint in the other. The name *Clara Jane* had been painted over and replaced by the new name for their ship: *Pandora*.

He shaded his eyes from the sun and admired the perfectly formed swirls of the letters. 'It looks perfect, Gunny. Splendid job!'

The man knuckled his forehead and grinned. Liam watched him as he energetically hauled himself back up to the ship's rail and pulled himself over on to the deck.

The temper of their crew was markedly different. These last few days, since Sir Thomas had cautiously issued Rashim a letter of marque, the men had been ready and willing to accept orders from not only Rashim, their elected skipper, but Liam too, now commonly acknowledged among the men as 'co-skipper' – a term none of them had heard of before but were happy to use.

The letter of marque had, of course, made all the difference to the crew's morale. There had been a number of conditions written into the issued licence, however. For one, should Sir Thomas issue a call to arms to defend the port from a Spanish incursion, they were duty-bound to drop whatever they were doing and muster to defend it. Another condition was that, while the manner with which they raided Dutch and French ships was entirely their own business, certain minimum standards of conduct were to be maintained when raiding Spanish ships. Mercy was to be given to crews who willingly hove to and surrendered. After the ship's cargo was 'confiscated', the ship and crew should be allowed to proceed on their way. (This courtesy, of course, did not extend to any Negroes, either crew or 'cargo'. As far as Sir Thomas Modyford was concerned, they were legitimate booty from which he expected his cut.) And that was the other condition: a third of their haul was to be paid to him as a 'safe haven tax'. A standard condition, he assured them, applied to all the licensed privateers operating out of Port Royal.

The carrack they had brought in was already in Sir Thomas's possession and being repaired by shipwrights and carpenters ready to be added to his small fleet of merchant ships that carried a steady supply of cocoa beans back to London from his plantations. The carrack was their goodwill gesture to him. Their down payment of his 'tax'. The word 'bribe' was never mentioned.

The carrack's cargo of wines and cloths, spices and several cases of silver coin, on the other hand, was theirs. They'd managed to sell most of it off to a merchant at a scandalously low price: they discovered, hours after shaking on the deal, that they could have made half as much money again from another merchant, conducting his business in a tavern next door. Nonetheless, the deal made, the haul had netted them enough money to give their lads a long-awaited payday, and enough left over to resupply and re-equip the *Pandora*. Which was the very business that Rashim was looking into right now, having mentioned something about the *rifling* of barrels and 'finning' of cannonballs.

Meanwhile, Liam had his own tasks to attend to. A dozen of their crew had opted to take their share of the money and cut free. There were plenty of other ships in port to try their luck with, and word was spreading among the taverns that a privateer captain by the name of Henry Morgan was looking to try his luck over on the Spanish Main – what Liam realized would, centuries down the line, be a number of different nations: Panama, Costa Rica, Colombia, Nicaragua. There were rumours the raid was likely to be a lucrative one. And, in any case, most of the men that left had been part of Henry Bartlett's cluster of malcontents. They'd be better off without them.

So, Liam had places to fill, crew members to recruit, sign up to their ship's charter, and Old Tom to help him with that.

Rashim looked up at the sign swinging from a hook above a narrow doorway, flanked on either side by the premises of a cordwainer and on the other by a pipemaker. He checked the address scrawled on a scrap of parchment. This was it: SCHWARZMANN'S — THE GUNSMITH. He pushed the door open, kicked sand off his boots outside then stepped into the gloomy interior.

'Hello? Anyone here?'

Ahead of him was a narrow passageway between two wooden-slat walls, and a low ceiling of thick cross-beams and floorboards. He made his way down the passageway and finally emerged into an open courtyard at the end, half of it in the deep shade of an awning of wooden shingles, the other half baking in the hot mid-morning sun. Rashim could taste the acrid odour of burning coals at the back of his throat. He could smell cordite and a number of other unpleasant chemical taints. A curl of smoke spun from the embers of a fire within a forge. It looked like the place was open for trade, going about its business, except for the fact it appeared to be entirely deserted.

'Is there a Mr Pieter Schwarzmann here?'

'Hello,' a deep throaty voice replied from beneath the shadow of the awning. A thickset man with bushy, ginger-coloured sideburns and wearing a blacksmith's leather apron waddled out into the sunlight, shading his eyes to get a look at Rashim.

'I am Pieter Schwarzmann,' he replied with a thick German accent, efficiently clipped down to little more than a collection of consonants and over-pronounced sibilants. 'And who iss this I am speaking to?'

'Rashim Anwar.' He took off his tricorn hat. 'Uh . . . that is, *Captain* Rashim Anwar.'

'Captain, iss it?' He weighed that up. 'Seems every man out here calls himself a Captain *This*, Captain *That*.'

Rashim met him in the sunlight and offered his hand. 'I have a ship, if that makes any difference.'

Schwarzmann's shoulders shook as he laughed. 'Of course you do!' He grasped Rashim's hand and squeezed it like a vice. Rashim winced.

'Ach . . . look, you have a lady hand! Iss smooth as a baby's bottom.'

Rashim pulled free and rubbed his crushed knuckles. 'Your name was recommended to me.'

'Of course! Best gunsmith on this island. Now vhat iss it I can do for you, *Captain* Anvar?'

'Anwar actually.'

Schwarzmann frowned. 'Iss vhat I just said.'

'Uh . . . right. Yes, of course. I thought you . . . it's the accent, I suppose −'

'Vhat accent? I speak perfect good English!'

Rashim looked around the courtyard. 'So . . . is it just yourself here?'

'*Ja*. Today, iss just me. My boy iss vorking on another job.'

'Good. That's good . . . because, you see, I wish to discuss a contract with you. In confidence, that is.'

'Confidence?'

'In secret. I want to employ you to do some work for me, but the details of it need to be kept between you and me. Do you understand?'

Schwarzmann shrugged. 'You the customer. Come . . .' He wiped the back of his hand across his forehead. 'Iss very hot out here. We go sit down.' He led Rashim over to the shade where he pulled a stool out beside a workbench and sat down heavily in a rocking-chair on the far side.

'Now, ve talk. Vhat iss this secret business of yours?'

'I want to extend the range and accuracy of my ship's cannons.'

Schwarzmann looked intrigued.

'I am not sure of . . .' He was going to say *I am not sure of my history*, but decided this German already seemed to regard him as enough of an oddity already. But, the fact was, his historical knowledge of anything before the twenty-first century was schoolboy knowledge at best. He wasn't sure whether the technique he was thinking of employing was in use yet.

'Mr Schwarzmann, I am not sure if you have heard of a technique called rifling?'

The man nodded. '*Ja*, of course. Back home in Stuttgart I have done this many times for a Jäger.'

'*Jäger*?'

'Gentlemen who like to hunt. Huntsmen. Men with much money and very nicely made muskets who want a flintlock fitted also.'

The process of rifling involved cutting several spiral grooves down the inside of a gun's barrel. The grooves applied a spin to the musket ball which increased both its range and accuracy.

'Ah, right. You've done this with muskets. What about cannons?'

Schwarzmann shook his head. 'This, *nein*. You have muskets on your ship and I can rifle all of them for you. But a cannon?' He smiled. 'For this you would need a large foundry.'

Rashim nodded. 'I suspected that. But what about applying some sort of curved fins to a cannonball?'

Schwarzmann was about to chuckle dismissively at that, but then narrowed his eyes as he gave it a moment's consideration. 'Hmm, like the fletching on a crossbow bolt?'

'Yes. But offset slightly, so the air resistance in flight would set it spinning.'

The gunsmith stroked his fleshy chin thoughtfully. 'These . . . fins . . . would need to be part of the ball's mould. Not attached, but part of the ball. They would –'

'Break off, yes, that's what I thought. But the cannonball would also need to be a different shape. Not round but elongated, like a bullet.'

'Bullet?'

Rashim pulled his scrap of parchment out. On the reverse side of the address he had sketched a design. He spread the parchment out on the workbench. The sketch looked like a stubby rocket: one end a cone, the other end with fins.

'This . . . iss . . . really . . . interesting,' said Schwarzmann as he studied it, stroking his fleshy chin. 'Hmm, this shape . . . this would travel well, I think.'

Rashim sat forward. 'Could you mould projectiles this shape?'

The gunsmith nodded slowly. 'It iss possible. *Ja*. But I would need exact measurements of the bore of your cannons.'

'Indeed.' Rashim did not have access to anything as precise as a simple ruler. Instead, what he had done was hold the parchment against the end of several of the cannons and marked their diameter on the paper. 'These cross-marks indicate the bore of our cannons. Could you work with that?'

'And these marks are accurate?'

Rashim nodded. 'I have also done some calculations on the length of the projectile and the required ratio length of the fins. See?' In one corner of the page, he'd jotted down dimensions in inches.

A smile spread across Schwarzmann's face. '*Ja*, I can make this.'

CHAPTER 36

1667, Port Royal, Jamaica

'Next!'

Liam looked at the list of names he'd scribbled down: seven men so far who Old Tom had agreed seemed to have enough experience to be worthwhile additions to their crew. To Liam's eye, they all looked convincing and scary enough: a procession of broad-shouldered men with deeply tanned faces, framed by scruffy beards and hair tangled into long, greasy coils. Each of them happy to make their mark on the *Pandora*'s charter — a list of terms and conditions that Liam had patiently read aloud to each man, since none of them seemed to be able to read a single word of it.

'Mister?'

Liam looked up at the next man in the queue. His gaze rose up a wall of rippling muscle barely contained within taut and frayed shreds of clothing, mended and re-mended with coarse stitching. His eyes finally rose to the top of this tower of gleaming flesh to fall upon a face as black as gunpowder.

My God, he's bleedin' enormous. Almost — but not quite — as large as Bob but, by God, almost.

'Uh . . .' Liam cleared his throat. 'And your name is . . . ?'

'Ma name?'

'Aye, please.'

'Ah gots two of 'em, mister.'

Liam smiled politely. 'Well now, we've all got two.'

'Ma owner give me the name James Dawson.'

'I'm Liam O'Connor and this is Tom.'

Tom nudged Liam. 'This one's no good, sir. He's a slave.'

The black man looked at Tom. 'Ain't slave no more, mister.'

'You a runaway?'

The man hesitated a little too long. 'Yup,' Tom nodded. 'He is. You don't want to take on a runaway. That's trouble right there, that is.'

'Ah'm a good worker, mister. Work hard. An' ah'm strong.'

Liam grinned. 'I can see that all right.' He turned to Tom. 'Why would he be trouble?'

'He's someone's *property*. Plantation owner more'n likely. Yer sign him up aboard the *Pandora* and his owner gets to finding out . . . you'll be done for stealin' his slave.'

'Well, it's not like he'll be my property. So, it's not exactly *theft*, is it?'

'Don't matter. They don't take it light here. Runaway slaves. Catch 'em and they hobble 'em. An' them they see as helping 'em out is just as likely to end up in the clinker.'

Liam had noticed one or two dark-skinned men among the crews coming ashore, frequenting the taverns. Men who appeared to be treated – more or less – as equals, men who appeared to be free to move from ship to ship, to offer their services to whomever they wanted. He didn't see how this one might not pass as one of them, provided he was dressed in more than rags. But perhaps Tom was right: taking him on was inviting trouble they didn't need.

He looked up at the giant. 'James . . . look, I'm sorry but –'

'Ah can work for you, mister. Pay me half as much as all them others. I work real hard.'

Liam didn't doubt that. More to the point, the man looked

utterly terrifying. Put a cutlass in each of his ham-shank fists and, as soon as the crew of some hapless Spanish merchant ship caught a glimpse of him, there'd be no need for a fight. Another notion occurred to him. Not that Liam had the time or any particular inclination right then to get involved in what was right and what was wrong. After all, if right and wrong was his guiding compass, then he'd have changed the way history goes a dozen times over already. But – he studied the man's face silently – wasn't Liam also in a similar situation? A product? Someone's genetically engineered property. And now just as much a piece of property on the run from them as this man standing before him.

Liam looked around the tavern; this giant was the last man in the queue. The flurry of interest that had stirred as he and Tom had set up their 'recruitment stall' had moved on to other things. It looked like a fight was brewing between two men on the other side of the tavern. Drunken voices were raised and others had gathered round, egging them on. All the same, against that growing noise, Liam lowered his voice slightly.

'We take you on and there's some kind of trouble? I'd say you assured me that you were free. That you lied to us. Is that clear?'

'They'd hang you for sure for lying 'bout that,' added Tom. 'You understand that, man?'

'Ah'm free,' James said again firmly. 'Tha's all I gots to say.'

Liam studied his face intently. A firm resolve was etched there. An acceptance that the risk of hanging was more than a fair price for the chance to escape a lifetime of slavery.

'Well, all right, then. You said you've got another name? We should probably use that.'

The man nodded. 'I was born Kwami. Kwami Okembo.'

Liam wasn't going to bother asking whether the man could read. Instead, he read out the terms and conditions of the ship's charter, while in the background the fight finally began. The gathered crowd tightened round the scrap and voices united in a rhythmic chanting. By the time he'd finished reading aloud the *Pandora*'s rules on behaviour and conduct and Kwami had made his mark — a large clumsy X — at the bottom of the document, the fight was over and one of the men quite dead.

Liam offered his hand. 'Welcome aboard, Kwami. The *Pandora* is the third ship along on the north docks. The schooner. I suggest you get yourself over there and stay aboard and out of sight until we're ready to set sail.'

Kwami enveloped Liam's hand in one giant fist and shook it violently. 'Thank you, Mister Liam! Thank you, Mister Liam!'

'That's all right. Uh . . . but one small thing, Kwami. Now you're crew, you should call me either *sir* or *co-skipper*. All right?'

'Co-skipper?' He frowned. 'Ain't heard of that word before.'

Liam shrugged. 'It's sort of a new thing. We do things slightly differently aboard the *Pandora*.'

CHAPTER 37

1667, east of Port Royal, Jamaica

The men — almost the entire crew — were crowded round the cannon, packed in and hunkered down in the low-ceilinged space of the gun deck. Gunny pushed the dry rammer down inside the cannon's barrel, gave it several twists to ensure it was clean inside, then pulled it out.

One of his gun crew passed him a measured amount of powder in a charger and he eased it into the open muzzle, careful not to spill any on the deck. He then used another clean rammer to push it down the barrel and gave it several firm punches of the ramrod to compact it at the end.

Liam looked round at the expectant faces of the crew. Rashim had told them all they were going to witness an experiment with a different-shaped cannonball. The men had yet to clap eyes on it so far. Sitting on the deck, covered by a yard of greasy tarpaulin, were three test moulds, and the German gunsmith, Schwarzmann, was standing guard over it, glaring at the crew and daring them even to try lifting the tarpaulin to get a peek beneath.

Gunny was now carefully ramming down a fistful of wadding against the charge of powder.

Liam wondered what the men would make of the odd, bullet-like shape. He winked at Rashim who returned an anxious half-smile, keen to get on with the test firing, to see if his design was going to work.

Gunny now quickly swabbed the inside of the barrel, clearing out any excess wadding and powder. 'Awl right. We're ready for the shot now, Skipper.'

Rashim turned to Schwarzmann. 'I believe it's time to reveal your handiwork.'

The German squatted down and grasped a corner of the tarpaulin; the crew all leaned forward, those further back straining to get a look. Liam noted Kwami's hulking silhouette right at the back, bobbing and leaning one way then the other to catch a glimpse.

'Thiss, gentlemen,' Schwarzmann announced with some pomp and ceremony, 'this iss the *future of naval warfare*.' With a theatrical flourish, he whipped the tarpaulin aside.

A gasp rippled across the gun deck as the men tried to make sense of the three stubby, dark shapes sitting on the deck: lead cones about a foot high ending with a pointed tip. The base of each was flat and they reminded Liam of modern-day artillery shells, except for the fact that each sported three slight fins. Not perfectly straight, they slanted up the side of the cylinder as if they'd been applied carelessly, or knocked and bent in transit.

With a grunt of effort, the gunsmith picked one of the cannonballs up and handed it to Gunny.

'Uh . . . which way does it go in the cannon, sir?'

Schwarzmann rolled his eyes and sighed. 'Flat end in first.'

The gunner eased it into the muzzle, the men all holding their breath with growing excitement as he carefully rammed it down the chamber until it was pushed firmly against the cushion of wadding at the bottom.

'Why does it have them fish-like fins on it, Skipper?' asked one of the men in the crowd.

'To make the projectile spin around its longitudinal axis,' replied Rashim. 'You may have noticed the fins are not straight. They are angled slightly; this is to create an aerodynamic profile that will stimulate a rotational force on it.' He shrugged slightly. 'In theory.'

Liam suspected not a single man there had understood a word Rashim had just said, but he noticed one or two of them nodding thoughtfully.

'The shot is loaded now, sir,' said Gunny.

The *Pandora* rocked gently in the sheltered cove. They were just a dozen miles eastward around the coast from Port Royal; they'd followed the coastline until they had come across this deserted and sheltered inlet. Now, floating on the calm turquoise water yards away was a pinnace with a small mast, bobbing patiently, waiting to be obliterated.

'When you're ready, Gunny,' said Rashim, 'take your best shot.'

'Aye, sir.' He moved round the back of the cannon and retrieved a smouldering length of tarred rope. He cupped it in his hands and blew on it until the tip glowed a dull orange. He waved the men back from the rear of the cannon. Not that he needed to: they were all very well aware of the cannon's recoil length – just under a yard. He hunkered down beside the touch hole and squinted down the length of the cannon's barrel, out through the gun port at their distant target bobbing gently on the water, judging the subtle movement of the ship, gauging the rhythm of it.

'Have a care!' he called out and, as one, every man on the gun deck clapped their hands over their ears as he pressed the smouldering fuse to the touch hole.

A spark, a momentary hiss, then the cannon boomed, lurching backwards, and spurted out a six-foot tongue of flame. Rashim,

Schwarzmann and several of the men quickly leaned out of the neighbouring gun ports to watch the arc of the projectile. But all they were rewarded with were a number of geysers of water erupting across the space between the *Pandora* and their target. Schwarzmann cursed under his breath.

'What happened?' someone called out.

'It . . . uh . . . it appears that one disintegrated,' replied Rashim. He looked pointedly at the gunsmith.

'Vell, that one I made vith *bigger* fins,' he said with a shrug. 'I vas experimenting vith sizes.'

'Let's try another one.'

Gunny nodded and set about swabbing the cannon and loading the next one. Again, the men held their breath as he hunkered down, fuse poised above the touch hole, and waited to get a feel of the gently swaying rhythm of the ship.

'Have a care!' He touched the fuse. Again, the hiss followed by the deafening *whump* of the cannon as it leaped backwards across the gun deck.

Liam this time was already crouched beside a gun port and caught a glimpse of the dark projectile hurtling across the water. A half-second later the pinnace seemed to explode amid a shower of splinters and jagged planks. A cheer erupted across the gun deck, almost as deafening as the cannon had been a second earlier.

'Bullseye!' someone shouted.

Liam could see the projectile had carved the vessel in two. Both ends of the boat bobbed independently and began to sink, surrounded by a soup of floating wooden shards.

'Beggar me! God 'elp me, straight an' true as an arrow!' Gunny looked round at Rashim, at the rest of the crew. 'Ain't never seen a ball travel that way!'

Schwarzmann nodded smugly. 'This, of course, iss vhat I expected.'

Rashim stroked his chin as he gazed out at the sinking ruins of the pinnace. 'There was most definitely spin. I saw spin on it.' He squinted out at the shoreline several hundred yards away. Emerging from the swaying fronds of palm trees were the crumbling remains of a church spire, or perhaps it might have been the ruins of a Spanish watchtower.

'Gunny, why not try for that?' he said.

'Our cannon don't 'ave the range for that, Skipper. Be lucky to make the beach at this distance.'

Rashim glanced at Schwarzmann. He shrugged a *why not?*

'Let's have a go anyway,' said Rashim. 'See how far the shot will go.'

Once again the gunner went about cleaning and loading the cannon with the last of the three test projectiles and again a stillness settled on the men as they held their breath and waited. Gunny narrowed his eyes as he stared intently down the length of the barrel. 'It'll not reach the building for sure,' he muttered, more to himself than anyone else.

'Have a care!' He touched down the smoking fuse.

The cannon boomed again, filling the gun deck with coils of blue smoke, and the men once again rushed to crowd the gun ports. Liam, still perched where he was, caught the blur of the shot racing over the floating debris of the pinnace, a straight line of flight that began to dip slightly right at the end as the power of the shot waned.

The ruins of the building exploded in a cloud of dust; its crumbling tower toppled forward and crashed down on to the beach. Above the palm trees, the sky was suddenly filled with birds of all colours taking flight.

The men on the gun deck roared like spectators at a town square execution.

'Good God!' gasped Schwarzmann.

Gunny, leaning beside Liam, sharing the same gun port, stared with his mouth slung open and catching the swirling smoke. He shook his head slowly. 'But that ain't possible. It surely ain't!'

'What range would you say that is?' called out Rashim above the raucous noise of the crew. 'Four . . . five hundred yards?'

'More.' Gunny rocked back on his haunches. 'More, sir. I'd say closer to eight hundred yards.'

'Iss incredible,' said Schwarzmann. He got to his feet and came to stand beside Rashim. He spoke in a lowered voice. 'Vith enough of these, Captain Anwar, your ship vould be . . . almost . . .'

'Invincible?'

Schwarzmann shrugged. '*Ja*. Perhaps.'

'We'll need to discuss your fee, Mr Schwarzmann. And how many of these projectiles you will be able to make for us.'

Liam got to his feet and joined them, grinning. He slapped Rashim on the back. 'Jay-zus, fella, that shot carved through the building like a hot knife through butter!'

'My fee?' said Schwarzmann. 'Perhaps ve should talk business upstairs, outside?'

Rashim nodded and led the way as the three of them ducked their way beneath timbers towards the ladder well. They climbed the steps and emerged into the sunlight and the cooling, teasing breath of a fresh breeze across the deck. A merciful change from the fetid heat down on the gun deck.

'I am curious, gentlemen,' said the German, dabbing at his forehead with the corner of his shirt cuff. 'Vhat are the plans you have?'

'Our plans?' Liam shrugged. 'The governor has licensed us as privateers. So, we plan to make some money, of course.'

'A *lot* of money,' added Rashim.

Liam nodded and smiled. 'And to make this ship of ours,

Pandora, a legend in the Caribbean. To make it a legend known on every sea by every sailor.' He glanced sideways at Rashim. 'That's right, isn't it?'

Rashim nodded.

'Mr Schwarzmann, sir . . .' continued Liam, 'we want to be sure that, centuries from now, the name *Pandora* is as known to every boy who dreams of pirates and swashbuckling buccaneers as . . . *Blackbeard* or . . . *Long John Silver*!'

Neither name seemed to mean a thing to the German. Of course they didn't. Nonetheless, Schwarzmann nodded slowly, appreciating the sentiment. He looked at them with the slightest hint of begrudging respect. 'You both, I think, vill achieve something like that.'

'So, then,' said Rashim, 'your fee . . . ? We should discuss —'

'I think, gentlemen, my fee vill *not* be a payment upfront, but instead a share of vhat plunder you manage to bring into Port Royal. A percentage.'

'A percentage?' Rashim looked at Liam. 'What do you think?'

Liam pursed his lips. 'We don't have a lot of money left right now. It makes sense.' He turned to Schwarzmann. 'If you're prepared to trust us, that is?'

Schwarzmann curled his lip. 'I trust no one. But iss like this — you don't pay me vhat ve agree on, then I stop making your veird shape cannonballs. Simple.'

Rashim nodded; they had an agreement of sorts. He offered a hand to him. 'Then let's discuss that percentage.'

CHAPTER 38

1889, London

'So much for Liam and his, "The three of us need to hold fast together. To stay a proper team",' Sal whispered. Weren't those his exact words? Wasn't that exactly what he'd said to her out in that windswept playground, when they were hanging round that abandoned school back in Harcourt, Ohio?

Now, it seemed, the first chance he had to cut free, skip off and do his own thing, that's exactly what he'd gone and done. She picked up her pen.

So now I guess the choices left for me and Maddy to make are not whether we carry on as a team, but where we want to live the rest of our lives. And who knows how long that is? Maybe I'm going to age-up like Liam will do and be an old woman before my time. Maybe I'll live hundreds of years. Who knows what our bodies were designed to endure?

I know one thing, though. I don't want to stay here. This dungeon isn't a home. And I guess if I'd known what I was back in New York, that archway wouldn't have felt like home either. It's a cage really. A prison.

She looked up from her diary. Maddy was fast asleep on one of their improvised beds, snoring, as she generally did. She usually slept well. The support units were sitting together on a pair of crates, bolt upright, but kind of 'asleep' in the way they often were, going into a trance, during which their computer minds could quietly get on with overdue housekeeping: compressing, sharing, archiving data. Sal wanted someone to talk to.

She turned to her left, towards a flat top Maddy had been using as a coffee table. 'Hey, SpongeBubba? You awake or are you charged down?'

SpongeBubba's squat-box frame turned round towards her. 'Hey, Sal!' The mug wobbled on his flat head, spilling cold dregs. Sal took it off and put it on the floor.

'I'm Ay-Oh-kay today!'

Too goofy-stupid for her to stomach right now. 'Must be great feeling happy-clappy all the time.'

SpongeBubba's eyes rolled. 'I'm a lab unit. I'm programmed by skippa to appear happy. I have no conceptual understanding of "happy", though.'

'I'm beginning to feel the same. Hey, SpongeBubba?'

'Yup!'

'If Rashim's gone for good, what does that mean for you?'

The unit stuck out a plastic bottom lip. 'No more skippa?'

'Yes. If you knew he was gone for good, or dead even, would that change your programming?'

'No, Sal. Not unless it was changed for me. My AI can be returned to the factory setting.' He looked up at her reproachfully. 'But then I'd be a boring old standard lab unit again.'

'No more squeaky voice. That might be an improvement!'

'I would not be SpongeBubba any more.'

Sal remembered Rashim saying he'd customized this unit to look like an old cartoon character from the beginning of the century. She vaguely remembered the cartoons too. 'SpongeBubba' wasn't quite the right name. Damned if she could remember what that stupid cubic yellow sea creature was really called.

'But you're not the real SpongeBubba. You're just an imitation of it.'

'I know.' He offered her a goofy grin. 'But I'm different from all the other lab units. And that makes me *special*!'

'SpongeBubba, if you could live any place, any time in the world . . . where would you choose to go?'

He frowned. 'I would choose where skippa needs me to be.'

Stupid question to ask a lab-bot, Sal decided.

'But skippa did once show me a Western movie. I like cowboys and Indians. They're *neeeat*!'

She smiled at the unit. It couldn't know how to 'like' anything. But it was obviously programmed, 'hacked' by Rashim, to appear to like things. Cute. Almost endearing actually.

'Cowboys and Indians, huh?' Sal could see the appeal of that. Wide-open prairies, crisp blue skies and rocky mountain skylines. A largely undiscovered frontier world full of adventure and all manner of possibilities. 'Nice idea. I like it.'

'Thanks!'

She had the name now. She had it! Came to her out of the blue. 'Sponge*Bob*!' she said.

SpongeBubba cocked an eyebrow. 'What's that?'

'SpongeBob SquarePants . . . that's the name of the character Rashim tried to make you look and sound like!'

SpongeBubba frowned. 'I prefer SpongeBubba! That name you just said sounds *stoo-pid*. And it's too long. Too many characters to fit on a command line. *Stoo-pid, stoo-pid, stoo-pid . . .*'

But Sal wasn't listening to his babbling. Her mind was elsewhere. Far away. She was seeing a small apartment. A faux wood-slat floor, cool to the touch. A wall-mounted flex-screen next to stylized portraits of Brahma, Vishnu and Shiva. The smell of coriander, turmeric, cumin and of rice cooking, an intoxicating smell wafting through from a kitchen. She could see glass sliding doors leading on to a modest balcony on which a clothes horse stood. Brightly coloured saris and head wraps were pegged to it and fluttered in the high-tower breeze. And beyond, emerging through the sulphur-coloured smog of pollution like stout cedar trunks from a bed of snow, other tenement blocks.

A crystal-clear memory of Mumbai. A child's memory. Because here she was, lying on the cool floor, gazing up at the flex-screen watching a rerun of an old cartoon called *SpongeBob SquarePants*. A memory triggered randomly by this discussion about a lab robot's wrongly remembered name.

My God . . .

No AI technician could have predicted she was going to have this exact conversation, surely? A conversation about an obscure and ridiculous cartoon character from the beginning of the century. And therefore – Sal's mind reeled – no technician was likely to say to him or herself, 'Oh, hang on! We'd better make up and put in a SpongeBob SquarePants memory for this support unit . . . you know . . . just in case the subject crops up?'

'My God,' she whispered.

Maybe her memory wasn't merely a montage of made-up things, just enough to convince a support unit that there'd been a life before this one. Maybe, just maybe, there was once a real girl that all those memories came from.

A real Saleena Vikram.

All of a sudden, Sal knew exactly where she wanted to go.

CHAPTER 39

1667, the Caribbean Sea

Two weeks later they had cast off from the north docks, the *Pandora*'s hull catching the tugging current ebbing out of the harbour, the sails quickly fluttering and filling with a fresh easterly breeze. Heading south, the ship leaned to starboard as the yards swung round on their iron braces to the right, pulled by the crosswind.

Liam steadied himself against the rail as the deck slanted over and the schooner began to build momentum, her bow beginning to carve through the smooth sheltered water of the harbour, then twenty minutes later, and further out from the shelter of land, she began to cut through lively waves that thumped and splashed against her hull. The wind was steady, occasionally gusting, tugging hard at the sails and pushing the ship over to a steeper angle.

With each lurch to starboard, Liam found his grin spreading wider. After several weeks moored up in the fetid heat of Port Royal the cool downdraught of wind from the mainsail felt wonderfully refreshing. The rolling motion of the ship beneath his feet was exhilarating, the steep angle of the deck . . . simply fun.

'I hate it when the ship leans over so much,' muttered Rashim unhappily. His knuckles were white on the rail. 'It feels like it's going to tip over.'

'She won't do that. The mast would break before the wind could turn over something of this size.'

'Right.' Rashim nodded. 'Very comforting.' Their journey west across the Atlantic had been mostly with the wind behind them – no leaning.

The course they were on now was taking them due south from Jamaica, down towards Puerto Bello, where the tapering end of Central America met the very top of the continent of South America; where a man with a plan would one day build the Panama Canal. The enterprise – as it was presented to the crew – was very simple.

The rumours were true. A pirate captain called Henry Morgan, something of a close personal friend to the governor, was planning a raid up to Spanish-held Cuba. Already he had enlisted a fleet of ten ships who'd signed up for the endeavour, and something like four hundred men had already signed his charter. It was going to be a big raid and news of its preparation was undoubtedly already making its way to the Spanish authorities. Which meant that up around Cuba they were going to be on their guard. Whereas south, down towards Puerto Bello, the regular transatlantic traffic of merchant ships would consider themselves comparatively safe, assured that most of the pirates in the area were going to be six or seven hundred miles further north, involved with this Cuban raid.

Hopefully, the ships they would undoubtedly stumble upon were going to be easy pickings, although perhaps not quite as easy as that storm-damaged carrack they'd happened upon. The men were all in a buoyant mood, eager to get their hands on Spanish loot, preferably a hoard of crudely struck gold escudos, or *doubloons* as the men called them. Their mood, their confidence that this enterprise was going to be a resounding success, Liam suspected, was down to Rashim's 'miracle shot'. That's what the

227

lads were calling it. He did wonder how much help thirty-six rocket-shaped cannonballs were going to be to them if they happened to stumble upon a whole fleet of Spanish ships.

Still, it was the confidence the men had that counted. That and the fearsome reputation among the Spanish crews that the pirates operating out of Port Royal had. From the stories he'd overheard being told in the taverns, quite often a raid was over with very quickly. A fast, intercepting approach with lots of noise and cannons booming, and the frightening, close-quarters sight of a hundred or more men armed to the teeth were usually more than enough to convince a lone merchantman to call it a day.

He caught a glimpse of Kwami being instructed by young William how to splice the bitter end of a rope. Dress that giant just right, a few leathery ears on a string, flintlocks on ribbons around his bull neck, a blood-smeared sword in each hand and a loud snarl . . .

Jay-zus . . . the stuff of nightmares.

'I think I'm going to be sick,' muttered Rashim.

'Well, for God's sake go and do it in your cabin . . . and not out here in front of the crew!' They finally had the crew's respect and confidence now. Rashim getting all pasty-paced and tossing the contents of his breakfast all over the afterdeck probably wouldn't help matters much.

'You are right.' He belched and held a fist to his mouth. 'I'll . . . just . . .'

Liam nodded. 'See you when you're done.' He watched Rashim stagger against the slant of the deck to his cabin door, pull it open and disappear inside. He turned back to look over the rail at the main deck below, at the deep blue sea, the rising-falling horizon, the ballooning sails, and heard the snatched notes of a fiddle being played along with an accompanying bodhrán.

'Ahoy there, m'hearties,' he muttered to himself, mustering his best piratey snarl. 'Ahaaarrr! Make way for the notorious Cap'n O'Connor . . . *aharrrrrr*.' Liam choked on a gob full of his own spittle. 'Aharrrrghhhh!'

'You all right there, sir?' asked Josh Culper, the helmsman. Liam had quite forgotten the little shrew-faced man was right there.

'Uh . . . yes . . . quite fine. I, uh . . . I swallowed a bug, that's all.'

CHAPTER 40
1667, the Caribbean Sea

'This is actually quite good,' mumbled Rashim, his mouth full.

Liam nodded, finishing work on the fibrous hunk of mutton in his mouth. 'Cookie picked up some spices in the marketplace. It's pretty hot, though – spicy-hot.'

'It reminds me a little of my mother's cooking. She used to make a prickly-hot Chicken Patia. All soyo-protein substitutes and vat-grown rice, of course, but the spices were real.' He spooned another mouthful from his bowl and nodded appreciatively. 'It's all about the spices really.'

'Aye. And it seems Cookie's decided to throw the whole lot in.'

'Liam, is that *really* our cook's name?'

'Our Cookie? Yup. Jeremiah Cooke.'

Rashim snorted a laugh. 'We have got a chief gunner whose surname is Gunny and our cook is called Cooke.' He shook his head. 'I suspect Teale was having a laugh when he hired the crew. I won't ask you the name of the poor sod who twines our ropes.'

Liam laughed. 'No, best not.'

They ate in silence for a while. Through the cabin door they could hear the noise of pots being banged and scraped on the main deck; Cookie was serving the rest of the crew with his spicy mutton broth.

'I wonder what's become of him,' said Liam. 'Jacob Teale. I still feel a little guilty about us casting him adrift.'

'I, on the other hand, don't. The man was a fraud. A liar. Nothing but a silver-tongued conman.' Rashim shook his head. 'And a bit of an idiot. Anyway, I'm sure he made his way to land somewhere and, as we speak, is busy conning some foolish merchant out of his savings.'

'True.'

Just then they heard the clump of boots up the ladder and across the afterdeck, the muffled sound of Old Tom's voice barking angrily. An exchange of other voices in protest then eventually a timid rap of knuckles on the cabin door.

'Enter!' said Rashim.

The door opened and Tom's face appeared. 'Awful sorry, sirs, I told these godless rascals you was both busy eatin' yer supper. But they insisted . . . said they got grievances they needed to air.'

'Grievances? With what?'

'Ship's charter, Skipper.'

All the men had had the new terms and conditions read out to them before they'd made their mark and signed on. Even the original men Teale had hired had been required to sign on again. New captain, new enterprise . . . new charter.

'They agreed to the terms,' said Rashim irritably. 'Tell them to go away and stop bothering us.'

'Rashim,' Liam cut in. 'Uh . . . our terms also included the right for the men to knock on the door and speak freely.'

Rashim gritted his teeth. 'Dammit, yes, I suppose you're right.' He nodded at Tom. 'All right, let them in.'

Tom stepped aside and allowed three of the crew to duck in through the low door. They removed their caps respectfully, a good sign.

'Hey, Gunny,' said Liam, 'we were just talking about you.'
Beside him was one of his gun crew, Lenny, and Jamieson, one
of the new recruits they'd picked up at Port Royal.

'Evening, sirs,' said Gunny.

'Tom says you gentlemen have a grievance?' prompted
Rashim.

'Aye, it's . . . er, it's about one or two of them conditions in
the charter, sir.'

'Which ones?'

'Well . . . the grog, sir. No alcohol on the ship.' Gunny
shrugged. 'Seems to all of us to be just a little harsh, that.'

'OK, look, James,' said Liam, 'there's a good enough reason
for that. And you above all the others should understand why.
You remember what happened last month? That fool, Cobbler,
blew himself up because he was drunk.'

'Aye, but . . . well . . . maybe that was because Cobbler
couldn't handle his drink?' Gunny backed that up with a hopeful,
half-hearted shrug.

'We didn't have that foolish rule on me last ship,' said
Jamieson.

'That's not really my concern,' said Rashim. 'On *this* ship,
I'm afraid we do.'

'That ain't right to 'spect us to work weeks 'n' weeks without
no grog. Me and some of the boys ain't 'avin' that!'

Liam shot a quick glance at Rashim. The man was openly
challenging their authority.

'Perhaps it would help if I explained why,' replied Rashim
patiently. 'We are carrying six kegs of gunpowder and a number
of barrels of highly flammable lamp oil aboard a vessel made
entirely of wood, tar, rope and –'

'Beggar that!' The man spat. 'We're all bloody well

experienced mariners 'ere. Not boys! We knows our way about a ship! 'Tis a stupid rule which we ain't minded to –'

'Shut yer gaping hole!' snapped Old Tom. 'How dare yer speak to the captains like that!'

Liam stood up slowly. 'Now you signed the charter and these are the conditions we *will* be operating under until we return to Port Royal. It's not negotiable.'

Be firm, Liam. He looked at Rashim. *One of us has to be.*

'The crew of this ship will remain sober until . . . until the job's done. Then, if you want, Jamieson, you can take your share and go drink to your heart's content as far as we're concerned. But, until that time, we're all staying sober and that's all there is to it!'

Rashim offered a placating smile. 'Think about it, we could encounter a ship at any moment. The crew, all of us, need to be in a constant state of readiness for that. Not drunk.'

Liam could see Gunny and Lenny were having second thoughts about challenging this issue any further. The point was made and quite reasonably so.

'That ain't our way!' pressed Jamieson, however. 'The men all agree with me.'

'Now look,' started Rashim calmly. 'It's basic common sense –'

'We want the charter changed! Or we –'

'You'll what?' *Jay-zus, Rashim . . . you've got to be firmer than this.* Liam took a step towards the men. 'You'll do what?'

'I'll –' he looked at Gunny and his mate for support – '*we'll* take steps.'

Liam realized he was trembling. Damned if he was going to let that creep into his voice. 'I'll tell you what you're going to do.' He reached for a deeper, more commanding tone. 'You will accept this rule, Jamieson, or we will clap you in irons and you'll forfeit your share when we get back to Port Royal!' Liam took another, hopefully intimidating, step towards him. 'Is that quite clear?'

To his surprise, and relief, the man's challenging stare dropped to the floor.

'I said . . . is that clear?'

'Aye,' he mumbled. 'S'pose.'

'Aye . . . SIR!'

'Sir.'

He looked at Gunny. 'And what's your other grievance? I believe you had a couple of them?'

Gunny shuffled uncomfortably. 'Well . . . some of the lads ain't too happy 'bout the Negro slave aboard.'

'Tha's right,' said Jamieson. 'Now we ain't 'avin' it that that Negro is gettin' the same share as the rest of —'

'Jay-zus!' Liam shook his head. Then felt a stab of sudden anger. 'GET OUT!' he snapped. 'OUT!'

Tom grabbed Jamieson's arm. 'Come on, you scabs, as the co-skipper said. Out with yer.' They ducked through the doorway, Gunny offering an apologetic nod back at them and knuckling his forehead before the cabin door closed behind them all.

Liam realized he was shaking with a mixture of nerves and . . . yes, outrage. He turned to see Rashim staring wide-eyed at him. 'That was . . . uh . . . that was a rather impressive display of testosterone there.'

'Some things . . . arghhh! Some things really get to me.' He took a deep breath. 'And that's one of them.'

'Racism?'

'Unfairness.' He sat back down at the table and looked at the cooling bowl of broth in front of him. 'Just . . . just *unfairness* . . .' He sighed. 'Every man out there stands an even chance of losing their life, right? So, why should one man's life be worth any less than another's? We can all stop a musket ball just as good as the next man!'

'Different times, I suppose,' said Rashim with a shrug, 'different values.'

'That's no excuse! People in this time know it's wrong just like you and I do. I'm sure of that. But it's too convenient, isn't it? Too easy to point at a slave in rags and say, "He's not the same as me." That's how one group of people enslaves another, by convincing themselves they're not even human. It's a cop-out!' Liam picked up his spoon and stirred the broth absently. 'The unfairness of it just annoys me, so it does.'

The silence in the cabin felt long and uncomfortable to Rashim. But there was something else. Something he felt he needed to say. 'So . . .' He leaned forward across the table and gently rapped his knuckles next to Liam's arm. 'So, now I think I've seen a different side to you.'

Liam looked up at him. 'And what's that?'

'I suppose . . . the Mr Serious side,' he said, grinning.

'What? Are you laughing at me?'

'No.' Rashim shook his head. 'No, definitely not that. On the contrary. I . . . just realize there's a bit more to you than I previously thought. You have *ideals*.' He smiled ruefully. 'There's not much of that in the future, in my time, Liam. Like everything else . . . not much of it left.'

Rashim regarded his colleague silently.

You may be an artificial — a meat product, my friend — but you are more human than most people I've met.

CHAPTER 41

1667, the Caribbean Sea

The shout came down the next morning, as Cookie and William were preparing a skillet of freshly cooked spiced yams for breakfast. Cookie growled at the boy around the pipe stem in his mouth, ''Ere we go . . . 'nother fine meal ruined.'

Liam and Rashim tumbled out of their hammocks, pulled on breeches and boots and met Old Tom on the afterdeck as he bellowed at the crew to muster for action.

'Lookout spotted several sails ten degrees off the port bow, sirs.'

Rashim slid down the ladder to the main deck, jogged along it and climbed the ladder to the foredeck, Liam right behind him. Bracing himself against the rail right at the front of the ship, he pulled out his spyglass, extended it and put it to his eye.

'I don't see . . . ahhh . . .'

'You see 'em?'

Rashim squinted into the lens, his lips silently moving. Counting.

'Well?' Liam shuffled impatiently. 'Spanish?'

'Uh . . . I am seeing yellow and red at the top of one mast. That's Spanish, isn't it?'

'Aye. How many? Two? Three?'

Rashim lowered the spyglass. 'Seven.' He looked at Liam anxiously. 'That's . . . that's too many for us to take on.'

Liam grabbed the telescope from him and made his own quick assessment. 'I make it six. The middle one isn't two ships . . .' He adjusted the focus. 'It's three-masted. Bigger than the others. It's not a carrack.'

Tom joined them, breathless from barking at the men. Liam handed him the spyglass. 'The ship in the middle, Tom, what is it?'

It was Tom's turn to squint into the lens. 'I see five fat sheep and a sheepdog.' He lowered the glass and handed it back to Liam. 'Two square-rigged masts, two lateen sails at the back, prominent forecastle. She's a galleon.'

'Is that a good or a bad thing?' asked Rashim.

Tom grinned toothlessly. 'It means you'll get a chance to try out yer fancy cannonballs this morning. She's a warship. This time around you'll have yerself a proper fight.'

Rashim paled slightly. 'Six to one . . . perhaps we might be taking on too many?'

Tom looked appalled. 'One warship . . . the rest of 'em most likely'll try and make a run for it. You bring the galleon down first, Skipper, the rest should be easy prey.'

'There, you heard him,' said Liam with a grin.

'Right. Yes . . . well then.' Rashim mustered his best effort at a bloodthirsty leer. It came across as an insipid grimace. 'Action stations . . . or whatever the correct term is.'

Tom turned and started bellowing orders. Within a minute, every last sail was unfurled gull-wing style, the wind that morning right behind them, every square foot of linen taut and thrumming. The *Pandora*'s bow carved through the sea and they bore down on the galleon now no more than a mile away from them.

The Spanish warship was now altering course, a large round sweep towards them, tacking into the wind.

Liam looked at Rashim. 'You all right? You ready for this?'

He shook his head. 'You know me well enough. Not particularly good at confrontations. So, no . . . not exactly.' He took in a deep, steadying breath. 'But I will be fine.'

'I'll take charge of the boarding party.'

Rashim smiled gratefully.

As the two ships rapidly closed the distance between them, Liam was down on the main deck handpicking two dozen men and ensuring each was adequately armed. Another six men were issued with the muskets that Schwarzmann had had rifled. The day before Liam had organized a shooting contest among the crew to identify their best marksmen. The general quality of marksmanship hadn't been particularly outstanding, but one of their new crew, a French huntsman called Pasquinel, had stood out. Liam ordered the man up to the *Pandora*'s crow's-nest with specific instructions to target the galleon's helmsman once they were close enough.

Meanwhile Rashim headed down to the gun deck to ensure Gunny and the teams of gun crew were ready. The *Pandora* had twelve cannons on each side. He ordered all twenty-four cannons to be loaded and ready to fire with the new elongated cannonballs: a foolish measure, since the pitch and sway of the ship might result in some of them sliding out. But Gunny knuckled his forehead and grinned at the order; these 'miracle shots' weren't going to roll anywhere.

Half an hour after the first sighting, the first cannons fired. Clearly meant as a hopeful attempt to warn them off, the shots splashed harmlessly into the sea a hundred yards short of the *Pandora*, sending plumes of spray into the air.

Up on the afterdeck, standing beside the helmsman, Rashim waited until their ship had sailed past the diminishing foam on the water where the plumes had erupted, halving the remaining distance between them. They were now closer to the galleon than they'd been to their target pinnace a few days ago.

'I'd say . . . now.'

'Aye, Skipper.' The helmsman spun the wheel to the right. The *Pandora* turned to starboard, presenting her ready-loaded port cannons towards the Spanish ship. Rashim pulled out his pistol and fired it into the air, the signal for Gunny to fire at will. A moment later a cannon roared, then a peal of one cannon after another, no more than a second between each shot, erupted down the side of the ship like a Mexican wave.

Rashim caught the blur of movement as the projectiles whistled across the water, one shot breaking up midway across. Then he saw puffs of impact. A cloud of splinters and shards erupted from the galleon's forecastle. Another two midway along the waist of the ship. A ragged hole was torn through the middle mast's mainsail. Two shots raced harmlessly across the low main deck, but the last shot in the volley found the most useful target. The short foremast juddered, an explosion of shards near its base, then began to sway forward and collapsed across the forecastle like a felled tree. Rashim heard a chorus of cheering coming up from the gun deck.

'Now let them have the other side,' cried Rashim.

'Hard to port!' yelled Tom.

The helmsman spun the wheel the opposite way and the *Pandora* leaned into the sharp turn, spinning round almost within one length of her hull, now bringing the starboard-side cannons to bear.

Even closer now, a second pealing broadside suddenly erupted: *whoomp, whoomp, whoomp, whoomp* . . . Horizontal mushroom clouds of blue smoke spat out from their side, each sonic boom punching Rashim in the chest, each shot making the whole ship vibrate and rock. More impact clouds of splinters and shards erupted from the galleon. The slender mast at the rear carrying one of the lateen sails spun off at its base and over the side, becoming a tangled drag of rope and sail in the ship's wake.

Rashim yelped with delight. 'Yes!'

The galleon, now hobbled, wasn't yet prepared to give up the fight. It wallowed clumsily, slowly, as it tried to turn and present its port-side cannons for a return volley. Down on the main deck Liam and his two dozen men were excitedly cheering. But he could see what was coming. They were close enough now that the Spanish cannons, if the ship completed its turn, were going to do some damage. He looked up at Pasquinel, wanting to signal him to take a shot at the helmsman. But there was no need.

Above, from the crow's-nest, the single crack of a musket. The French huntsman wasn't waiting for an order. Liam saw the man at the helm double over and drop to the deck. The helm began to spin wildly, rebelling against the laboured turn they were attempting.

Jay-zus. It can't be going this well . . . can it?

The galleon had lost what momentum it had and was now listlessly bobbing in the water. Once again, the *Pandora* began to swing round, this time to starboard, a final approaching tangent that would bring her around on the galleon's far side, in close, close enough for them to throw hooks and board.

'Get ready, lads!' he shouted. The men roared a chorus of something. Might have been *huzzah*. Might have been a hearty, nautical, piratey *a-harrrrr*, he couldn't tell.

Over the rail, now they were close enough, he could see the Spanish sailors, a scramble of men preparing themselves for the boarding action. More than that, he could see the damage their cannons had already done: jagged, frayed ends of pale wood freshly exposed, smears of bright crimson spattered across sails that now flapped uncontrolled. The prow of the *Pandora* was past the prow of the galleon to their right, just twenty yards of water separating them. On her forecastle Liam saw a man in a shining cuirass with long dark hair waving a sword to muster men for the fight.

This is it. Again, Liam noted that the trembling pre-fight fear that had always plagued him in the past was absent; instead, he was calm. A chilling, killer's calm. A relief not to feel his stomach churning, to want to vomit with fear, the pressing need to empty his bowels . . . but really . . . *this* calm? *What the hell does that make me – a psychopath?*

'Ready your hooks, lads!' he shouted.

Over the rail he could see the faces of the Spanish crew armed with muskets and swords, determination etched on their powder-smudged faces. Men who may have lost the opening act of this skirmish, but were far from ready to surrender. He wondered how ready he and his own men would be to take on a close-quarters fight if the opening exchange of fire had gone the other way.

Just then the deck beneath their feet convulsed as cannons below erupted. The *Pandora* lurched backwards as the cannons fired a united volley instead of a stepped peal. Every man staggered to keep his footing.

Virtually point-blank. Undoubtedly devastating. The narrow space between the ships became an instant thick fog-bank of powder smoke and, out of it, sharp splinters of wood rained down on them like hail. On to the deck beside him an arm landed with a soft thud, like a joint of meat tossed carelessly from the back of a butcher's cart.

And then the smoke began to clear.

CHAPTER 42

1667, the Caribbean Sea

The *Pandora* had been leaning to port as she'd fired her last salvo – the tail end of their sharp final turn to bring them in alongside the galleon – consequently her cannons had been angled forty-five degrees upwards. The point-blank volley had punched twelve gaping holes up, through the top side of the hull, through the main deck, shredding the rail and the men waiting behind it ready to repel them. Twelve jagged bites along the ship's waist exposing a ribcage of decks and bulkheads.

Through the clearing coils of smoke, Liam caught sight of a charnel house of severed limbs, grotesquely mangled bodies tangled with frayed splinters of lumber.

'. . . sir?'

Liam felt his shoulder being thumped. He turned to see Old Tom, mouthing something, his voice lost against the ringing in his ears. His hearing was beginning to return.

'The order?' The man tried again. 'To board, sir?'

Liam nodded. 'Let's GO!'

The order was passed along the rail and, with a chorus of wild yipping and howling, his men leaped up on to their bulwark, some jumping across the narrow space between the ships, some swinging across from shrouds. Liam did likewise, climbing over the rail. Two yards separated him from the ragged edge of the galleon's splintered deck. He hopped across a void

242

of slapping water below on to a plank of deck that flexed and creaked precariously beneath his weight. He leaped to the right, on to decking that appeared more stable, as fibres cracked and the plank cascaded down into the dark crevasse between the ships.

He could hear the fight starting somewhere to his left, but he could see nothing. The smoke was still thick and the front end of the Spanish ship was a confusing tangle of clutter. The deck was slippery with blood, a mess of debris; rigging from the collapsed mast draped a spider's web of low throttling loops of rope and tatters of sail. He picked his way through the mess, ducking beneath the spar of a broken yardarm only to find himself thumping heads with someone coming the other way.

'Ow!'

The other man groaned. He looked up at Liam as he rubbed his painful forehead. Both of them grinned at their mutual clumsiness, a shared second of acknowledgement that, when you can't see a damned thing, leading the way with an outstretched hand was probably a smarter move than leading with your forehead.

'That was stupid,' Liam muttered.

The man seemed to understand, grinned, nodded. '*Si . . . Somos burros torpes.*'

The moment passed. The Spaniard, a barrel-chested man with a red cloth cap with a frayed gold-thread tassel that hung down the side of his face, produced a machete and pointed the tip towards Liam.

Liam countered with the tip of his cutlass. 'Look . . .' he said softly, 'why don't we let each other pass?'

The man said something, then suddenly lunged low at Liam's gut. Liam stepped back and parried hard, swinging his cutlass, successfully deflecting the blade, knocking it out of the man's grasp. But he lost his footing on something loose on the deck behind him and tumbled over on to his back. The man landed on top of him, knocking the wind out of his lungs.

He felt a strong hand round his throat, squeezing so hard that he thought he could feel the cartilage of his Adam's apple snapping, breaking, cracking. The man's other hand was out of sight, fumbling for something, then he saw it, a small blade. Liam dropped his cutlass – useless now, too close to use the blade – and reached for the man's wrist as he tried to lunge at Liam's neck. The knife, a short oval-shaped blade, glinted in the space between their grimacing faces, Liam could feel its tip tickling, teasing the skin beneath his left ear as he struggled to hold it at bay.

No . . . no . . . no . . . no . . .

The Spaniard was using his weight, pushing down on the blade with his shoulder. He pursed his lips, *shushing* Liam, pleading with him to make this an easier death for him.

'No . . . please . . .' Liam gurgled.

'Shhhh . . . shhhhh . . .'

Liam's other hand was trying to prise free the man's vice-like grip on his throat. He gave up on that and instead reached for the man's face. He dug a thumb into his right eye, pressed hard enough that he could feel his thumbnail digging deep into the socket. The man frantically shook his head from side to side, trying to shake off Liam's hand. And that was enough: his attention was off the blade.

Liam rocked to the right, then flung his body to the left, rolling the man over the top of him, and now he was on top. The weight transferred, now he had the upper hand. He gave up on gouging the man's eye out and instead quickly transferred his spare hand to work the blade round until it was now pointing towards the man's neck. Their eyes met. Liam could see the man knew what was coming.

'*Shhhh* . . . is it?'

The tip of the blade dug into the man's neck. So easy now to push it in all the way to the hilt. After all, this wouldn't be his first time or his second. Or his third. Killing . . . too much of it and it would become an easy thing to do. Too easy. The man gurgled desperately, eyes wide with fear. Liam bared his teeth and snarled a curse. He turned the blade round and smacked the man senseless with the hard end of the hilt. He climbed off the unconscious man quickly.

Through the thinning smoke he could hear the distant ring of blades, the yipping, excited cry of his men, the pitiful moaning and crying of those hapless men caught in the broadside.

He struggled through the tangle of drooping ropes and fluttering sails and finally emerged into a clear space on the main deck to see a mere handful of the Spanish crew left, less than a dozen able-bodied men, most of them bloodied and already scored with cuts . . . but still making a determined effort to fight back to back. They were pushed up against the rail on the far side of the ship, defending a number of the wounded they'd managed to drag back from the carnage wrought by the cannons. Liam's men had surrounded them and were feinting, lunging, probing like hunting dogs baiting cornered game.

Liam pushed forward. 'Quarter! Give them quarter!' he cried above the screams and shouts and clatter, ring and scrape of blades. His voice was lost in the cacophony. He could see familiar faces pulled into rictus grins of blood-lust, excitement, terror. Even the giant man, Kwami – so far he'd only known him as a softly spoken gentle giant – seemed caught up in the mania, wide-eyed and caterwauling as he swung a hatchet in front of him. A frightened Spanish sailor half his size was desperately parrying the blow with the stock of a broken musket.

Jay-zus.

Liam pulled the pistol from his belt, cocked it and fired it into the air. 'Stop!' he screamed. 'Stop! ENOUGH!'

His men finally seemed to hear him and began to disengage and take a step back. Further along the deck, he could hear other smaller skirmishes playing out, but here, this one right in front of him, became a lull . . . all eyes now resting on him expectantly.

He stepped forward, his pistol tucked back in his belt. Hands held out, showing he was holding no weapons. 'That's it!' he said to the Spaniards. 'That's enough!' He looked at them, sailors most of them. Two of them were wearing cuirasses of tin-plate armour and braided tunics. Soldiers, then. But none of them seemed to be officers. None of them probably spoke a word of English.

It's going to have to be with gestures, then.

Liam approached them slowly, then for want of any better idea, dipped his head with a salute. 'You will be unharmed, I promise. There will be no slaughter,' he said to the Spaniard nearest him. The man was shaking, wide-eyed, holding a rapier in the bulging knuckles of one hand.

Liam reached for his belt and the flask of drinking water there. He uncorked it, held it out to the man. 'It's all done, it's finished,' he said soothingly. 'You're done here. Why don't you drop your weapons? Eh?'

The man seemed to understand his intention if not his words. Slowly he nodded. Then he released his hold on the sword and it clattered on to the deck at his feet. The other Spaniards followed suit. Liam handed him the flask then turned to his men. 'The ship's ours, lads.' He sighed, took in several deep breaths. 'The ship's ours.'

Rashim and Liam found each other a few minutes later. They spoke across the space between both ships, the hulls bumping and creaking against each other.

'My God, Liam!' Rashim's face was glistening with sweat. 'My God, that was . . . that was *incredible*!'

Incredible? No. It was hard. There were going to be moments of it he'd want to forget. It had been savage, primal even. But at least it was done. 'Where are the other ships?'

'Two of them are right out there.' Rashim pointed towards the prow of the ship. 'They've dropped their sails! Not even trying to make a run for it!'

Liam craned his neck to see. Sure enough, he could make out the dark outline of their hulls a mile away. Their sails were down, untethered and flapping uselessly in the wind.

'What about the others?'

'Not that far.' Rashim's bearded face split with a smile. 'I can chase them down!'

'I don't know . . . I . . . will we not be spreading ourselves too thin?'

'You stay with the galleon, we'll be back!'

'No! Hang on! Look, this is enough.' Liam nodded at the waiting carracks. 'That's enough for one day, surely?'

Rashim shook his head. 'Good God, Liam! Where's your sense of adventure?'

Adventure?

'Look, Rashim. I think this is enough of a win for us, OK? It's enough!'

Rashim laughed at that. 'Rubbish . . . there's an even bigger win waiting for us out there. I just have to go and grab it.' He turned away from the rail and began calling out orders for Old Tom to ready the men to set sail immediately for the pursuit.

'Wait! Hey! Rashim!' But he was shouting at his friend's back. 'Rashim!'

Tom's baritone voice echoed across the deck and the *Pandora*'s crew were already scrambling up the rigging to the lowest yards.

'Goddammit! Rashim!'

The *Pandora* lurched slowly forward, beginning to pull away. Liam caught sight of Rashim again, scooting up the ladder to the afterdeck to stand beside the helmsman.

'Rashim!'

His friend looked back at him and Liam could see the flash of a broad smile on his face. He waved back at Liam, then cupped his hands around his mouth. The afterdeck passed by him as the *Pandora* pulled away. Rashim shouted out something across the choppy water, but it was lost against the bark of orders being passed down the ship, the hiss of the hull cutting through the waves, the lively rustle and snap of the sails finding the wind.

Liam cursed as he watched the high rear of the schooner as she pulled away from them.

'We're supposed to be a bleedin' team, here,' he muttered. 'Dammit . . . a team.' He cursed his gallivanting friend for treating this like some kind of a game.

Over the rear rail of the receding ship he caught sight of one last good-natured wave from Rashim, and it was then that he finally figured out what his friend had called back to him.

This is fun!

CHAPTER 43

1889, London

Sal wanted to do this quickly. She wanted to be gone before Maddy and the support units came back from the market. She didn't want to have a big shouty row with her. She didn't want Maddy trying to coerce her into her way of thinking – and she knew Maddy could do that easily. If shouting at her didn't work, she'd implore Sal to stay because, after all, all they had now was each other. And, God help her, if it wasn't going to be a row, it would be worse: a tearful goodbye.

I can't face that.

So, this was the cowardly way. Sal had spent the night struggling to write a farewell note. So much to say and none of the words she scribbled down quite seemed to get on paper what she felt.

I love you, Maddy, like the big sister I never had. I love Liam too. There was a time, which now seems like ages ago, when I thought we were almost like a family, the three of us ...

It went on – a couple of pages of emotional outpouring. Rambling, meandering thoughts that filled up the last few pages of her diary, but it added up to something more coherent than she'd ever be able to do face to face.

'I'm sorry, Maddy,' she'd muttered as she left the diary open on the bed, somewhere it would easily be found when she got back. Right now, though, she had computer-Bob to deal with and he was fussing like an old woman.

> **Sal, has Maddy approved this time-stamp request?**

She looked at the webcam. 'Yes, Bob. She and I discussed this earlier.'

> **What is the purpose of the mission?**

'Research. I'm . . . I'm going there to acquire some useful data.'

> **What useful data?**

Damn him. 'That's not necessary for you to know right now.'

> **I require approval from Maddy. This is not normal protocol.**

'Bob, look, there are no protocols left. No procedures. We've just been making things up as we go along for a while now if you hadn't already noticed.'

The cursor winked silently on the dialogue box for a while as Bob weighed up his response. Finally . . .

> **Sal, I sense discord among the team.**

She nodded. 'Oh, you can say that again.'

> **You appear to be distressed. You are crying.**

Self-consciously she swiped at her cheeks to dry them. 'Yes . . . yes, well done, you. I guess you've spotted things aren't so great with us right now.'

> **I am concerned. Why do you want to visit this time-stamp location?**

She laughed. So easy to underestimate Bob's intelligence. Inside his human frame the same AI appeared to be almost completely human now, if a little dry and humourless. But the same intelligence presented on-screen as no more than text in a dialogue box made it easy to think of him as nothing more than a rather clever, human-friendly operating system.

'I want to know who I am, Bob.' She dabbed at her red-rimmed eyes. 'I *need* to know who I am.'

> **You have chosen a location and time from the memories you have of your life before you were in the agency?**

'Yes . . . I remember being right there. At that precise time. I'm sure of it.'

> **Sal, do you intend to meet yourself?**

It wasn't really meeting herself in the way that would cause a whole heap of time-travel-related cause-and-effect problems. No. She was meeting someone else. She would be meeting her progenitor. The girl she was copied from. Her *original*.

'I remember being right there, Bob. Or at least I remember Saleena Vikram being there. I just want to see her for real. See if she looks exactly like me. Sounds like me. I want to talk with her.'

Maddy had gone to her supposed home in Boston in the hope of finding the same thing. And what had she found? Strangers living there. *But maybe it's different for me.* Sal was sure her memories weren't a patchwork quilt of borrowed scenes. What she recalled seemed like a real life. A complete life lived by a real person.

> **How will this help you?**

'It'll keep me from going completely insane, Bob. That's a start, isn't it?'

Again the softly blinking cursor. She wondered what loops of code he was running through in there. What possible code could he have in those linked PC circuit boards to make a value judgement on her state of mind right now?

'Bob . . . I need to know if I was once a real person.' She could feel fresh tears welling up. 'If I could have just that, to know that I lived one proper life once upon a time, it . . .' She shook her head, not really certain yet exactly what that might mean to her. 'It would help me. Does that make any sense? Any sense at all?'

> **I am unable to answer that, Sal. There are too many unquantifiable variables.**

She pressed her lips together. Of course. How the hell could she expect him to even begin to understand what she was feeling? She couldn't even understand it herself. There was a desperate feeling of hope in there somewhere. Hope for what, though? If she did find herself standing in front of the real Sal Vikram, what then?

'Bob, please . . . let this one through. I have to go.'

> **I will suspend normal procedure.**

'You'll do it?'

> **Affirmative. I am logging the time-stamp in and initializing the displacement machine now.**

She suppressed a whimper. 'Why?'

> **I am concerned for you, Sal. You are experiencing emotional distress. This trip may ameliorate that.**

She looked back at the webcam. *Concerned?* Dry and clinical as his response was, 'concerned' was the most human response he'd ever come up with. Right then Sal wished she could hug this thing. But what to hug? The mouse? The keyboard? The monitor? If he was inhabiting his fleshy meatbot frame, then she would have at least had the opportunity to wrap her arms round him – as far as they could reach – and plant a kiss on one granite-hard cheek.

'Thank you, Bob.'

> **Will you require the normal return-window procedure?**

She shook her head. 'I . . . I don't know.'

> **You do not intend to return?**

'I'm not sure what I intend to do. Perhaps . . .' She shrugged.

'I don't know yet. I suppose it makes sense to have a way back if . . . yes, best set up something.'

> **In that case I will program a two-hour return interval. A twenty-four-hour interval. A week interval. Is that OK?**

'Yes, that's fine.'

> **Information: I will inform Maddy of your location when she returns.**

Sal nodded. 'That's fine.' She looked at the diary lying wide open on her bed. 'She knows where I'm going and why.'

> **The displacement machine has a full charge already.**

She got up off the stool, touched the screen gently in front of her. 'You know something? You're the best, Bob.'

The cursor jittered to the right.

> **Information: correct.**

CHAPTER 44

1667, Port Royal, Jamaica

'How much?' Schwarzmann's eyes bulged.

Rashim sat back in his seat and stroked the thick thatch of dark bristles on his chin. 'Seven thousand doubloons.'

'Seven *thousand*!'

Liam leaned forward and ran his fingers down their ledger. 'Seven thousand three hundred and seventy-eight pieces of eight, to be precise.' He looked up at the gunsmith. 'That is your five per cent share as was agreed between ourselves, Mr Schwarzmann. Not a penny more, sir.'

'*Mein Gott!*' He shook his head and gasped several long, wheezy breaths. 'I am not complaining, Mr O'Connor! That . . . iss . . . that iss . . . incredible!'

'Liam? Would you do the honours, old chap, and hand this gentleman his well-earned plunder?' said Rashim. His voice was slurred somewhat. The afternoon had been spent in the King's Head, the tavern that was now serving as their informal 'office'. They'd gone through their accounts and paid each crew member his share. The rum was flowing freely and Rashim, despite a promise to Liam that he'd not touch a single drop until all the account work had been settled, had finally weakened and was on his second jug.

Ninety-three men, each of them handed a bulging hip pouch of coins containing just over eight hundred doubloons, and each of them doffing their caps, knuckling their foreheads with a wide grateful smile, as they'd backed away. Seven men had died, their shares returned to the communal pot. Thirteen of the surviving crew had received additional compensation payments for injuries sustained. Five hundred for the loss of one man's arm. He'd gleefully walked away with his bound stump swinging uselessly. Another had been equally ecstatic with his additional two hundred piece of eight compensation payment for the loss of his eye; the other one bulged wide and round as he cradled his pouch and shook their hands vigorously.

All said, a rather satisfying afternoon spent in something of a carnival atmosphere. News, of course, had spread across Port Royal shortly after the *Pandora* and the crippled galleon, the *Santa Maria*, had docked. Every harlot, every merchant, every pedlar, every craftsman in the town had descended upon the tavern as the crew had queued patiently for their pay, the line snaking beneath the low-timbered ceiling of the inn out into the baking sunshine of Queen Street. An impromptu market had appeared out of nowhere and blocked the street directly outside the tavern as merchants offered silks, liquors, pipe tobacco, smoked boar jerky at double, triple their normal prices to the drunken men partying in the afternoon sun.

Rashim took another slug of rum and set his tankard down heavily on the barrel-top table beside him. 'I presume we can repeat our business arrangement with you, Mr Schwarzmann?'

'For certain!'

'The arrangement, of course . . . will remain *exclusively* with us?' added Liam.

The German nodded emphatically. He looked around, lowering his voice. 'Your miracle shot, I will make just for you. How many more will you require?'

Rashim turned to Liam. 'Liam?'

He consulted their ledger once more. 'We used a total of forty-two. Nearly all of them. We counted seven shots that disintegrated, though.'

'Then make us twice the number!' said Rashim. 'I have some suggestions on a refinement of the design, but –' he shrugged – 'I'm a little the worse for wear right now. We'll discuss that tomorrow.'

Schwarzmann smiled and offered a courteous half-bow. 'Tomorrow, sir. At your convenience!'

They watched him weave his way through the press of bodies in the tavern and now, with one last payment to settle – Sir Thomas Modyford's 'tax' – they were finally done with business matters for that afternoon.

Liam looked down at the ledger. 'After we've restocked our ship with essentials –' the tip of his quill hovered above the parchment as he did some quick arithmetic – 'this expedition will have made us a tidy seven thousand pieces.'

Rashim grinned at him. 'Marvellous!'

Liam looked out of the small leaded window beside them. Outside in the street, the market looked like a fair, a miniature festival. He caught sight of Gunny and his cannon crew dancing inelegantly in a clumsy circle as a fiddle and bodhrán played for them. He spotted their little helmsman, Culper, swaying, quite catatonic, held on his feet by two painted ladies giggling at his drunken mutterings. He saw Kwami trying on a variety of different brightly coloured shirts and smocks being presented to him by a haberdasher who held up a mirror for the large man to check himself in. Liam smiled at that. Kwami looked like a man of means now, someone important. No longer a slouching giant in rags staring at his feet, but holding himself proudly.

'Isn't it amazing how a few yards of silk can transform a person?'

'Whazzat?'

'Rashim,' said Liam with a sigh, 'you're drunk. I thought we'd agreed to save the partying until after —'

'Oh, please . . . who are you? My mother?'

'I'm just saying . . . you and me, we agreed to keep our wits about us.'

Rashim wafted the comment away like an unwelcome fart. 'Pfft . . . I think we have earned ourselves a good time, have we not?' He leaned forward and slapped Liam's arm. 'Come on, Mr O'Connor . . . I was beginning to think you and I could enjoy ourselves a little!' His brown eyes locked on him intently. 'Isn't this damned wonderful? You an' I, partners in crime.' He stroked his beard. 'Partners in time?'

Liam looked at him closely. 'Rashim? Hang on! Are you wearing eyeliner?'

'Indeed.' He shrugged. 'Why not? It's what gentlemen of leisure wear.'

'Sirs?'

Both of them looked up to see Old Tom. Standing behind him was the captain of Modyford's guard, looking as sour and humourless as the last time they'd met.

He stepped forward. 'Gentlemen —' somehow he was still managing to make that word sound like a poorly veiled insult — 'Sir Thomas has invited you, Captain Anwar, to dinner at his plantation residence this evening.'

Rashim pursed his lips thoughtfully then smiled. 'Lovely. Why not?' He nodded at Liam. 'I presume my best friend here is invited too?'

The officer shook his head ever so reproachfully at Rashim's drunken slur. He turned to Liam and offered him only a slightly less disdainful glare. 'Of course . . . you two are a pair, aren't you?' He sighed. 'Yes, you are both invited. A carriage will be sent for you at six bells on the clock.'

'Marvellous! A party!'

'And where should the carriage pick you . . . *gentlemen* up from?' He addressed his question to Liam, the sober one of the two. 'Should I send it here or to your ship?'

Rashim shrugged, deferring to Liam to handle the details as he pulled himself up out of his chair, grabbed his empty tankard and wove his way towards the tavern's serving counter.

'I think we'll be taking rooms here for the foreseeable future.'

'Very good.' The officer turned to go, then hesitated. He turned back. 'Might I suggest you encourage your friend to sober up before you arrive?'

Liam nodded. 'Oh, for sure I will.'

'And if you have clothing more . . . *suitable* for an evening at a governor's residence, may I suggest you wear it?'

Liam looked down at his sweat-stained cotton shirt. Despite having been vigorously scrubbed in a bucket of seawater, it was still spotted with one or two dark sepia spatters of blood.

'Aye . . . right, yes.'

CHAPTER 45
1667, Port Royal, Jamaica

'Oh . . . oh God,' groaned Rashim, burying his face in his hands, 'I think I'm going to throw up.'

'No, you're not. You're going to be fine.'

'No . . . seriously, I think I . . .' Rashim suddenly got up, reached for the carriage door, wrenched it open and stuck his head out. Liam listened to him heave – the miserable sound reminded him of some unfortunate wild boar squealing. He decided there was more where that was coming from and rapped on the carriage roof for the driver to stop his horses.

The rocking and bumping along the dirt track ceased and Rashim dropped down on to the sunbaked dirt and finished emptying his guts into a thicket of dried reeds at the side. He straightened up, wiped his beard with the back of his hand and climbed back aboard the carriage.

'Better?'

'Better . . . although my head feels like there's a gravity-spin separator thumping around in there.' He pushed long strands of sweaty hair back from his forehead and massaged his temples. 'What in God's name kind of toxic additives do they put in the alcohol here?'

'You probably wouldn't want to know. I do believe it serves you right anyway.'

The journey took an hour and a half, winding uphill through

thick copses of tall mahogany and cedar trees, beneath which thickets of cane and reeds clustered. They passed by several cocoa plantations. With the sun already set and the sky becoming a deep-sea blue stained to the west with the last hint of a peach dusk, the crops of cocoa beans were still being tended to by dozens of slaves. Liam spotted them: dark forms in rags moving slowly among the rows of squat, shrub-like trees, plucking the yellow cacao pods from the low branches and tossing them over their shoulders into large wicker baskets on their backs.

By eight thirty in the evening the carriage arrived at Sir Thomas Modyford's plantation, the winding dirt track becoming a long, straight, wide approach between orchards of mango and orange trees. At the end it became a grit driveway that circled round a small cultured rose garden before a grand-looking one-storey building. There were other carriages parked, their horses untethered and gathered beneath a sheltered porch where their heads dipped into long troughs of water.

The carriage door was opened for them by a black slave wearing a white powdered wig, breeches, white stockings and a short waistcoat.

'Thanks,' said Liam. The slave started at that and stared wide-eyed at him for just a moment, then immediately dropped his gaze to the floor.

One of Modyford's servants came out to greet them with a crisp bow and ushered them inside through the residence's portico entrance into a hall with a cool stone-tiled floor. He excused himself to announce their arrival to Sir Thomas. As they waited, Liam savoured a refreshing breeze on his face, wafting down from above; he looked up at a large swaying reed fan, like a ship's rudder on its side. It was being tugged to and fro from a length of rope by a slave sitting cross-legged on the floor.

They could hear raised voices of conversation, the convivial sound of a party already in progress. Rashim looked edgily at Liam. 'I have to admit I feel a little bit out of my depth here.'

Liam nodded. He felt the same way, as if they were pretenders, fakers, about to be unmasked before a mocking audience.

'Uh . . . so, Liam, any pointers on how a person is meant to behave at a seventeenth-century drinks party?'

'What, you think I've been to a thing like this before?'

Rashim looked at him. 'You are the experienced time traveller, are you not?'

'Not *that* experienced.' He shrugged. 'I suppose we've just got to brass it out, act the part of swashbuckling privateers. But be polite.' He nudged Rashim gently. 'And do not get drunk.' Rashim looked waxy and pale. 'You're not going to hurl again, are you?'

He shook his head and smothered a queasy belch. 'I don't even want to *look* at another drink,' he muttered miserably. 'Unless it's a dehydrogenase booster.'

The servant returned and beckoned them to follow him into the main reception room. 'His Excellency will receive you now.'

They followed him through wide-open mahogany double doors into a large room with long walls of mint-green painted plaster, punctuated with oil paintings, portraits of – Liam presumed – members of Modyford's family. Candles, dozens of them, glowed from chandeliers and a sideboard along one wall, bathing the room in a rich amber glow. Tall window shutters were wide open allowing a modest breeze into the stifling room and a view of the gentle slopes of Sir Thomas's plantation.

The room was filled with guests: elegantly dressed ladies wearing tight-laced corsets and flowing skirts of satin brocade. Liam imagined that if Maddy was standing right beside him, she'd be geeking out at the opulence. But there were more gentlemen than ladies, most of them sporting luxuriant shoulder-length periwigs. Every now and then Liam could see fingers discreetly reaching up and scratching beneath them. He stifled a nervous giggle; a strong gust of wind through this room and it would be wall-to-wall shaved heads – a gathering of Shaolin monks.

Sir Thomas Modyford broke off conversation with a couple of fabulously fat and insanely rich-looking fellow plantation owners and made his way over.

'Ah! If it isn't the man himself, the talk of Port Royal, Captain Anwar!' He stuck a hand out and Rashim grasped it limply.

'Well, yes . . . and my co-captain here.'

Modyford nodded a little dismissively. 'Oh yes, something like O'Connor, isn't it?'

Liam nodded. 'Aye, sir, exactly that.'

Modyford's attention shifted straight back to Rashim. 'Now I do hear that your privateering expedition was a splendid success.' His voice lowered somewhat. 'I heard it said you brought in a jolly large haul?'

Rashim nodded.

'Well, later we can discuss the *tax* you owe on that, but . . . for now, tell me all about it.'

'We were rather lucky, Your Excellency.'

Modyford wafted the formal title out of the way like an intruder. 'Just address me as *Sir Thomas*, my good man. And, after a few drinks alone with fellows I find agreeable, I'll even dispense with the "Sir".' He nodded at Rashim to carry on.

'Well, we surprised a convoy of ships that were in the process of evacuating goods and gold from Cuba. Apparently the Spanish caught wind of the preparations going on for Henry Morgan's raid.'

'Captain Morgan is an arrogant fool. Too big for his boots. And perhaps too ambitious and slow off the mark. A fleet of ten ships and five hundred men is what I heard he took to Cuba. And what have they managed with that? A paltry haul. His investors have lost fortunes on that mess of an enterprise!

'But you –' he smiled admiringly – 'you, sir, with just one ship and your small crew of, I imagine, wholly ferocious and bloodthirsty devils, the lot of them, battled – what was it? – a *dozen* Spanish galleons and forced the damned lot of them to surrender?' Modyford slapped Rashim's shoulder and laughed. 'It seems you are quite the miracle worker, sir!'

Liam wondered whether to step in, correct the governor and tell him that it was six ships and only one of them a warship, but Rashim replied first. 'It was a very fierce struggle, Sir Thomas,' he said with a shrug of false modesty, 'but, you see, I had the wind behind me and the element of surprise.'

'Now, Anwar, I think we both know there was a little more to this victory than that. Hmm?' Modyford's jovial manner changed suddenly. He narrowed his eyes suspiciously and studied Rashim intently, as if by glare alone he was going to ferret out any untruths from this story.

'Oh yes, Captain Anwar,' he said drily, 'I'm quite certain you're not being entirely honest with me, are you? Perhaps there was a little *something else* tilting the fight in your favour?'

Rashim's mouth flapped open and closed uselessly. He glanced at Liam for a prompt, for something helpful to say. But Liam could do little better. The cannonball design was the one thing they both agreed needed to be kept entirely to themselves.

'Uh . . . I . . . not honest, Sir Thomas? Er . . . what exactly are you . . . ?'

Modyford's face suddenly creased. He laughed and slapped Rashim's shoulder roughly. '*Courage*, man! I'm talking about damned balls-to-the-wall courage and fighting spirit, sir! I suspect you bore down on those Spaniards like a bat from the bowels of Hell, like the Devil himself. Scared the wits out of the lot of them!'

'I . . .' Liam nodded almost imperceptibly at Rashim to let Modyford believe that. 'Well, we did approach the convoy quite quickly, I suppose. Like I said, we had the element of surprise on our side.'

'Too damned modest by half, sir!' he roared and shook his head. 'Good Lord! So many of the so-called *captains* out here on this island are little more than thugs and hooligans elected by their men to command their ships. A rabble of drunkards and thieves with little or no knowledge of naval tactics, navigation or nautical skills. Morgan, for example, all bloody talk. The man has lost me . . . well, let us just say the fool has lost me a small fortune. But you, Anwar, I suspect you're the man I should back. A man I can rely on to keep the Spaniards at bay. Keep them steering a wide berth round Port Royal.'

Modyford shrugged. 'Even if King Charles does firmly disapprove of me encouraging your kind, it's reputation, you see. It's all about *reputation*. As long as you pirates . . . my apologies . . . you *privateers* are putting the fear of God into the Spanish, then they'll not have the *cojones* to invade us. Not while we have the likes of you to call on to defend Port Royal!'

'Uh . . . yes, Sir Thomas.'

'Anyway. Good God, enough of wretched matters political. Enjoy yourself! This party is in your honour! You are the talk of Port Royal, man! The all-conquering hero!' He clapped his hands together and bellowed across the heads of the other guests. '*Somebody get this thirsty fellow a drink!*' He looked back at Rashim. 'You really do look as pale and colourless as a freshwater eel. A drink, sir, that's *exactly* what you need!'

Rashim smiled queasily. 'Marvellous. Yes. A drink. Thank you.'

CHAPTER 46

2025, New York

Sal felt the gentle touch of firm ground beneath her feet and immediately opened her eyes.

Times Square once more. It seemed her whole life now revolved around this urban acre. She'd seen this distinct convergence of streets in so many guises: an irradiated ruin, a monotone tribute to a fascist dictator, an expanse of jungle populated by reptilian hominids, a sleepy coastal town with a distinctly French ambience, a mature cedarwood forest inhabited by a tribe of native Americans.

Now it was a more familiar Times Square. But not the one she'd got to know so very well back in 2001. This was how she imagined — no, remembered — it was. Definitely a memory. Father had taken her to New York in 2025 on a business trip. And this was what she remembered. A city still unaware that it was dying.

There was the cinema. There the ticker-tape display. There the Times Square ticket booth, the Paramount Building. And the streets were busy enough — although not quite so busy as 2001, but still lively. She saw Greyhound buses, the new hybrid-version yellow cabs, trucks and coaches, and electro-bikes. Hundreds of them. Thousands of them. She remembered those things seemed to fill every street in every city. They certainly had in Mumbai.

She looked up and noticed that the skyscrapers leaning over her on all sides each sported a number of wind turbines: the traditional windmill and the newer egg-whisk designs, and endless arrays of glinting solar panels.

Yes, of course. The first of the major peak oil shocks had already begun to occur by now. Sal remembered her history. Saudi Arabia's mammoth oil reserves had suddenly gone dry in '23. The world's single largest producer of oil had, without warning, disconnected itself from the international supply loop intending to preserve what little it had left for itself. Within weeks of that day, gasoline, diesel – *petrol* as the British insisted on calling it – became a tightly rationed commodity. As expensive per pint as the most expensive of liquors. And the cars sitting outside everyone's home became, almost overnight, a worthless one and a half tons of scrap metal waiting to be collected by someone. Sal looked around. It was all so familiar.

She watched the intersection lights beside her change and a cloud of electro-bikes jangled bells at each other as they jostled for space. They swarmed past her like a cloud of insects, each one with a small electrical engine that hummed like an angry bumble-bee in a jam jar.

'I've definitely been here before,' she whispered.

No, not you, a pernicious, spiteful voice in her head reminded her. *The* real *Saleena Vikram has. Not you, though*.

She ignored her own malicious inner voice because she had better things to think about. Something to do. Somewhere she needed to go to. She looked at her watch. It was just gone 11:30 in the morning. Which meant she had half an hour to make her way up to Central Park.

That's where Father, *Papaji*, had taken her. To see the

enormous skyfreighter come in over the top and collect another load of scrap metal from the park.

'They come in every day at midday, Saleena. It is an amazing sight, I am told. I will take you to see it,' Father had said to her.

She dodged her way across the road, weaving through the jangling, buzzing electro-bikes, and headed north up 7th Avenue to Central Park. She could feel goosebumps on her arms, a shiver of excitement blowing down her neck to her spine.

My father . . . and me. They're somewhere up there. She looked up 7th Avenue at the press of pedestrians. *Somewhere up ahead of me.*

CHAPTER 47
1667, Port Royal, Jamaica

'A second ship?'

'Yes,' replied Rashim. 'Sir Thomas said he'd provide it for us if we wanted. And you would be the captain of it, Liam. How do you like the sound of that? Captain O'Connor?'

'Aren't you already a Captain O'Connor?' piped up Will.

'Co-captain, Will,' Liam corrected him then looked at Rashim. 'And, as it happens, more like a first mate really.'

'Nonsense,' exclaimed Rashim. 'You and I, we're *partners*, Liam. Even, *equal* partners in crime.'

'Some more equal than others,' Liam muttered then wandered over to the table where Will was perched on a stool practising writing letters of the alphabet with a quill, pot of ink and a scroll of parchment rolled out before him. Liam studied the boy's copied letters and nodded. 'Good, very good, lad. Much better. Now . . . once again.'

As Will scribbled and scratched away, Liam gazed absently out of the small windows of their rooms in the King's Head tavern down on to Queen Street, bustling with traders and merchants. 'Why do we need a second ship anyway? We did well enough with just the one last time.'

'If we'd had a second ship, we could have caught *all* of that convoy, instead of allowing two of them to slip away.'

Rashim had returned from chasing the carracks to the

captured galleon six hours later at twilight. He'd been excited at how much they'd managed to plunder, but gnashing his teeth at what more they might have had. Although they'd all hove to – and been waiting patiently to be plundered – Rashim and his men had taken so long to get round to them that two of the ships had got tired of waiting and sneaked off with the dimming light.

'If we'd had two ships, we could have herded them like sheepdogs all the way back to Port Royal.'

'Two ships, Rashim, will mean taking on more crew, more supplies for us to buy in, more paperwork.'

'And so . . . ?'

'So, it's more work, so it is . . . for me mostly. Plus –' he crossed the creaking wooden floor towards Rashim's bed – 'this isn't about you and me building up some pirate business empire. It's about somehow getting the name Pandora into a future history textbook or Wikipedia page!'

Rashim glanced pointedly at young Will. The boy was concentrating on his handwriting and, more than likely if he had heard, or was listening, that outburst wasn't going to make much sense to him. All the same, Rashim lowered his voice. 'Wikipedia page? Liam, your friends are now based in 1889. If we cause a time ripple that generates a Wikipedia page in the future, they are never going to know about it.'

'Bad example. I meant more like . . . I don't know, an article in a newspaper or perhaps a famous book, like *Treasure Island*, that uses the name Pandora in it.'

'Liam, like it or not, I do believe we're stuck here. I've been thinking about this. Maybe . . . possibly . . . just possibly, there's a chance that Maddy and Sal will pick up on something we do back here. In 2001 and with the Internet, they would have stood a much better chance. But in 1889? They only have the basic database of history they took with them. Since there's no displacement protection field, yes, that database is susceptible to changing if a time wave ripples through . . . but it would only change the data that was taken along. Not add articles to the data. So, if her database doesn't contain a big fat article on pirating in the Caribbean in the 1600s, we're . . . rather stuck here.'

Rashim settled back on his bed. 'So, why not make the most of it? We could end up being extremely wealthy men, Liam. Plantation owners, governors ourselves one day!' He leaned up on one elbow. 'You and I have such privileged knowledge in our heads, the broad course that history will take, knowledge of technology ahead of this time.' Rashim grinned. 'Look . . . I studied most of a chemistry degree in my teens. I could formulate a gunpowder that produces greater explosive energy and virtually no smoke. Think how that one thing could change the fate of wars, of nations? Perhaps that's the next innovation I'll work on to give our ships the advantage!

'Liam . . .' Rashim sat up. 'I almost . . . almost don't want to be rescued. This –' he gestured at the room, the small lead-lined windows and the sharp sunlight streaming in through them – 'this is everything! This is a world I could be happy in. You and I are going to become extremely wealthy, powerful gentlemen. We could end up owning Jamaica. Think of that! Owning a whole country!'

Liam turned away to look back at Will scratching away on the parchment, listening to the voices carrying up from the busy narrow street below. There was much in what Rashim was saying that struck a chord with him. God, yes! To be a king, a pirate king. To be free from worrying about timelines, cause and effect, contamination. To simply kick free and be an adventurer.

Jay-zus, what's not to like about that?

'And two ships, Liam? Guess what that means.'

He turned round. 'What?'

'Technically speaking, that's a fleet. People would have to call me *Admiral* Anwar.' Rashim giggled at that.

Just then they heard a sharp knock on the door.

'Who is it?' called out Liam.

'Tom, sir!'

'Enter!' bellowed Rashim.

Old Tom's face appeared round the edge of the door. 'Uh, sirs, beggin' yer pardon, but we got somethin' downstairs that needs yer comin' down and seein' to.'

CHAPTER 48
1667, Port Royal, Jamaica

Liam and Rashim emerged from the tight stairwell into the tavern's drinking hall to find the owner looking less than pleased with them.

'I won't have it, gentlemen. I won't have you turning my premises into a gathering place for their sort!'

'What's the matter?'

The tavern owner led them towards a back room, little more than a sweat box of timbers built on to the rear of the tavern. It was where his patrons were encouraged to take their painted ladies – or outside. He pulled open an oak door. 'You tell them this isn't no safe haven for damned Maroons.'

Liam's eyes adjusted to the dark, windowless space; shafts of sunlight speared down between slats of wood and the loose-woven reeds of the lean-to roof. 'I let 'em in here seeing as how they just weren't going to leave until they got to meet your friend. So, you talk to them then get 'em out of here!' The taverner turned and left the room.

There were a dozen or more slaves sitting patiently on the dirt floor, dark skin glistening with sweat in the humid and rank shack. They wore dirt-stained, sun-faded rags, frayed and threadbare, and wooden clogs – only one of them seemed to own a pair of shoes. It was he, their spokesman, who stood up.

'You not the Dark Beard man. Where he?'

Liam sighed. 'Oh right, I suppose you want to meet Captain Anwar.'

The man's eyes lit up. He smiled and nodded eagerly. 'An-wah! Great Ship Captain An-wah!'

Liam moved aside, out of the doorway, to allow Rashim to step in.

Rashim nodded politely. 'Morning.'

The slaves, as one, leaped to their feet, a collective gasp rippling among them as they pressed forward. Their spokesman turned round and angrily snapped in a glottal language. Holding out his hands to stop them crowding in on Rashim, he hushed them down then finally turned back to Rashim and Liam.

'We hears you take slave as ship man. He now is free man. Work for you?'

'Kwami,' said Liam, 'he's talking about Kwami.'

'Many knows this. You good man, Ship Captain An-wah. Good man.'

Rashim stroked the bristles on his chin. 'Uh . . . well, I don't know about that, but uh, yes, we do have a black gentleman who's been enlisted on the payroll as it happens.'

The spokesman narrowed his eyes, working his way through that sentence.

'Negro,' muttered Liam. '*Blacks* is what the plantation owners call them.'

'What?' Rashim looked at him. 'Negro is the *polite* term?' he whispered.

'Aye. In this time.'

'We good work, Mr Ship Captain. Work very hard for you. You take us on ship too?'

Rashim bit his lip thoughtfully for a moment then finally pressed his lips together. 'Well now, to be honest, we're after sailors really. Ship men? You understand? Men who actually know how to work on a ship? So –'

The man nodded vigorously and smiled widely. 'Work! Yes! Ship!'

Liam wondered how much understanding was actually going on.

'So, really, I'm sorry . . . do you understand? I can't take you on our –'

'We work. Work men. Ship men!' The spokesman reached out, grasped Rashim's hand and placed it on his upper arm, then flexed a bicep. 'See?' He encouraged Rashim to squeeze the muscle like a baker checking a freshly baked loaf.

He did so reluctantly, smiling at the man. 'Yes, jolly good. Very nice muscles, but . . .'

The spokesman grinned. 'Good worker. All us. Hard worker.'

'They're Maroons, sir,' said Old Tom. 'Runaway slaves. Nothing but bloody trouble for you, sir, an' that's the honest truth.'

'Hmmm . . .' Rashim nodded thoughtfully. 'Trouble we could probably do without.'

'Rashim?' said Liam. 'A word in private?'

They stepped out of the back of the tavern into a yard of hard dirt, gnarled tree roots emerging like unearthed bones, brittle brown fallen palm fronds and a graveyard of discarded broken clay jugs. The hubbub of Queen Street was muted by the tavern. Above them, on the low branches of a breadfruit tree, a parakeet squawked noisily.

'Tom's right, they are runaway slaves,' said Rashim. 'Someone's property and someone will be wanting them back.'

'Rashim, people are going to talk. People must have seen them come here. Anyone can see they're slaves, so how long before word gets back to whichever plantation they came from?'

'I don't know. Not long?'

'Not long. That's right. And they'll be hauled off and God knows what will happen to those poor sods.'

'Well, that's . . .' Rashim sighed. 'Well, that is just how it is, Liam. I know it is not right, but you know this even better than me – the past is full of ignorance and injustice. We don't have to be a part of it, but that doesn't mean it is down to us to put it all right.'

'You know they'll probably hang? All of those men in there? Whoever owns them will want to make an example of them.'

Rashim kicked at the dirt with a boot.

'And we just turf them out, do we? We hand them over when they come? So, where does that put us?'

'What do you mean?'

'I mean . . . does that make us innocent bystanders? Or does that make us just as bad as the slave owners?'

'It does not make *us* as bad. You and I did not enslave them.' He looked at Liam. 'And do not try to make this simpler than it is. Those slaves . . . do you want to know who *first* enslaved them? More than likely a rival African tribe. *Then* they were probably sold on to white traders or corsairs for a few beads. So who, I wonder, Liam, wins the bad-guy contest? The tribal chief who can happily enslave his own people and sell them on, or me, for not taking some moral stand right here?'

Liam squatted down and sat on the sun-bleached wood of a discarded cask. 'I'm not a do-gooder, Rashim. I'm not anyone's hero. I'm not even sure what I am any more. But . . .' He stopped, searching for a way to finish the thought. 'But I feel I kind of understand what it is to be a *product*. OK, not a slave . . . but, yes, a product.'

'You're not a product, Liam. You're a person, a human. You're my friend.'

'A human? Because me, Maddy and Sal — I don't know — somehow broke our programming, became more than the tools we were originally designed to be?'

Rashim nodded. 'Yes.'

'We ran, Rashim. We *ran* from our slave master. And that's how we became free.'

'Oh, so that is your angle, is it? That's how you want to get to me? Liken those slaves to you and the girls? That this is a similar situation?' He shook his head. 'Pfft, that is moral blackmail.'

Liam looked down at the dirt between his boots. 'Kwami is a good hire. Those other slaves will be just as good, work just as hard. What's more, freed slaves frighten the Spaniards. You saw that. They'll make a good crew.'

'They may, they may not . . . the point is they're not *free* to hire!'

'They would be if we bought them.'

Rashim frowned. 'So, now all the money we make, we throw away on charitable causes?'

'All right, then, not giving it away. What if they *owed* us? Paid us back from their share of the plunder? With our last trip, Kwami would have almost, maybe even already, managed to pay for himself.'

Rashim laughed. 'You're saying our pirate ship becomes some sort of a floating bank? A banking corporation for slaves to come knocking on to apply for a mortgage to buy their freedom?'

Liam hadn't taken the thought that far, but that seemed to more or less sum it up. 'Aye. The Pandora Banking Corporation for Slaves.' He shrugged. 'Now that's something that might catch Maddy's attention.'

'You're an idiot.'

CHAPTER 49

1889, London

Maddy slowly closed the diary and looked up. Bob and Becks were staring at her expectantly.

'Sal's gone and left us . . . as well,' she said finally.

'Saleena is now no longer part of the team?' asked Becks.

'That's right.' Maddy tossed the diary back on to her bed. 'Matter of fact, there isn't really much of a team left anyway.'

'Where has Sal gone to?' asked Bob.

'She didn't exactly say, but I can probably make an educated guess.' She crossed the floor and sat down in front of the computer monitor. 'Computer-Bob?'

> **Yes, Maddy.**

'You just sent Sal back to Mumbai, didn't you?'

> **Negative. The time-stamp she gave me was for New York, 2025.**

'Uh?' She wasn't expecting that. Sal's written goodbye – and it had been a heartfelt goodbye that Maddy suspected she'd been thinking about writing for quite some time – had said she wanted to go back to her life, to see her parents again. Not something Maddy could blame her for wanting to do. After all, she'd done just that herself in Boston. But surely she knew that was only going to end in tears. Maddy's 'home' had turned out to be someone else's.

No sign of her parents. Parents which she now suspected had

never actually ever existed, or if they did, the fading recollection she had of them – Jane and Robin Carter, middle managers at a software company, sensible, nice, middle-class, college-educated suburban parents – was of someone else's parents. A *borrowed* fading recollection.

'New York?'

> Yes, Maddy. The time–stamp she gave me was for Times Square, New York, 11:30 a.m., 7 April 2025.

'Why there and then?'

> I do not have that information, Maddy.

Then she remembered. Sal had told her once, while they were enjoying the sunshine and hotdogs in Central Park, that her father had taken her here. Maddy recalled the year . . . 2025, because it seemed so bizarre that New York could sound so different, so quickly. She'd talked of the 'scrap metal mountain' in the park, the giant walls being built round the island of Manhattan to hold back the rising Atlantic Sea. The streets with no cars on them any more.

'*New York without cars? Ya got to be kidding me,*' she remembered saying.

The year she'd said was 2025.

'I get it,' said Maddy. 'She's gone to New York to find her father. To find herself.'

'That is not logical,' said Becks.

'No . . . I guess it's not. But I can see why she might think it's worth a shot.' She turned to face the support units, standing behind her like bookends. 'For a while I was thinking the same, that maybe all the things I remember about my past life were taken from someone else. A complete person's memories?'

There was something comforting in the idea of that. All right, they may be *borrowed* memories, but if they told a complete, cohesive story of a life lived, perhaps even one that had been tragically cut short by an accident or an illness, then that was at least something to hang on to, right?

But Maddy was almost certain now that all the things she could remember were bits and pieces pulled together by someone in a hurry. A work memory: a photograph of some cluttered office space occupied by any games developer. A childhood memory or two. No problem . . . some home-made videos of a water-pistol fight on a front lawn on a hot summer's day. Or some kid blowing candles out on a birthday cake. Jesus, you could get that kind of footage off YouTube, or any other number of video archive sites.

Maddy was almost certain there had never been a 'real' Maddy Carter. Her memory was a mishmash of bits and pieces, like forensic evidence gathered from a murder scene, bagged and tagged and filed in her head. Enough bits and pieces there for her to subconsciously join the dots and create the narrative of the life she'd once lived. Just enough fleeting memories to allow her to convince herself she'd once had a life.

'She's got to do this . . . I can see that,' said Maddy. 'But I'm pretty sure it's gonna end in tears.'

'Explain, please,' said Becks.

'She won't find her father in New York. She won't find herself.' Maddy shrugged. 'The best she might find is some tourist filming footage that one day will end up in her head. Footage she thinks she saw.'

This is going to break her.

Maddy had half a mind to use the same time-stamp and go after her and try to talk her out of doing this. But she realized that, having gone this far, Sal wouldn't come back willingly. She'd have to drag her back kicking and screaming. And then what? Sal would just try it again next time Maddy's back was turned.

She has to find out for herself.

And then . . . ?

Maddy wasn't sure. Looking at the log screen, it appeared that computer-Bob had set up return windows for Sal. But whether that was something she'd actually asked for or was Bob just following the usual displacement window protocol of setting up a return, there really was no knowing. If she returned, she returned.

If not?

Then, Maddy guessed, she was choosing to 'do a Liam'. Although why the hell she was choosing *then* of all times. *Then* – 2025. Within ten years the post-oil recession would bite hard. The conflicts that would eventually lead to the oil wars in the Middle East were already stirring. And, if all of that wasn't enough, a whole bunch of environment-related hurt was coming their way: the seas rising in earnest, the toxic blooms, food shortages . . . it was going to get worse for everyone, year on year.

Backwards . . . that's the direction to go, surely? Backwards, girl. Not forwards.

CHAPTER 50
1667, Port Royal, Jamaica

'Which ship is these victuals for, sir?' asked the labourer.

Liam craned his neck to get a look at the load piled in his handcart. Sacks of coarse-milled oat grain. The *Pandora* was already fully loaded with her stockpile of non-perishables.

'That one over there.' He nodded at the low-decked and sleek brigantine berthed right next door.

The man squinted as he picked out the name of the boat, freshly painted in white on her side. 'The *Maddy Carter*?' He wrinkled his nose at that. 'Odd name for a ship, that.'

'Perfectly fine name,' replied Liam distractedly as he scanned his shopping list of supplies and ticked this particular item off. He watched the labourer as he, his boy and the mule pulling the cart rattled another dozen yards along the dockside towards the loading ramp. It rocked and wobbled across a couple of yards of water, up towards the sloop's low waist. A few moments later Old Tom had roused half a dozen of her new crew to form a human chain, and they energetically began to toss the sacks of oats one at a time to each other, up the wooden ramp and over the rail on to the deck at the top.

Liam listened to the song — little more than a melodic chant — that the black men sang, something from their distant, almost forgotten home. Tom was shaking his head and muttered derisively as he began to lend a hand.

Just then the sound of approaching cartwheels and hoofs caught Liam's attention. He turned to see a carriage emerge from the top of Queen Street, turn left and rattle along the rutted dockside towards him. The horses were finally brought to a halt by the driver in front of where the *Pandora* was tied up. A door swung open before the driver could get a hand to it and Sir Thomas emerged blinking into the daylight, cursing the wretched man for being too old and slow.

He studied the activity going on all around him: the *Pandora* was now taking on casks of drinking water, each being carefully rolled up her ramp and lifted aboard by waiting hands at the top. He finally spotted Liam and made his way over.

'Splendid! Splendid! Good to see you fellows are busy.' He looked around. 'Where's my good friend? Where's the man who's going to earn me a fortune on my investment?'

'Rashim's aboard the *Pandor*–' Liam caught sight of him, sliding down the ladder on to the main deck, then weaving his way round the rolling casks down the ramp and on to the wharf.

'Sir Thomas!' he called out as he made his way over. 'A pleasant surprise! We were not expecting you.'

No, we weren't, thought Liam. If they had, they would have made sure the slaves were down below decks and well out of sight.

'I see you renamed the sloop I gave you,' said Modyford. 'What was wrong with the *Charlotte*? Lovely name,' he said, sounding a little hurt.

'Oh . . . well . . .' Rashim looked at Liam.

'It's a superstition thing, Sir Thomas. The second ship of a fleet should always have a name with the initials M.C.'

The governor looked perplexed. 'Really?'

'Oh yes,' said Liam with a nod. 'An old maritime custom, so it is.' He tossed the ball back to Rashim. 'Isn't that so?'

'What? Oh yes . . . lots of ships with that, uh . . . that . . . those initials. Um . . . the *Marie Celeste*, uh . . . the *Marie Curie* . . . the *Miley Cyrus* . . .'

'Can't say that I've heard of any of those,' grunted Modyford. 'What odd superstitions you sailor fellows have!' He looked around again at the buzz of activity surrounding their two ships. 'Ready to set sail again?'

'Tomorrow morning, Sir Thomas.'

'Marvellous! No point delaying. The Spaniards will be hungry for their next convoy of silver from Puerto Bello. More ships on the way already, I imagine.' His beady eyes finally rested on the chain of men tossing the sacks of oat grain to each other up the ramp.

'Whose are those Negroes?' He shaded his eyes. 'Some of them look vaguely familiar.'

'Ours,' said Liam quickly. 'They're ours, Sir Thomas.'

Modyford's gaze rose up to the *Maddy Carter*'s rigging where he spotted another couple painting the shrouds with pitch.

'Slaves working aboard a ship?' He looked at Liam. 'They're only good on land, I've been told. The water spooks them like it does horses. Where did you buy them?'

'They were uh . . . part of our last haul, Sir Thomas,' said Rashim. 'Spanish slaves . . . I suppose they must have trained them up to be at ease on water.'

Modyford nodded thoughtfully. 'A group of slaves escaped from Sir Hunnyford's plantation a few weeks ago.' He shrugged apologetically. 'That's why I ask; some local scoundrel might have rounded them up and, instead of returning them to their rightful owner, sold them on to you.'

Liam shook his head. 'No, Sir Thomas, they're certainly not local ones.'

'Good. Because if they were Hunnyford's Maroons, I'd have

them taken over to his plantation, whipped, beaten, then hanged in front of the other slaves.' He nodded firmly. 'Have to make a prompt example of runaways. Be quite ruthless, I'm afraid. Even if killing them means losing all the money you paid for them. Otherwise the idea of escaping into the jungle spreads like wildfire among them. Makes them all quite unmanageable. Then, of course, you'd have to do away with the lot of them and start over with a new batch. Hugely expensive. Hugely disruptive.'

'That seems a little harsh,' said Rashim.

Modyford looked at him incredulously. 'You have to understand, my good man, the idea of *freedom* is an infection that any responsible plantation owner must be constantly vigilant for. And it is just like an infection: it spreads, corrupts. Before you know it, the disease has got a hold and you are left with savages running wild. Chaos. This entire colony relies on my harshness, as you put it. Relies on the fact that every slave knows, as a cast-iron certainty, that if he runs and he is caught . . . he will most certainly hang for it.' He looked at Liam. 'Am I right?'

Liam nodded. 'Of course you are.'

Modyford's gaze remained on the slaves a while longer then he looked back at Rashim. 'So, your raid will be on Puerto Bello itself?'

'Indeed. Word is there is silver stockpiling there as they wait for a new convoy of ships.'

Modyford nodded. 'With Morgan's continued clumsy raids along the Spanish Main, and your recent successful raid, they will be more wary now. More warships accompanying their merchant ships. Perhaps even bringing more troops to garrison their ports.'

'Which is why we are planning a quick hit-and-run shore raid,' said Rashim. 'Before reinforcements arrive.'

'Very shrewd, my friend.' He looked around once more approvingly. 'And you say you are setting sail tomorrow?'

'At first light.'

'Very good.' Modyford smiled. 'Captain Anwar, I can't wait to see what my investment in you will earn for me this time around. Godspeed and good hunting.' He turned and headed back to his carriage.

CHAPTER 51

1667, off Port Royal, Jamaica

'Sorry, Jamesey, we got no more spicy mutton,' said Cookie. 'All gone. Just the broth now. And the bread.'

Jamieson leaned forward and looked down into the serving pot. By the light of the gently swaying oil lamp hooked to a beam above, they were clearly down to a sludge pool of steaming thick gravy at the bottom.

'Dammit! I been splicing rope and un-caking salt all day. I'm bloody hungry!'

'Sorry, friend. Look, Jamesey, the broth's got the flavour of mutton right through it. Just as good for you.'

'I need some bloody meat!' Jamieson looked at the men standing behind him in the queue, their wooden bowls empty. 'We want mutton, Cookie! Not bloody gruel!'

'Sorry, lads. I'm out of it tonight.' He addressed Jamieson. 'You'll just have to make sure you're front of the queue tomorrow night, won't you?'

Jamieson glared at him, then turned to look at the man who'd just been served the last few fatty chunks of meat. He was already sitting down and dipping a spoon hungrily into the thick spiced broth.

'Ain't right, Cookie,' he muttered. 'Ain't right. Worked twice as hard as anyone today. Spliced the ropes once over again cos those fools ain't done it right the first time. What's more,

286

dammit, I already served on this ship. I ain't a newcomer.' He ducked under a looping shroud, crossed the main deck and stood over the man who'd just had the last of the meat. He was squatting on his haunches as he ate, wooden clogs off his feet and placed tidily in front of him.

'What the hell're you smiling at, Negro?'

Jamieson looked at the other runaways, all twelve of them huddled closely together, squatting the same way and all grinning anxiously up at him, small white teeth in night-black faces. 'You slaves *laughin*' at me?'

'My name . . . John,' said the one with the clogs. 'Not Neg-ro.'

'No, it ain't. Your *real* name is some fool-sounding Diji-Bungo-Bongo savage name.'

'My name John. *John Shoe*. Not slave now. Ship man, like you.' He said that still politely smiling, which angered Jamieson even more.

'No, you ain't! You ain't a damned sailor. You're *deadweight*. All of you useless dirty plantation Maroons! Can't even tie a simple bloody *clove hitch*. Good for carryin' an' fetchin' an' not much else!'

John Shoe's smile quickly faded. 'We learn. We work.'

'You'll learn nothing. You and your kind's dumb as mules. Shouldn't even be on this ship.' Jamieson bent down and picked up one of his wooden clogs.

John Shoe dropped his bowl on the floor and reached out to grab hold of the other one. 'Mine! My shoe!'

Jamieson held the weathered clog by its toe and shook his head, amused by the thing. 'What? This is so goddamned precious to you, you *named* yourself after it? Mr Shoe!' He laughed at that. 'You Negroes! What the hell ya goin' to do with yer money anyway? Buy more of these?'

'Give me shoe!'

'Oh, you want it back? Go fetch it!' He tossed it over the rail. It disappeared into the darkness followed a moment later by the sound of a faint splash.

'Jamie-son!'

Jamieson turned to see Kwami standing on the other side of the deck. '*You* go fetch!'

'Oh, now . . . there we are!' Jamieson replied, raising his voice for everyone to hear. 'There we are, gents! So, this is what a Maroon looks like soon as he got a bit of money of his own! Tryin' to dress up like some *fancy gentleman*!'

Kwami crossed the deck and stopped a stride short. He looked down at his clothes, smarter than most of the other men. He wore a silk scarf round his broad neck. 'Better this things . . . better than just drink!'

'What? Oh, you think those pretty clothes change you? Huh? Make you better than me? Better than a man who's served seven years at sea? Weathered countless godless storms and got me scars, front an' back, fightin' them Spaniards!' He shook his head. 'See? I've *earned* the bloody right to call myself a sailor! But you? All you have is a fancy yard of silk.'

'I am a seaman.'

'Oh, are you? Is that it? We *equal* now?'

'You drink too much, Jamie-son.'

Jamieson clamped his lips shut; he was shaking with rage. He drew a knife from his belt.

'Hoy! Jamesey man,' called out Gunny. 'Why don't you put that thing away? There'll be mutton again tomorrow.'

'Shut up, Gunny!' He turned to Kwami, the knife held out at arm's length, its tip wavering and glinting in the space between them. 'I'll give you a scar then maybe you might start to look like a proper –'

Out of the gloom a hand suddenly emerged and wrapped round Jamieson's wrist. 'Whuh?'

Liam twisted it sharply and the blade clattered to the deck. With his other hand, he snatched a fistful of Jamieson's dreadlocked hair and yanked it back hard. Liam grimaced as he caught a fetid blast of the man's breath. 'Yup, Rashim, he's been drinking again.'

Rashim emerged into the pool of light cast from the oil lamp above Cookie's serving pot. 'Drinking. That's one breach of contract.' He walked over, stooped, picked up the knife. 'Fighting among the crew? That's another breach right there.' He gestured at Liam to follow him to the ship's rail. Liam pulled the man roughly by his hair.

'Goddammit, you let go of me, *boy*!'

'Ahh,' said Rashim with a smile, 'and insubordination. That's another. Three strikes.'

'This ain't right!' growled Jamieson. 'THIS AIN'T RIGHT!'

'Really?'

'Them damned Negroes! They're no good! They're a waste of –'

'Every man aboard my ships will have a chance to prove their worth, Jamieson. That's how this works, you see? No good? Then off you go and work somewhere else.'

'Them runaways is no good! You'll see that, by God!'

'Well, we shall just have to find out for ourselves, won't we?'

Rashim looked out into the darkness. Across the shallow harbour the faint flicker of nightwatchmen's fires along the north docks glinted on the becalmed water. A five-minute swim ashore, no more than that. He nodded at Liam.

'You really are more trouble than you're worth,' Liam muttered into Jamieson's ear. 'Off you go, then.' With a hard shove to Jamieson's chest, he pushed him over the rail. The man disappeared into the darkness and a moment after the splash had subsided they heard the even sound of strokes as he began to swim for shore.

'Oh, and if you find that shoe floating out there . . . !' called Liam. 'Do us a favour and toss it back aboard, will you?'

Rashim made his way towards the swinging lamp and stood beneath it. 'Gentlemen, let me be very clear on this. You all signed the charter. So, there will be no drinking, no fighting until the job is done.' He stroked his chin. 'And there you have it.' He was about to turn and go.

'Actually, one more thing. Jamieson raised a valid point. Every man will do his job, earn his share. Or they will forfeit it. There will be no favourites.'

CHAPTER 52

1667, off the coast of Puerto Bello

'No, no, no!' Gunny shook his head impatiently. 'Yer doin' it all wrong!' He snatched the swab off the young black man. 'What's yer name again?'

'David,' he mumbled, looking down at his feet.

'You twist it as you push it down, right? Twist it? Understand?' Gunny demonstrated, pulled it out of the cannon's barrel then handed it back to him. 'Now you do it.'

The young man reluctantly eased the rag-covered end in and warily began turning the pole cautiously, slowly in his hands, wide eyes regarding the cannon as if he was foolishly prodding a slumbering giant with a stick.

'Faster! You got to do it quicker than that, boy!' He looked at his other trainees, all of them standing well back from the cannon. The first swab and load he'd done on his own to demonstrate, then fired a shot of wadding. The boom had terrified his trainee gun crew such that they'd scrambled in alarm towards the far end of the gun deck. It had taken him nearly ten minutes to coax them back towards the still smoking cannon. He'd even sat astride the warm barrel to show them it wasn't some monster that was going to rear up and swallow him whole.

The swabbing finally done, the rod extracted, he beckoned at them for another volunteer to step forward. 'Come on, who's next?'

They shuffled uncomfortably.

'Come on, it ain't gonna bite.'

One of them stepped forward. Gunny smiled. 'Aye, good man . . . what's yer name?'

He nodded. 'Simon, boss.'

'*Gunny* is good enough. Now . . . here, take this.' He handed over a small bag of powder. 'This is the stuff ya got to be wary of.' He slapped the top of the cannon. 'Not this ol' thing. Without the powder, this is just a big ol' chunk of iron. Now . . . Simon . . . we put that charge bag in the mouth and then we're gonna ram it all the way down. Just like I did last time?'

The man nodded. Eased the packet of powder in, then took the ramrod from Gunny and pushed it carefully all the way down.

'And a couple of firm pats.' Gunny watched him do that. 'Good. Now . . . we ram down some wadding.' Gunny reached for a handful of straw wadding and pushed it into the barrel. 'Now, Simon, push that all the way down and a couple more pats.'

Job done, he nodded. 'If we was firing in battle, the next thing would be the cannonball, but . . . we ain't gonna waste any of those today. We'll just fire the wadding again.' Gunny grinned. 'So, who wants to be the gunner and fire this big beauty?'

The trainees stared back anxiously.

'Look, lads, it really isn't going to —'

'I will.' John Shoe stepped forward.

'Good man. Come here . . . this end of the cannon.' He pointed to a small hole on the top of the rear end of the cannon. 'This, John, this is what wakes our monster up. The touch hole.' Gunny produced a foot-long metal rod with a sharpened tip and pushed it into the hole. 'Clearing it for blockage and now piercing a hole in that bag of powder.'

'Charge . . . bag.'

Gunny nodded. 'That's right. Well remembered. Then . . . we pour a little more powder into the touch hole. That's called the primer.'

John nodded, his intense face lined with concentration. 'Primer.'

'Now, my friend –' he produced a linstock with a smouldering twist of rope on the end of it – 'we're ready to fire.' He looked at John. 'You ready?'

John licked his lips nervously, nodded quickly. 'Yes, boss.'

'Get down low, look along the barrel . . . that's it. Now see our *Maddy Carter*? That's our target. We want to aim right at her hull. See how we're swaying slightly, that she's goin' up an' down as we sway?'

John nodded.

'We want to aim for just above her hull. We want this cannon to fire just a finger above because the shot will drop in flight. You understand what I'm saying?'

'Yes, boss.'

'But we gotta light the touch hole about two seconds before we want it to fire. Cos that's how long it takes for the primer to burn through to the charge bag. So, the gunner has to judge the timing of the sway and, when he's ready, call the warning, "*Have a care*".'

'Have . . . a . . . care?'

'That's right, it means everyone stand clear of the cannon and cover their ears.'

John nodded. The smouldering rope quivered on the end of the linstock.

'Don't be afraid, man.' Gunny rested a hand on his shoulder. 'S'gonna be just fine.' He took a step back. 'So . . . when you're ready, John . . . just touch that hole.'

Gunny glanced at his other trainees. All of them were

grimacing in anticipation. 'No running away this time, lads, right?' He squatted down to look out of the porthole of the next cannon along and waited.

John hunkered down, his chin almost touching the cannon's barrel as he narrowed his eyes and stared down it out through the gun's porthole at the rolling horizon and the low profile of the ship two hundred yards away, watching it sedately rise and fall. Finally . . .

'Have . . . care!' He touched the rope to the hole and stepped smartly back as the primer sparked and fizzed. The cannon boomed and leaped back.

Gunny watched the wadding fly out across the water and disintegrate fifty yards out, descending to the water and leaving arc trails of smoke. He turned to look at his trainees, half expecting them to have vanished once again. But they were still there, standing amid the swirls of smoke, hands still clasped over their ears.

The shot was good. Perfectly judged. As John Shoe had touched the hole, so Gunny had absently tapped his thumb on his thigh.

He nodded. 'Good work, lads! I think we can make a gun crew of you.'

The gun deck echoed with their delight, perhaps tinged with a little relief, a high-pitched yipping and howling. He stepped over a coil of rope towards John and slapped him firmly on the shoulder. 'And you, sir, I think have the makings of a fine gunner.'

John Shoe beamed with pleasure. 'Thank you, boss!'

'Gunny, right? That's what you call me.' He turned to the others, still yipping with excitement. 'Right! Let's do this again.'

Liam watched a plume of smoke drifting in the wake of the *Pandora*. The faint intermittent boom of cannon drill had been going on all morning. And to his right, on the *Maddy Carter*'s main deck, it was being complemented by the crack of musket fire as the French marksman, Pasquinel, put some of their new recruits through the basics of loading and firing. Just as they had done with the cannon drill, they made sure some of the runaways were being included. The sooner the rest of the crew saw these men could carry and use weapons as well as them, the sooner the mutterings about them would cease.

He shaded his eyes and scanned the afterdeck of the *Pandora*. There he could make out the distinct form of Rashim, taking another sun reading with his sextant. He seemed to take a nerdish delight in playing with the device, constantly reconfirming their position with increasing precision and reminding Liam how easy it all was. In this time, the art of navigation and those who practised it well were treated with the same reverential awe and respect as people in the twenty-first century seemed to treat quantum physicists. As if the practice was some dark art that only the anointed few, those with almost other-worldly intelligence, could comprehend.

He suspected that half the time Rashim was actually merely posing with the thing. Secretly savouring the knowledge that half his crew were quietly watching his mysterious little fiddlings with the sextant and the jotting down of cryptic notes and muttering to each other, '*Aye, see that man over there? Bleedin' genius 'e is.*'

Liam smiled. Perhaps that's what Rashim missed the most being stuck here in the past, the chance to show off his geekery, his pointy-headed rocket-science knowledge. Precious little opportunity to do that here in a world without computers, where the cutting edge of science was a clockwork model of the solar system or a course of leeches for any given illness.

Perhaps it was glory-hunting, vanity on Rashim's part, that

he was tempted to take on Modyford's suggestion that they try their hand at raiding Puerto Bello itself. At first glance a rather foolhardy proposition. The small settlement was at the end of a narrow bay protected on the way in on one side by a fort, San Felipe, with twelve cannons, on the other side by another fort, Castillo Santiago with thirty-two cannons. The settlement itself was overlooked by a third fort, San Geronimo, with a company-strength garrison of troops permanently stationed there.

Recklessly foolish at first glance, but then Puerto Bello was the shipping point for all the gold being brought up from Peru, bound for Spain. It was stockpiled in the garrison fortress, building up and up until another convoy of Spanish merchant ships arrived. Then it was hastily loaded aboard and the ships turned round, hoping to make best speed back for Spain: the first leg of the journey, through the Caribbean, was the most hazardous as they hoped desperately to avoid being spotted by any pirates.

Modyford had suggested the stockpile at Puerto Bello might be even greater than normal given the last-minute exodus of valuables from Cuba in advance of Morgan's poorly concealed and loudly trumpeted preparations for the raid.

The bay, sketched out on parchment by one of Modyford's spies, looked daunting: long, narrow and clearly overlooked by the fortifications. But then it was the other smaller details that changed everything, the kind of details an unassuming fisherman wandering around could easily pick up. The garrison was grossly under strength. San Felipe should have had a hundred men, but in fact had less than fifty. Castillo Santiago, the main fortification, should have had two hundred men, but was down to approximately sixty, many of whom were untrained as gunners. San Geronimo, in the town, wasn't even finished and was occupied by an army engineer, seven labourers and a dozen work mules.

Easy pickings. And knowing these titbits, Liam was now almost as fired up about this raid as Rashim. Perhaps in two days' time they'd be sailing back to Jamaica with a greater personal wealth stowed in the two ships' holds than the governor of Jamaica himself.

It's got to be all about speed and stealth; about disguising how few of them there were . . . convincing the Spanish soldiers they were staring out into the night at a much larger invasion force.

Liam smiled. They had a rather simple yet ingenious plan lined up.

CHAPTER 53

1667, San Felipe, Puerto Bello

The single crack of a musket shot did the job. Within a minute, Liam could see a pair of softly glowing oil lamps bobbing along the stonework wall of San Felipe and, silhouetted against their amber aura, the heads of several men looking out into the dark in the direction the shot had come from.

'All right, Will . . . light 'em up, lad!' he whispered.

Will struck a flint, lit the end of his torch, then ran along the line of men, touching his torch against theirs. Soon all thirty men of Liam's landing party held a flaming torch in each hand and were lighting others that had been stuck into the ground next to several dozen crudely constructed 'scarecrows': four- and five-foot-tall stakes of wood with crossbars tied to them and rags of clothing draped over them topped by woollen caps. Soon just over a hundred torches flickered in a long, uneven line a hundred yards down the slope from the fort.

It had taken them nearly seven hours since anchoring in the next cove. All but a skeleton crew had been left behind on each ship; the rest had rowed ashore and crossed the rugged terrain by the pale light of the moon and stars. Liam's raiding party numbered thirty. Rashim had taken the rest, a hundred and seven of them, and rowed across the bay to duplicate the very same ruse on the landward side of the other fort, Castillo Santiago.

Now Liam could see the glow of a dozen lamps along the wall, and could faintly hear Spanish voices calling to each other.

'OK . . . so we've got their attention now.'

He reached for the white parlay flag beside him and grabbed the torch that Will was holding. 'You stay right here, Will.'

'Be careful, sir.'

'Oh, I plan to be.'

Liam strode forward, sweeping the flag to and fro in front of him, up the steep, boulder-strewn hillside towards the south wall of the fort, hoping desperately that the flickering torch he was holding in his other hand was clearly illuminating the flag. Fifty yards short, he heard a solitary musket crack and saw a tongue of muzzle flash. A shot whistled close by.

'Hey! Parlay!'

A voice from the wall barked a command, which Liam could only hope was a ceasefire order. 'I wish to speak to your commanding officer!' he yelled. He approached another dozen yards, the steep incline finally giving way to more even ground now. A small wooden doorway creaked open at the base of the wall and three men emerged, one of them carrying an oil lamp in one hand.

'I want to speak to your commanding officer!' Liam called out again.

'English?' a heavily accented voice crossed the ground to him.

Irish actually, he nearly found himself replying. And then realized that would be a lie anyway.

'Yes! English!'

One of the men stepped forward, leaving the other two behind. Liam and the lone Spaniard slowly approached each other until they were half a dozen yards apart.

'Do you speak English?'

The man, young and slender, still blinking sleep out of his

eyes, tilted his head and shrugged as he finished buttoning his tunic. 'Little English. *Si*. Yes.'

'Are you the fort commander?'

'*Si*, Captain Mendoza. Yes. What . . . is . . . this?'

'This is a raid, sir. Your fort is surrounded. I have a two-company strength with me. Two hundred muskets trained on you and your men. And . . . *five* ships out in the bay ready to bombard your fort on my command.' Liam took another step forward. 'There's no need for a massacre, Captain. I strongly recommend you surrender.'

The young officer glanced past Liam at the line of flickering torches, the dancing light catching the glint of musket barrels here and there. Liam could see his lips move as he quickly made a rough count.

'Your men will not be harmed, sir. They will be disarmed and they will be confined to this fort, but none will be harmed. You have my word on this.'

The officer huffed indignantly. 'Other men . . . soldiers . . . come from Puerto Bello soon. They see your flame . . . they come.'

Liam shook his head and smiled. 'We know how few men you have garrisoned here. Less than fifty in this fort. We know the men in Castillo Santiago number less than a hundred. No one will be coming to relieve you. Captain, you should surrender.'

'My men . . . will fight.'

'And if they do, you understand what will happen? They will all die.' Liam turned and gestured at the line of torches downhill. 'These are not soldiers, you understand. They are pirates. There is no honour among them, no discipline. I am a gentleman, sir, but those men down there? They are *animals*. Buccaneers. Maroons. *Wild men*. Once the fighting starts, there will be no quarter. No prisoners taken. And you, sir . . . I will try my best to protect you, but . . . I can make no promises.'

The officer took a moment to digest that. 'Surrender. My men . . . not harmed?'

'You have my word. You must understand, it is best for you that this does not become a fight.'

Captain Mendoza took another moment before finally nodding. 'What do you want of me?'

'Have your men stack their muskets outside your gate. I will count the muskets when you are done and will expect to see no less than fifty. Do you understand?'

'*Si.*'

'And also the powder for your cannons. This should be set outside your gates as well. When this is done, your men should return to their barracks and they will be kept there and guarded until our business here is finished.'

'What is your *business*, *señor*?'

'The gold in Puerto Bello. Nothing more. This town will not be looted. The civilians will not be harmed in any way.'

'You can *promise* this? With your wild men . . . your savages?'

'I can give them orders. They follow them . . . *mostly*.' Liam shrugged. 'Just help me, Captain Mendoza. Let's not make them too angry, too *uncontrollable*, with an unnecessary fight up here on this hill. Eh?'

The officer narrowed his eyes and once more gazed down at the flickering torches and the glint of drawn blades and musket barrels among them. He could hear the faint cries and yips of excited voices coming up the hill towards him. A chilling sound. Men clearly spoiling for loot and, failing that prize, thirsting for a Spanish scalp or two as a consolation.

Finally he nodded. '*Si* . . . I agree this.'

'Good. Then you have an hour to place your arsenal of

301

weapons outside. Is that understood? When you are done, signal to me.'

'*Si, señor.*'

Liam nodded. 'Better get started then, eh?'

The officer dipped his head with a quick cordial salutation then turned to make his way back to his waiting men. Liam waited until he was out of earshot before letting out a long, ragged sigh of relief.

Bleedin' hell. That was easier than I thought it was going to be.

CHAPTER 54

1667, Castillo Santiago, Puerto Bello

Dawn was nearly breaking by the time Rashim had his larger party of men in place. The plan had been to attempt the same ruse on Castillo Santiago – under cover of night to appear to be a much larger force. But with the sky growing paler and the sun soon to breach the horizon, another approach was going to be required. At least, if Modyford's spy was to be believed, they did in fact have the numerical advantage: 107 men to approximately 60.

Almost double. But that advantage would be negated if they had to storm and take the fort. Surrounding the fort on three sides was open ground, ground that had been hacked clear of trees and undergrowth to provide the defenders with a clear line of fire. Even clearer now the last of the night had slipped away. Any approach was going to be immediately spotted by the fort lookout and they were going to come under musket fire and, by the look of it, within the arc of fire of at least two cannons on each side.

'Marvellous,' he muttered.

The situation was quite clear. The fort had to be taken before they could do anything else; it was positioned in such a way as to not only command the entrance to the bay but also overlook the small settlement of Puerto Bello. If they simply attempted to skirt round it and head towards the town and the third –

unfinished – fort, Geronimo, Castillo Santiago's cannons could fire at leisure on them. Equally, they needed to bring their two ships into the bay and right up to the town to load their plunder aboard. The ships would be vulnerable to those cannons too.

Rashim needed to take the damned fort.

'Monsieur Anwar,' said Pasquinel. 'Your orders?' The Frenchman stood beside him, surveying the situation for himself as he leaned against the long barrel of his own hunting rifle, his bearded chin resting on the muzzle. 'You 'ave a problem, I think, yes?'

'That wretched fort is my problem.' Rashim looked around. On the left side of the fort, a few hundred yards away, he noted a small hillock topped with a few sparse silk cotton trees. 'What accurate range do you have with that rifle of yours?'

Pasquinel noted the same hill, narrowed his eyes and sucked air between his lips with a soft whistle. He reached down to the ground, grabbed a fistful of powder-dry dirt, tossed it into the air and watched it drop in a dusty cloud down to his feet. 'No wind today. Is good.' He looked again at the hill. 'From there?' He nodded slowly. '*Oui*, I can be accurate.'

'How accurate?'

Pasquinel drilled a finger on his temple. 'Head, maybe.'

'Beyond range of their muskets?'

'Yes, of course.' He smiled. 'But not their cannon.'

The hillock appeared to be high enough to look down on to the fort. Especially if he could gain an extra few yards in height and climb one of those trees.

'Well, perhaps while they still seem to be fast asleep . . . you can make your way over there without being seen?'

'*Oui*.'

'And –' Rashim had the vaguest notion of a plan B forming – 'if you watched me very closely from there, perhaps I could nominate a high-value target for you to take out?'

His brow rumpled. 'Pardon?'

Rashim explained the roughly formed plan he had in mind. Not so much a plan as an opportunity that might just present itself. When he'd finished, the Frenchman was grinning, sly as a fox.

Colonel Fernandez watched a dark-skinned man wearing a frock coat with fancy lace cuffs and a tricorn hat that boasted a plume of ostrich feathers stride across the weed-tufted ground towards his fort. He was carrying a white flag above his head. And that was the first sight that unsettled Fernandez. The second thing that unsettled him was the sight of dozens of other armed men stirring at the edge of the woodland nearby.

Dozens? For all he could see it might just as easily be hundreds.

'*Madre de Dios* . . . are we being invaded?'

He had warned the regional governor that Puerto Bello was surely soon going to become a likely target for the increasingly ambitious and greedy English pirates. Fernandez had warned him time and time again that the defences for the bay were scandalously inadequate and ill-prepared for a land raid. He had warned him the land raids on Cuba might well be duplicated here one day soon. Well, now it seemed the day had finally come.

The garrison drummer was sounding the alarm for his company of men to muster to their stations on the walls. But it was barely a company, mostly made up of old men who should be telling war stories to their doting grandchildren, and young boys, many still too fresh-faced to warrant the use of a razor.

He watched the approaching man hesitantly pacing towards

the wall beneath his fluttering flag of truce, finally coming to a halt.

'Good morning!' the man in the tricorn hat called up. 'Am I speaking to the commander here?'

English. These are *pirates, then.*

Fernandez nodded. 'Colonel Fernandez. And who do I have the courtesy of speaking to?'

'Captain Rashim Anwar – privateer licensed out of Port Royal and on the governor's business.' He took off his plumed tricorn hat and bowed theatrically. 'We have come to steal all your gold!' he added, smiling like the devil himself.

'You come to seek our surrender, I take it.'

'I wish to discuss terms with you, Colonel.'

Fernandez stroked the silver-grey bristles of his waxed moustache as he surveyed the men in the distance, stirring restlessly in the shade of the trees like a pack of hungry wolves. It wouldn't hurt to hear what this olive-skinned man had to say. Perhaps in doing so the pirate captain might let slip some crucial details of his plans. 'I will listen to your terms, Captain, but, understand this, I will not surrender this fort to you.'

The fort's oak gates cracked open for Rashim and he was ushered in and quickly escorted up some stone steps to meet the colonel standing on the cannon emplacement above the gate.

Rashim found himself facing the man he'd greeted moments ago over the battlements: a short, moustachioed man in his fifties with a pronounced pot belly, exaggerated by the high waistband of his white breeches. He was accompanied by a younger officer in his thirties, who looked ashen-faced at the figures moving menacingly back and forth beneath the distant trees. There was another older officer with thick dark grey mutton-chop whiskers and the uniform of an artillery officer.

'Fernandez, is it?' said Rashim.

'*Colonel* Fernandez,' he replied stiffly. 'Now say what you have to say.'

Rashim nodded, then glanced quickly over the battlements at the paling sky and the glow of the sun peeking over the top of the nearby hill. 'My fleet are assembled several miles down the coast.' Fleet? Strictly speaking, it was technically a *fleet* . . . of two. 'Our spies have informed us of how under strength your garrison is. How few men you have, the state of disrepair of your fortifications, how few of your cannons are serviceable —'

'Then your spies have been unreliable. Our garrison is at full strength. And our cannons are all working. In fact . . . this gentleman —' Fernandez nodded to his left, at the man sporting thick sideburns — 'my chief of artillery, Sergeant Vasquez, is a renowned gunner. He will be certain to annihilate your ships the moment they attempt to enter this bay.'

Rashim glanced at the man. Dark eyes glared at him from beneath wiry grey eyebrows that flared out like dragonfly wings. He'd decided this colonel was *the one*. But, on second thoughts, perhaps the artillery sergeant was as much if not more important.

'My ships will focus their firepower on this fort before proceeding up the bay, Colonel. I have, uh . . . five — *six* ships, each of them carrying twenty guns. A hundred and twenty cannons to your two dozen.'

Fernandez smiled, clearly suspecting an exaggeration. Rashim inwardly cursed his inability to tell a lie fluidly, without fumbling the words, or all too obviously scratching the tip of his nose.

'Then, *pirate*,' said Fernandez, 'enter the bay and show me the strength of your fleet.'

The ashen-faced younger man spoke quickly in Spanish to his colonel. The old man replied angrily, snapping at him. Shutting him up. He looked once again, nervously, out at the men gathered at the edge of the treeline.

307

'Your second-in-command seems less assured of victory than you, Colonel.'

'He is young and inexperienced,' he replied gruffly.

Rashim smiled at the young man. 'You're quite right to be frightened. My men are the most vicious —'

'Captain Anwar,' cut in Fernandez, 'if you have terms to discuss, please proceed with telling us them. Otherwise —' he splayed his hands — 'our business here is concluded.'

Rashim realized his business here was concluded. The colonel wasn't about to surrender, no matter what terms Rashim offered. Any further talk was wasting time. In any case he now had what he wanted. Information.

'I see, Colonel, that you are a brave man. That surrender here is out of the question. In which case, sir,' Rashim dipped his head politely, 'allow me to wish you the best of luck.' He extended his hand towards Fernandez. The colonel looked at it awkwardly for a moment then grasped it firmly. Rashim felt the slightest tug of regret at that.

Rashim let his hand go and turned to the artillery sergeant. 'And you, sir, good luck also to you. May your cannons not . . . uh . . . not misfire and your balls fire true . . . or something.' Colonel Fernandez translated that into Spanish. The sergeant's scowl deepened, but all the same he acknowledged the gesture by grasping Rashim's hand and shaking it roughly.

Rashim lifted his tricorn hat and bowed theatrically. 'Good day, gentlemen,' he said and turned to go.

'Pirate!'

Rashim turned back to face them. It was the young officer who had just called out. His cheeks were red with anger, or perhaps they were burning with the shame of being passed over.

'Pirate, why is it you not shakes *my* hand?' He extended his own, waiting for Rashim to grasp it.

'I . . . I, uh . . .'

He wanted to leave. Now. He needed to be on his way down to the gate, escorted through it and heading back to his men. Now. Rashim glanced once again over the battlements at the hill, at the gnarled guango tree on its brow, and fancied he saw the stirring of movement in its branches, the glint of gun metal. He hoped to God he'd made it perfectly clear to the Frenchman to wait until he was well clear of the fort before picking off his targets.

But just then he saw a flicker of muzzle flash, a puff of smoke emerge from the branches of the tree. A half second later, a sizeable chunk of the back of Colonel Fernandez' head exploded and, as he slowly, lifelessly, dropped to his knees, the distant sound of the shot finally arrived.

CHAPTER 55

1667, Castillo Santiago, Puerto Bello

Pasquinel was already certain his shot was true without waiting for the smoke to clear to see for himself. Already he was tapping in a measure of powder from his horn into the long barrel, while balanced on a branch. He braced his back against the trunk to help hold his balance as he needed both hands to recharge his gun.

The short, round-bellied Spaniard was down now, he could see that. The other men standing on the platform appeared to be in shock or still trying to understand what had just happened. Good.

He loaded in the next ball with some wadding and quickly thrust it down the barrel on to firmly pressed powder with his ramrod.

Still standing there. One of the Spaniards was now stirring, the other thickset one. That was his other target. The other one whose hand Captain Anwar had shook. He shouldered the rifle, rested it in the fork of the branch directly in front of him and squinted down the weapon's long barrel, his leathery cheek resting against the warm metal.

Pasquinel sighted the thickset man. He was now squatting down beside the other. Now understanding, turning round to look out across the battlements at the surrounding sparse terrain. Now looking directly at him, or at least looking at the tree in which he was perched, and realizing that was where the shot must have come from.

Pasquinel raised his aim ever so slightly: two hands' breadth at this distance to allow for the drop in-flight, three hands' breadth to the left to allow for the gentle westerly breeze this morning. He pulled the trigger and his view of the man's wide-eyed face, his dark sideburns, the still-frozen other Spaniard and Captain Rashim looking almost as alarmed as the man about to die – the entire scene was suddenly lost behind a billowing cloud of swirling powder smoke.

The artillery officer staggered backwards over the body of his colonel, clutching at his throat. He fell over the colonel and continued writhing on the floor with a gurgling sound as the gentle peal of the second shot finally arrived. The young officer stirred to life, at last understanding both men hadn't spouted gouts of blood and gristle for no reason. He leaped across the platform and grasped Rashim roughly by the arm.

'*Madre de Dios!*'

The young man quickly locked him in a half nelson and spun him round to use him as a shield. Rashim now found himself hoping to God that Pasquinel was not attempting to line up a third shot in an attempt to 'save' him.

'You trick us!' the officer gasped. He locked his other arm tightly round Rashim's throat. 'You . . . you *mark* us to your men out there!'

Rashim nodded. 'They have . . .' He struggled to talk, his voice a choked burbling. 'They have orders to target the officers first. You're next.'

The man's eyes darted from the hillock to the treeline to the rooftops and the spire of Puerto Bello's nearby church.

'Surrenderrr,' gurgled Rashim. 'Save . . . save your men. Save yourself.'

The young officer looked almost ready to make that decision. As he dragged Rashim from one side to the other, Rashim caught a fleeting glance of the low stone walls of San Felipe across the bay. Above it, the Spanish flag was no longer fluttering. In its place hung *their* flag raised high above the gatehouse.

'Loo–!' Rashim managed to squeeze out of his windpipe. He pointed across the bay. 'Loo–! There!'

The young man followed the direction he was pointing, then also noted that the fort's colours had changed.

'Oooh . . . *Dios mio* . . .'

'S'overrrghh,' gasped Rashim. He struggled to loosen the man's iron lock on his windpipe. 'It's over. San Felipe has already fallen. Do you see?'

The man's white-knuckled fist loosened around Rashim's throat. He wriggled and pulled himself free, gasping for breath for a moment.

'So . . . uh . . . why not do yourself a favour?' Rashim finally managed to croak. 'Surrender?'

CHAPTER 56

2025, New York

Central Park was just as she remembered it. The lake was drained, leaving a large concrete basin, and that's where they'd started stacking the city's cars, buses, coaches, trucks that operated using petrol. Several large industrial compactors had been installed beside the dried lake – 'car crushers' – that day and night had for the last few years been grinding their way through cars and spitting out jagged cubes of compacted metal and plastic.

But the cars had been arriving in Central Park on the back of trailers, faster than the compactors could make cubes. The vehicles, piled haphazardly on top of each other like discarded, rusty toys, had spilled out beyond the lake. Now the authorities had chain-linked a perimeter that took in most of the centre portion, including the Ramble, Strawberry Fields, Bethesda Fountain.

Children's playgrounds, all soft tarmac and roundabouts and swings, bandstands and park benches, giant outdoor chess sets and coffee 'n' bagel stands, all buried beneath a forest of six to seven-storey rusting towers of useless vehicles, all waiting their time, like prisoners on death row, to be crushed into cubes and carried away.

Sal watched the enormous airship finish winching up the last pallets of crushed metal into the dark bowels of its belly. It hung like a low storm cloud casting a shadow across most of the park.

She'd been late, though. She wanted to get here for midday, because that's how she remembered it. Father and her, standing here, or hereabouts, gawping up at the huge vessel as it carefully navigated its approach over the tall city skyline and then descended into the open space above the park. Midday, they'd been standing right here. Watching the ship arrive and begin the loading process.

Now it was twenty past. There'd been an incident down on Broadway and the bus (an electric one, of course) she'd decided to take up to the park had been caught in a traffic jam. She'd pleaded with the driver to let her off and walk, but after patiently saying no to her three times he'd closed his plastic talk-hatch on her to shut her up.

Sal realized she'd arrived five minutes too late. The pair of them would have been standing here five minutes ago, Papaji and Saleena. That stopped her short. She realized she'd thought of the girl as someone else for the first time. Not Father and *me* . . . but Father and *Saleena*.

An odd thing. A strange sensation, seeing the person she 'was' as another person entirely. Some stranger who was standing with Father . . .

Instead of me.

Those three words crystallized something in her mind. Brought to the foreground a notion that had been lurking around in the background like a ghostly apparition sulking in a dusty attic.

Who's to say you're not the real Saleena Vikram? Hmm?

She watched another fifty-foot-wide pallet of scrap-metal cubes being lifted up into the sky, swinging gently on carbon-fibre cables and chains as it ascended. Again, she scanned the onlookers. Thirty or forty people, a few tourists among them, but mostly the motley assortment of alcoholics, addicts and vagrants that had begun to use the park as a flop centre. On colder nights those abandoned cars with windscreens and side windows still intact afforded at least some protection from the elements.

No Mr Vikram and his twelve-year-old daughter.

Sal cursed. She racked her brains to try and remember where they'd gone to next. Was it the museum? No. That was already in the process of being closed down. Where else? She couldn't remember. That day's memory had been all about this spectacular sight. She knew where Father had booked them into for the week, though. She remembered the name of the hotel. Remembered that seedy area. She remembered Papaji had apologized to her after they'd checked in. He'd told her it had looked prettier when he'd booked it online.

'So, can I help you?'

The hotel certainly wasn't an expensive one. It was at the southern end of Broadway, in Lower Manhattan, where neighbourhoods like Little Italy, Chinatown and Soho converged. Once upon a time, Father had said, this was a nice place to live. A place where artists and poets met, where waiters hoping to one day be actors hung out with clerks hoping to one day become playwrights and planned scripts they hoped would one day end up on Broadway.

Bohemian, that was the word Father used.

Now it looked like a place only unpublished writers, unappreciated artists might choose to live. Every shop, what few of them there were, sported tough wire grilles over their windows and doors. Every counter inside seemed to have another grille to protect the lowly paid, sullen-eyed till-jockey beyond.

'Miss?'

Sal looked at the hotel clerk. He was sitting on a stool behind his own protective grille, his attention more on a vintage comedy digi-channel than it was on her. Some milk-skinned, lanky young man was goofing around in a kids' ball pool squawking 'Bazinga!' for some reason. The clerk seemed to find it funny.

'I . . . I lost my hotel room key.'

'Lost your keycard? That was stoopid of you, wasn't it?' He sighed. 'I'll have to code you a new one. What's the room number?'

'I . . . uh . . . I can't exactly remember that.'

He tore his eyes away from the flickering flex-screen on the foyer wall behind her. 'Seriously?'

'I'm with my dad. He remembers that kind of thing. Sorry.'

Another sigh. The clerk leaned forward and tapped on the grubby, old-fashioned touchscreen terminal in front of him. 'And the name is . . . ?'

'Vikram. Mr Sanjay Vikram. Room for two.'

The clerk tapped, swiped, tapped, then looked up at her. 'No. No Mr Vikram staying here.'

'What?'

'I said, no Mr Vikram.'

'But . . . but . . .' Sal frowned. That wasn't right. They did stay here. They did. The Douglas Hotel. She remembered the name. She was certain of that. Details. She was good at remembering details. Things like goddamned bloody hotel names for instance.

'We stayed . . .' She corrected herself. '*We're staying* here!'

'Maybe you just got the wrong hotel, sweetheart.' He offered her the faintest flicker of a sympathetic smile. 'There are a bunch of other hotels just like this one around here. Maybe you're in one of those, huh?'

'Can you please check again?'

He shrugged and did so. 'Sorry. Nothing. No Mr Vikram.'

Sal remained where she was, waiting, hoping for him to suddenly say, 'No, wait! Hang on . . . I guess I must've spelled it wrong. Here we are . . .' But he didn't. Instead, he went back to watching the vintage comedy stream and she remained where she was, standing on the scratched and worn parquet floor of the hotel's small foyer.

'This *is* the Douglas Hotel?'

The man sighed irritably at her and pointed towards the door, to the street outside, to an identically shabby-looking hotel on the opposite side. 'That's the Douglas Hotel.'

'Oh,' she said and smiled apologetically. 'I get right and left mixed up sometimes.'

But he was already ignoring her, smirking at the old sitcom.

'OK, thanks anyway,' she said finally and stepped out through the wire-mesh reinforced double doors past a couple of old men drinking from brown paper bags down three steps on to the sidewalk. She gazed across the busy road at the hotel opposite, mentally preparing herself to have the same conversation all over again with another impatient and bored desk-jockey.

The wrong side. She'd got the wrong side. She was beginning to question her memories. Beginning to doubt them.

What if they were never here, Sal? That sniping, told-you-so voice of hers.

What if you're really like Maddy? Huh? Not even a copy of a real person. Made up. Just a piece of fiction. A jumbled-together library of memories. A Frankenstein's monster.

'Shut up,' she whispered.

You're going to cross the road, to the correct hotel this time, and find out there's no Mr Sanjay Vikram and daughter staying there either.

'Shut up!'

And perhaps it's for the best. I mean, can you really do what you're thinking of doing? Huh? Can you?

Sal hadn't thought through in detail what she planned to do. But some foggy notion appealed to her that, like that old fairy tale of *The Prince and the Pauper*, she might somehow swap places with the real girl.

Come on, 'swap places'? Like the real Saleena's going to want to do that? Of course she wouldn't. You'd have to replace her . . . you know what I'm talking about, don't you? You'd have to get rid of her, Sal.

All of a sudden she felt sick, dizzy. Yes, she realized that's what she'd been subconsciously planning. To kill herself. To replace herself. To become the imposter in someone else's life.

She stopped on the edge of the sidewalk and stared across the bicycle and rickshaw traffic at the far-side hotel. Perhaps it was best she didn't cross the street and check in there. They were probably not even staying there. In fact, there probably never, ever was a Saleena Vikram. Why would she be any different to Maddy?

'I'm a Frankenstein girl too,' she uttered quietly. The nagging voice was quite right. This was a completely stupid idea.

Then, of course, her eyes made lies of those words as she spotted a middle-aged Indian man leading a young girl by the hand, out through the hotel door opposite, down several steps on to the sidewalk. The girl was chatting to her father, animated, excited, swinging her father's hand as she talked. He laughed back at her. A kind, caring, proud laugh for his daughter.

'My God . . .' Sal rocked dizzily on her heels. 'Shadd-yah.'

CHAPTER 57

1667, Puerto Bello

Liam led his men in a convoy of three pinnaces, rowing across the bay and beaching on the silt and shingle that sloped down from the small settlement of Puerto Bello. As they made their way up on to the settlement's main thoroughfare, a rutted dirt track running east–west from Castillo Santiago into Puerto Bello and the modest village square overlooked by the settlement's one church, Liam saw Rashim proudly striding towards him along the track, leading his small army of pirate cut-throats and desperadoes.

He spotted Liam and gave him an exhilarated grin. 'Liam! Good God! This is like taking candy from a *sleeping* baby!' They clasped each other by the arms.

'Jay-zus!' laughed Liam. 'We didn't need to fire a single shot! They thought we were an invading army and just caved in! It was incredible!' He looked up the dirt road towards the low walls of Castillo Santiago. 'How was yours? I heard a couple of shots.'

'Our French frontiersman took out a couple of their officers –' Rashim shrugged a little guiltily – 'while we, uh . . . while we parlayed. I'm not particularly proud of that. But that was all that was needed,' he added quickly. 'No more bloodshed required.'

They led their men down the track towards the town square,

the men merging together into one column of cheering, chattering, excited sailors. As they passed by the few single-storey mud-plaster homes coated with peeling white paint, window shutters rattled hastily shut. Ahead of them an old muskreet man yanked on the reins of his donkey to force it off the track and out of sight.

'The place looks deserted,' said Liam.

'Oh, they're there . . . keeping out of sight, hiding in their homes.' Rashim glanced back at their rabble army. 'Which is probably best for everyone.'

'Aye.'

The track opened on to a small square before the town's church: a modest space of rutted, sunbaked dirt, roamed by chickens and roosters, with a well plumb in the middle. The men spilled into it, spread out and began inspecting the square for things they could steal. Liam heard a chicken squawk and turned to see Cookie holding a flapping chicken in his hands. He twisted the bird's neck, the squawk ended abruptly and he tossed it into a bag on his shoulder.

We need to keep our men focused.

They were now fanning out, stepping into alleyways, rat runs between shacks, poking their heads into open, unshuttered windows. Looking for loot. Or worse. The town of Puerto Bello was effectively all but taken, albeit with only a couple of shots fired. Their men were conquerors, victors . . . and their attention now was wandering, seeking what they expected as theirs – the spoils of victory.

'Rashim?'

He'd noticed and nodded. He cupped his mouth. 'Gentlemen! The big prize isn't this town. There's nothing here!'

Heads turned sharply towards him, eyes wide, mouths opening ready to roar in angry complaint.

'The prize, gentlemen, is over there!' Rashim added, pointing across the town square, along a dirt track that led out of the far side of the settlement and up a gentle slope towards what appeared to be a small building site. Stacks of masonry blocks cut from coral beds nearby, bags of sand and piles of lumber, a framework of wooden scaffolding along a section of wall still to be built.

'One last fort, San Geronimo . . . all the gold, all the silver is being stored in there. In a strongroom. Waiting for us to collect it!' As one, over a hundred heads turned to look up the slope in unison. 'So, uh . . . what are we waiting for . . . *lads*?'

The men roared with delight, many casually dropping the modest bits and pieces they were attempting to loot and instead started striding out of the town square and up the track heading towards San Geronimo.

Rashim looked at Liam and winked. 'I do believe I am getting the hang of this.'

Ten minutes later, as they waded up the gentle slope through tufts of knee-high grass under a sun that was beginning to find its strength that morning, a volley of musket fire opened up.

Liam heard the bee-like hum of balls whipping past, the soft percussive *thwack* as several hit their targets. 'GET DOWN!' he shouted. They all dropped to the ground, a rattling of sabres, cutlasses, muskets and flintlocks mixed with a smattering of curses.

Liam turned to Rashim. 'I thought Modyford's spy said this one wasn't garrisoned yet?'

They squinted through the tall grass at the unfinished front wall and spotted the flicker of light blue tunics and yellow cuffs and collars moving among the support struts of scaffolding and stacks of coral bricks.

Rashim bit his lip. 'Hmmm . . . so much for "an army engineer and seven labourers".'

'Soldiers . . . there can't be that many, though.' Liam closed his eyes, recalling a snapshot image of the uneven, unfinished wall as he'd dropped down to the dirt; a dozen plumes of smoke, certainly no more than eighteen curling out towards them. 'Less than twenty,' he said quickly. 'We can rush them, *now* . . . before they finish reloading!'

Rashim stroked his chin thoughtfully.

'Now, Rashim . . . not in thirty seconds' time. *Now!*'

'All right . . . yes . . . OK, we –'

Liam wasted no time. He scrambled to his feet. 'Charge 'em down, lads!' He began to sprint up the last twenty yards of slope. 'CHARGE 'EM DOWN!'

A roar rippled along the swaying grass and heads and shoulders emerged, men clambering to their feet and yipping and hooting excitedly, like a room full of bored schoolchildren finally excused from a morning of dull lessons to play in the sunshine outside.

Rashim reluctantly pulled himself to his knees, wondering why men like these so willingly hastened towards each other with deadly intent and childlike joy, when a single wound in this time – a single cut! – could lead to infection and a lingering death of fever and agony . . . *Where exactly is the 'fun' in this?*

Upfront he caught just a glimpse of Liam, waving his cutlass in wide, rallying loops above his head, his mouth wide open, roaring encouragement to his men. And he envied Liam that. He envied the young man's recently discovered fearlessness. God, he envied that.

CHAPTER 58

1667, Port Royal, Jamaica

Sir Thomas looked at the scruffy man standing in front of him. 'So, Jamieson you said your name was?'

Jamieson nodded edgily, shifting from foot to foot. 'Aye, Your Lordship. *Jamesey*, the lads call me.'

The governor sucked his fingers clean of mango juice then steepled them beneath his chin. 'And you are absolutely certain of this? Of what you have just told me?'

'Oh yeah, Your Honour. Them Negroes on the ship was yours all right. They got yer mark on their arms. I saw it with me own eyes.'

'To be certain they are mine, Jamieson, describe the mark for me, will you?'

Jamieson closed his eyes as he concentrated. He'd seen it several dozen times. The Negroes had all made some effort to conceal the branded mark on their upper arms, wrapping cloth strips round their arms, but the work aboard any ship and the complete lack of privacy ensured every square inch of a man was exposed at one time or another.

''Tis the letter of yer name, sir, "M" but with a crown, is it? Sittin' atop the letter?'

Sir Thomas nodded slowly. The crowned 'M' was his personal design and one he was rather proud of: the 'M' for his family name, the crown to clearly demonstrate his loyalty to the King.

A simple and quite distinctive design, the raised lines of seared and scarred tissue defined very well against a slave's dark skin. Quite easy to spot a Modyford slave.

'And you say they have a dozen of them aboard the *Pandora*?'

'A dozen? Yes, Yer Lordship. Split between both ships. The *Maddy Carter* and the *Pandora*.'

Twelve. Indeed.

In the last month alone, fourteen of his slaves had gone Maroon: simply vanished from the plantation and slipped into the surrounding jungle. His men, attempting to hunt them down, had come across one of them, quite dead from starvation, but the rest he presumed had joined the growing band of wild savages, *Maroons*, that inhabited the interior wilderness of Jamaica. They were becoming a problem that needed addressing. Every now and then a supply wagon on the dirt tracks that linked the plantations and settlements spread out across the island was raided, the driver inevitably killed. In the past that had been an infrequent enough event to be an occasional nuisance, but now it was becoming a problem of increasing concern.

There were terrifying stories from the island of Hispaniola of the entire slave population of the plantations rising up and killing their handlers and masters. Something that could so easily occur over here if the slaves got a collective mind, and will, to do it. The wild Maroons were a law-and-order problem, but perhaps also, more worryingly, a potential source of inspiration for the many others toiling in the fields. Something needed to be done about them, decided Sir Thomas. They needed to be rounded up and put down like feral dogs.

He gave the scruffy sailor standing in front of him a coin for his story and dismissed him. No doubt the man had a grievance of his own against Captain Anwar, but his description of the branding was wholly accurate. More to the point, substantiating the man's story, there had been some sightings just before Anwar's two ships set sail of a group of unescorted, 'wild-looking' Negroes hovering around Port Royal for several days.

Sir Thomas ground his teeth angrily. Hiring slaves as crew, though. 'My God, you stupid, stupid man!' he whispered. If ever there was a thing that would make his slaves and those of every other plantation on the island down tools and rise up in revolt, it was the knowledge that some reckless fool of a privateer captain was happy and willing to hire Negroes for his crew. The Negroes would need to be made an example of. Captain Anwar and his Irish colleague too. The hangman's noose for the lot of them.

And if he was to revoke the letter of marque right now, in their absence, their raid on Puerto Bello could be considered a flagrant act of piracy. The plunder would be entirely forfeit.

Sir Thomas Modyford smiled. 'In other words . . . mine,' he muttered.

He reached across his desk for a pot of ink and a quill. With one hastily scribbled note, he could quite legally make an important example of this man and show that Negroes were fit for the field and nothing else: two-legged beasts of burden and nothing more. An important example not just to the slaves, but to all of those lawless criminals who considered themselves brethren of the sea, with their funny liberal notions about electing their captains and all being equal before God.

More than that, he could use this to demonstrate to King Charles II that he was doing *something* to rein in the rampant piracy in the Caribbean.

And, of course, last but not least, the Puerto Bello plunder — and there was surely going to be a lot from this raid — would be entirely his.

CHAPTER 59

1667, San Geronimo, Puerto Bello

'What is it with those guys?' Rashim muttered as he slumped to the ground beside Liam. 'Why the hell won't they surrender?'

Liam was busy inspecting his arm. A musket-ball fragment had torn a ragged hole in his forearm. He peeled back the strip of cloth he'd ripped from his shirt and tied round it. Already the blood had congealed to a thick crusty syrup.

'How's the arm?' asked Rashim.

'All right. It'll be fine.'

'I suspect your blood is laced with a heady cocktail of antibiotics. The wound you sustained back in Rome healed without any help, didn't it?'

'Aye. Didn't stop it hurting like buggery, though,' replied Liam, tightening the bandage once more.

Rashim cast a glance at their wounded, a line of a dozen men squirming in the long grass nearby, moaning and whimpering. Uphill, another dozen or more of their men lay dead. The wounded, most of them from musket fire, were unlikely to survive their injuries. The wadding that came for free with each musket ball was embedded deep in their flesh, wadding alive with bacteria that would eventually turn a wound into a festering, fatal infection. Sword injuries, by contrast, though more horrific to look at than the small puckered entry hole of a gunshot wound, were more survivable.

'What a screw-up,' Rashim said. 'I thought all the hard work was done.'

Liam nodded. The skirmish had settled down into a stand-off. After three unsuccessful charges up the slope towards the unfinished wall the morning had ended in stalemate. Quiet now, save for the moaning of the wounded and peppered with the solitary crack of an opportune shot fired every now and then.

'It looks like you've no option,' said Liam, 'but to do it.'

Rashim sighed. He turned to look downhill, across Puerto Bello and out at the bay. Both of their ships were more or less in place, anchored near the shallows and in easy cannon range of San Geronimo.

A drastic last resort and one Rashim was reluctant to deploy. A bombardment was a sledgehammer to break a nut. 'God knows, there might be priceless things in that hoard that we'll end up blasting to bits.'

'It's mostly gold and silver coins. It'll survive a pounding.'

'Incan treasures, fine-plated gold statuettes, jewellery. Who knows what goodies they've transported up from Peru?'

Liam nodded at the men squatting among the tall grass and boulders nearby. 'I think our men are not that fussed, Rashim. If there's gold and silver up there, they'll be just as happy with mangled nuggets of it.'

'Hmmmm . . .' He reached for the parlay flag lying on the ground beside him. The white rag was holed several times with shot: the defenders, it seemed, were far more eager to fight than talk terms. 'I'll try once more,' he said with a sigh. He nodded at their ships in the bay, side by side, presenting this way a total of twenty-four cannons between them. 'Perhaps those stubborn morons in the fort have noticed the ships by now.'

Five minutes later, standing downhill from the building site, Rashim and Liam waited beneath their fluttering flag for someone to emerge from the bricks and scaffolding to talk to them. Finally someone did. A short man in a tattered and blood-spattered uniform. A bandage was wrapped round his forehead over one eye. He limped down towards them, using a musket as a crutch; one leg was bound with bloody rags.

'Jay-zus,' Liam whispered, 'you'd think this fella would have had enough.'

Finally he drew up in front of them, wheezing from the exertion. Closer now, Liam could see he was unremarkable-looking: a gaunt, middle-aged man with a badly clipped toothbrush moustache and a balding head lacerated with scratches and cuts. Out of uniform and not looking like he'd just emerged from Hell, he might just as easily pass as a mere bank teller, a humble backstreet tailor, a hotel doorman, a shoeshiner. Nothing to suggest heroic officer material.

Rashim spoke first. 'Do you understand English?'

The man nodded. 'Yes, I speak this well.'

'I am Captain Rashim Anwar. And this is my partner, Captain Liam O'Connor.'

The Spaniard nodded politely. 'Captain Raoul Garcia.'

'Look, Mr Garcia,' said Liam, 'we think this has gone on long enough. You and your men have fought honourably.' He looked back at the distant outline of the forts either side of the bay. 'Far more honourably, I might add, than the other officers and soldiers back there.'

Garcia smiled. 'I am not a soldier. I am an engineer.' He hunched his narrow shoulders humbly. 'The title "Captain" is a temporary one while I build this fort.'

'Then you've put real officers to shame.' Liam took a step closer. 'Why not surrender, sir?' he asked. 'Enough men, yours and ours, have died this morning already.'

'I have a duty to protect this property of my King.'

'Do you see the ships out there in the bay, Mr Garcia?' Rashim stepped to one side. 'They are now within accurate range of your fort.'

'Yes,' he nodded. 'I have seen them already.'

'We, uh . . . we really don't want to do this if we can avoid it, but if you don't surrender I will have to give the order for them to fire on San Geronimo. They will bombard you. You understand?'

'Yes, I understand.'

'The fort will be flattened . . . you, your men will die.'

'I understand this . . . but my men and I have a duty.'

'Look,' said Liam, 'why don't you put it to your men? We'll give you ten minutes. Let them have a choice?' Liam looked at Rashim and Rashim nodded. 'If you surrender, none of your men will be harmed or taken prisoner. In fact,' Liam scratched at the binding on his wounded arm, 'any men who wish to join us . . . including yourself, Captain Garcia, will be welcome and entitled to a share of the booty.' He smiled. 'Clearly you are all courageous men, good fighters.'

The engineer nodded politely. 'I thank you. I must decline your offer. But I will put it to my men.'

'A pistol shot will be fired to mark when your time is up,' said Rashim.

'I understand.' He turned and began to limp up the hill towards the fort. They watched him until he disappeared from view among the piles of building materials.

'Now there's courage,' said Liam. 'The real bleedin' thing right there.'

Rashim nodded. 'Dying for duty . . . that would be a foolish, old-fashioned notion in my time.' He pulled out a leather flask of water, uncorked it and took a slug. 'In the latter half of the twenty-first century, Liam, war is a . . . a *remote* thing. Soldiers

329

sit in comfortable, air-conditioned command-and-control centres, remotely directing drones, assigning waypoints and capture points to squads of combat clones. Like a game. Just like they're playing a child's computer war game.' He offered the flask to Liam. He took it and chugged down several mouthfuls.

'There's no courage in the soldiering of my time, Liam. No courage, no honour. Just relative target values and successful hit ratios.'

Liam handed the flask back to Rashim. 'I hope he surrenders. I'm not sure I can bring myself to do this.'

'We don't have much choice. Our men won't charge the fort again . . . and I wonder whether they'll lynch us if we walk away now empty-handed.'

The ten minutes felt like ten hours. Finally the time had elapsed without any sign of movement from the fort. Rashim pulled out the pistol tucked into his belt, poured a small measure of powder into the barrel and tamped it down. He cocked the flint.

'For what it's worth,' he muttered then fired the pistol into the air.

The shot echoed across the slope, the tongue of smoke carried across the gently stirring grass by a languid breeze. The sound of the shot, Liam had been hoping desperately, would be the final necessary incentive to stir the men inside to emerge with their hands in the air. Instead, all he saw was the flash of a light blue tunic among the coral-white masonry, somebody shuffling into position, readying himself for the final showdown.

'Jay-zus, Rashim . . . are we actually going to do this?'

'We've left ourselves with little other choice.' He tucked the pistol back into his belt, turned downhill to face the ships anchored in the bay and waved his arms. Old Tom would be watching with the spyglass.

They waited. Aboard the *Pandora* Liam could just about make out individual blobs of colour, the tunics of the skeleton crew left aboard. There seemed to be movement going on there. Rashim waved his arms again.

'Come on,' Rashim muttered. 'Wake up, you –'

A plume of white smoke erupted from the front of the ship, followed by another further along, and another – the first boom finally reaching their ears a moment later. Liam heard the buzz of a shot passing overhead, a buzz that sounded vaguely like the whir of a propeller spinning. Then impact. One then another against the unfinished front wall, sending showers of coral shards and wood splinters into the air.

They ducked down into the long grass as razor-sharp flecks of coral brick spun towards them and the low walls of the fort disappeared behind an increasing fog of swirling dust and debris. The first twenty-four-cannon volley ended. They waited in expectant silence for the cannons to be reloaded and watched the dust slowly settle, Liam still hoping that this first volley would be the final encouragement for Garcia and his men to emerge.

CHAPTER 60

2025, New York

She followed them north through Greenwich Village, up along Broadway and back towards Times Square. Papaji and Saleena Vikram taking in the sights and sounds and smells of New York. Father and daughter enjoying their day together. And, as the afternoon spun away into evening, Sal had watched them from the street outside as they stepped into a fast-food restaurant for some dinner. From the street, among jostling pedestrians and amid the jangle of bicycle bells, the beehive hum of electric-engine vehicles and the intermittent beeping of traffic lights, she watched the two of them through the grubby glass.

She watched them settle down in a cosy window booth, pick up menus and discuss what they were going to eat. Saleena pointed at the food pictures and asked her father something. Again, he smiled and laughed. A harried-looking waitress arrived and quickly took their order.

Sal felt a tear roll down her cheek. 'I want to be you,' she muttered as she watched Saleena Vikram chatter away to her father, as she pulled out and inspected the things she'd bought in various shops that afternoon. Gaudily coloured clothes and gel-plastic bangles. A Pikodu flexi-mag that lit up her face as she opened the cover to wake up the display and started on the easy puzzles.

The waitress arrived with a tray of chicken wraps and fries

and tall cardboard cups of Pepsi, and Sal watched the pair of them hungrily tuck into their junk food. Two real people in this real world. No monsters, mutants, dinosaurs, hominids, Nazis, eugenics. No time waves, churning storm fronts of infinite realities. No chaos space haunted by ever-encroaching apparitions. None of that.

Just this very real, ordinary moment between a doting father and a contented child.

They are perfectly happy, do you see, Sal?

She nodded. She *did* see that. And, even though this world was inevitably doomed to gradually get worse and worse, there was still a decade or two of relatively stable normality for this girl and her parents. A normal family life. Because . . . Sal was convinced of this now . . . the one memory she had in her head that was false – that didn't seem to fit with all the rest – was the memory of her death. It was almost as if that last moment of her life was bolted on to the complete memory of a thirteen-year-old girl.

Perhaps Saleena Vikram didn't die in a fire and a collapsed building just over a year from now? Maybe that fire never happened. Maybe she'll go on to live another forty, fifty years . . . then, as an old woman, die like everyone else when that virus finally happens.

I don't think you want to do what you were planning.

Her nagging voice was right. She realized she couldn't do that. She couldn't do what was needed if she wanted to replace the girl. Even if she could do the deed, Papaji would know his little girl was not right, had changed somehow. Sal could never imagine herself being that happy, that carefree. It would be an act at best. A sham. All that had happened to her in the last year – because it all added up to that by now, surely – made her a wholly different person to this girl.

Sal tugged her hood up for warmth: the evening was getting cool now.

Saleena is who you should be . . . not what you are, Sal. You're damaged goods now. With all that you've seen, all that you know about the future, do you honestly think you can be that carefree and happy girl? I don't think so. What's more, you're not even properly human. You can't be her.

Those words hurt. But they were also right.

You'll never be that girl, Sal.

She swiped at the tears on her cheeks. She knew that now. It didn't need saying.

But you can do something.

'What?'

Make sure Saleena Vikram and her papaji and mamaji have a life.

Sal frowned, trying to make sense of that.

If you can't live her life, then you can make sure she does, Sal. Wouldn't that be something? To know that somewhere a version of you will have everything you've ever wanted. A family. A normal life.

CHAPTER 61

1667, San Geronimo, Puerto Bello

They advanced towards the fog, Liam, Rashim and the other able-bodied men of their raiding party. Liam pulled his neckerchief over his mouth and nose to filter out the fine abrasive particles of coral dust swirling around him.

The wooden scaffold frame was now an uneven bed of shattered lumber; the ground was painted white as if a snow cloud had passed over this slope. They picked their way over sharp-edged rubble, shattered blocks of brittle coral that scratched and cut at ankles and shins.

The front wall was entirely gone, replaced with a bed of white granules and glistening boulders that resembled the crumbling ice skirt of a retreating glacier. And, among all the white, here, there, the odd splash of dark crimson and the pale, dust-coated parts of bodies lacerated, *minced*, by countless spinning razors of coral.

Rashim led the way through the thinning clouds of dust into the fort's main compound towards some low-roofed buildings beyond, while Liam found himself squatting down amid the rubble. At his feet, the head and shoulders of Captain Garcia emerged from the debris. Quite dead. He wiped some of the chalk-white powder from the man's face.

'Stupid,' he whispered softly, stroking the dust away from his glazed, open eyes. 'Stupid.'

A heroic and utterly pointless death that would never even make a footnote let alone the main text of a history book. No. Such mentions were reserved for kings, princes, dukes, lords; stupid aristocrats dreaming vainly of glory and leading nameless men to needless ends.

'This, Captain Garcia?' He shook his head. 'This? Just to protect a rich Spanish king's stash of gold?' And, what's more, it was stolen gold and silver. Not even King Philip's. Not really. Stolen from countless minor Incan chieftains. A European king's *loot*.

Just then Liam heard voices calling out. Someone wolf-whistled. A man broke into hearty singing that spread to some others.

'Mr O'Connor, sir!' someone called out. 'You should see this, sir!'

'Liam! My God! Over here!' Rashim's voice.

Liam stood up, picked his way out of the rubble into the compound. On the far side, beneath a partially staved-in sunshade of terracotta tiles that had cascaded down and shattered on the ground, Rashim stood in the archway of an entrance to a single-storey building. Two thick oak doors strengthened with iron braces hung wide open allowing the midday sun to sweep into a dark, windowless interior. Liam made his way over until he stood just outside.

'The strongroom?'

Rashim's grin was almost too much for him to bear right now. He was chuckling like a naughty boy; like a sweet-toothed glutton who'd just discovered a vault full of chocolate. 'Oh yes . . . oh good God, yes! Go on in, Liam . . . go take a look!'

Stepping into the shadows inside, he could hear the scrape and heavy metallic jingle of hands stirring, scooping through coins, muted gasps and stifled cries of shock and joy. His eyes adjusted to the interior gloom and finally he could make out a little more detail. A long, narrow room lined with thick oak and iron caskets, several of which had already been prised open. He approached one. Kwami was beside it, looking goggle-eyed down at a glinting mound of doubloons. Easily a ton of Incan silver in that one casket alone had already been melted down and recast as thick, wide discs of Spanish coin, each one shimmering back at Liam the surly, humourless profile of Philip IV of Spain.

Rashim joined him. 'I think we just hit the mother lode, Liam.' He placed a friendly hand on Liam's shoulder. 'I think we have just made ourselves richer than the governor of Jamaica himself.'

CHAPTER 62
1667, Port Royal, Jamaica

'Looks like yer got yerself a welcoming party,' said Old Tom, pointing towards the north wharf of Port Royal.

Rashim pulled his spyglass out, extended it and put it to his eye. Through the lens, close-up images of the wharfside danced unevenly as the *Pandora* swayed gently as she moved from the choppier waters of the open sea into the calmer waters of Port Royal harbour sheltered by the Palisadoes spit.

The bucking image danced along several merchant ships tied up, loading or unloading bales of trade goods, past the low, half-submerged fences of a turtle crawl, back again on to the tree-trunk thick support struts of a jetty, then finally on to a blur of startling crimson and crisp white. Soldiers standing to attention in two tidy ranks on the jetty. Beside them he spotted Sir Thomas's carriage, the door open and a stockinged leg caught in the sunlight leaking inside.

'Someone must have spotted our approach,' said Rashim. 'We've got Modyford and an honour guard waiting for us.'

'Let's have a look.' Rashim passed Liam the spyglass. 'Oh yeah . . . lazy bugger! Letting his men roast in the sun while he slobs out in the shade?'

'Privilege of rank.' Rashim adjusted the cuffs of his jacket. 'It's what I'd do.'

'Still . . .' Liam passed the spyglass back. 'Nice of the fella to make an effort, I s'pose.'

'Sirs? A point of caution if I may . . . ?'

Rashim and Liam looked at Old Tom. 'What is it?'

'Might it not be best to keep our Negroes below decks?'

Liam turned to look at the main deck. John Shoe, Kwami and the other black men were quite noticeable lining the ship's rail along with the others, hooting and waving their caps excitedly.

'He's right, Rashim. We should probably hustle them out of sight.' Liam was expecting a quick, compliant nod from his partner; after all, confrontation, making a stand on a point of moral principle, wasn't exactly his strong point.

'No,' he replied. 'Let them stay.'

'Huh?'

'Let them stay. Let Modyford see them.'

'What? He'll go mad! Those are *his* slaves!'

'Then we will buy them off him.' Rashim's grin was loose and mischievous. 'We could probably buy this whole port, Liam.'

'Yes, yes, we probably could, but . . .'

'We're rich, Liam. Ridiculously rich. And that makes us powerful and –'

'We're rich *only* while we have those silver and gold coins in *our* hold.' Rashim glanced at him quickly. The point was clearly not wasted on him. The loot was theirs right now, but what was to stop Sir Thomas ordering his honour guard to board their ship and help himself to it?

'Hmmm. Perhaps a little caution should be exercised, then,' said Rashim. 'Tom?'

'Skipper?'

'Have someone row over to the *Maddy Carter* and tell them

to hold their position in the harbour until they hear otherwise.'

'Right y'are, sir!'

The loot – just under half a million pieces of eight – was split between the two ships, in case one of them floundered. Rashim's paranoia at work there.

'So, what're you thinking?' asked Liam.

'We shall tie up and, I suppose, uh . . . address the slave issue.' He jutted his bearded chin out. 'I'm certainly not going to hand them back. Far as I'm concerned, they're crew. They're my *men* now. Not his *cattle*.'

'That's admirable enough.' Liam looked again at the approaching wharf and the soldiers, perhaps thirty of them, standing to attention. 'But he's brought them soldiers along for a reason, Rashim. I think we've got a problem.'

'Relax. I'll talk him down. He will have a decent price for his slaves and a very nice twenty per cent of our haul.' Rashim flashed white teeth at him from the dark nest of bristles on his chin. 'He's going to be a very happy gentleman this morning.'

'All the same, let's have our lads ready for a scrap . . . just in case.'

'No, we'll be fine.'

Liam looked at him. 'Seriously . . . Rashim, let's have some muskets loaded and to hand. Just in case?'

For a moment, just for a moment, Liam saw a flicker of irritation, perhaps even anger, cross his face.

'Remind me. Who's the captain here?'

'*We* are, Rashim. *Both* of us. Remember?'

'Hmmm . . . well now, technically speaking, *I* am the captain. The men elected me, Liam, not you, to lead this –'

'Rashim, this probably isn't the best time for us to be squabbling about who's the big boss fella, OK? I'm just saying let's be a little prepared, huh? For any eventuality?'

The irritation lingered on his face a moment longer then finally melted away to be replaced with a rueful half-smile. 'Yes, yes . . . maybe you are right.' He nodded vaguely apologetically. 'Would you see to that, then?'

'Aye.' Liam turned and headed down the ladder to the main deck to organize the loading and discreet, out-of-sight-but-easily-to-hand distribution of their supply of muskets. It would have been better if Pasquinel was aboard this ship, but instead he was on the *Maddy Carter*. All the same, there were at least seven men that he knew were half-decent shots and cool-headed in a moment of heat. He picked them out of the cheering, hooting, waving mob gathered along the waist of the ship, tapped them lightly on the shoulder and quickly explained that this morning's triumphant homecoming *might* possibly get a tad hairy.

The *Pandora*'s sails dropped and, as the last of her gentle momentum brought her in to rest a dozen yards short of the wooden wharf, lines were tossed ashore fore and aft. Two teams of dock workers grabbed them and hauled together with chorused 'hoys', bringing the ship closer in. Close enough for a long boarding plank to be raised from the wharf to be rested across and tied to the rail of the *Pandora*'s low waist.

As they finished securing the boarding ramp, Liam finished passing out the loaded muskets. '*Keep it out of sight*,' he whispered to each man. '*Only on my command, all right?*'

'Sir Thomas!' Rashim called out from the afterdeck. 'You'll be pleased to know the raid on Puerto Bello was a magnificent success!'

Modyford finally emerged from his carriage into the sun. He adjusted his wig, squinted up at the ship's rail then muttered something to the captain of his guard. Then he acknowledged Rashim.

'Captain Anwar,' he called up. 'Good to have you back.'

Liam thought he detected an icy tone in the man's voice.

'So? Is there no invitation to be extended for me to come aboard?'

Rashim nodded. 'Uh . . . yes, yes, of course. Please! Come on up.'

'Why, thank you!' Modyford nodded courteously. 'Lead the way if you will, Lieutenant Hamshaw.'

'Yes, sir.' The surly officer barked an order to his men. They quickly clambered up the boarding ramp and dropped down over the rail on to the ship's main deck, forming a protective, outward-facing circle, their muskets — bayonets already fitted — held ready at hip height.

Sir Thomas Modyford slowly climbed the plank and Lieutenant Hamshaw offered him a hand as he clambered awkwardly down on to the deck.

Rashim climbed down the ladder and approached the soldiers warily. 'Uh, Sir Thomas, is this . . . er . . . is this entirely necessary?' He tried to inject a little levity into his voice. 'After all, come on, we're business partners here, right?'

Modyford bristled at the overfamiliarity. 'I, sir, am not generally in the habit of conjoining my business affairs with common thieves, liars, scoundrels.'

Liam caught Rashim's eye. *Be careful, fella.* He suspected something must have happened while they were away.

Something's changed here.

'Thieves . . . did you say, Sir Thomas?'

'You heard me correctly, man. Damned bloody thieves!'

Liam glanced around at his hand-picked men. Eyes on him from various corners, nooks and crannies around the edge of the deck, wanting to know what next. Now?

'You have stolen property of mine aboard your ships.'

342

Modyford picked out one of the crew standing nearby. 'You! Negro! Show me your arm!'

The man looked terrified. He shook his head frantically, but Sir Thomas was in no mood for that. He strode across the deck, grabbed the man roughly by his wrist and lifted the loose sleeve of his smock. 'There! My mark!' He turned to glare at Rashim. 'You, sir! You distinctly assured me the Negroes in this crew were Spanish slaves!'

'I was . . . I must have been mistaken, Sir Thomas.'

'Mistaken? No, sir . . . you lied!'

Rashim tried levity again. 'Oh well . . .' He chuckled nervously. 'What's a little fib between friends, eh?'

Oh no . . . Liam shook his head . . . *not the right approach.*

'WHAT!' roared Modyford. 'Good Lord, you are no *friend of mine*! You are certainly no associate or business partner of mine either! You are a thief, sir! What's more, you and your crew are guilty of acts of piracy –'

'Piracy? But . . . but we have a letter of marque signed by yourself, sir –'

'You have no such thing!' Modyford turned quickly towards Lieutenant Hamshaw. 'Lieutenant?'

'Sir?'

'Arrest this man!'

Liam took in a sharp breath. 'To your arms!'

Across the deck a dozen men moved quickly, accompanied by the metallic rattle and scrape of guns being scooped out of hiding places, shouldered and levelled at the soldiers. Hamshaw barked a response. 'Present and aim!' The soldiers likewise shouldered their muskets, picking out those crew holding weapons.

'Make your aim the governor!' shouted Liam.

Modyford's eyes bulged with alarm as musket barrels shifted towards him. 'What the devil is this?'

343

'If anyone fires a gun this morning, Sir Thomas,' said Liam, 'more than likely at least one shot's going to find its way to you!'

Modyford was gasping urgently, hyperventilating his panic out with long, wheezy, rattling puffs of air. Liam noticed a dark patch spreading across his breeches.

'Sir, my men have their mark! On your command, sir?'

'NO! Hold! H-hold fast!'

The main deck was a crowded and complex sculpture. It reminded Liam of a period painting of some famous naval battle, a freeze-frame image from history. Silent except for the ragged breathing of several dozen men close enough to each other that every fired gun was guaranteed to hit someone.

Stalemate.

'May I suggest,' Rashim offered, 'that you and your men go back the way you came and leave the shi—'

'I will pardon any man, right now, who lowers their aim!' shouted Modyford. 'A pardon! Do you hear?'

'I said, get off the ship!' Rashim replied sharply. '*Now!*'

Perhaps in that moment, if a sudden unexpected sharp puff of air *hadn't* ruffled the sails above them, the loose sleeves of linen smocks, the light silk of scarves and lace ruffs of those standing stock-still, then events might just have unfolded very differently.

In the split second before the first twitchy, sweaty finger reacted in panic to the sudden gust and the first musket erupted, Liam thought he saw in his peripheral vision an odd shimmering in the air. But that was forgotten the moment the first plume of grey-blue gun smoke ballooned across the narrow deck.

There was a cacophony of muskets discharging. Liam felt a shot whisk past his cheek out of the fog; heard the gasped *ooff* of someone in the smoke being hit in the chest, the scream of another man, the cry of alarm of another.

The peal of gunfire diminished, but the smoke hung heavy all around them. Liam could already hear the rattle of musket balls tumbling down upended barrels, the frantic scraping sound of ramrods. Lieutenant Hamshaw barking an order for his men to form up on him. Modyford screaming in panic. The clatter and ring of a cutlass parried by some soldier's bayonet.

The smoke thinned into ghostly swirls and through it Liam could see the fight had become a push and shove mêlée over the squirming bodies of those who'd been caught in the volley fire. This close to each other, no one was going to have time to completely recharge their gun. The rest of their crew had decided to throw themselves into the fight with every available weapon to hand: hatchets, knives, boarding axes and winch handles.

Hamshaw's men tightened into a defensive knot round Modyford and together they shuffled back across the deck towards the boarding ramp. In the thick of the scrimmage Liam saw Kwami's huge bulk swinging a long-handled axe at a pair of soldiers, desperately trying to force a gap between them to get to his former owner. But Modyford was now already stepping up and over the rail.

In frustration, Kwami threw the axe he was holding at the man in the hope of knocking him off the ramp, but it passed by harmlessly as Modyford jogged down the ramp towards the wharf.

Don't let him get away. The man was rich, powerful, connected and now undoubtedly determined to make it his life's mission to see him and Rashim hanging from a rope. Better he was dead than alive.

Liam had a shot left unfired in the pistol he'd scooped from its hiding place. He swiftly levelled his aim at the man as he backed up against the side of his carriage and fired. The shot ricocheted off the carriage beside Modyford's head, sending stinging shards of wood into the man's cheek. He turned sharply to look at Liam, his luxuriant auburn-coloured wig falling off the back of his head as he did so.

The soldiers were now attempting to follow his retreat, the rearmost throwing their legs over the rail and scrambling down the ramp, a couple of them simply throwing themselves over the side.

'Dammit! Let them go!' shouted Rashim. He looked around for Old Tom and quickly found him. 'Tom? We have to go . . . now!'

The quartermaster nodded. 'Cut her free fore and aft!' he bellowed through cupped hands. 'All hands to the sails! We . . . are . . . leaving!'

Someone swiped a blade at the boarding ramp's tethers and kicked the ramp off the rail. It clattered down between the ship's hull and the wharf into the water below. The mooring rope upfront whip-tailed as someone sliced at it and the gap between ship and wharf almost immediately began to widen.

Liam had begun reloading his pistol, but Modyford was now almost completely obscured by the soldiers gathered tightly round him. But he saw the man's face, a cheek running with blood, his sore-encrusted scalp rudely exposed to the sun, a snarl of outrage like a wide-open gash across his face.

'I WILL HUNT YOU DOGS DOWN!' he roared, his eyes still locked on Liam. 'I WILL HAVE THE KING'S NAVY AND I WILL HUNT YOU DOWN!'

The aft mooring rope cracked like a whip as someone cut it and the *Pandora* started to turn and pull away with more urgency. The sail above Liam unfurled and began to flap with a noisy rustle. The wharf began to recede quickly. Modyford's shrill voice, carrying promises of hanging, disembowelling, quartering across the water to them, also began to diminish.

Rashim came to stand beside Liam, watching the redcoat soldiers now drawn up in a line along the edge of the wharf. They had nearly finished recharging their muskets, slotting ramrods back into their holders. Hamshaw raised his sword to ready a command.

'HEADS DOWN, LADS!' called Liam. He pulled Rashim down with him as the soldiers fired a parting volley. The rail above them was smacked by a couple of well-judged shots and rained shards of wood down on to them. The rest of the musket balls hummed harmlessly over the deck.

They both slowly stood up again. Then Liam laughed nervously. 'Hey! Morons! You missed!'

Rashim shook his head and tutted like a disappointed tutor. 'Really, that's just childish.'

CHAPTER 63

2025, New York

There were one or two dusty, cobwebbed corners of the archway that looked almost the same as she remembered. Almost as if they'd left it behind yesterday. The room right at the back was mostly as she remembered it. No generator now, no growth tubes, of course. In one corner were stacks of flattened cardboard boxes that were turning to a brown, soggy mulch at the bottom where seeping water was making its way in.

Sal worked her way forward into the main room. It had clearly been used by some other business, several in fact, by the various telltale signs of occupancy. For instance, someone had at one time tried to paint the brick walls white, but the mortar and the bricks were so crumbly it looked like they'd given up halfway along one wall. Someone else had replaced the tube light on the ceiling – the one that had always flickered annoyingly – with a low-energy halogen bulb.

The wall against which the computer table, monitors and PC cases had stood was now lined with sheets of plywood leaning up against it. There were tatters of paper stapled across them, layer upon layer. Sal looked closely at them. Flyers, adverts for events, staple-gunned to the ply. It seemed the last business using this premises was some sort of printer for flyers or bill posters, or something.

The little archway alcove where their bunk beds used to be

was occupied by a couple of large metal wheelie bins. She lifted the lid and winced at the smell of decay that wafted out.

This was our home. Once. But it felt desecrated now. Twenty-four years of use by various other occupants, businesses, vagrants, drug addicts — even urban foxes — had left their mark.

The entire concrete floor of the archway was soaking wet. In places water sat in shallow puddles. Not from the occasional drop of water that had always found a way down through the tons of brickwork above to drip annoyingly on the floor. This was floodwater.

She splashed her way across the floor, to the middle, then coyly probed a circular puddle with her toe. It was several inches deep. She smiled. That was the shallow crater of concrete their displacement machine had scooped out of the floor over and over.

Sal felt a warm feeling standing here in their archway. Returning to this place that for a while had been a home of sorts. A place that had once echoed with Liam's guffaws, Bob's rumbling deep voice, Maddy's rock music, the soothing chug of the filtration pumps in the back room. A place where they'd played board games on a makeshift table between the bunk beds. Where Liam had been introduced to the delights of the Nintendo 64 games console. Over there, where their long wooden kitchen table had stood surrounded by a mix of mismatched chairs and a couple of old threadbare armchairs. How many evening meals had they eaten together around that? How many pizza boxes had been piled up there, cans of soda, cartons that had once held noodles and foo yong.

She smiled. And how many bizarre conversations had they had between them? Three teenagers from three very different worlds brought together to live in this one. Sal remembered delighting in hearing Liam describe what it was like to be a steward on the *Titanic*, and he in turn had been fascinated by all the modern things the twenty-first century had produced.

Now it was just a damp, empty archway once more. And soon, perhaps within five years, it would be submerged beneath the rising sea.

Sal made her way towards the open shutter door. A different one, she noticed. She ducked under it and stepped into the backstreet. That was no different. Graffiti-covered brickwork and trash piled in heaps against the far wall. She turned to her left, towards the end of the alley that used to look out across the East River. There was no view now. A large concrete slab, lined with thick metal support braces, obscured it. The levee wall was fifteen feet high, built along this side of the East River to protect Brooklyn. But it had failed in several places a couple of years ago and most of Brooklyn had been flooded. The waters had receded but the flood damage remained. There had been some talk of regenerating the area and bolstering the levee walls, making them higher, thicker, stronger. But that idea had died when Brooklyn was flooded again the following winter.

The sea was rising. No way the city authorities were ever going to win that particular fight. Sal looked up at the wall. High above it she saw the grey underbelly of the Williamsburg Bridge. Even that, high as it was, was a victim to the rising tide. It was no longer used. Being a bridge to the abandoned Brooklyn it was now, basically, a bridge to nowhere. All closed off either end.

No hiss of traffic from above. No occasional rumble of a train passing overhead. Not any more. It was an iron, brick and tarmac relic of better times. She could see twigs and leaves wedged into the corners and joints of the ironwork. The nests of seagulls and terns.

When Foster had first brought them outside the archway, she

remembered it had been dark. She recalled stepping out beneath the shutter door, turning to look that way and gasping with delight at the lights from Manhattan shimmering across the calm water. The buzz of life and energy. New York right at the very pinnacle. The night before those two beautiful towers, those proud inverted chandeliers of light, would be gone.

Now . . . twenty-four years later, there was this — a dying city. Not dead just yet but the writing was writ large on the wall.

Sal wondered if it had been such a good idea coming here. After tailing Saleena Vikram and her father for another day, she had decided to let them go. Eventually Sanjay Vikram might notice they were being followed everywhere by a shabbily dressed girl who bore more than a passing resemblance to his daughter. He might call the cops. There would be questions she couldn't answer. She would probably end up being sectioned by the authorities for her 'own protection'. And then no chance of making the one-week return window.

If that's what she planned to do. Sal wasn't sure of that yet. Her head was all over the place. But she'd been hoping that a visit to the archway would lift her dark mood. Hoping to find something from the past to make her smile. Instead, she was standing alone in a part of New York that was dead. Necrotic flesh on the side of the Big Apple. Brooklyn was now inhabited by rats, dogs, foxes and quite probably a few rough-living tramps and addicts, taking refuge on the drier first floors.

Coming here was a stupid idea.

CHAPTER 64

1667, Port au Prince, Hispaniola

Liam studied the busy shoreline of Port au Prince ahead of them as their crew rowed them ashore.

'Looks no different to Port Royal to me. Smells the same too.'

'The only difference is that it is not run by the English.' Rashim looked at Liam. 'Which, given we are now fugitives, is the relevant difference.'

'Aye.'

Port au Prince was the principal settlement on the island of Hispaniola. An island that over a hundred and thirty years later would be called Haiti. It was *officially* a Spanish territory, but their hold on the island, and their interest in holding it, had lapsed over the last fifty years. And now French and Dutch privateers, buccaneers had moved in and established several coastal settlements, principal among them being Port au Prince. It had been Pasquinel's suggestion that they make for this place. The port was a lawless haven for all manner of scoundrels escaping the long reach of vengeful governors and monarchs.

Liam regarded the hotchpotch of wooden buildings on stilts, shingle roofs at all manner of random angles, spilling tendrils of smoke from countless cooking fires. There was, of course, a bustle of activity along the shoreline, but not the ordered work of trade ships being loaded and unloaded. Instead, he could make out random knots of people, light-skinned and dark-skinned, in coloured smocks and shirtless. Sailors – pirates – working on repairs to their beached pinnaces. On one side there seemed to be a fight in progress: two groups of men swinging drunkenly at each other. Further along a beach party seemed to be in full swing. A bonfire flickered and tongued sparks into the evening sky. Around it figures danced, staggered, slumped and Liam could hear a lively tune played by an accordion and sung along to by several men who didn't seem to agree on the words or even the tune.

Not nearly so ordered as Port Royal had been. There seemed to be no stone-built structures, no sense of a town centre, or a main street, no apparent warehouses. And no forts to protect it.

'A frontier town,' said Liam.

'What?'

'Like in them Western movies?' said Liam. 'Total anarchy. No one's in charge here.' He made a face. It meant any man with a grievance and a loaded pistol to hand could settle his argument without fear of facing a charge of murder. Although, that said, the same man faced the equally likely chance of being 'settled' in return.

'It's more than that, Liam. More than anarchy.' Rashim smiled. Liam could see the glint of the reflected firelight in his eyes as their pinnace bucked gently on the waves as they began to break on the gently sloping shingle towards the beach. 'It's perfect.'

'What do you mean?'

'It's a power vacuum. No laws here. No navy. No militia. No soldiers. Every man for himself.' The crew drew in their oars and the boat was carried by one last lazy wave up on to the soft white sand with a soothing hiss. The men climbed out and splashed into the withdrawing surf. Liam and Rashim followed suit, wading up through the water on soft fine sand that gave beneath them like virgin snow.

To their right, the party round the fire continued without even a solitary curious glance their way. New arrivals. No big deal. The business of cavorting, singing, drinking continued unabated.

Rashim stamped his wet boots on firmer, drier sand. He took in a deep breath of air that smelled both inviting and repulsive: the mouth-watering smell of a suckling pig being roasted on a spit nearby more or less negated by the stench of a sunbaked pile of offal and faeces further along the sand from which Liam thought he could see a rotting pair of bare human legs sticking out.

'Lovely,' he said with curled lips.

Rashim wrinkled his nose, assuming the smell was what Liam was referring to. 'That's one of the first things we'll sort out here. Hygiene.'

Liam looked at his friend standing there in the fading twilight, with his hands on his hips, taking in the raucous chaos of Port au Prince like some invading general. The scene reminded him of something else Liam had seen back in New York. Another film that he'd stumbled upon while channel-hopping on their TV. He tried to remember the name of the film but nothing came to him. He remembered, though, one scene in particular . . . wandering through a large house stuffed to the gills with teenagers. Every room seemed to have its very own party going on, every person staggeringly drunk, wild-eyed and out of control. Pranks and japes were being played, stupid pranks. Idiots thumping beer cans into their foreheads in an attempt to crush them flat, but leaving bloody gashes instead. 'Aw, that's just a typical frat party,' Maddy had said. Liam didn't have a clue what one of those was, but this . . . this looked a lot like one.

It also reminded him of a painting he'd once spent several hours studying in one of the many history books he'd pored through. A painting by an artist called Bosch. Something called *The Garden of Earthly Delights*. A depiction of Heaven and Hell. On the left, Heaven: a scene of order and tedious tranquillity, green rolling pastures and hills, fair people in flowing silk robes looking piously at their navels. On the right, however, a macabre scene of grotesques and freaks, fires lighting an endless dark wilderness populated by leering faces and guffawing simpletons.

Pretty much a medieval frat party.

Their men were gravitating towards the fire, drawn by the smell of sizzling pork.

'Liam,' said Rashim, watching them go. 'This is the perfect place for us.' He turned to look at him, the nearby bonfire lighting his eyes and making them glint and shine like the flickering embers of a dying brazier. He put an arm round Liam's shoulders. 'Now isn't this *exactly* what we were looking for? Hmmm? The sort of place you and I can rule just like kings.'

CHAPTER 65

1889, London

Maddy didn't notice the first tiny ripple when it happened: she was far too busy researching where she wanted to live out her years. Trawling through their vast digital encyclopedia of world history, she joked with the po-faced support units sitting beside her.

'Hey. Look at me, eh? Just like someone picking out a holiday online.'

Because that's how she figured she must appear to anyone looking on: some college kid picking out a gap-year tour of exotic places to visit. Ancient Rome?

Nah, been there, done that.

Egypt in the time of the pharaohs?

Too hot.

Tudor England?

Too much beheading going on.

Elizabethan England?

Too much Catholic-burning going on.

Renaissance Italy?

Hmmm . . . She rather liked the fancy clothes and the idea of looking up Leonardo da Vinci and maybe posing for a portrait or two. But then decided that the poor sanitation, plague and a little too much zealous persecution of heretics was somewhat off-putting.

Maddy had awoken that morning in their dungeon, entirely alone, save for the meatbots, the stupid-looking lab unit and computer-Bob. Her circle of friends. All robots together. After all, that's kind of what they all were, including herself. AIs of one sort or another. So, alone then . . . but not lonely. And surprisingly upbeat. Last night, after computer-Bob had opened the first recall window, recharged and then opened the twenty-four-hour recall window for Sal, and she had failed to appear, Maddy had taken herself to bed. She'd pulled a blanket over her head and quietly sobbed tears of self-pity until she'd fallen fast asleep.

But this morning . . . stepping outside their side door and watching Holborn stir to life, smelling freshly roasting coffee beans, woodsmoke, horse manure, hearing the toot of a far-off train whistle, she realized she still had a burning desire to live on, to explore the rich variety of history. There really was so much to see, to experience, to taste. And maybe she'd take Bob and Becks along for the joyride as travel companions. OK, Bob could be a bit stiff, formal and not the greatest laugh, but he would be her protector. And Becks . . . hadn't Becks's AI begun to loosen up a bit before she died? Maybe not exactly a party girl, but she'd made a couple of lame stabs at being funny.

Maddy was beginning to build a picture in her mind of a life she *could* lead. A life after the agency, after being a TimeRider . . . and it was beginning to look inviting. She'd be just like that weird British TV show character, Dr Who . . . wandering from adventure to adventure with her two trusty sidekicks.

She clicked on through the historical timeline on-screen. 'How does Ancient Greece sound to you guys?' She turned in her seat to look up at them. 'Uh? Hey . . . Bob, we could enter

357

you into their Olympic games. You'd win pretty much everything. You up for that?'

Bob regarded her coolly. 'If that is what you wish.'

'Attaboy.'

Maddy was about to pull up some details on Ancient Greece, the Peloponnesian wars, the Persian invasions . . . when it all went dark. Seconds passed. For a moment Maddy thought it might be the Holborn Bridge power generator shorting out again. The thing had a habit of doing that every few days. The lamp beside the monitors flickered on again; the computers began to whir and reboot.

As they waited, Maddy looked at Bob and Becks. 'Do you think that was a time wave?'

'I am unable to tell at present,' replied Becks. 'I will observe outside.' She turned and headed for the door.

'It is possible that was a wave,' said Bob. 'We know of at least one potential source of contamination.'

Not Sal. It wouldn't be her – she was way past them in the timeline. Whatever nonsense she was getting up to it would affect only the years after 2025.

'Liam?'

Bob nodded. 'Liam. Or it could be someone else.'

The monitors flickered on with the W.G. Systems logo as they finished rebooting. Then computer-Bob's dialogue box appeared on-screen.

> **Maddy, I have just experienced a run-time interruption.**

'I know. We just lost power for a few seconds.' She was about to ask Bob whether he'd detected any changes of data on their history database, but then realized that, with no protective field up and running, computer-Bob would have no 'before and after' comparison to make. If history had changed in some way, it would be there in its new form, on disk, and Bob would be none the wiser that the information had changed.

But I might be . . . ?

'Bob, open the history database. I think we might have experienced a wave.'

> Yes, Maddy. Do you believe the wave was caused by Liam?

'That's going to be my starting assumption. So, let's start looking from the year we first lost sight of him, 1666.'

> Affirmative.

She had another thought. Sal was going to feel this wave when it passed up the timeline and eventually reached her. She was going to have access to more information in 2025. An Internet, for starters. If she was thinking along the same lines – supposing it might just have been caused by Liam – the first thing she'd want to do is come back.

Right?

Or was she too far gone? Too messed up in her head to care about anything any more? It was worth a go. The power was on and the displacement machine was busy charging.

'Bob?'

> Yes, Maddy?

'Let's recharge and run the one-week return window. Maybe Sal's decided to come back for that one.'

She had a sinking feeling this one was also going to be a no-show.

CHAPTER 66
2025, New York

Stop looking at me like that.

Sal scowled at the people who walked past the mouth of her alley, looked into it and saw the bedraggled Indian girl sitting on a wooden orange box. She hated the momentary look of disgust on their faces followed a second later by self-reproachful relief that it wasn't them sitting there. It was that look – relief – that stung.

She was well aware that she didn't look so great. A week of sleeping rough in and about Manhattan was liable to do that to a person. Particularly in this time, where she noticed people had become hardened, ossified by the increasing hardships of life. No different really to her installed memories of Mumbai. In an increasingly resource-poor world, isn't the first casualty always humanity? Charity? Compassion? Love?

A week roaming the streets of Manhattan and she'd begun to see in everything the effects of the oil shortage: the lack of imported goods, the price of food. The infomercials on the huge screens over Times Square talked of avoiding waste, recycling, tips on how to grow food on roof-top gardens, window ledges and balcony grow-baskets. And the news itself . . . ? It seemed every leader in the world had recently gravitated towards the Middle East in an effort to talk down Iran and Israel from going to war with each other. Images of convoys of transport vehicles loaded with tactical nuclear warheads constantly being shuttled around from arid canyon to rocky gulley. Constant manoeuvring, as both sides kept their nuclear arsenal mobile. Those were going to be the first opening moves of what would become a decade of mini-wars as world powers jockeyed to control the last super-reserves of oil in the ground.

It was a big mistake coming here. Sal knew that now. And the day after she'd decided to let Saleena and her father go about the rest of their holiday unmolested, Sal had impulsively decided she just wanted to give up. Stay here . . . not even try to return to 1889.

There had been a dark moment. Two days later. The darkest moment, when she'd managed to find a way through the closed-off pedestrian entrance on to the Williamsburg Bridge. She'd walked halfway along it, worked herself through a gap in the rusting protective mesh grille, swung her legs over a handrail and stared down at the swirling grey water of the East River.

How long had she stared down like that? Three hours? Four hours? Wanting to let go, but not quite managing to convince her hands to release their grip on the rail. The instinct to survive desperately fighting with her. Her mean voice — that voice of reason — told her it was probably OK to die if that's what she wanted. She was never meant to have lived anyway. And it would be quick.

But her body had other ideas.

She'd hung there for hours, her cheeks wet with tears and chilled by the gusting breeze. Here was where her short life, her short story, would finally come to an end. And no one . . . *no one* was ever going to miss her, ever going to know that she'd even existed.

The fact is she decided not to jump. Sal couldn't say exactly why. Fear of the fall? Instinct? It certainly wasn't a glimmer of hope or inspiration that saved her. Just that she couldn't quite bring herself to do it.

The next day, though, the thing happened. A time wave. A subtle one, not a churning storm cloud on the horizon, but the subtlest shimmer like heated air above a sunbaked interstate highway.

A time wave.

If she ever lived to be an old woman and had grandchildren on her lap, perhaps she'd end up muddling the sequence of things and say that it was that time wave that saved her life, gave her hope and prevented her from jumping to her death. But no . . . nothing so poetic. It had come the day after she'd nearly thrown herself off the Williamsburg Bridge. What had saved her from jumping was fear. That was all.

The time wave itself was a mere shimmer. But it was also a reminder that there was something still worthwhile in her life. A job.

A mission.

Now she looked out of her dirty alleyway at the holographically projected news screen opposite. A newscaster was reporting some war going on in Africa as beneath her the time ticked seconds away. The time was approaching midday. The one-week window was nearly here.

The time wave meant something important. It was a clear sign. Almost certainly it was Liam. Either he was trying to cause a disruption in the past in order to get Maddy's attention or he was just being careless as he enjoyed his frolicking in history. Either way, Maddy was undoubtedly going to go back and get him.

But it was also a sign for *her*, she felt. A reminder that she'd given herself a personal goal. Something to live for, to ensure . . .

You're going to die an old woman, Saleena Vikram.

That meant she needed to get back home to Maddy and their London dungeon.

She'd been busy these last few days. She managed to beg, forage for, steal just enough money to buy herself an hour in one of the digi-stream cafes down the rough end of 5th Avenue. She'd found a place crammed with immigrants plugged into several rows of digi-consoles, desperate to contact loved ones. Rows of cubicles filled with worried faces wearing headsets. A clamour of conversations in a dozen different languages. She'd paid for her hour, found a vacant cubicle plugged into a console and then began to look for a clue to the time wave's point of origin.

Sal looked at the clock again. Just seconds to go. What worried her now was that the time wave might have altered things in the past – for example, enough that Holborn Viaduct, along with the world's first commercial electrical generator, might never have been built – that there would be no return window.

She anxiously counted the seconds down until it was past midday.

Please . . . please . . . please . . .

She'd found a sign. Oh God, it was a sign all right. A cry, a loud bellow through history from Liam. A big ol' completely unambiguous, unmissable come-here-and-get-me!

'Come on . . . open, please,' she whispered.

At fifty-three seconds past midday Sal's plea was answered. She saw the rubbish in her alleyway begin to stir restlessly, paper and plastic bags suddenly chasing each other in childlike circles. Then, without fanfare, without a sound except for the soft thud of displaced air, there it was: a dark orb of swirling, oily reality.

Sal was on her feet in an instant, down the alley, and thrust herself into it, not sparing a thought, a moment's dread, for the seconds of milky-white horror beyond.

1889, London

She emerged into the gloom of the dungeon, stepping quickly out of the mist and almost knocking Maddy over.

'Sal! It's Liam!' she howled. 'It's Liam!' Maddy stopped, held Sal steady by the shoulders, looked at her, then wrinkled her nose. 'My God, what happened to you?' She grimaced. 'You smell like a garbage bin!'

'Living rough.' Sal blew out the answer quickly. Not important right now. 'Maddy, the time wave. You got it here too, right?'

She nodded. 'Oh, I got it all right!'

'It *is* Liam, isn't it? It's Liam and Rashim?'

'Yup!' She smiled. 'Apparently the pair of them decided to name a frikkin' pirate ship after me.' Maddy giggled. 'They . . . they named a whole frikkin' *port* after you, Sal!'

'I saw that on a database,' said Sal. 'Not exactly subtle.'

Maddy clucked and laughed. 'Liam doesn't do subtle. For Christ's sake, he and Rashim even named a whole frikkin' island nation Pandora. Can you believe that?'

Sal nodded. 'I saw that too. It's like their own country or something.'

'Yup. What used to be called Hispaniola then later Haiti.'

They stared at each other, Maddy grinning so much that some of it leaked across on to Sal's face. 'I guess he did want to come back after all.'

The emotion was too much for Sal and she began to sob into Maddy's shoulder.

'Hey, you poor bedraggled thing.' She let Sal cry herself out, deep racking sobs of relief coupled with tears that trickled down Maddy's neck and soaked into her blouse. She let Sal have this because she clearly needed it.

So, it seemed Liam and Rashim hadn't intended to escape the present and go play pirates. For whatever reason that transponder ended up in someone else's hands, quite clearly they'd resorted to whatever measures they could to make their mark in history, to ensure Maddy would spot them here in 1889. No mistaking that as their intention.

I mean . . . Fort Bob? Republic of Pandora? The good ship Maddy Carter? Only an idiot like Liam would be so recklessly unsubtle about the whole thing. Clearly he was thinking along the same lines as her. '*Come get me and then together we'll fix this contamination – hopefully – before it ripples forward to Waldstein's time.*' On the other hand, Maddy suspected he wasn't even thinking that analytically. '*Just come get me . . . and Maddy can figure out the rest.*'

She smiled as she soothed Sal's juddering sobs.

Typical Liam.

The news was mixed, though, and she was going to need to share this with Sal once she was done sobbing on her shoulder. Maddy now had his where-and-when-abouts, but – *and isn't there always a goddamn 'but' when it comes to our luck?* – the news from the past, from *1687*, didn't end particularly well for Liam and Rashim.

It wasn't good.

Maddy decided to give Sal a few more minutes before breaking the news.

CHAPTER 67

1687, Port au Vikram,
Republic of Pandora

Liam looked again at the note in his hands. He read the first sentence once more. The opening words of this despatch told him all he needed to know.

Your Excellency, it is with the deepest regret . . .

The rest was all political flattery and an excuse that sounded less than convincing.

'Oh well,' he muttered. He dismissed the courier with a nod and tucked the note in his waistcoat. 'Nothing I didn't already expect.' He adjusted his neckerchief and collar, placed his tricorn hat firmly on his head and inspected himself in the ornate gilt-framed mirror beside the door of his private suite of rooms.

He still cut a lean figure despite the advancing years. If there was an accurate age that could be applied to him, he'd be about thirty-seven. Not that Liam ever celebrated his birthdays; there wasn't exactly a day he could point to and call it the day of his birth.

Thirty-seven.

The way things were headed, like as not there wasn't going to be a thirty-eighth.

Silver streaks laced through his hair and peppered his full beard. That plume of hair on his left temple was now a

Frankenstein streak of ghostly white. He buttoned his cuffs, his morning coat, cinched tight the sword belt round his middle. If today was going to be the day . . . then, damn it, he was going to be a smartly dressed corpse by the end of it. Liam opened the door and stepped out into the hallway. An elderly doorman bowed respectfully.

Liam patted him on the arm fondly. 'George, you should go home to your family. Today the fighting will happen. You should gather your wife and children and find a way off the island.'

He strode out across the hall, into the sunshine filling the courtyard in front of the governor's mansion. A stable boy had his horse ready and helped him up into the saddle.

'You as well, lad. Best you go home now. The English and the Spanish are coming.'

He steered his horse through the small courtyard, a beautiful place that he was truly going to miss. A small orchard of mango and orange trees. A place he came to meditate. To try and recall that old life he'd once lived long ago as a young man. He remembered their names, of course, those two girls he'd once thought of as sisters: Madelaine Carter and Saleena Vikram. But he struggled now to remember precisely what they looked like. He recalled a vague impression of Maddy, of frizzy, reddish-blonde hair and pale, freckled skin. Sal with her jet-black hair and intense, dark brown eyes.

So long ago now. Twenty-one years. There were things he remembered and so much he'd forgotten about that time. Most of it seemed like an impossible dream. He retained a fading memory of airships and mutant monsters, herds of dinosaurs, skyscrapers and knights, castles and Romans. All of those things had seemed to merge into one confused story that no longer made much sense to him. Indeed . . . just like a dream, although he knew those things had once happened in his life.

But since then another whole life had filled the many intervening years. A good life if the truth of it was to be weighed out. A life with a woman he'd loved, married and lost. Fleur, a beautiful woman, once upon a time a plantation slave, and for twelve happy years his true love. She'd died giving birth to his child three years ago. The physician had said it would have been a boy, if he'd lived. But the poor wretch was so malformed he would not have lived for very long. It was kinder that way.

Liam had grieved and still did in the quieter moments of any given day.

He coaxed his horse out through the mansion gate. He was met with a salute from a captain of the Republican Guard. The uniform was a flamboyant one: a deep blue tunic with gold cuffs and braids, yellow breeches and tricorn hats topped with a yellow parrot's feather. Rashim's design, of course. Those were the affairs of state that interested him the most: their small nation's flag, their modest little army's uniform, the names of the ships of their naval flotilla. The ephemera of nationhood.

'Where is Lord Governor Anwar?' asked Liam.

'Overseeing the defensive works on the east side, sir. The English main body has been sighted.'

'Thank you.' Liam looked at the captain and the half a dozen men guarding the entrance to the governor's mansion. 'You gentlemen should rejoin your unit. We'll need every man we have this morning.'

'But your . . . your home, sir?'

Liam looked around at the busy thoroughfare, Lady Rebecca Street. Shopkeepers and merchants were busy at work, hammering wooden planks over their doors and windows. Quite understandable. Once the British and Spanish soldiers entered

Port au Vikram, there'd be looting. No hammered planks would protect his mansion, though. All that he owned would be confiscated and handed over to Edward Pullinger, the British general commanding the forces that had landed on the east end of their island.

'Don't you worry about my mansion, Captain. It's the fight that matters now. That's *all* that matters now.'

The captain nodded gravely. 'Yes, sir.'

Liam steered his horse up Lady Rebecca Street, observing the panic and mayhem all around him: families packing all their worldly goods on to the backs of carts and donkeys, in a hurry to evacuate the port by boat or hide in the jungle wilderness of the island. He didn't blame them. Most of these families were black or of mixed race. Most of them had once been slaves from Jamaica, Cuba, Hispaniola, or they were the children of slaves. Once Port au Vikram fell, Liam imagined General Pullinger would treat the majority of the citizens of Pandora as assets to keep for himself, to share among his senior officers or sell on to pay for the military campaign's mounting costs.

He'd always suspected this day would finally come. The Republic of Pandora had become too much of a thorn in the sides of the English and the Spanish. Their fleet of ships had intercepted too much Spanish gold. Their small nation's constitutional promise of freedom and equality for every citizen had caused far too many slaves to abandon their plantations.

This day was always going to happen. Sooner or later.

Perhaps the surprise was that it had taken the new English king, James II, so long to negotiate an alliance with King Philip IV and his successor King Charles II of Spain and coordinate an expeditionary force between them to invade Pandora and squash this tiny *upstart* republic.

Liam wiped dust from his cheek – and a tear.

They'd managed to make a special place right here on this island. He and Rashim, and many of the old crew, now old friends, from their ship the *Pandora*. They'd arrived here in this thrown-together shanty port that was lawless and brutal and dangerous, and turned it into an oasis of freedom, fairness, enlightenment and stability. Which in turn, over the years, had attracted hundreds of merchants and craftsmen and traders as well as many thousands of slaves seeking a new beginning.

Given another twenty years, perhaps other islands in the Caribbean might have followed their example and formed a loose coalition of island states with the same values. Safety in numbers.

Liam faintly recalled there'd been another goal. A hope that their actions would echo through history and those girls he now barely remembered might step through time and come back for them. Perhaps even join them and live here in this roughly hewn piece of Heaven. But that goal had increasingly become secondary, receded and eventually been almost completely forgotten as the day-to-day shared running of their small nation had occupied every waking hour.

Liam's horse took him past the new marketplace, past the old Catholic church and the recently built All Faith church. Past the wooden palisade of Fort Bob and up the gentle slope of Foster's Ridge to where defence works were being hastily erected.

Among the hundreds of men, civilians and militia alike, working shirtless in the cloying morning heat to dig out trenches and build up earthworks, he spotted Rashim and colonel of the militia, William Hope.

Rashim had not weathered twenty years quite so well. Too much good living had ended up as a thick belt of fat around his waist. His once lean jaw now carried jowls beneath his dark beard. To call him a *round* man now would be unfair. *Stout* would be a little kinder.

Liam reined his horse in, climbed down and joined them.

'Good morning, Will,' he said.

The young man saluted him. 'Morning, sir.' That small motherless boy had grown into a fine and capable young man.

'How goes the work, Will?'

'As you will see, our artillery battery is well protected on three sides by the earth walls.' He pointed at shallow trenches either side of it that stretched along the modest ridge overlooking Port au Vikram. 'We also have splendid firing positions for Pasquinel's company of sharpshooters.' William grinned. 'We will make them pay heavily for their approach, sir.'

Liam nodded, shaded his eyes from the sun and studied the distant encampment of the combined British and Spanish expeditionary force. He could just about make out rows of canvas tents, the fluttering of regimental flags. His eyes had once been far better.

'Liam, here . . . use this.' Rashim handed him a spyglass. 'You might not like what you see, though,' he added quietly.

'Thanks.'

Through the lens he could make out much more detail. The army was breaking camp. Across the intervening mile of scrub, bushes and rock, through a lightly shimmering heat haze, he could see lines of English deep crimson tunics and Spanish sky-blue coloured tunics forming up into regiments. He could see General Pullinger had also rather shrewdly thought to bring along a number of artillery pieces.

Liam made a rough estimate of their strength. Five, maybe six thousand troops and so far he'd counted six pieces of artillery being hooked up to teams of mules.

He lowered the spyglass and noted Rashim was looking at

him with an expression that communicated what Liam already knew to be true.

We're not going to hold this position for long.

'What's the news from the French, Liam?'

Liam reached into his pocket for the note, pulled it out and passed it to him. 'I'm afraid there will be no assistance from them.'

There had been a hope, the promise of some very late, eleventh-hour help.

'What? Why?'

'The despatch states their ships were blockaded by the Spanish.'

Rashim rolled up his dirt-smudged shirtsleeves then wiped sweat from his forehead. 'Swines! They chickened out on us, that's what happened.'

William Hope looked at both Lord Governors. 'We're on our own?'

Liam nodded. 'Rather looks that way, Will.'

Across the open ground, they heard the distant rattle of regimental drums starting up and the faint trill of flutes and piccolos.

CHAPTER 68

1889, London

'The siege of Port au Vikram in May 1687 by General Sir Edward Pullinger was a spectacular victory for the combined British and Spanish expeditionary force,' read Maddy. She held in her hands a thick hardback book entitled *London Illustrated: Famous British Military Campaigns*.

She had taken a trip to the British Museum's library. It was the book an excitable young man interested in all things military – and, quite possibly, Maddy too – had eagerly recommended to her: a large, heavy tome full of line illustrations of various battles and maps and patriotic portraits of national heroes like Lord Nelson, Wellington, Chelmsford and Pullinger.

'The forces under General Edward Pullinger secretly landed on the east end of the self-proclaimed *Republic of Pandora*,' she continued, 'and marched the length of the island through jungles and swamps in less than a week, catching the disorganized army of rebels by surprise. The rebel army – a motley assortment of cut-throats, pirates, criminals, but predominantly runaway slaves under the command of their self-appointed leader "Lord Governor Anwar" – had little time to prepare for the landward attack of their home port.

'General Pullinger camped and rested his men overnight outside the island's main settlement, Port au Vikram and, on the morning of June the fifth, advanced his army up towards a hilltop overlooking the port where the rebel army had hastily erected crude defence works.

'The battle commenced just after midday and was won by the heroic and disciplined English troops within the hour. An eyewitness among General Pullinger's general staff reported that, "the slave army, easily outnumbering our modest force of advancing troops, took one look at the ordered redcoats advancing uphill on them and abandoned their posts like crows scattering from a field of corn".

'Pullinger's men took the ridge overlooking the port and observed the swarms of rebels descending down the far side of the slope, casting their weapons aside and fleeing into the labyrinth of ramshackle buildings of Port au Vikram and into the jungle surrounding it. Heartened by the early success of taking the ridge, General Pullinger boldly led his men down into the port . . .' Maddy looked up at Sal. 'I suspect this is not exactly an *impartial* account of events, by the way . . .'

Sal nodded at her to read on.

'. . . where they finally located the notorious rebel leader, Rashim "Blackbeard" Anwar cowering in the lavish rooms of his stately mansion, behind a gathered human wall of servants.'

'What about Liam?' asked Sal. 'Is there not any mention of Liam?'

Maddy ran her finger down the page until she found something. 'Anwar's lesser partner and second-in-command, the other half of the notorious "Pirate Kings of the Caribbean", was an Irish ex-sailor called *Lionel* O'Connor. O'Connor was caught attempting to flee the British soldiers in a pinnace that was being rowed out to the last remaining ship of their pirate fleet still moored in the bay, the *Madelaine*, a thirty-gun frigate formerly known as HMS *Reliance*, a Royal Navy ship of the line captured by "Blackbeard" Anwar's pirate fleet several years earlier.'

'Lionel O'Connor? They got his name wrong!'

Maddy shrugged. 'I guess that's a handwriting or typo error.' She carried on. 'An officer among the soldiers that arrested *Lionel O'Connor* reported that, "the Irish fellow screamed, cried and pleaded as he was manhandled, like a scolded child". He claimed that "*he was forced by Blackbeard to commit all his crimes upon fear of death by him*".'

Sal shook her head firmly. 'That's not like Liam. He wouldn't say that.'

Maddy sighed. 'Come on. You know what they say about history? That it's always written by the victors, right?' She turned the page. 'So, I guess we can assume there's a little creative licence going on here.'

Sal shook her head indignantly. 'Liam wouldn't scream and cry,' she muttered angrily. 'Not our Liam.'

'Forget that,' said Maddy. 'The important point is, Sal, they lost this battle . . .'

CHAPTER 69

1687, Port au Vikram, Republic of Pandora

Liam took advantage of the lull in the fighting to recover his breath. The slope leading up towards their defensive trench was littered with the splayed and squirming bodies of redcoats in the long, dry grass.

Three times that afternoon they'd made an attempt to take the ridge – three unsuccessful times. However, their last attempt had come within a whisker of succeeding. They'd been almost upon them and the fighting had become the vicious business of hand-to-hand mêlée. But the withering fire of Pasquinel's platoon of sharpshooters and the disciplined volley-fire of the First Company of the Pandora Republican Guard – drawn quickly back from the hand-to-hand fight and assembled in three lines – had whittled the English troops down until they began to break and retreat down the hill.

Liam looked at the lengthening shadows. Not much was left of the day. They'd done far better than either he or Rashim could have hoped. The advance on their modest 'capital city' had been stalled for the entire day. And that had bought invaluable time for the port's citizens to flee for their lives. He looked back down at Port au Vikram and saw that a few figures were still moving frantically through the narrow streets, dragging carts behind them, but that many of the ships and boats that normally filled her busy wharf and shallow bay had hours ago weighed anchor and departed.

He hoped the majority of them would manage to evade the English and Spanish ships combing the seas out there, perhaps to find refuge in Tortuga, or on one of the other many small islands nearby.

He caught the eyes of one of Pasquinel's sharpshooters, the platoon sergeant, scraping the inside of his barrel clean of sooty build-up with a ramrod.

John Shoe.

Liam smiled wearily, walked over and squatted down beside him. 'How're you doing there, John?'

'S'fine, sir.' He grinned. His dark face was smudged with dirt and dried blood. 'We show 'em proper soldiers we fight as good?'

He patted Shoe's shoulder. 'You and your lads are the proper soldiers here, John. That's the truth of it.' Liam noticed that John was carefully holding three musket balls in his hand. 'How much shot do we have left?'

John's defiant grin faded. 'No good. Little. Three, mebbe four volley-fire left.'

Then the very next charge, they'll take the ridge from us.

He looked along the line of men crouching in the shallow trench, a mixture of the dark green of the sharpshooters' uniforms, less than a dozen of them left, and the deep blue tunics of the Guard, perhaps a hundred able-bodied men in all. Among the bodies tangled with the dead English soldiers, he recognized Kwami's huge frame. He'd caught a glimpse of the man not five minutes ago, in the thick of it, roaring defiantly above the din of the fighting. Liam spotted the whippet-thin frame of Pasquinel, his red woollen *coureur de bois* cap lying in the dirt beside him.

And there lay William, a shot to the temple and he was done. The closest Liam had come to feeling like a father was caring for the small boy. Watching him grow into this brave young man. Liam clamped his jaw and screwed down hard on the grief that threatened to spill out.

Good men, all of them, friends even: friends he'd known well for the last twenty years, ever since their short, notorious and very successful career as privateers.

'Well, to be honest, there's not much left for us to put up a fight with,' said Rashim quietly.

Liam looked up at him, relieved to have the distraction of his friend at his side. 'Exactly what I was thinking.'

Rashim hunkered down beside him, equally exhausted, muddied and bloodied. His long, wiry grey hair had worked loose from its ribbon. Liam was so used to seeing him immaculately tailored and impeccably tidy. Now he looked wild and unkempt.

'Look at you,' Liam tutted. 'You've really let yourself go.'

Rashim laughed breathlessly. 'You look hardly any better, my friend.'

They silently watched General Pullinger regrouping his troops, moving a fresh regiment of foot soldiers in to replace the last routed regiment. A new untarnished line of crimson tunics, bone-white breeches and glinting bayonets. Men ready and eager to get into the fight at this late stage.

Liam tapped Rashim's arm. 'A quiet word.' He got to his feet and Rashim followed him. They took a few steps away from the trench and their men readying their guns for the next assault. The final assault.

'I think it's time, Rashim.'

'Time?'

'To call a halt to this.'

'Surrender?'

'Aye.' Liam glanced back over his shoulder at the near-empty bay and the all but deserted streets below. 'We bought them the day. Which is more than we hoped for. From what I can see it looks like most of them have managed to get away.'

'Indeed.' Rashim nodded. 'The wharf is empty.' Anchored alongside a protruding spit of land was one last ship. 'The *Madelaine* is still there, though.'

'Ah, I see.' Liam grinned. 'Don't tell me you fancy returning to the sea and resuming your career as a notorious pirate captain?'

'Too old for that sort of mischief now.' Rashim slapped his thick torso.

Liam looked at their men, all of them preparing for a fight that they must surely know they were going to lose. They were all going to die. That or be taken prisoner. And if they surrendered, their fate would be no better. A final warning letter had arrived from King James II himself some weeks ago declaring that if arms were taken up against General Pullinger's expeditionary force the penalties would be most severe. Any white man taken alive would be tried and hanged for sedition and piracy. Any black man taken alive would almost certainly be returned to a life of slavery.

The sun was approaching the horizon now and soon it was going to be dark. They had another hour at best until the sun breached the horizon and a quick twilight blended into night. By the look of what was going on downhill among the English lines, it seemed Pullinger was acutely aware of that and keen to take this ridge and finish the battle before dark.

An hour? Liam figured they'd be lucky to last another ten minutes once the fight began in earnest again. If the remaining men of John Shoe's platoon of sharpshooters, and the rest of the Guard were down to three volleys left, it would be over almost before it started. Perhaps there was a way he could buy these last few score men a chance to get away. They deserved that: a chance to escape under cover of dark. Some of them, he knew, had families anxiously waiting for them down in the town: women and children who wouldn't leave the island without their men.

'Rashim? What do you think?'

He turned to look and saw that Rashim was already pulling his unruly, wiry hair back into its ribbon, doing the best he could to tidy himself up. 'I am damned if I will surrender myself to them looking like a complete tramp.'

CHAPTER 70

1687, Newgate Prison, London

And have I regrets? I suppose I must have. But I wouldn't change any part of my life. I know that I have filled my - what? thirty-seven? thirty-eight? - mortal years with more memories than any man who has ever lived. Now that's not a bad thing to be able to say.

I look back on this last dawn and realize I'm lucky to have lived two lives. This one as a privateer, a pirate, a self-made king. I've two decades of proud memories in my head. And it's memories that are ultimately the currency we end up trading in, not money.

Rashim and I very nearly created a small piece of Heaven in the Caribbean. A place in which there was fairness and equality. A place with values a century ahead of those that will be written down by a bunch of founding fathers in Philadelphia.

We can both be proud of that.

I have heard since our deportation here to London and the very public show trial that was held last month, our beloved port has become known as Port James. The island itself - our Republic of Pandora - is henceforth to be known as New Dominion by order of an act of Parliament. It seems a number of our citizens were rounded up on the island and, true to King James's word, the white ones were hanged then and there, the black ones enslaved. I also have heard that the entire island of New Dominion is almost entirely owned by Lord Pullinger and the Member of Parliament who championed for the support and royal sponsorship for this invasion, Lord Thomas Modyford.

There it is. So much for hopes and dreams.

Liam O'Connor, 17th November 1687

'Bloody c-cold this morning,' whispered Rashim, as they left Newgate Prison. He was wearing both a loose white cotton shirt and a dark felt morning coat over the top, but still shivering.

Liam looked up at the overcast grey sky. A fresh breeze nipped across the Thames, coaxing white crests from the muddy water.

'It is a bit on the fresh side.'

'I should have p-packed a jumper.' Rashim managed a faltering smile. 'Maybe next time.'

The execution cart rattled along the cobblestone road parallel to the Thames. Liam watched London Bridge recede behind them, still standing proud despite the great fire that had threatened to engulf it some twenty years ago.

The north side of the street was lined with spectators that had gathered to watch the execution procession led by the Lord High Marshal on horseback. There were jeers and the occasional badly thrown missile that arced over their heads and into the river, but most of what they could hear was excited cheering. Not for them, not in support for them, merely an expression of the carnival atmosphere that accompanied a public hanging.

The cart finally turned right, in towards Execution Dock, and came to a halt facing on to the river. A 'stage' of planks erected on wooden beams that protruded out over the Thames awaited them. Beyond, boats and dinghies, pinnaces and ferries hovered out on the choppy water: 'paid for' seats for those who wanted the best possible view.

The chaplain who'd been sharing the cart with them and quietly reading aloud prayers from the King James Bible stepped down first then offered Liam a hand to help him.

'I'm all right, thanks.'

Rashim followed, stumbled on the cobbles, which provoked a ripple of laughter from the watching crowd behind them.

'Pay them no heed,' muttered the chaplain. He helped Rashim to his feet. 'This will be your last chance to confess your sins, my son. Will you not let me hear you?'

Rashim shook his head. 'It's . . . it's n-not something I believe in.'

'God forgives whether you believe in him or not. I beg you to reconsider –'

Liam turned round. 'Will you not just let him be?' he snapped, then offered the chaplain the ghost of a smile. 'The kindness you can do us, sir, is to let us get this over with as quickly as possible.'

Rashim nodded again. 'Y-yes. P-please.'

Liam stepped close to him. Both their hands were bound behind their backs. To untie his hands, to allow him to hold his friend, put an arm round Rashim, would have been a kindness too.

'It'll be all done and dusted in five minutes. Just brass it out, eh?'

Rashim looked at him, ashen-faced. 'I . . . I envy you, Liam.'

'My good looks, is it?'

He sputtered a nervous, chittering laugh that sounded like the puffing of a small steam engine. 'N-no . . . no f-fear. I envy th-that.'

'*I'm frightened too,*' he confided with a whisper. '*Just damned if I want these mawkish souls seeing it.*'

The Lord High Marshal beckoned for them to be brought up the four wooden stairs on to the stage. The hangman stepped towards them and gently grasped Liam's shoulder. 'Come along now,' he said softly. 'The drop will be quick enough, boys.'

They took the steps up on to the stage, the wood planks echoing hollowly and creaking beneath their boots.

The hangman positioned Liam by the shoulders, squarely in the middle of a long trapdoor. He nodded tacit approval. 'Perfect. Good man.' He placed Rashim on the trapdoor beside him then reached up to pull down the nooses of rope hanging from the frame above.

'Liam?' hissed Rashim.

'Yes?'

'They . . . they never f-found us. Never did c-come for us.'

He's talking about the girls.

'I know that.'

Rashim's face twitched with a glimmer of hope. 'P-perhaps it's n-now? Perhaps this is w-what they w-were waiting for all . . . all along?'

Liam gave that a moment's consideration. *No.* He vaguely remembered how it all worked, the rules, the dos and don'ts. Not right here. Not with an audience. They wouldn't open a window here. If a rescue had been coming, it would have arrived before now, surely? But Rashim didn't need to hear those thoughts. Instead, he turned to him and nodded.

'Yeah, it's possible,' he said. 'Perhaps.'

The hangman had Liam's noose in his beef-pink hands and eased it over his head. 'Lift your chin just a bit, there's a good lad.' Liam did so and he fitted the rough hemp rope snug under his jaw, checked the knot and gave it a firm testing tug. He then set about the same ritualistic process for Rashim.

Liam looked up at the featureless grey sky. Bland. A monotone. It reminded him of something from long, long ago. And then he quickly had it – that curious white mist that you had to step through to reach the past. That other strange dimension.

Chaos . . . yes, that's what we called it. The chaos dimension.

Only he didn't recall the chaos dimension having seagulls. The birds swooped and fluttered out over the river, hovering on the breeze as if delaying their onward journey a moment or two to watch this spectacle like all the other onlookers gathered that morning.

'All done here!' announced the hangman.

Beside him Liam could hear Rashim's ragged, panting breath: in and out, in and out, in and out like a blacksmith's bellows. And now . . . *now* the fear was finally biting Liam. He gritted his teeth. He wasn't going to show them the slightest hint of scaffold-terror.

I won't give them that. I won't!

He closed his eyes and thought of his long-dead wife, Fleur: her long dark kinks of hair, her brown eyes, her full lips. A million and one unique little things she did, habits she had, sayings she whispered into his ear in the still of a hot night. Sayings and homespun, inherited tribal truisms from her old world.

Then the girls, *his* two girls, his all-but-forgotten sisters-in-time. Comrades bound together by their fate. Closer than family. Closer than brothers and sisters. And that big clumsy man-mountain – the support unit, *Bob*. A compressed lifetime of memories. A precious thing and, best of all, all of those memories were entirely *his*. Not someone else's. Not a fiction conjured up by some lab technician.

His.

He could hear Rashim whimpering next to him and spared a thought for his friend of so many years, his partner in crime.

'Hey! Hey, Rashim?'

'Uh . . . huh . . . ?'

'Why are pirates so big and scary?'

Rashim turned to look at him. Wide-eyed, his skin as grey and colourless as the sky above. 'I . . . I d-don't . . . I . . .'

'Because they arrrrrrrre.' Liam offered him a lopsided grin. 'Get it?'

Rashim managed a flickering smile.

Then, with the clunk of a lever, the trapdoor opened beneath their feet.

And they dropped.

CHAPTER 71

1889, London

'. . . both were hanged by the neck at Execution Dock in London until they died. As was customary for pirates, their bodies were left dangling above the Thames at low tide until "three times covered by a high tide".' Maddy looked up at Sal and saw tears in her eyes. Beyond her, even Bob and Becks looked more sullen than normal.

'Their bodies were then cut down and quartered, their heads cut off and displayed on spikes on London Bridge . . .'

Maddy closed the book. She'd read out enough of that.

'They tried . . .' Sal said, 'they tried to call out for us . . . They named everything they could with words we'd pick up on.' She looked up at Maddy. 'And we missed them. We were too late.' Sal pressed her lips together, holding back tears. 'Oh God, poor, poor Liam.'

'No, screw it. Hang on. It's not over yet.'

Sal cocked her head.

'Think about it! We can intercept them earlier, Sal. Earlier! There's nearly two decades of them in the past. Two whole decades when we now know exactly where they are and what they're getting up to!'

'Maddy is correct,' said Becks. 'Liam and Rashim can very easily be reacquired now.'

'See? The ice queen agrees with me!' said Maddy with a smile.

'I know that all sounded pretty grim, but this is *good* news! We've got a baseline date and location to work backwards from in order to identify a precise window to open. We just need to do some more research, hit some history books and stuff.'

Sal nodded and wiped her cheeks. 'Right . . . I get it.'

Maddy shrugged. 'So, it's all good.' She smiled. 'We've found them. We'll figure out a time-stamp and go back and get them long before they get hanged!'

Sal still looked morose.

'Sal? I thought you'd be happy!' Maddy felt a little exasperated. They had an end marker – this admittedly grim account of the execution. There would almost certainly be written records made by the Admiralty Court clerks of the trial and, in those records, eyewitness accounts of the various acts of piracy conducted by Liam and Rashim, along with the dates they occurred. Enough there to start with. Failing that . . . they could pick any time they wanted in the two decades preceding, find somewhere on the island that was quiet and pop back. Surely it wouldn't be too hard to go back, look around, ask some questions and be pointed in the general direction of where Liam and Rashim were holding court? But, ideally, what she wanted was a specific eyewitness account. Something relatively early in their long entrenchment in the past; after all, retrieving a middle-aged Liam would be kind of weird. She just needed to fish around for some witness account that gave them a precise enough time and place.

'We'll get them back, Sal. Sheesh . . . this is going to be the *easy* bit! You'll see.' She looked up at the two hovering support units. 'We'll have them back in time for tea.'

'I know.' Sal nodded. 'I know we're going to get them back . . . it's just . . .'

'What?'

'It's just . . . I dunno, the thought that . . . *that* –' she nodded at the closed history book on the table in front of them – '*that awful thing* . . . actually happened to Liam and Rashim.'

Maddy followed her gaze and all of a sudden the buzz, the exhilaration, the happiness felt clumsily ill-judged and misplaced. She had no real understanding of how time really worked, whether it was a line or looped back on itself; whether the future and the past were parallel rail tracks that ran side by side, or whether there were an infinite number of universes in which every possible event, every possible timeline was played out. But she realized, as she looked at the history book proudly announcing its coverage of 'Famous Military Victories', that somewhere, in some dimension . . . both Liam and Rashim had experienced death by hanging.

The thought sobered her and she moderated her tone from the *boo-ya-we-scored-a-touchdown* tone to something a little more reserved.

She gave Sal a hug. 'Let's go find them and bring them home. Eh?'

CHAPTER 72

1889, London

> **Ready to open the portal again in one minute, Maddy.**

'Thank you, Bob.'

They'd tried this several hours ago, but the pre-release build-up of energy in the displacement machine had caused a copper wire to melt and the whole process had collapsed and left them in momentary darkness. It had taken her and Bob most of the afternoon to diagnose the fault and replace the Victorian-era cable with a length of far more reliable electrical flex that they'd brought with them from 2001.

Time to try again.

She turned to look at the marked squares in the middle of the dungeon's floor. The spherical return portal would — hopefully, this time — appear a foot above the floor over there.

With Becks and Sal spending a couple of days picking through relevant books in the library, they had managed to isolate a perfect time-stamp, the perfect window to open. Just as Maddy had expected, there were in fact extensive notes on the trial of the 'Notorious Pirate Kings of Pandora'. The trial, it seemed, had caught the public imagination and been followed by many of the people of London. She'd even found notes on it in Samuel Pepys's diary who, it seemed, had bought tickets to attend one of the big prosecution days of the trial.

God, there'd even been a *novel* written about them. A novel written by none other than Charles Dickens entitled *The Pirate Tyrant*. There'd been a play too, by John Dryden – *The Pirate and the Plantation Owner*.

But it was the very precise testimony of Lord Thomas Modyford that had given Maddy the most accurate time and place. The most reliable window of opportunity.

> **Thirty seconds.**

All right, it wasn't the perfect place to extract them from: there would be witnesses. But then half of them would be pirates and therefore full of all manner of superstitious claptrap, and not to be trusted in anything they said. The other witnesses were Modyford himself and a number of soldiers. Perhaps this window might result in some minor contamination. There might possibly be a need for them to go back and tidy things up. On the other hand, perhaps not.

History has a course it 'wants' to steer after all.

But, by Modyford's account of things, there had been a moment of confusion during the incident he'd spoken of at the trial; there had been 'much smoke, shouting, fighting, bedlam . . . the firing of muskets in close order'. Enough confusion presumably going on, then, that one might excuse the account of something quite so strange as a person simply disappearing in the middle of it all as the product of post-traumatic shock.

> **Twenty seconds, Maddy.**

Either way, fix or no fix required after rescuing them, this location was too good for her to pass up.

'Stand clear, guys,' she said needlessly. The displacement machine's hum was building towards its inevitable crescendo, the moment of its energy release, like an archer releasing his bowstring. Their electric lamp dimmed, the computer monitors flickered as the current pooled in their time machine.

> **Ten seconds . . . nine . . . eight . . .**

She smiled at the thought of Liam and Rashim actually ending up as characters in a Dickens novel. She would have liked to have read it before bringing them home, or at least found some way to preserve a copy from the corrective sweep of the ensuing time wave. What a souvenir that would make.

> Five . . . four . . . three . . .

She felt the build-up of static electricity in the room, her hair lifted ever so slightly by it, goosebumps along her arms. Then the strong puff of displaced air and all of a sudden they were looking at a churning spherical pattern, a Van Gogh oil painting of blue sky and blue sea, wooden planks and twisty-turny figures in bright crimson.

'OK, Bob . . . go grab them for me.'

1667, Port Royal, Jamaica

The sudden unexpected gust of wind across the deck made the lifeless sails above them all snap and rustle. It was enough to disturb the finely balanced stalemate. A musket discharged. That was enough to convince every other sweaty finger currently resting on a trigger to twitch convulsively.

The mid-deck suddenly filled with plumes of powder smoke as a dozen guns clapped and boomed in a discordant symphony. Liam felt something hot skim his ear. Instinctively he ducked down, fearing another shot in his direction. As the boom of gunfire faded, he heard the clash and ring of blades, the barking of voices in the swirling mist.

He drew the cutlass from his belt and turned and readied himself for the figure moving quickly out of the smoke towards him. He raised his arm in readiness to get in an early swipe across the man's midriff. As he did, the figure drew closer, became clearer . . . and much bigger.

Bob's granite-slab face emerged through the last tendrils of smoke like an Easter Island monolith rising from a haunting sea mist. Liam could see he had already collected Rashim, grasping him by his collar. Rashim was struggling and flailing instinctively: he obviously hadn't yet seen whose giant crane-like hand had grabbed him from behind. Bob extended the other enormous hand towards Liam.

'Come with me if you want to live, Liam.'

1889, London

A handful of heartbeats and a chaos dimension eternity later, the three of them tumbled out of the mist into darkness and a tangle of limbs and curses on the cold, hard floor of the dungeon.

As Liam lay on his back looking up at a curved ceiling of damp bricks, gasping, trying to make sense of the last jumbled ten seconds of his life, he heard something shrill and irritating hooting merrily.

'Skippa's home! Skippa's home!'

Then into his field of vision, looming over him, a pair of faces he knew so very well. A pair of faces he'd begun to worry he might never see again.

'You all right down there, boys?' said Maddy. 'Don't bother getting up now.'

And Sal. She didn't wait. She dropped down on to her knees and planted a kiss on his cheek. 'Welcome home, Liam.'

CHAPTER 73

1889, London

Liam watched the barges on the River Thames from Blackfriars Bridge. Watched them coming in to be loaded and unloaded: a ballet of industry and manpower in the beating, smoky heart of London.

There had been a time wave that had arrived only minutes after he and Rashim had stumbled through into the dungeon. It almost seemed random. Sometimes a wave took hours to arrive, sometimes days; in this last case, for whatever reason, it had merely been minutes. A small wave, not a roiling bank of black filling the sky but a shimmer that had seemed to affect nothing more than the words on the pages of countless books in countless libraries around the world.

Maddy said it was a shame that the wave had arrived so quickly. She'd wanted to show him and Rashim the two history books she'd pinched from the library. She'd said their unintended long stay in the past had led to quite an adventure. Apparently he and Rashim had become rather notorious figures of seventeenth-century English history.

According to her, they'd both lived another two whole decades in that time. And during those years they had built a budding nation on the island of Hispaniola. They'd also become something of a problem to England and Spain, enough of a problem that they had sent an army and a fleet of ships across the Atlantic to deal with them.

Maddy also told them what their fate had ended up being; that both he and Rashim had been hanged like common criminals in a place a stone's throw from where this whole unintended adventure had begun. London Bridge.

Liam had spent seven months in the past this time, longer than in Kramer's time. Longer than in King John's time. Seven months as a pirate. He was fascinated by the notion that, if Maddy hadn't come across Modyford's account of their escape from his attempt to arrest them for piracy, he would have gone on to live a very different life.

He wondered if, in that other life, his twenty years' living as some sort of king of a pirate kingdom, there had been people he may have got to know and love. A weird thought that. That he might have had a wife and children and all that business.

Jay-zus . . . twenty years would have made me nearly forty.

An old man. Sort of.

Rashim would have been closer to fifty!

He wondered how he felt about being back. Was he glad to be here? Yes and no. He wasn't going to tell Maddy that he'd missed her and Sal, that there had been many times he'd pined for them, yearned to return to their homely dark dungeon. She'd only make fun of him. There had been times when he thought they were going to be stuck there for good. So, yes . . . he was glad to be back with the girls. The support units. Back home with his odd, odd family.

But then there had been several times he'd wished he could be back there. Golden moments that would be so hard to explain, to describe to someone who hadn't experienced them. Moments like, for example, watching the last of the sun vanish behind a table-flat horizon. The sound of a lazy sail slapping against the stout oak of a ship's mizzen-mast in the still heart of night. The soothing creak and groan of a ship's hull. The tarry smell of caulked wood mixed with the ever-present tang of salt. The bad-eggs smell of powder smoke and the reek of damp hemp rope. The downward thump, the upward rise of our girl, the *Pandora*, bearing three-quarters to the wind as she rides through lively, white-topped crests and leaves a tamed trough in our wake.

Aye, she was a good ship, the Pandora. *A fine ship, so she was.*

Last night in the dungeon, while the others were asleep and Liam lay on his bed of mattresses and packing crates, he'd cupped one hand over his ear and fancied he could actually hear the distant rumble of the sea. Even though he knew what he was hearing was the rush of his own blood. But, listening to that, he could almost feel the gentle rise and drop of a ship at sea and pretend that the darkness of their dungeon was the darkness of the gun deck. And imagine he could see his crew, his lads, curled in their hammocks, stirring, fidgeting, farting in their sleep.

Liam wondered what became of them all.

He hoped it was not the same fate that Rashim and he might have gone on to face one day.

I hope those good fellas – young Will, Old Tom, John Shoe, Gunny, Pasquinel, Kwami – I so hope they all managed to make an escape and find their own destinies, whatever those may be.

CHAPTER 74

1687, somewhere off the coast of Florida

He looked up through the rigging at the clear blue sky and savoured the warmth of the sun on his face. He closed his eyes for just a few seconds and let his senses drink in the moment: the gusting wind against his cheeks, the sounds of his ship cutting through a choppy sea, the crew about their business. The smell of woodsmoke coming from the galley and tobacco smoke from his clay pipe.

A perfect morning.

He remembered some words of wisdom from that Irishman who'd once saved him. *'Make sure you catch those precious moments, lad. Hold them close like a lover and cherish them.'*

So long ago now he could barely remember what he'd looked like. Slim, dark-haired, with that strange grey tuft of hair and the modest fluff of a young man's beard. That man for a while had been like an older brother, no, almost like a *father*, to him. God, he wished he could remember his full name.

He could just remember the first. That was all now. But that same name is the one he'd proudly christened his young son, waiting for him back home in Nassau, New Providence.

All so long ago now and memories can play tricks on you. Is that really what happened? Did he just disappear over the side during that fight? He and the darker man, Captain Anwar? That had troubled him for years . . . that they could just leave them like that. So suddenly. Vanish amid the smoke as it were.

He bore them no ill will, though. If they'd escaped too, then good for them. Somehow he was certain that's what had happened. They'd escaped and not been shot, killed and fallen dead over the side. They'd made their escape and, what was more, he had an instinctive feeling that those two were still alive somewhere.

He smiled. *Wherever you are, Liam . . . I wish you Godspeed*.

Just then a call came down from the crow's-nest. The first mate, Jacques Pasquinel, climbed the ladder up to the afterdeck. 'Skipper! Sighting of a Yankee merchant ship off the port bow!'

Captain William Hope grinned.

'Well, what're we waitin' for? Let's go get 'em!'

Epilogue

1889, London Bridge, London

Sal too had taken herself for a walk to get away from the gloomy confines of the dungeon. She was watching the very same barges coming in to disgorge their cargoes and fill their open holds with sacks of coke, bundles of leather, spars of pig-iron to be transferred back down the river to smoke-stacked factories hungry for more raw materials from which to mass-produce items to be sold across the colonial empire. But she was watching the work from London Bridge. If both had known where the other stood, they might even have been able to make each other out, less than half a mile apart, and offer a friendly wave.

She looked down at the cold grey river, polluted with chemicals from tanneries, potteries, textile factories. Even less inviting than New York's East River had been.

Everyone was back, safe and sound, and history seemed to be back to how it had been before Liam and Rashim had meddled with it. The same as it ever was. But not quite the same. She realized she loved Liam and was so relieved that he was home, safe, unharmed. Loved Maddy too. And yes, she was even fond of Rashim and the support units. Even that stupid yellow lab unit.

But the more she thought about it, the more she dwelled on it, the more she cared for a certain girl who wasn't going to be born for another one hundred and twenty-three years. Saleena

Vikram. A very real girl who Sal was determined was going to live a long life.

Sal was merely the ghost of that girl. The pale copy. A lost echo of her.

Yet here she was with the others a century and a quarter before Saleena Vikram's due time, with a machine that could so easily derail the delicate sequence of events that would eventually lead to a young man called Sanjay Vikram meeting Abeer.

You can't let that happen, her nagging voice chimed in softly.

Sal nodded. She quite agreed.

'I promise you, Saleena Vikram, I won't let them do that to you.'

HISTORY AS WE KNOW IT

1666
TimeRiders go back in time to witness the Great Fire of London . . . .

1889
TimeRiders' new base of operations in Victorian London

THE PRESENT:
the world as we know it today

HISTORY ALTERED

1666
But Liam and Rashim are kidnapped by a gang of pirates in the chaos of the fire

1667
Liam and Rashim are press-ganged into joining a pirate crew, but they stage a mutiny and become successful captains of a pirate ship

1687
Liam and Rashim set up their own anti-slave, libertarian republic Pandora

1889
The Spanish and English unite in a successful conquest of the piratical Republic of Pandora

THE PRESENT:
a world in which the Republic of Pandora is a mere footnote in history

TIME RIDERS

2001 20 1957 2066
1912 1941

THE ADVENTURE DOESN'T STOP THERE

NEXT STOP: THE MAYANS . . .

JULY 2013

BECOME A TIMERIDER AT
WWW.TIME-RIDERS.CO.UK

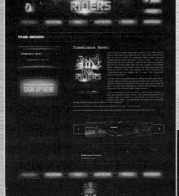

- Keep track of all the *TimeRiders* action with **ALEX SCARROW'S BLOG**

- Enter mindblowing monthly missions to win **EXCLUSIVE PRIZES**

- Enjoy must-have **FREEBIES** including music and wallpapers

- Challenge yourself with online **DIGITAL JIGSAW PUZZLES**

- Hit the top of the leader board with the addictive **LOST IN TIME** game

- Follow **MADDY'S BLOG** posts from 2001!

And much, much more

- **Plus sign up to the *TimeRiders* newsletter and receive all the latest news as it happens . . .**

www.time-riders.co.uk

  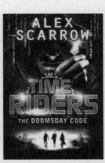 

WANT MORE ACTION? MORE ADVENTURE? MORE ADRENALIN?

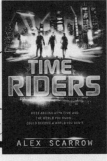

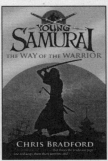

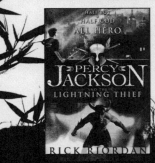

GET INTO PUFFIN'S ADVENTURE BOOKS FOR BOYS

It all started with a Scarecrow.

Puffin is seventy years old.
Sounds ancient, doesn't it? But Puffin has never been
so lively. We're always on the lookout for the next big
idea, which is how it began all those years ago.

Penguin Books was a big idea from the mind of
a man called Allen Lane, who in 1935 invented
the quality paperback and changed the world.
**And from great Penguins, great Puffins grew,
changing the face of children's books forever.**

The first four Puffin Picture Books were hatched in 1940 and the
first Puffin story book featured a man with broomstick arms called
Worzel Gummidge. In 1967 Kaye Webb, Puffin Editor, started the
Puffin Club, promising to **'make children into readers'**.
She kept that promise and over 200,000 children became
devoted Puffineers through their quarterly instalments of
Puffin Post, which is now back for a new generation.

Many years from now, we hope you'll look back and
remember Puffin with a smile. **No matter what your age
or what you're into, there's a Puffin for everyone.**
The possibilities are endless, but one thing is for sure:
whether it's a picture book or a paperback, a sticker book
or a hardback, **if it's got that little Puffin
on it – it's bound to be good.**